One Dead Diva

One Dead Diva

PHILLIP SCOTT

alyson books
los angeles | new york

© 1995, 2003 BY PHILLIP SCOTT. ALL RIGHTS RESERVED.

MANUFACTURED IN THE UNITED STATES OF AMERICA.

THIS TRADE PAPERBACK IS PUBLISHED BY ALYSON PUBLICATIONS,
P.O. BOX 4371, LOS ANGELES, CALIFORNIA 90078-4371.

FIRST PUBLISHED BY BLACKWATTLE PRESS (AUSTRALIA): 1995
FIRST ALYSON BOOKS EDITION: JANUARY 2003

03 04 05 06 07 a 10 9 8 7 6 5 4 3 2 1

ISBN 1-55583-759-X
(PREVIOUSLY PUBLISHED WITH ISBN 1-875243-21-6 BY BLACKWATTLE PRESS.)

CREDITS
COVER PHOTOGRAPHY FROM PHOTODISC.
COVER DESIGN BY LOUIS MANDRAPILIAS.

CHAPTER 1

A few months ago, the reigning operatic star of Sydney held her annual bash. Dame Norma Clutterbuck, known and revered by millions of operagoers the world over, threw open her well-appointed Palm Beach weekender to feed the starving cognoscenti. Some people bent over backward to get an invitation. A lot of people bent over backward and failed to get an invitation.

The shindig had all the hallmarks of success: indigestible hors d'oeuvres, sexy waiters, a swimming pool full of bodies designed to look good in a swimming pool—and, as usual, Dame Norma managed to snare certain guests who were notoriously hard to secure. One was a bankrupt entrepreneur who owed his friends a small fortune and was presumed to be in Rio de Janeiro. Many of those friends were also present. They were delighted to see him, clapping him on the shoulder and beaming with bonhomie. Later, when he was in the pool, they would all be contacting their lawyers.

The regular icons and magazine-cover faces were there, the habitual partygoers, rich or famous neighbors, clusters of homosexuals—and there may have been one or two people who liked opera. There was food and drink to feed a moderately hungry army.

There was also a tragic incident, which set this year's party apart. A promising young soprano, scheduled to make her debut with the Opera, fell off the steep cliff at the back of the house and died on the jagged rocks below. I suppose this incident was hushed up to some extent. I certainly didn't hear about it at the time, in spite of my interest in opera. Now I know a good deal about it; in fact, I know everything.

I wish I didn't.

CHAPTER 2

*T*his bit is fabulous. Just into Desdemona's "Willow Song," Act IV of Verdi's *Otello,* she sings the word *salce* three times in the most exquisite pianissimo, echoed by the cor anglais. And then...she floats the most gorgeous high note, supported by a big, warm, wet cushion of strings on the word *cantiamo* ("Sing to me"). Some sopranos belt it out—sing me through the back wall and out onto the median strip. Not Renata Tebaldi. She gets it absolutely right, even in the stereo remake.

We were just up to the second *salce* (my favorite), when a deep rumbling made its presence felt somewhere off to the south of my left speaker. Tebaldi's high note never had a chance. By then the rumble was overwhelming. Cracks appeared in the wall. I made a grab for the remote, but because of my bandage I couldn't get a grip on it. It skidded to the floor, taking a full mug of cold coffee along for the ride. (This has happened so often I invested in a coffee-colored rug, but the shade never seems to match.)

I turned off the music and glanced at my watch. It was one minute after midnight. Really, that did it! Is there a curfew or not?

I live under Sydney Airport's flight path, you see. About two meters under it.

It's bad enough during the day. I mean, nothing kills an alfresco Sunday brunch quicker than a Lufthansa 747 blow-drying your bouffant. I'm used to it—the noise, the fumes, the interrupted thoughts that never recur—but new guests are quite taken aback. Tanned young things from the eastern suburbs turn ashen. Witticisms dry like Sorbolene cream on their lips—words destined to be forgotten or recycled. People start

2

exclaiming things like, "My God, is it already 1:30? I promised to visit my grandmother's grave this weekend...."

Yes, Sundays are bad enough. But when you can't even call the wee small hours your own! I was livid, and at my age that's not good.

I picked up the phone and dialed the Aircraft Noise and Pollution Line, an initiative set up by angry locals. There'd be no one there, probably. It's only manned Monday nights between 6:30 and 9. (Concerned Lesbians have less free time than you'd think. Before this boot-scooting craze yahooed into our lives you could get through on Thursdays, too.)

They answered. Boot-scooting must be passé.

"It's me again—Marc Petrucci. Look, this has got to stop. I just had a jumbo go over. It sounded more like a bloody herd! Is there a curfew or not? Here it is, after midnight: There's coffee everywhere, my big moment with Tebaldi has been ruined probably irretrievably—there's another crack in the stairwell, and I'm dangerously livid!"

"Please, who is this?" asked a sleepy Vietnamese voice.

"Oh. Sorry."

I replaced the receiver. My dialing is sometimes a tad inaccurate. It's probably the bandages.

There was nothing to do but start the opera over from scratch. It doesn't take long to get back in the mood. Renata can do it for me in a few seconds. Some of my friends spend hours watching American porn just to achieve the same effect, a sense of heightened realism I suppose you'd call it. Arthur, an acquaintance of mine, gave me a Jeff Stryker six-pack for Christmas with titles like *Bigger than Ever* and *Harder than Calculus*. You can have it! I've hardly even glanced at it. I'll take Puccini any time. I mean, if people knew what opera was really like—well, it would be illegal in Tasmania.

I'm Italian, of course. My given name is Gianmarco, but I've been Marc for about forty of the last fifty years. (Better that than John.)

A few people call me Dotty as well. This appellation dates back to a party in the late '60s where I made a memorable appearance in drag. It's not something I do on a regular basis or to fulfill any long-felt want, but this particular gathering was a "Friends of Dorothy" party. We had such things in those days. Naturally the place was chockablock with Oz characters and a dozen Judy Garlands in various stages of deterioration, so I avoided the obvious and arrived instead as the slinky and sexy Dorothy: Dorothy Lamour. The resemblance was uncanny. The name stuck.

Unfortunately, Dotty doesn't sound too slinky. As names go, it's up there with Vera Vague. It has connotations of clumsiness, which I'm very touchy about. I mean, clumsy is something Italians are not supposed to be. We're suave and smooth and have sleek tapered fingers that don't drop saucers of olive oil or get chopped up by coffee grinders. All except me. I could have been quite a passable pianist if my hands had stayed out of trouble, but that was not to be. My early potential was quashed by a broken wrist on the morning of my major piano exam. I was shaking hands with a particularly robust priest. Robust priests are such a worry.

If I'd become the first-rate pianist I had it in me to be, I might have gone into opera professionally as a repetiteur. It's a repetiteur's job to accompany singers as they learn their parts, hence the name. These lowly creatures repeat passages over and over again for hours, and eventually the singer gets a sketchy notion of how it ought to go. Then, miraculously, overnight, all is forgotten—so the process has to be repeated anew every day for months.

It's similar, and equally enthralling, to teach a foreign tongue to rich school children. That's how I spent many unhappy hours of my life, until I had one of my accidents, fortunately on the premises, and a hefty comp payment freed me from slavery.

At the same time an aunt in Rome, a marchesa, left me a block of flats overlooking the Vatican. She died of spite, I think.

Things had reached the stage where she was forced to sell one apartment per year just to raise the money to pay tax on the building. Italian taxes are like that: crippling, if you're honest. My aunt paid up, against the advice of family and professionals alike. In the end, she would no longer give the tax department the satisfaction. She died happy.

I sold the building for two reasons. One was money, the second was my dislike of the Vatican. Heretical of me, I daresay, but the Pope and I disagree on so many issues that we simply had to call the whole thing off. Sorry, Mary. I'll regret it someday, no doubt, when it's too late.

Despite this windfall, I still work. I don't sit around all day listening to opera—well, not every day. I give private lessons in Italian. You may have seen my ad in the gay papers: It's the one without the "actual photo."

It took me a few attempts to get the wording right. Some of the gentlemen who phoned up at first read too much between the lines. They seemed to think taking Italian was the next step after Greek. I was asked questions like, "Do I need latex gloves?" and, "Do you have your own toys?"

It soon sorted itself out. At the moment I have a few regulars. One is an importer who deals with Italian companies. (I think he has a boyfriend in the Mafia; I don't want to know.) Another client is a rich lawyer who made too much money one year and bought himself a villa in Tuscany. Now he's having a midlife crisis and wants to live there until the crisis is over. He's allocated eight months for it. What luck! Some of us are forced to sit out our crises at home.

Oh, I'm not complaining. I can't say I'm going through menopause just yet, even though I'll be fifty next month. If and when I do fall apart, I know I'll have La Tebaldi to ease the way.

I poured another even colder coffee and sloshed it into the microwave, pausing only to jam my thumb closing the door. (It never rains, but it hurts.) I re-cued the "Willow Song." I hit the couch and coaxed myself into the appropriately orgasmic state.

This time, it was the phone.

"Caro! I have to come 'round at once!"

"What?"

"It's me, Paul."

"I know, I know. I was just about to go to bed."

"At this hour? Rubbish. You don't even start to function till the planes stop. Who's that I hear? Our own Joan, friend to the poor little ethnic person?"

"Of course not! Really—"

"Relax, babe. I know it's Tebaldi. Listen, please let me in. It's late and everything, but I'm desperate!"

Paul is another of my pupils—or was. He's twenty-two, give or take five years, and has a pleasant light baritone. When he came to me, he momentarily aspired to be in the chorus of the City Opera. Every so often they hold open auditions, and I helped Paul prepare his audition piece. He failed to knock 'em dead. In the meantime he's been singing in one big musical after another, eight shows a week. I must say, he makes the cutest cat.

"Surely you don't want a lesson now?"

"We could run over a few basics."

"You're flirting with me, Paul."

"And don't you just hate it. Come on, Marc. I can't go back to my flat tonight. Let me camp on the couch, and I promise I'll use up all the hot water in the morning. Please!"

"All right. There's nothing wrong is there?"

"Just the usual. Somebody's going to kill me."

CHAPTER 3

*P*aul bounded furtively through the front door. He bounds everywhere, with the grace not of a gazelle so much as a terrier.

Today's hair color (terrier-esque) was a reddish brown; Last week it was bottle blond. As for the rest of him, it's generally more consistent. Paul is on the compact side but fit, as befits a dance-party maniac. He has olive skin and dark eyes—in fact, he looks more Mediterranean than I do. His most attractive feature (as far as *I* know) is his smile: It reveals small but perfectly white, even teeth, the upper set pointing slightly inward. When he smiles, there is a cheeky glint in his eye that suggests he has just done, or is about to do, something naughty. It's probably true.

He flung himself all over the couch.

"Was I followed? Never mind. Let's have a drink. My God, what's happened to your hand now?"

"Nothing."

I'm always embarrassed about these minor catastrophes.

"Silly me. I'd forgotten ornamental bandages were the new look for the modern bachelor."

"If you must know, I tangled with an electric whisk. Making flummery."

"Flummery? You funny old thing." He gave me a sympathetic hug." Caro, you're the reincarnation of my grandmother."

"I bet you say that to everybody. Would you like some?"

"With champagne, please."

We adjourned to the kitchen—or rather, I adjourned, he bounded. I'm quite fond of desserts. I have a light touch with them, unlike most other things. I tore this recipe out of an ancient magazine I found once in the ER waiting room.

Flummery is a fruity, frothy concoction. I've known many over the years.

"Last time I had this it wasn't pink."

"I put a little of myself into my creations."

"Oh, yuck."

"Well, the Scots make blood sausages don't they?"

"Whew, there's a heap of booze in it."

"No there's not."

"Must be your blood alcohol. Think I'll take a rain check. It's the champers I really need."

He snuggled up behind me, as insufferably coy as a Disney character.

"So, Bambi, which of your army of boyfriends is going to kill you this time?"

"How did you guess?"

"I didn't come out in the last shower! Why else would you be here, when you could be wrecking your hearing on the dance floor?"

"It's all so silly. You see, I promised Stephen I wouldn't tell Geoffrey he had a boy on the side, and I promised Geoffrey not to tell Stephen about his boy either."

"And you told them?"

"No, but they found out. The boys on the side were me."

"Ah."

The ins and outs of Paul's private life make *Queer As Folk* look like an Amish community during Lent.

"And then, the other night a very handsome man came to the dressing room to take Rodney out to supper. But Rodney was in the shower, so I accidentally went instead. I had the best crème brûlée."

"So Rodney's going to kill you?"

"No, Stephen is. I introduced Rodney to Geoffrey."

"If your life gets any more complicated, you'll have to turn straight."

"*Caro mio.* If you knew anything about the world, you'd

know that heterosexuals are the biggest sluts this side of the Royal Family. Why do you think they're always crashing our dance parties? Besides, I don't think I'd make a good straight man. Last month I escorted a young lady to a party, and she jumped off a cliff and killed herself."

"That's not funny."

"I know. I feel awful. Jen was a mate of mine. Lovely voice. We were backups together in *Rocky Horror* before she went legit. We had a lot of laughs. You remember, I was going to arrange for her to take Italian lessons with you so she could chat up conductors."

"Oh, yes. Is that the girl? That's terrible."

"Poor love. It was at a very posh function up on the peninsula. Dame Norma Clutterbuck's summer place, excuse me! Jen's fiancé was away, and she asked me to go with her. All the opera big shots were there, so I was going to network myself into a frenzy. Next time they held auditions, I'd drop a few names and voilà!—in via the back door, as it were."

"I'm sure it doesn't work like that."

"Helps if you've got talent. Anyway, poor Jen's little dive put a stop to that. Dame Norma discovered the body and went *troppo*. Locked herself in the en suite and refused to budge. Everyone else scattered. A waiter or somebody called the cops."

"My God. Were you interrogated?"

"At length, by a very charming policewoman. The kind who wears the uniform on her night off."

I must admit I was a little put out. This tragic waste of a young life, though unfortunate, was nevertheless first-rate gossip. I'm always the last to know.

"Get that look off your face. I was going to tell you! It's just that affairs of the heart took over. Can I have a top up?"

"No."

"Oh, come on. It's for medicinal purposes. I haven't thought about that nasty business for a while. I'm getting myself upset."

I poured him another full glass of champagne.

"Lovely!"

"Why did she do it?"

He sipped appreciatively. "Who, darling?"

"The girl who jumped!"

"Oh, yes, good question. I think she slipped. Suicide wasn't in Jen's bag of tricks. I hate to traffic in clichés, but she had everything to live for. She was on the verge of being a huge new discovery."

"Had she done any singing?"

"With the Opera, you mean? Not in public. They've been holding workshops of a new commissioned work. Invited audience only. It's one of those local things the company doesn't want to produce and music lovers don't want to hear."

"I'm glad you haven't prejudged it."

"Caro, you hate modern opera as much as the next diva. Tebaldi never sang one, I'm sure!"

"True."

"Jen told me it was dire. Murder on the voice, impossible to learn, frocks were crap—unrewarding in every way. Sixteen workshops! Can you believe it? And it got worse every time. But she thought she was making an impression. A couple of people took her aside and told her great things were expected."

"Well!"

"Talk's cheap. If I had a job for every time I'd been offered a job, I'd be a retired millionaire like you."

"I'm nothing of the sort!"

"Of course you are. Everyone knows you mutilated yourself and got a record compo payout." He glanced toward the cupboard door. "That's the champers gone—do you have any spirits?"

I persevered. "You said she had a fiancé?"

"They were tying the knot next month."

"Not a very good reason to end it all."

"No. Of course, we all know marriage is pure hell on earth, but that comes after you sign the book. I don't know the boyfriend. He's a repetiteur, a genius apparently. She was raving about him. Jen knew the meaning of the words *career move*."

I bent low to grab a bottle of Scotch I keep under the sink in case the washing up becomes too tedious. Paul suddenly sat bolt upright—the seated equivalent of bounding.

"Wow!"

"Why thank you."

I straightened up. An alarmingly smug look had appeared on his cute face.

"No, caro. Don't you see? It's as plain as my cousin's hairdo! Jen didn't jump, she was pushed! It was murder!"

"Really, Miss Marple."

"Yes, yes! Why would she kill herself? And she was far too ambitious to fall. No, it was foul play, I'm convinced."

"Get me Scotland Yard."

Paul jumped to his feet and grabbed me by the shoulders.

"Let's investigate!"

"What? Who?"

"Let's do some sleuthing. I want to get to the bottom of this."

"You generally do."

"Marc, take me seriously. I mean it. She was a friend and a mega-talent. And a potential pupil of yours: all that money down the drain."

He switched off the light and flicked on the flame of his cigarette lighter. Eerie shadows ran up the walls.

"And...she was *murdered!*" He laughed maniacally.

I switched the light back on.

"The police must have considered that possibility. If they think it was suicide—"

"They don't know Jen like I do."

"But they know murder when they see it."

"I won't rest until justice is done. Anyway, if it wasn't murder, so what? No skin off our pecs. We're just having a little poke around, our own private investigation. Caro, we'll have the best time! You obviously need an adventure like this in your life, you're bored to wracking sobs."

"I've got safer things to do."

"Like making flummery? Come on. It'll be fun."

He bounded up close and whispered, "Don't you want to have fun, caro?" He placed his lips on my own, stroked my hair, and gave me a long passionate kiss.

I'm a sucker for that kind of logical persuasion. Even so, I'm not a complete pushover.

"There's the couch, Paul. The sheets are in the closet."

"What's a closet?"

"I hope you don't mind listening to a couple of Verdi arias before nye-nyes, exquisitely rendered by Tebaldi."

"All right, if you don't have Tina Turner's version. What about our murder thingy?"

"We'll think about it in the morning."

"Yesss!"

"But God knows what we'll do or how we'll do it."

"Love will find a way. 'Night!"

Paul flung himself onto the divan and within seconds was dead to the world, sleeping the sleep of the superficial.

CHAPTER 4

I had a particularly bad night's sleep, due to the gradual formation of a hangover, plus the odd nightmare.

In the worst of these, I was chased to the edge of a cliff by a trio of screaming banshees answering to the names of Stephen, Rodney, and Geoffrey. Paul was floating innocently above it all, passing the time singing the "Willow Song" from *Otello*. I tried to call for help. I looked down and saw my feet sinking into the cliff top, which appeared to be made of flummery. In a desperate panic I screamed out, "I want to have fun!" Suddenly I was alone, which is what often happens when I say things like that.

As a blinding dawn broke, I was awakened by the loud jangling of my throbbing head. The Annual Sleaze Ball seemed to have forsaken it's traditional home at the Sydney Showground and relocated inside my skull.

I throbbed and zigzagged toward the bathroom.

"Eighteen…nineteen…hundred and twenty. Morning!"

Paul was on the lounge-room floor, doing pushups.

"Fresh orange…juice is…on the table…hundred and thirty! Plenty left."

I soured the O.J. with a look and continued on my not-merry way. As you get older, you lose many of the attributes of youth. The first to go is the ability to spring out of bed in the morning and carry on as though nothing had happened. I can't face people or even familiar household objects until I've spent half an hour fixing myself up. Paul knew this, the tactless little rat. Ruddy good health is a fine thing, but there was no need to rub my face in it.

Eventually I emerged, fresh as a pressed daisy.

"What's for breakfast?" I asked, before Paul could ask me.

"How about a toasted bagel with smoked salmon and hollandaise?"

The old taste buds creaked back into life.

"Sounds perfect. I'm not certain I've got all the ingredients."

"Don't panic. I know a marvelous little café that does them like a beauty. Hurry up and get dressed, caro."

My protests were drowned by the roar of a passing air force. Reluctantly, I propped my eyelids open and out we went.

Café Butt was the newest thing in Oxford Street's eateries. In fact, it was so new they hadn't had time to finish the decor. One of the inside walls was bare, crumbling brickwork; the other two were sloppily half-painted in ochre and canary respectively.

The crumbly wall was held together by a piece of metal sculpture. Beneath it was a simple hand-painted sign: MADONNA AND CHILD, $11,500. Either the Madonna was leaning right down to the floor, or Baby Jesus was suffering from acute elephantiasis of the testicles. I suspected the latter. The most remarkable feature of this piece of Art was a small blue sticker attached to Jesus's forehead. It read: SOLD.

Beside a gleaming cappuccino machine lounged two or three gay persons of indeterminate sex. I assumed they came with the establishment, as they all wore black, but then I noticed the customers were wearing black, too. There seemed to be about a dozen people inside—it was hard to tell in the dark—but there was no sign of coffee or food. Everybody was waiting to be served.

Through a large hole in the wall I could see the chef in his polished, unused kitchen, casually chatting on a cellular phone. He looked as though he had never eaten a meal in his life, let alone prepared one.

At a table near the window sat two filthy teenagers poring over an elegant mah-jongg set. Paul and I took the table behind them.

"Must we sit near the window? It's so bright."

"Caro, see and be seen."

"I thought you didn't want to be seen. By certain people who wish you ill."

"From here I can see them first. Then up goes the menu. Whoo! Hi!"

He waved to a couple of slim young things across the road. They crossed over, sashayed up to the café and leaned in to our table. I hadn't realized there was no glass in the window.

"Murray, Laszlo, this is Marc."

"Hi." A quick look told them all they needed to know: I was over thirty. They forgot me instantly.

"Paul, you're looking faaab."

He was, too, owing to the fact that we had to stop at his flat on the way for a change of outfit. That may sound simple, but it was as complex as any operation devised by John le Carré. First, I had to go to the building alone and knock. If anyone answered the door, I had to pretend to be searching for a Mrs. Smith. If no one answered, I was to let myself into the flat, then call a public phone around the corner where Paul was waiting for the all clear. While he changed, I had to stand sentry and whistle "Sempre Libera" from La Traviata at the first sign of trouble. Trouble being Stephen. Of course, I had never met this Stephen, which made trouble a little tricky to identify.

Luckily the whole thing went without a hitch. After twenty minutes, Paul had swapped his black T-shirt for a white one and we left.

Now the T-shirt was being roundly admired, and I must say it did look appetizing with the sleeves rolled all the way up to the neck. There was a little pair of sparkly red shoes embroidered across the left nipple that I hadn't noticed before. Paul has a ton of sex appeal at first sight. It's only when you get to know him that it somehow dissipates.

"Stephen was very pissed last night at the Flinders. You'd better keep out of his way," gloated Murray.

"He needing to kill you," said Laszlo, who was Malaysian.

They both laughed at this amusing prospect.

"I'm not worried. I've got big strong Marc to protect me," quipped Paul. The boys looked at me with slightly renewed interest.

"Want a coffee?" Paul asked.

"Haven't got all day, love," said Murray.

"We going get the papers," said Laszlo. "Bye, honey!"

They rushed off in the direction of the closest telephone link to Stephen.

I was not overwhelmingly delighted at being dragged into this soap opera. Paul knows I like to keep a dignified distance from his sex life. "You silly queen," I remonstrated, "why do you do this?"

"I've got to make a living, sweetheart." This answer came from a pale, skinny waiter who had silently sneaked up on us.

"Oh!" I blushed. "I didn't mean you were a silly queen, I meant my friend."

"I am though. What do you want?"

"Err, a bagel with smoked salmon."

"They're off."

"Oh. What else is there?"

"It's on the blackboard." He pointed into the darkness. "I'll come back."

"No!" screamed Paul. "We'll just have two strong cappuccinos."

"Right away, handsome." He turned on his heel and vanished into the gloom. We never saw him again.

"Now," said Paul. He had on his Serious Look. "This murder. Let's get down to business. We must establish what we know and what we don't know. Let's start with what we know."

"Brilliant."

"Well. The victim's name was Jennifer…what was it? Burke, I think. Jennifer Burke. That sounds about right."

"I thought you knew her well."

"We worked together. I knew her first name well, the rest not so well."

I looked at him skeptically.

"Don't grill me! "

"Did she have any family?"

"Not really. She was from New Zealand. She arrived here with nothing, which isn't unusual, is it! God, I'm witty. Anyway, that was about six years back. She danced, sang, and looked pretty. We did a couple of shows together. *Me and My Girl* was the first, I think. And she absolutely refused to tour with it to Auckland."

"Ah! What does that tell us?"

"It tells us the money was shit."

"Or she may have had some reason for not wanting to go back to New Zealand."

"Of course she did, darling! Have you ever been there?"

"I'm just trying to establish some motive. She could have had a falling-out with her family."

"What, she had a fight with her mother, so six years later the old girl flies all the way to Sydney and shoves her daughter off a cliff? Doesn't hold water. I think the fiancé did it."

"Was he at the party?"

"No, he was in Brisbane doing something or other."

"Then he couldn't have done it."

"I suppose not, but it's usually the partner in these cases, isn't it? Where's our fucking coffees? Look, they're just sitting there on the bench getting cold. No trace of that woozy waiter! Popped next door to the peep show, I bet."

Paul hopped up and jetted over to get the coffee. I had the distinct gut feeling that our murder investigation was starting off on a disorganized foot. I had half a mind to tell Paul to put it all behind him and concentrate on avoiding his own demise at the hands of a crazed bimbo. On the other hand, I was excited. The "spy vs. spy" stuff at Paul's flat while he changed shirts had given me a fair old tingle. Suspense can be addictive.

In the old days, suspense was part and parcel of our lifestyle. When I used to drink at the Frisco Bar, long since defunct, a raid was often in the cards. Every brandy, lime, and soda could have been your last. You never knew if the fellow in the tight corduroys and tank top chatting you up was in plainclothes, poised to charge you with "expostulating in a place of worship" or some such summary offense dating back to the Middle Ages. It gave the whole cruising procedure a frisson that's no longer there. Nowadays we have gay liaison officers. I knew one or two back then as well, but they were strictly unofficial.

And then there was the operatic aspect of this affair. I was intrigued at the thought of mixing with some of the country's top canary fanciers. It's my passion, after all, though I can't say I'm a regular attendee at the Opera. For one thing, I can't afford it. For another, there's the problem of Surtitles, the translation they project onto a strip above the stage. Who wants to read what the singers are singing about? That's not the point! But you can't avoid it. You find yourself becoming gradually mesmerized by these prosaic drawn-out phrases, like on those long-distance flights with their endless maps and updates on the temperature outside and how many kilometers you are from Kuala Lumpur, until you find yourself screaming, "Stop! I don't want to be told!"

For me, opera is a more intimate, domestic affair. My association with the art began early, as a babe in arms. My grandmother had grown up with the mother of a great star—you guessed it: Signora Tebaldi. I was taken to the great lady herself one afternoon, in all my linen and finery, to be shown off. She took one look and said, "I can never have children. My voice would suffer." Divas always talk about themselves, but as she seemed to refer obliquely to me it was taken as a compliment. I became famous round the market as the Baby Renata Could Never Have. This special relationship was cruelly curtailed when I was whisked away at the age of two to Australia—a place where, in those days, no diva would be seen dead (except Melba, and she was).

Paul returned with the rapidly cooling beverages.

"Now, Paul," I said, "If we're going to do this, let's do it properly. Put me in the picture. Where exactly is this cliff-top where the fatal act took place?"

"Ooh, you make it sound *molto* spooky! Well, Dame Norma Clutterbuck has a summer place up on the peninsula. It's right at the end, on a—you know, a hill. There's fabulous panoramic views on all sides, and she's only there six months of the year— isn't that pathetic? And the house! You simply wouldn't believe some of the kitschy stuff she's got. It's so camp you could die! Anyway, the house faces west I think. That's where the road is. You must have seen pictures of the garden in *New Idea*."

"I don't read *New Idea*."

"Really? Your loss. Then the land gets steeper at the back, behind the pool and tennis courts, and it's a bit bushy. There's a sort of track through to the cliff edge, and you've got the ocean down below. You can see the water from the house but not the cliff because of the trees. I remember because we were looking out at one point, checking out a cute boy in the pool."

"Did you see anyone go onto the track?"

"I don't remember. People seemed to be popping off into the shrubs all afternoon."

"How many guests were there?"

"Oh, hard to say. Fifty?"

I was somewhat taken aback. "Fifty? How the hell are we going to find fifty people and talk to them?"

"A few of them left straightaway after lunch."

My excitement was rapidly diminishing. "Paul, I'm afraid this is impossible. We're not the police. We can't simply barge up to someone and say, 'Where were you on the night of such and such?' In fact, we can't even look as though we're investigating anything. You hardly know any of these people, I don't know them at all, and we're not even sure if it was murder!"

"A challenge, isn't it?"

"Why did the police think it was suicide and not an accident?"

"Oh, well…there was a note."

I made an expansive theatrical gesture of despair, knocking my coffee off the table and bang into where Paul's lap would have been if he weren't an agile youth with dance experience.

"Caro, do you ever finish a cup of coffee?"

He wiped down his bench with a handful of the café's recycled tissues.

"I'm sorry, but really! A suicide note says it all, don't you think?"

"Oh, she was always doing that. Writing little goodbye things, threatening to kill herself. Several times she promised to end it all if I didn't lend her my blue eyebrow pencil. I told her to stick it up her arse. Everyday dressing-room talk! It meant nothing, I swear."

"I think you killed her to get your eyebrow pencil back."

"Not a bad theory."

"What can we do about these millions of partygoers?"

"We'll have to narrow it down. Jen didn't know everybody there. They weren't all opera people. A lot of them were FOC's."

"What?"

"Friends of the caterers."

"I see. And friends of the caterers don't murder people?"

"Not if they want to get invited to more parties."

"Hmm."

"And it was late afternoon when she died. Most of the hangers-on had gone. Professional partygoers don't limit themselves to one a day! The staff were tidying up. Now that I think of it, I wanted to go, too. But Jen had to talk to somebody first. She wouldn't leave until she'd done it. She was a great networker."

"Who did she want to talk to? About what?"

"I don't know. They all sat up and took notice of her in *Phar Lap*. She probably wanted to follow it up. Don't look confused, caro—*Phar Lap* was the commissioned opera they were workshopping. Jen played the daughter—that is, not the horse's daughter, somebody else's daughter."

He hooted with laughter.

"I just remembered! Jen said it was a shame the horse was a baritone role because they had the perfect girl to play it!"

"So she had enemies."

"One or two, I suppose. That's showbiz." His big brown eyes took on a watery aspect. "Oh, Marc, fuck it. I'm going to miss that kid."

I patted his hand. "There there, don't go to pieces. We need to think clearly and work out our modus operandi."

"Work out what? It sounds like a tampon." He had recovered. "HAR HAR HAR" (*Splutter*).

The grunge-filled silence was shattered by an appallingly loud and grating laugh from the recesses of the café. My face dropped. I knew that laugh.

"What was that?" Paul was wide-eyed.

Approaching us at a rate that precluded avoidance was one of the ugliest men on earth. A pitted face the color and texture of a disused brickworks, sprouting hardy tufts of gray hair in unusual and/or unnecessary places; teeth so weathered they seemed to predate the horseless carriage; shoulders sagging, dragged earthward by a commedia dell'arte potbelly; most unforgettable, perhaps, the eyes—heavy and red-rimmed from a potent combination of alcohol and conjunctivitis. All this would have been forgivable if he hadn't had that laugh.

"We-hell! HAR HAR HAR! Marc Petrucci out for a Saturday nosh with his young gentleman friend. Don't introduce me then, you rude bugger. Roy Coxedge!"

He thrust out his palm to Paul, who took it as though he were handling a sick eel.

"Paul Silverton," I intoned. "Roy and I go back years."

"Yes, longer than we'd care to remember, ay? HAR HAR." Roy patted the back of my neck as he pulled up a chair.

Paul looked absolutely horrified. I knew what he was thinking. "Roy," I gushed, "is that gorgeous wife of yours with you?"

"No, worse luck. Shaunna's got a charity do on this afternoon. She had to stay up at the property and get organized. She doesn't mind. She loves a bit of hard work."

Shaunna is as gracious and charming as Roy is overbearing and charmless. She was a Logie Award–winning soap opera star, if that isn't a contradiction in terms. Most people were amazed when she married Roy, even though he does own Cox Bros. Wines and has a certain cachet among the red-drinking set.

Roy was studying political science when I met him in another life at university. It was clear even then that he would end up in wine: When cardboard wine casks were invented, he was the one who removed the silver bag and throttled out the last few drops. Now, of course, it's Select Vintages. He set an empty glass on our table.

"That was a first rate shiraz. I'd have left you some if I'd seen you before."

"Bit early for me."

"Rubbish! Never too early for a good solid red. But look, have you ever seen the property? I'm upgrading like buggery! You must pop over and let me show you around. I keep some great stuff out of sight of the tourists. A real drop, none of that cellar-door Chairman's Selection crap."

"Roy is a winemaker." I explained to Paul. "You might know his wife, Shaunna Campbell."

Now it was Paul's turn to gush. A spotlight might have been turned on him. "Shaunna Campbell? I was brought up on her! She's just heaven! I adore everything she's ever done."

"I don't. She was married twice before I snagged her! She'd like you, though. Flattery will get you everywhere with Shaunna." Roy turned to me. "Bring your friend along…" With a twinkle in his eye, he raised his already deafening voice, "As long as he's not a *poof!*"

Every single head in the room turned.

"HAR HAR!"

"Roy, I've just remembered an appointment. We'll have to go."

He took no notice.

"Jesus, you should've come down last month for the festival."

"Oh," said Paul. "The Malanga Festival?"

"That's right, sonny Jim."

"I'm afraid—" I began.

"Yeah, I run me own Arts Festival now. Well, Shaunna runs it. I just stand around and get pissed. HAR HAR!" He became unattractively solemn. "Beautiful music, lovely stuff. Bloody classy, too. We had a string quartet, coupla pianists, a singer— now *he* would have been right up your alley! Amazing young fella. Bit weird, I thought at first, but by Christ he can sing. Fucking incredible."

A tall, tanned, bald gentleman was weaving his way over to our table. He wore a neat sports jacket, casual slacks, a perfectly creased white shirt open at the neck, and a fetching gold bracelet. Everything about him was cultivated and attractive. In a mild singsong voice he said "Thank you, Roy. It's gratifying to have my own opinion vindicated."

"There you are," boomed Roy. "You sure took your time in the mens'. Bit constipated, ay?"

Paul spluttered into his coffee. The strange gentleman merely smiled and shrugged. Meanwhile, Roy was rounding up another chair.

"Have a seat, Charlie. I just been chewing the fat with this old bludger Petrucci. Marc, this is Charles Mignon, the critic."

"How do you do?" said Charles amiably.

"And this is Marc's friend...ah, Paul."

"Hi!" Paul said.

Charles stared. "I'm sure we've met," he said.

I can't say I fell off my seat at this. It's one of Paul's stated aims in life to meet, charm, and, if possible, seduce anyone who is ever likely to do him any good. Critics fall automatically into this category.

"Marc's a music lover," said Roy. He sat back with folded arms, as though daring me to refute this claim.

"Yes."

Charles looked at me expectantly.

"Err, I always read your reviews with great interest," I said, "especially the opera. You always seem so...reasonable."

He blushed, charmingly. "Do I? But I'm nothing of the sort. It's simply my tone. I'm quite unreasonable. I hold very hard and fast prejudices."

"Oh, so do I. I'm a great Tebaldi fan."

"Hmm. Yes. Well, she knew when to quit, I'll certainly give her that." He sounded reasonable. "Her *Butterfly* was well sung. Couldn't act, of course." As I was speechless, he went on. "I'm not particularly fond of that period at all. Give me the older masters—Lully, Handel, Gluck. A purer musical experience. Their work had nobility, a quality entirely lacking in contemporary life."

I was about to stick up for the Italians when Roy barged in. "I was telling Marc about young Raoul's recital at the festival. That's his sort of stuff, Handel and what-have-you."

Charles glowed. "Raoul is a very exciting talent. My protégé—I suppose I should make that clear! A male alto of extraordinary range and power, quite unlike the weak countertenor voice you may be used to. Indeed, I think he's headed for great things on the opera stage. So many of the major castrati roles are gods or mythical heroes. And..." he winked lasciviously, "Raoul is nothing if not godlike."

"Baroque opera doesn't have quite the following...that ...you know, normal opera has, err, I don't think," I concluded lamely. I don't know why I said such a tactless thing. On the other hand, he had dismissed Tebaldi: He deserved to suffer.

He leaned forward and took my hand in both of his. "That is definitely the view of the Sydney City Opera, as I have come to discover. My suggestions for a more comprehensive repertoire have fallen on deaf ears. Still, they can't afford not to listen to me. I'm too dangerous to ignore!" At this he brightened. "Surely there is room for a wider spectrum. Are we not enriched by diversity? Any true music lover would appreciate hearing Gluck and Handel operas sung the way they should be sung as they were originally—with strength and purpose! With nobility!"

He leaned back, and stared at Paul.

"We met at Dame Norma's soiree. You were taking photographs. Are you a professional?"

"Not really," said Paul with unjustifiable modesty. "I just took a few private snaps."

"You didn't tell me that," I said.

"I forgot."

"I only ask," Charles continued, "because Raoul needs publicity photographs. They must be taken by a true artist who appreciates male beauty. At least that's my opinion, and I'm usually right." He smiled disarmingly.

"Well," Paul consulted a mental diary, "he could come and see me on Tuesday—"

"Where?" I interrupted sarcastically. "In your studio?" Paul was, of course, no more a photographer than I was a nuclear physicist.

Paul came down to earth. "Yesss. I'll have to get back to you."

An awkward silence ensued. It seemed like kismet to find myself confronted by someone who had been a guest at the fatal party. It was now or never in the sleuthing stakes. I decided to get Charles's perspective.

"So, Charles." I settled back with that old Hercule Poirot glint in my eye, the picture of alert bonhomie. "What did you make of that terrible and mysterious accident at Dame Norma's?"

"You needn't be ghoulish about it," he snapped, pulling me up short. "Of course, it was appalling. Who knows what the future had in store for that young woman? And yet, I must say,

I disapprove of suicide, especially in this day and age. It's so passé. When you consider the great suicides—Sylvia Plath, Diane Arbus, Mishima—who would follow an act like that? It's been done too often and too well. Done to death, you might say. I don't mean to be insensitive, but as a critic I am trained to make comparisons of this nature."

Coming from Charles, this sounded perfectly fair. I even found myself nodding in agreement. (He had that effect.) However, I could sense Paul getting hot under the collar.

"I took Jen to that party, honey, and she never gave me the impression for one split second that she wanted to jump over a cliff! What's more, she wasn't the type. And I'll bet she'd never heard of Sylvia Sims or Mitsubishi!"

"Now, let's not have a row!" urged Roy.

Charles was immediately apologetic. "I'm sorry. I'd forgotten you were her friend. Of course, it was a tragedy—no one denies that. As a matter of fact, I heard her sing in the new opera they're hoping to mount, *Phar Lap*. She was good. Made a silk purse out of a horse's arse, but don't quote me!"

"HAR HAR! I can't stand that modern rubbish either." Roy stood. "We've got to get going, but let's make some arrangements here! I'm off overseas on Monday—the Cambodian market, you know, opening up like you wouldn't believe. I'm floggin' them a vintage I call Khmer Vin Rouge. A nation of wine drinkers in the making."

"Cambodia?"

"We gotta dump our crook stuff somewhere! Now let's see...we're having some people to stay...when?"

"First weekend in December," Charles prompted.

"Right. Consider yourselves invited! No getting out of it."

"I'd love to see your place, Roy," I said.

"Me too," Paul chimed in.

Roy clapped me hard on the shoulder, leaning heavily as he staggered to his feet. "You beauty! I'll look forward to it. Let's roll out the old red-stained carpet. We might even persuade Raoul to give us a number, eh?"

"I'm sure he would be delighted," Charles purred.

"Well, so would I. Marc, I'll call you with directions. Charlie, stay here while I get the car."

As soon as Roy had gone, Charles came over all conspiratorial. "I must confess, I'm buttering him up. I'm hoping Roy will produce a full-scale opera at his next festival, although he has none of the facilities as yet."

"Sounds like a big expense. Is he keen?"

"Raoul's recital got him interested in the old masters. I'm working on him—doing my damndest!" He smiled amiably. "Gluck's *Orfeo* is the obvious choice, I think. It's relatively familiar. You must back me up."

"When it comes to music, I would have thought Roy was more into Lloyd Webber."

"Oh, not a bit. We don't have to worry about *Phar Lap*."

"What?"

Charles grinned. "We're at cross purposes. You're talking about the well-known Lloyd Webber! I meant the other one."

I was momentarily confused. "You mean the cellist?"

"No, no." Charles rocked with glee at the information he was about to impart. "Another composer! Local fellow!"

"Yes," Paul added, "there's two! Isn't it heaven? The man who wrote *Phar Lap* is called Lloyd Webber as well! Jen thought it was hysterical!"

"Delicious irony," agreed Charles. "Randolph Lloyd Webber. No relation, I understand." He chuckled. "My God, who'd be a composer nowadays? I saw young Randolph only the other morning. I was out getting some of the new-season orchids. It's a hobby of mine, and there's the poor boy working ten hours a day in a nursery, trying to write his music at the same time. So much for subsidies! Different in Lully's time and even Haydn's. They simply attached themselves to the Court or to some nobleman, and they were set for life. Roy's the closest thing we've got, and he has to be constantly jollied along or he'll lose interest. Progress? I don't think so."

A red BMW skidded into a no-standing zone outside. The horn honked, a more melodious variation of Roy's laugh. Charles stood, squeezed my hand, and kissed Paul lightly on the lips.

"See you again soon, I'm sure."

"Which nursery was that?" asked Paul quickly.

"In the market for an orchid, are you?" Charles inquired. "It's the Upstairs Nursery at Bondi. Most unusual place. It's on the second floor, above a sex shop. The name escapes me."

"Wet Dream."

"I thought you'd know it. Bye!"

I watched Charles sprint lightly out to the car, and wave a tanned arm as they sped away.

"What an agreeable man," I enthused. "Not at all what I imagined critics to be like."

"I can't stand a bar of him," said Paul.

"Why not?"

"Caro. Don't you know an old lech when you see one?"

"He's no older than me."

"You're a sweet, motherly old thing. He's a scumbag."

"I thought he was very pleasant. A touch ignorant when it came to sopranos of the '50s, but otherwise charming."

"He wasn't charming up at Dame Norma's. He was boring and pushy. Everyone hated him."

I somehow couldn't picture it. However, I could picture Charles Mignon putting the hard word on Paul. Very definitely.

"I had the impression he was keen on you."

"Oh yes, he was all over me for about two minutes. I know he's important and everything, but he's not my cup of Spanish fly. There's something about him—he's so insincere! If there's one thing I look for in a casual encounter, it's sincerity."

"By the way, if I were you I wouldn't go around telling every interested party your murder theory. Let them think the girl committed suicide."

"I know, but Charles irritates me. He's a manipulator."

"Doesn't take no for an answer, you mean."

Paul looked abashed.

Blithely, I changed the subject. "What about these photos you were taking?"

"Oh, yes. It slipped my mind. I fancied a few shots of myself sampling the lifestyle of the rich and loud."

"Do you have them?"

"They're not developed yet."

"We must get it done this morning. There's a print-while-you-wait place across the street."

"I haven't used all the film yet!"

"That doesn't matter."

"Oh, it's all right for you with your wealthy aunts and everything! I'm on a budget. I'm not throwing away half a roll of film. It costs money."

"You don't mind throwing money away on cold piss-weak coffee!"

Paul glanced about. The staff were their customary absent selves. "Who said we're paying for it? Let's go. *Andiamo!*"

He took my arm and leapt to his feet.

"Wait, we can't. Go where?"

"To the Upstairs Nursery, of course, to interview our first suspect."

"Err, yes, all right. What makes you think this Lloyd-Webber fellow's a suspect?"

"I've met him. He's nuts."

"Oh."

"You can talk to him while I use up my film on adorable hunks at the beach."

He hustled me out of the café, but not before I managed to leave an $10 note behind for our bill. As we crossed the street I looked back to see one of the customers at the next table languidly reach over and pocket the money.

CHAPTER 5

"*B*y the way," I said as we motored toward the notorious beachside suburb of Bondi, "how do you think you can get away for a weekend? Mustn't the show go on, et cetera?"

"I'll take a sickie."

I feigned ignorance. "But suppose you're not sick?"

"I'll act sick! I'm a professional actor, you know."

"Would it work? You tend to radiate good health. God knows why."

"Don't worry, darling, it's the easiest thing in the world. After the Friday show, I'll take a long hot shower then run straight to the stage manager and say I've got a sweat and I'm coming down with flu! They loathe the thought of flu spreading through the company. They practically beg you to stay away!"

"And what about all those tired businessmen and little old ladies who forked out their life savings for a ticket? Hardly fair to them, is it?"

"As long as the chandelier falls down and the helicopter lands, they're happy. They don't care about the actors! As far as they're concerned, we could be trained apes lip-synching the Original Cast Album."

"I can see how they'd get that impression."

His face fell. "There may be one small problem. I just remembered. We've had sixteen cases of suspected flu this week already—including Rodney, and no way was it his turn!"

"Maybe he's really got it."

"Probably. That's just the sort of trick he would pull. Anyway, if this keeps up, management is going to clamp down. Start asking for doctor's certificates and stuff."

"Don't they trust you?"

"Exactly! We'll see what happens, but I might have to join you on the Sunday. Could you live without me for one day?"

"Perfectly well."

"You're welcome to that revolting Roy."

"Paul! Don't speak about my friends in that tone."

"Well, he is! Ear hairs! Yuck City!"

"Beneath those ear hairs, there beats a heart of gold."

"Yes, yes. Beauty is only foreskin deep. I know. There's a park!"

I swerved, a Chicago 1930s–style U-turn. Parking is at a premium in the beach suburbs. Unfortunately, this space was taken after all. Lying in the gutter was a heavily tanned, scantily dressed youth, casually enjoying the aftereffects of some lethal combo of designer drugs.

"What a tragic waste of human potential," I remarked.

"What a tragic waste of a parking space," said Paul. "That's where we're headed," he added, as we drove past a sleazy old shop. The large windows were blacked out and stenciled on them in red droplet lettering were the words WET DREAM.

In marked contrast, there was a doorway in the same building painted in a rich green hue with a sign saying UPSTAIRS NURSERY, 1ST FLOOR. Around the sign's perimeter was an elaborate vine motif with apricot-colored petals, cherries, gold leaf, and God knows what else sprouting from it. It was so cutesy, not even a queen could have done it. That meant only one thing: hippies.

We found a park in the approximate vicinity of New Zealand and bought frozen-yogurt cones to see us through the long walk back.

"We don't look much like hard-boiled detectives, do we?" Paul laughed. "You with your summer berry and me with my crunchy butterscotch. We really should have tumblers of neat whiskey."

"Wouldn't want to draw attention to ourselves."

"What are we going to say to this character?"

"Well, I've been thinking about that. I thought I'd pretend to be a journalist from an international opera magazine."

"Brilliant, caro! And I'll be your fabulously cute jet-setting boyfriend."

"You can be my assistant and take notes," I cautioned. "I'll get him talking about his work, and you bring the conversation 'round to Jennifer and the party. Let's pop into that newsagent and buy a notepad and pen."

He took my hand. "Marc! Our very first expenses! We really are serious!"

A passing homophobe snorted in disgust. In reply, Paul lifted my hand to his lips and kissed it. This sweet but unexpected act caused me to drop the frozen yogurt, which landed directly on my shoe.

"Damn."

"Never mind, caro. We're dealing with a heterosexual. You don't need to look your best."

As we mounted the stairs, the weather seemed to become more tropical. Eventually the stairwell opened out into an enormous greenhouse. Large-leafed specimens of vegetation were growing everywhere. The roof was glass, double-glazed, with a noxious yellow tint giving everything a jaundiced glow. The humidity was unbearable. Moisture from the nursery must have been seeping through to the sex shop below in torrents. I don't suppose it bothered the patrons.

Nobody seemed to be around. Paul set off on safari to the further end of the shop while I checked things out in the nearby rain forest.

Exotica was the order of the day. Trees with flat variegated leaves, oozing leaf sweat, towered above me. Lord knows how they got there, but they'd clearly been thriving for a very long time. The blood-red irises of a Brazilian ornamental passion fruit pulsated with unnatural health in the hot artificial glare. Splashes of orange in the deep green turned the scene into a painting by Rousseau. I expected a tiger to stalk out of the undergrowth. Sweating ever more profusely, I was seized with a sense of foreboding, of the unnamed, unknowable terrors of the jungle.

Near me loomed a large brown object smothered with tendrils and moldy with moisture. It was a cash register. Behind it sat a huge woman with coifed hair, wearing a flowing muumuu festooned with toucan motifs. She stared me straight in the eye, unflinching. She seemed kindly, in a terrifying way.

"You have returned to the heart of darkness," she intoned. "We are of the earth. These are our roots. I feel the presence of a kindred earth spirit. The rain forest is our life source. You have come home to your primal womb. We are at one with the living forest, the fecund blossoms, the birds. WAAAAAAAARK!"

I stepped back.

"Soon you will return to the corrupt decaying world. You must take with you a part of the life force to replenish and revitalize your inner being. Might I suggest a Colombian sticky-stamened umbrella tree? Everything about you says sticky stamen. And read my book, *Women Who Thrive With the Moisture*. You must get in touch with your feminine self."

"I don't really want a—"

"Of course, I understand. You feel unwilling to remove a portion of the life source. You find it spiritually abhorrent. Have no fear. The rain forest will nourish you, and in time you will nourish the forest. We are one."

"I—" I was about to explain my presence when I slipped on the damp floor. Reaching out to steady myself I grabbed onto a low hanging vine covered in purple flowers and, I discovered, thousands of tiny sharp spikes. As I pulled the vine, a branch of an exotic shrub snapped off.

"What the fuck are you doing? You can pay for that!" snarled Earth Mother. She began flicking through a price list.

I staggered back onto my feet, my good hand looking like a pincushion. "Yes, yes, all right. I'm actually here to do an interview." She beamed, radiating cosmic warmth. "With Randolph Lloyd Webber." She ceased beaming.

"Why?" she asked.

"I'm from the international opera magazine *Opera del Mondo*. We're researching an article on contemporary music theatre. Naturally, we are interested in Mr. Lloyd Webber."

"You sure you've got the right one?"

"The composer of *Phar Lap*."

"Yeah, that's him. He's in storage."

"Pardon?"

"Out back. Turn right at the camellias. Don't take too long, if you don't mind."

I continued my prepared spiel. "The magazine is based in Milan. I'm the official Australasian correspondent. I've written many articles—"

"Yeah, yeah. See if you can mention the shop in your piece."

"I will, yes, naturally."

"And the book!" she called after me. *"Women Who Thrive With the Moisture*, Frangipani Press, $39.95."

After some searching, I found the camellias. Paul was amongst them, sniffing contentedly. "Caro, where have you been?"

"I had to get the owner's OK for the interview. It's journalistic protocol."

"Who, that silly old drag queen?"

"Is she...?"

"Of course! She used to be called Victoria when she worked the Toucan Room. Then she put all that weight on. Now she's bigger than the whole State of Victoria. She owns the sex shop as well."

"Do you know her?"

"She was at Dame Norma's party. Sat by the pool all day reading palms and drinking Long Island iced teas. She was completely off her face by midafternoon."

"We should put her on our list of suspects, even so. Now,

Mr. Lloyd Webber should be around here somewhere, in a storage room."

"There's a door behind those what's-in-a-names."

"Let's try it. Mind that vine, it stabs you."

As we went through the door, the change of atmosphere almost knocked our socks off. The air was icy, chilling us to the marrow. Piles of cut plants were lying about, and an unpleasant odor of decay drenched the air. If the rain forest was the life source, this Cool Room was the morgue.

A sneeze brought to our attention a thin young man. He was pale with dark hair and a small dark goatee. His eyes were red-rimmed and streaming, as was his nose. In his long, pale hands he held a pair of secateurs with which he was unsuccessfully battling the thick stems of a bunch of proteas.

"Die you bastards! Aaachoo!"

"Mr. Randolph Lloyd Webber?"

He glanced up angrily. "What do you want?"

"I'm Marc Petrucci, and this is my assistant Paul. We're from the international opera magazine *Opera del Mondo*. Could we talk to you for a moment about your work?"

Randolph smiled a dazzling smile. "Please do!" He flung the proteas with secateurs attached into a corner. "Take a seat."

There wasn't one, so we stood. "We're researching a piece on contemporary composers in the operatic arena."

"That's great. Where will I start? The basic structural elements? I work in the area of polymodality, I'm not against tonality per se, but I like to stretch the ear. I explore the ambiguities of tonality, I suppose, using motivic development in a polymodal context."

I was nonplussed. "Are you getting this down?" I asked Paul.

"No."

Randolph, meanwhile, was staring at Paul. A strange, troubled look came over the young man's face. "I know you from somewhere. Aren't you Jen's friend from the party?"

"Jen? Party?"

"Yes, you are. The homosexual."

"Guess that's me," Paul admitted candidly.

"You're a dancer, aren't you?"

"That's what I told people. I was really on an undercover photo assignment for the mag."

"What?"

"The opera mag. Opera Thingo. What's it called again?"

"*Opera del Mondo*," I prompted.

"Don't you know the name of the magazine you work for?" Randolph asked suspiciously.

"Of course I do, honey. I'm just a dizzy queen."

I thought it best to interrupt. "I'll conduct this interview, thank you, Paul." I turned to Randolph. "*Opera del Mondo* is based in Milan. I am the official Australasian correspondent. I've written many articles on opera and music."

"I'm sure."

"Paul is a freelance writer and photographer I recently picked up."

Paul smirked at this. I must admit, it didn't sound quite right.

Randolph, however, seemed convinced. "So. Where were we? Post-Darmstadt, yes." He was about to break into another frenzy of jargon; instead he broke into a frenzy of sneezes. "Aaaah! Aaaachooo! Oh, bugger."

"Aren't you well?"

"Oh, it's this place. I can't stand it. I'm allergic to everything! I've got a permanent cold from running in and out of the Cool Room. Look at my hands, look at them!" He was getting excited. "They're red raw from stripping roses and wiring wreaths! Victoria's a slave driver, the fat old lush, she never does a thing. She's only interested in her exotic plants." He leaned forward conspiratorially. "Half of them are illegal imports you know. She sneaks them into the country somehow. In her big fat dresses, probably. Quarantine would impound them like a shot! See that thing over there, the sticky stamened umbrella tree? That's one of them. It's noxious! If it got out of here it would run riot. The whole city would disappear within a week! There'll be big trouble one day. Aaachoo!"

"How appalling," I ventured, "that a young composer of such talent should be reduced to this."

Paul winked at me in admiration.

"Oh, I must suffer for my art," replied Randolph. "That's just the way it is. I write at night. That's how come I'm so tired. I tend to get a little overexcited when I don't sleep. Things go through my head—the music, other things. I mean, *Phar Lap* is ancient history as far as I'm concerned. I've worked that seam. I'm on a different tack now: microtonality."

"This sounds interesting."

"It's utterly fascinating, the only way to go. It doesn't necessarily invalidate my previous tonal field, but it extends it enormously. The possibilities are exciting, as I'm sure you appreciate."

"Yes, I can see that. Micro...yes."

"Microtonality."

"My readers would probably be interested in your personal definition."

"Oh, it refers to division of the scale. Why divide the octave into twelve tones, when it can be divided into twenty? Or thirty?"

"Is that possible?"

"Not with conventional instruments, nor with opera singers of course. Most of them can't even sing one bloody note properly."

"Well, we're mainly interested in your operatic work. What are your views on sopranos? The great stars, Tebaldi for instance."

"I don't know her. I don't think very highly of singers. They know nothing about music and they care even less!"

"I see." I let it pass. "I believe the late Jennifer Burke's performance in *Phar Lap* was highly regarded."

That pulled him up short. "Yes, yes. She's the exception. Was, I mean." He stood. "I can't talk about that." He paced across the room, kicked a nearby shrub to pieces and with a sigh leaned against the solid trunk of the umbrella tree. Paul and I followed.

"A tragedy," I said. "How many young singers can do justice to contemporary work?"

Randolph shook his head. "She was so…wonderful. You must know," he said to Paul. "You were her friend."

Randolph's whole frame was shaking. Paul gently put his arm around him.

"Don't worry," he said softly. Randolph shifted his weight against Paul. "We won't write anything about her."

"No, you must. Write about how good she was. I'll never find another interpreter like her. She had such a feel for my work. And she did more than just sing: She lived it! I can't believe what happened, it's impossible! Why does this always happen to me?"

Paul kissed him gently on the neck.

"Please don't do that."

"I'm sorry."

"I know you mean well. I'm all right now." He blew his nose. "She's better off, you know. Better off dead than married to that idiot. She knew it, too. The poor thing, she was so confused. So vulnerable. She wouldn't listen to me."

"Did you try to talk her out of it?" Paul inquired.

Randolph's old suspicious look came over his face again. "I'm afraid that's personal."

"That's all right. Only I did, too."

"You did?"

"Oh, yes," Paul confided. "I've never met him, but I didn't think Jen was ready to tie the knot. Not with her career and everything. She wouldn't listen to me either."

"No, no. She wouldn't listen. And look what happened!" He sniffed. "Oh, God. Look, Mr. Um—"

"Marc."

"I'm sorry, I can't do this interview today. You'll have to come back another time."

"I'll try."

"Please do. I'd love to talk about *Phar Lap*. I can give you a detailed deconstructional analysis, but not right now."

"Ah, well, too bad," I said. "On a lighter note, what is your opinion of the music of your namesake?"

I don't remember ever having seen such a transformation in my entire life. I suddenly knew what Vesuvius looked like before it went off.

"To whom do you refer?" said Randolph. At least I think that's what he said. His jaw was locked tight.

"The other Mr. Lloyd Webber," I lightly hinted.

"Never heard of him."

"You know," Paul added helpfully. "The popular one."

"I...said...I've...never...heard...of...him. God damn it!" Randolph, his eyes blazing, made a fist and whacked it hard against the sticky-stamened Colombian umbrella tree.

"Aaaaaaaaargh!"

The force of the jolt dislodged a large Colombian tarantula, which flopped onto Randolph's shoulder and scuttled inside his shirt. He screamed and threw himself on the floor. "Help! It's biting me!" he yelled.

"Where is it gone?" cried Paul, also hysterical.

"On my back. Aaargh!"

Paul swiftly stepped forward and gave Randolph's back a vicious kick. Then he jumped to one side (a perfect jeté).

"Ow! Now it's on my stomach."

Paul stepped forward again.

"No!" screamed Randolph. "Don't kick me again! Take my shirt off! Help me."

"I can't," cried Paul.

I edged forward. "Put your arms up," I ordered. Randolph did so and I tore his thin cotton shirt over his head, flinging it immediately to the floor where Paul jumped vigorously all over it.

There was no sign of the spider on Randolph's body. Paul prodded the shirt gingerly with his toe. The tarantula didn't appear to be there. It was sitting on my hand.

"Fuck!" Paul aimed another well-placed kick, this time at my wrist. The momentum sent the spider spinning through the air. We all ducked for dear life. It cleared us and plopped to earth at the feet of Victoria the shop owner. She stepped forward and with one massive heel crushed the creature out of existence. She did not look happy. I don't know how long she had been there.

"If you have everything you need, perhaps Mr. Lloyd Webber could get back to work."

"Yes, of course. Well…" I looked down, but Mr. Lloyd Webber would clearly have difficulty getting back to work. He was unconscious.

"Randolph!" she snapped. "Clean this shit up!"

He didn't stir.

"He's been poisoned to death by that monster," Paul suggested.

"Possibly. I think he's fainted." She seemed greatly unfazed.

"We'd better call an ambulance," I said.

"I'll send him to Emergency in a taxi. Ambulances cost an arm and a leg." She glared at me. "The plant you attacked is priced at $65. We accept all cards. Then I would thank you to get out."

She waddled back toward her post.

Paul smiled at me. "Our second expense," he said.

CHAPTER 6

*E*merging from the roar of a jet engine came the plaintive sound of Desdemona's prayer. She is about to be strangled by the insanely jealous Moor of Venice. She is innocent, but her aria seems even more poignant to us (the audience) because we know she will soon be dead. Naturally, death never prevented Tebaldi from reemerging after the final curtain to acknowledge the prolonged applause of her loyal public. Quite rightly, too. That's where opera differs from real life. In life there are no bows. It's just curtains.

I could have heard any of Tebaldi's great roles that evening— she was a renowned Butterfly, for example— but I picked Desdemona because I was thinking specifically about jealousy.

In my short but jam-packed career as a murder investigator, jealousy was playing a major part. There was no doubt the unstable composer of the opera about a horse was plagued by jealousy. What had Randolph said? "She's better off dead than married to that idiot... She wouldn't listen to me and look what happened..." Those two statements alone were enough to convict in my book. I considered the scenario: Wildly in love with the only woman who could sing his difficult vocals, desperately jealous of her elusive fiancé, Randolph had cornered Jennifer at the cliff. Perhaps he asked her to marry him. When she rebuffed his advances, he lashed out in fury.

It was a feasible theory, one that might have occurred to Barbara Cartland. Even so, certain details worried me. For instance, Randolph's portrait of Jennifer as the epitome of doe-eyed vulnerability did not match Paul's description of her at all. One version was early Shirley Temple, the other mid-to-late Joan Crawford. Who was right?

My thoughts turned to young Ms. Burke herself. I knew

nothing about her. Indeed, I knew nothing about anything. Unlike the police, I had no way of finding out the exact time of her death or the precise movements of every living creature in the vicinity. My investigation would have to be based on psychological insight and sudden flashes of brilliance.

But now it was time to sleep. I washed my face and absentmindedly fastened the laundry window I'm always forgetting to close. I changed the dressing on my hand: It seemed much better. I'm a pretty fast healer—lots of practice.

I lay in bed, listening to Tebaldi's soft warbling downstairs, making my plans for the morrow. Paul had left me to go off and put in a perfunctory appearance at his matinee. We had agreed to meet in a few days' time. Fortunately, he had somewhere else to stay until his personal affairs stabilized.

One thing had become clear at the florist's: I couldn't drag him around with me to interview our suspects. They would all remember him as Jennifer's escort. So Paul had been dumped as *Opera del Mondo*'s note taker—his handwriting was indecipherable anyway—and his next job was to get the party shots developed and identify everybody in them. I suspected the film exclusively featured pretty young men. I would have preferred a photo finish of the murder, but pretty young men wasn't a total loss.

I decided my next interviewee should be the grande dame herself, La Clutterbuck. Start at the top. My opera magazine ruse had worked with Lloyd Webber, and I had no reason to suppose it would fail with her. If anything, I expected her to be even more cooperative. Divas eat publicity!

I was not certain how to set up this interview. I couldn't just turn up at the florist's where she worked, because she didn't work there. I had intended to ask Randolph Lloyd Webber for her number, but the dance of the leaping tarantula drove such thoughts out of my mind. I decided to ring the Sydney City Opera first thing Monday morning.

Meanwhile, there was tomorrow to consider. Paul had given

me the address where he'd collected Jennifer on the fateful day. It was a theatrical boarding house, "digs" as they call it, in the half-dilapidated, half-renovated inner city suburb of Surry Hills. The place was run by a retired actor, Roland Greaves. He was a delightful old chap according to Paul, especially if he had his teeth in. I thought I might pay him a visit for morning tea.

I dressed down for the occasion, befitting my assumed role of Jennifer's Uncle Marc from Auckland. As a relative, I thought, I'd have an excuse to enquire into the intimate details of Jennifer's daily life. I decked myself out in some old vaguely academic gear: corduroy pants the color of overcooked tandoori chicken, a tweedy jacket, a shirt that matched nothing within a kilometer of the rest of the ensemble.

From what I knew of the working actor's habitat, I assumed the apartments would fall well on the dilapidated side of the tracks. When I found the place, I was taken aback. The apartment block was clean, trendily appointed, and quite palatial. It was designed in the Spanish hacienda style, white stucco with little dysfunctional archways, which are normally detestable and repugnant. But somehow it worked. Was it the subtle highlighting of the paintwork? The sensitive plants so perfectly arranged? No two ways about it, I was confronted by an example of Good Taste.

I cast an eye over my attire. I looked shabbier than ever. The old clothes were a mistake. I removed my jacket and left it in the car. Then I untucked my shirt. Now I looked like a fashionable painter, which was an improvement, though judging from the clash of my outfit I must have been a fashionable color-blind painter.

I pressed the buzzer for Apartment 1, presuming that to be Mr. Greaves's residence. There was no answer. I was about to buzz again when the wrought-iron gate swung open and an exquisitely dressed elderly gent stepped out. Without noticing me, he slammed the gate shut and locked it. He replaced the key in his beige leather shoulder bag and started to stride away.

"Mr. Greaves?" I said.

He swung around. "Yes? I'm so sorry, I didn't see you there."

"I buzzed."

"Did you? I sometimes miss it at my age."

Paul was right. He had false teeth. Nice ones, too.

"What can I do for you?" He looked me up and down. "I'm full up at the moment."

"Oh, I don't need a room. I'm Marc Petrucci. I wanted to talk to you about Jennifer Burke. I'm her Uncle."

"Are you? Your name's not Burke."

I hadn't anticipated this, but he answered it for me.

"On the mother's side, I suppose. I rather thought she was Maori. Opera singers are, nowadays. Well I'm not surprised she had Italian blood. A beautiful voice! Yes, indeed. Reminded me of the young Renata Tebaldi."

You could have knocked me over with a souvenir program.

"I adore Tebaldi!" I gushed.

"Don't you agree, then? Lovely spinto tone." He touched my arm. "You're an artist of some sort, are you? I can always tell. You must be a photographer; a painter would never wear those colors."

"I'm strictly an amateur." I didn't say what sort of amateur. (Sleuth was the answer.) "I must say, Mr. Greaves.."

"Roland, lovey."

"Roland, I must say that when I was told Jennifer lived in theatrical digs, I didn't expect they would be so…pleasant!"

"Thank you for the compliment. I've had my share of want and make do—it's an up-and-down profession, God knows—but about ten years ago I landed a very nice series of commercials. Rather set me up. Remember Doctor Drane? The sink and toilet doctor?"

He presented his profile, adopting a warm, reassuring smile. He looked totally unfamiliar.

"Oh yes, of course! I knew you looked familiar."

"Paid a fortune in those days. They don't anymore, since ads were deregulated. I've seen the American Dr. Drane, incidentally. The man's a charlatan! Wears the worst hair hat. Anyway, I used the money to invest in art. I have rather good taste, if I say so myself. And I had this place fixed up nice. Why should actors live like rats in a sewer? I know too well, love. Touring in rep—now, that was a slog and a half!"

I gritted my teeth to stifle a yawn. Surely I wasn't going to get his whole life story here on the street?

"Look, we're getting along rather well, aren't we! I'd love to chat all day long about that dear girl, but I have to rush off to the fish market. Why don't you come to dinner this evening?"

"Oh, I couldn't impose—"

"No, please. I cultivate the spontaneous gesture, you mustn't mind! I'm having a few friends over. Please come, Marc Petrucci."

I smiled. "Very good."

"I was always a quick study. When we did *Midsummer Night's Dream* in Worthing, I got my Bottom up in less then a week. Right! To the fishies! See you 7:30 for 8! Apartment 6. Oh, of course, you know that—you buzzed. TAXI!"

In a booming voice that would stop traffic, which it did, he hailed a passing cab and was gone. I considered myself invited.

CHAPTER 7

*J*returned that night to Roland's building considerably more spruce. All afternoon I'd agonized over
my lie about being Jennifer's uncle. It had seemed
like a good idea at the time, but now I was bound to be exposed
as a fraud. Of all the things a fond uncle should know, such as
how old she was, where she was born, who her parents were,
what she looked like—I was completely ignorant. I supposed I
could play the black sheep of the Burke family, banished for
homosexual crimes against humanity and forgotten. That might
explain it. But banished from where? I'd never even set foot in
New Zealand. It would be tricky.

The only thing to do was construct a story: I'd been searching for Jennifer, the only member of the family who hadn't
ostracized me. I discovered she'd been living in Sydney, right
under my nose, and was almost onto her when she upped and
died in mysterious circumstances. The family had been
informed, but not poor neglected Uncle Marc. Naturally, I
wished to find out more. Who could blame me?

Since I didn't exist, it seemed feasible to invent myself.

The only alternative was to pretend I was suffering from the
onset of Alzheimer's. I seriously considered this option: It fit my
knowledge of the case perfectly.

I buzzed at the gate and waited. Gazing up at the white wall
I noticed an unusual watermark. Written in faint rust were the
words EL TORRO. Wasn't that a misspelling? A sign must have
been removed, leaving the rusty mark behind. But why take it
down, unless you were pedantic about spelling mistakes? *My
God*, I thought, *I'm becoming a detective!* I realized I'd been
waiting for five minutes. I buzzed again.

"Yesss?"

"It's Marc Petrucci."

"Marvelous! Come on up. Top floor. Don't worry if the security door at the bottom of the stairs is locked. I'll buzz it when I see you."

Admirable security arrangements, I thought, *but not strictly necessary. What can you steal from actors?*

It was a fair climb to Apartment 6. Roland embraced me like a long-lost boyfriend. He was wearing a light linen suit with a navy blue paisley cravat, exactly the kind of outfit rich queens wore when I was a youngster. It took me back. So did the quiet background music: classic Stan Getz bossa nova from the '60s.

"Marc. How exciting. Come in. My, you've scrubbed up well!"

"Thank you."

"You're punctual, unlike the others. But never mind, we can chat away till they come. Ciggie?"

"No thanks."

"You'll have a drink."

"Oh, here's some wine by the way." I handed him a bottle of Abruzzi white.

"Lovely, Italian like yourself. I'll put it away for a special occasion." He laughed. "What's your poison, love?"

"What do you have?"

In answer, he strode to a sideboard and swept up a sheet of paper which he handed to me. It was a computer printout of an alphabetical list of drinks: everything from absinthe to Zambian jungle juice.

"A campari and soda, thanks."

"Right away. Ng! Ng!"

"Are you all right?"

"Sorry?"

"I thought you were choking."

"No, I called\ 'Ng! Ng!'"

An attractive young Asian boy emerged from somewhere, wiping his hands on an apron.

"Remove your apron, darling, we have a guest."

"I won't. My clothes will smell like the fish. Hallo."

"Marc, Ng. Ng is my houseboy. Get us a couple of campari and sodas, would you?"

Ng smiled sarcastically. "Oh, sure, darling. I stand around pouring drinks all night, if you want the bloody dinner ruined. No worries."

"He calls me darling because he has trouble with Roland." He rolled the *r* in Roland with Shakespearean relish.

"Roland, Roland, Roland!" Ng snapped back. "Is the man gives trouble, not the word."

"What's the matter, love? Got your period?" Roland turned to me. "Good help is so hard to find."

"I need a hand in the kitchen. Right now!"

Roland sprang to his feet. "'Scuse me, Marc. I have to give Ng a hand job in the kitchen—right now!" They both giggled. Ng slapped Roland lightly on the bottom.

"Come to the kitchen. I make us a drink there," said Ng, extending his hand to me, "if Roland stop playing Auntie Mame for five minutes."

"We'll slum it," said Roland, looking slightly crestfallen.

I had not had a chance to take in the room, but as I got up I noticed several large paintings. A couple I recognized as Max Kreijns. And was that a Lloyd Rees? Hard to say, under the strong light.

"No Brett Whiteleys?" I asked.

"Heavens!" he exclaimed. "Grant me some originality!"

Two canvasses that rather frightened me were hanging opposite each other in the hall: They were oil portraits of a woman. She had deep-set dark eyes and a grim mouth. In both pictures she was nude. In the first she was wrapped painfully in chains and screaming in the style of the well-known Munch figure. In the second she was arranged like one of the many portraits of Saint Sebastian, in agony, with her body pierced by fine arrows. Unlike Saint Sebastian, the arrows were all lodged around her crotch area. She also wore a joke-shop arrow-through-the-head. This touch should have lightened the whole thing, but it didn't. If anything, it made the work even grimmer. I shuddered.

"An art lover, I see," remarked Roland.

"I don't appreciate much art, but I know what appreciates."

"Oh, very witty. These two are self-portraits by my dear friend Lavinia Cooper. She'll be joining us for dinner. She's bringing her new girlfriend along. Ng and I are beside ourselves with curiosity!"

Hope we're not having shish kebabs, I thought. I was relieved to find the kitchen quite ordinary, with no artwork of any kind. There was a simple round table, a large stove with a bouilla-baisse bubbling away, and a bench where Ng was in the midst of dissecting something edible.

"Sit down and relax." Ng said. "Cooking sherry do for you?"

"Fine."

"He wants Campari," snapped Roland.

"Yes, really? Next time you write your little computer list you better go out and buy the stuff."

"Sherry's OK, honestly," I said.

"Good," said Roland. "It's really quite nice sherry. I'll get them. Ng?"

"Thank you, darling."

"I suppose you expected to see old playbills all over the walls, didn't you."

"Well—"

"But I don't live in the past. I love the theatre, I love thespians, and I adore gossip, but as for me, I made my mind up back in Chelsea! I really wasn't much of an actor, you know. No future in it. I got sick of playing rapists in high school soaps."

"Too close to home, I think," added Ng.

"Shut up, or I won't sponsor your grandparents."

"I'd like to ask you about Jennifer," I said, "before the other guests arrive."

"Oh, and there's so much I must ask you! The poor girl, I can't believe she's left us."

"I like her," Ng said.

"We all did," said Roland. "She was feisty. You have to be, in that business. Not the perfect tenant, though, I'm sorry to say. She had a few gentlemen leaving in the early hours of the morning."

"Oh," I said. "I'm sorry."

"It's one of those house rules that was made to be broken, I suppose. But you understand, I own all this original work. One worries about security."

"Of course. Who were they, these gentlemen? Did you know them?"

Ng interrupted. "How can you gossip about that poor girl? Shame on you. Cut up the ginger."

Roland continued. "Well, that's where you have to admire her. One of the fellows was a critic! So she told me."

My ears pricked up. "Did you see him?"

"I only got a glimpsette. Older man, bald. I still have a full head of beautiful hair myself."

"She washes it twenty-five hours a day. Sweetheart, can you rinse a few things for me?"

"Must I? I am wearing linen, you know," said Roland as he went to the sink. "If it gets wet, it shrinks."

"So does your dick."

In the ensuing chilly silence, I decided to go out on a limb. "Did Jen ever mention me?"

"No, she never talked family, just showbiz and opera. We chatted for hours about that."

Ng, meanwhile, regarded me quizzically. "You Jen's uncle?"

"Yes, that's right."

"Yeah. She talks about you, no worries. Uncle Mike."

"Marc, darling," said Roland.

"No, no. Uncle Mike for Michael. Sure."

"It's Marc, you idiot. You misheard." Roland smiled. "It's

not his first language, you understand."

"No idiot!" said Ng. He picked up a carving knife. "You like I cut your throat?"

"Don't do that. There's a dear."

"Give me ginger, darling. Thank you."

"What did she say about me?" I asked tentatively.

"Oh, not much," replied Ng. "Said you were a fag." He winked.

"Charming," said Roland.

"Yes, well," I replied, "the family can't really handle it. I'm the black sheep. I was just trying to find Jennifer after all these years when this tragedy occurred."

"I'm very sorry," Roland murmured sympathetically.

Ng looked puzzled. "You not see her at Christmas, Uncle Mike? She spend Christmas with you."

I decided to contradict Jennifer. After all, she was dead.

"No."

"Don't understand. She so excited about it."

"I haven't seen her for years."

"Knowing Jennifer, she was probably seeing some married man, and she told Ng it was her uncle," said Roland.

"Why?" said Ng.

"Because you never keep your mouth shut. She didn't want it spread all over the Asia-Pacific basin. It was probably that critic."

Ng was unconvinced. "No. She not like him. It was her uncle, the fag. Very rich businessman, she said."

I started to break out in a sweat. "It was someone else, I'm afraid. I'm not a rich man, more's the pity."

"Marc's a photographer," Roland announced. "Are you exhibiting anywhere at the moment?"

"Um, no."

"My dear, you're perspiring. It's awfully hot in here, we'll go back to the lounge. I'll freshen up our drinks."

"You go. I come in a minute," said Ng.

As we stood, I heard a faint buzz.

"Door, darling," said Ng.

"Oh, yes."

Roland went to the door, while I braced myself in an armchair. Would she be wearing the chains or the arrows tonight? However, it was not the formidable artist who arrived, but a young man. He had a baby face, big brown eyes, and tousled dark hair. His body was sexy and very muscular, and he wore jeans with patches and a black *Cats* T-shirt with the sleeves cut off. I was immediately on my feet.

"Come in, you gorgeous thing. Rodney, this is Marc."

"Hi," said Rodney, squeezing my hand very very lightly. "Are you famous?"

"No. Sorry."

He flung himself onto the couch and shot a dazzling smile at Roland. "Champagne'd be nice. Where's Ng?"

"In the kitchen where he belongs. I'll get your champers."

Humph, I thought. *I got lousy old sherry. An uncle's drink.*

"You chat to Marc, lovey. He's a photographer," waved Roland as he positively pranced out. "Rodney's one of my boys." He laughed. "One of my actors, I should say."

Rodney snorted in contempt. "I was never one of his boys."

"You live here, then?"

"Yeah. On the ground floor, worse luck. They still get old buggers turning up at all hours."

"Hmm?"

He leaned forward conspiratorially. "The place used to be a brothel. Didn't you know? Check out the mirrors everywhere."

He was right. There were quite a few of them—even on the ceiling and above the divan.

"El Torro," he continued and leered lasciviously. "Never heard of it, right?"

Of course! It did ring a bell. A decade earlier it had been notorious. Needless to say, I had never availed myself of its services.

"I hadn't realized," I said. "It was famous in its day."

"Yeah. Before my time. That's how old Rolex made his money I reckon. Not from all this shit." He indicated the art with a dismissive gesture. "Oh, 'scuse me," he added. "Is some of this stuff yours?"

"No, no. My work is"—I was groping here—"a bit different."

"Yeah?"

"Yes."

"That's cool. I do nude posing from time to time. Strictly on a cash basis, if you're interested."

"Oh."

"Just posing, but…"

It was time to change the subject. "Roland tells me you're in show business. A dancer?"

"Yeah. Got a night off. Touch of flu."

"Maybe you know my niece, Jennifer Burke?"

"The girl that committed suicide?"

"That's right. She lived here. Did you know her?"

"Nah. She was mates with a friend of mine, Paul Silverton. They worked together. He knew her real well."

"I didn't, I'm afraid. Now it's too late, of course."

"I'm in her old room, I think."

"Oh. That's interesting. I'd love to see it."

He looked at me strangely. "You oughta talk to Paul."

"Yes. Where would I find him?"

Rodney laughed. "Good question. There's a few people want to know the answer to that one. I hear he's living with some old opera queen who's paying him for sex." After a short pause he asked, "What's the matter?"

"What?"

"You've gone all red."

"Have I? Oh. It's just that…I'm quite fond of opera myself."

"Ah. I understand." He leaned across and placed his hand on my leg. He looked me squarely in the eye. "You'd like to fuck me, wouldn't you."

"No! Well, I mean yes, but—"

"Darling, here's your drink. What's going on?" Roland returned, followed by Ng, who I noticed had gone to the trouble to remove his apron for the new guest.

"Thanks," said Rodney, "this guy was trying to race me off. Hi, Ng."

They had lots of little cheek kisses with very pursed lips.

"I don't blame you," said Roland to me, "but don't do it when the lesbians are here."

Rodney pulled a face. "This isn't champagne, is it?"

"It's flat Italian champagne. From the Abruzzi region. Here you are, Marc. I've got you one, too."

"Door," said Ng and skipped off.

"I never hear it," said Roland.

"I bet you heard it ten years ago," said Rodney.

Roland gave him a sour look. "I didn't live here then."

Suddenly, the room was full of sound and fury. At least that was my impression as Lavinia Cooper swept in, laughing, kissing, and hugging everything in sight. I recognized her from her self-portraits, although there were subtle differences. She wore not chains but tight jeans with a colorful shirt carefully untucked. She had short red hair, curly rather than spiky, set off by large hand-tooled wooden earrings, and a tasteful gold nose-ring. She was also considerably wider in the hips than her painted likeness.

When I was introduced, she squeezed my hand and called me "doll," as though we'd known each other all our lives. Perhaps we had, and I'd momentarily forgotten: That's how good she was at schmoozing.

"You didn't wear your chains tonight," I remarked lamely.

"My what?"

"Chains. In the portrait—"

"Oh, yeah!" she laughed. "I always forget those bloody pictures are here. Let's have a look." She dragged me with her. "Hmm. Great tits. She was three—no, four—lovers ago." She turned back to the others. "That reminds me—Everybody! Be quiet! I'd like you all to meet my fabulous new lover and soul mate, Jude. Isn't she a spunk?"

"Hello," murmured Jude.

If Lavinia was larger than life, then Jude was smaller. The most accurate description of her would be nondescript. Jude also wore jeans and had short hair, but there the resemblance to her lover ended. Her face was pale and thin, with no lips to speak of and lifeless pale-green eyes. She was softly spoken, well groomed, and forgettable, like a highly trained receptionist.

"Don't give her a lot to drink," said Lavinia. "She goes berserk." I looked at Jude again: She merely sighed and gazed lovingly at her friend.

Dinner was served. It was inevitable that our host would seat Jude and I together—we were the odd ones out. Rodney snuggled between Roland and Ng, in the spotlight as it were, with Lavinia next, leaning forward to effectively seal off the group. Because Ng was up to the kitchen most of the time, I was stuck between Jude on one side and an empty chair on the other.

The conversation, as much as I could catch of it, seemed to concern mutual friends of Lavinia and Roland's: art dealers, primarily, who it seemed were a race apart, related to the piranha.

Lavinia talked about her work. I gathered she only ever painted self-portraits—the face anyway if not the body—in differing historical and hysterical contexts. Her lifelong ambition was to replace every male icon in the history of art and the world with a female portrayed by her.

"I started in the '80s. I was kind of separatist in those days, but don't let's get all gooey and nostalgic. I suppose I should move with the times, slip into something a bit coalitionist, but I enjoy painting myself too much! It's what I'm good at." She laughed self-deprecatingly, as people often do when they're serious.

"Lavinia's being courted by the Mardi Gras committee," Jude confided to me. "They've wanted her to design the poster for years, but she won't."

"No?"

"How can she do a self-portrait with men in it? It's not part of her overview."

"Ah."

"Her vision is very specific."

Ng served the spicy ginger fish dish. It was utterly delectable and left a tingling hot aftertaste. The Italian white had long since disappeared, and we were on our third bottle of Queen Adelaide. I was being careful, not wishing to run into a Breathalyzer on my way home, but Jude was knocking the vino back with gusto. It had not loosened her up one little bit. Not yet.

"What do you do?" I asked her. "Are you in the art world?"

"Not at all," she replied. "I work for the Opera."

"A singer?" I asked, as I refilled her glass.

"I'm in finance."

I couldn't believe my luck. Here was an insider I could pump for information under the perfectly legitimate guise of small talk. We could yack about her favorite arias and singers and eventually bring the subject round to Jennifer. I jumped in.

"I love opera, being Italian, you see."

"Do you?" she yawned. "It bores me rigid." She excused herself and went off to the bathroom.

I must have looked put out, because Lavinia suddenly turned and patted my hand. "She hates talking about the Opera. She's always got some hassle or other—it's a rats' nest. I take no notice."

"Who is it you're keen on?" Roland asked me. "Callas, isn't it?"

"No, no, Renata Tebaldi."

"Of course. I know the most wonderful story. Have you

heard about the fake Tebaldi?"

"No," I answered, intrigued.

"It's gorgeous. A friend of mine was sharing in London with a young singer—must have been the late '70s—"

"Sharing what?" interrupted Lavinia.

"Herpes, probably. Can I tell the story? The singer told my friend he was having lessons with Tebaldi! He'd answered her ad in the *Times*. She was a wonderful teacher, this boy said, but very expensive."

"But Tebaldi never taught."

"Yes, my friend knew that. What's more, he'd heard the real Tebaldi sing many times. He said he'd love to meet her, so the boy arranged for them all to have coffee at the Savoy. The two of them waited for ages, and finally this dumpy little woman turned up, and it quite clearly wasn't Renata."

"Dumpy? Tebaldi is elegant!"

"Yes, yes! This impostor said she was on cortisone for her arthritis, and it had changed her face! She was an utter fraud. So my friend made up his mind to ring the great diva herself and tell her what was going on. And he did."

"Really! How did he get through?" I thought the answer might prove useful to me with Dame Norma.

"He looked up the Milano phone book. The maid answered, said the Signora was out at the hairdresser's or something, and asked if he could call back. He said it was important—you know, all that palaver."

"Phone etiquette! It gives you the fucking shits," said Lavinia.

"Anyway, he got onto Tebaldi, told her about the fake and she was livid! But did she sue, or have the woman arrested? No. In typical elegant style, she had a full-page ad placed in the London papers: Signora Tebaldi wishes to state that she resides permanently in Milan, and that she does not teach, as she considers her voice to be a unique gift from God."

They laughed. "What a class act!" Lavinia crowed. "Old

Norma would have personally cut the woman's throat with a blunt butter knife!"

"Who?" asked Rodney, who was looking bored and pretty.

"Dame Norma Clutterbuck, the opera star," I said.

"Oh, yeah. The fat one."

"Do you know Dame Norma?" I asked Lavinia.

"Not really. She bought one of my pictures, so she's got some taste. Jude knows her, reckons she's a cow."

"She's getting fifty times what she's worth," said Jude, who was returning to the table. I noticed she was unsteady on her feet and slammed back into her chair rather heavily. "But," she added, "not for much longer."

"Oh, fabulous! Gossip here!" exclaimed Roland. "Lights! Action!"

"I shouldn't talk," said Jude.

"You haven't said a bloody word all night," said Lavinia, "Here's your chance to shine. Go for it, hon."

"We're queens," added Roland, "Tell us everything."

"I can't talk about fees," said Jude with a sly look that indicated that she enjoyed her sudden elevation in dinner party status. "But what I can say…"

"The old diva's being forcibly retired," Lavinia butted in.

"She should have gone years ago," said Jude. "Everyone in the company thinks so. They've all got a use-by date, even the stars. Have you heard Norma recently? Sounds as if she's gargling with gravel."

I was amazed at the sudden torrent of vitriol. Were all opera people this cynical?

"But surely," I suggested, "even if the voice is past its prime, she's still a great artist with interpretive gifts gained only through experience?"

Jude eyed me as though I were a cockroach she'd found in her bouillabaisse. "Interpretive gifts!" she snorted. "She couldn't interpret surprise if she sat on a land mine. The tragedy is, there are better people being passed over because of these big-time has-beens. And they're paid astronomical sums! It makes my job hell. There's no value for money, none whatsoever. Try and balance a budget when you've got to throw half of it away. And Edward's no help—he's such a hopeless neurotic. Locks himself in his office and spends all day pacing up and down, biting his fingernails."

"Edward?"

"Edward Quinn, the man I work for. He's the company administrator."

"He's a wimp," added Lavinia. "But tell them why Dame Norma's on the outer."

"It must never leave this room," smiled Jude for the first time that evening.

"Everybody knows anyway," continued Lavinia. "The Dame's been having it off for years with the chairman of the board, till he dumped her for some hot young number."

Jude filled in the details. "All these productions she's had over the last few years, especially that tired old *Girl of the Golden West* everyone's sick to death of, have all been pushed through by Sir Fred. He's immensely powerful. He's on the boards of three of our major sponsors."

"Surely the chairman of the board doesn't make artistic decisions?" I asked.

"No," said Jude, "the artistic director does, but Sir Fred puts pressure on, and as he's responsible for so much of the money we get—"

"Somebody gives them a donation every season," said Lavinia. "Eight hundred thousand bucks!"

"Who?" asked Rodney, showing an interest at last.

"It's anonymous," said Jude. "I'm sure Sir Fred knows where it comes from, but that only makes it worse. Our hands are tied! The chairman ought to be on our side, on the side of moderation and balance. He should act as a brake on these artistic people who never care about costs. That's what the damn board is for, isn't it? But he's worse than any of them! And if he wants

Girl of the Golden West again, that's what we get. The public's bored with it, the critics have always hated it, but Sir Fred wants it. Next year we're planning yet another revival."

Roland was salivating. "And he's found himself a new protégé to star in it? How wicked! Dame Norma must be foaming at the famous mouth!"

"She sure is!" laughed Lavinia. "She'll be out of pocket, too. I hope she's invested her money wisely."

Jude drained her glass with a single swig. "I've had a hell of a day. I am going on a bit."

"You certainly are, dear," cooed Roland, "and it's fabulous! So who's the new girl?"

Jude frowned. "I don't know," she muttered.

"Marc, maybe this chairman of the board had his eye on your niece!" To the enquiring looks around the table, Roland explained, "Marc is Jennifer Burke's uncle."

The effect of this statement was extraordinary. It shut Lavinia up, for one thing. It propelled Ng hastily back to the kitchen. Most of all, it caused Jude to flush bright red and burst into tears.

Lavinia was at her side immediately, lending a hand and soothing her with a gentle back massage. "I meant to tell you," Lavinia whispered loudly to Roland. "Don't bring that subject up. She's not really over it. They were very close. There you are, doll. Get it together."

"I'm sorry, everyone," sniffed Jude. "I've had a few too many drinks. I've said too much, probably." There was an uncomfortable silence. "Lavinia, would you take me home?"

It was tactless of me, but I refused to let the opportunity pass.

"Jude," I said soothingly, "I haven't seen my niece since she was very small, because of family problems I won't go into, but I recently discovered we were both living here in Sydney. I'd almost tracked her down when this terrible thing happened. Now, at last, fate has brought me face-to-face with someone who knew her well. Please don't go." I looked soulful. If they had Oscars for dinner-party moments, mine was in the bag.

"I'm sorry," Jude said, and blew her nose. "I'll be OK."

Lavinia resumed her seat.

"Jen mentioned you," Jude continued. "She told me the whole story."

Roland and Rodney looked intrigued. I felt prickly under the collar. *What whole story,* I thought? I hoped she wouldn't start asking detailed questions—such as "Who are you?"

"Would you like to see a recent picture?" she added.

"Please."

She reached down to her handbag and produced from it a snapshot of a young woman on the steps of the Opera House. The girl was blond, cute, and smiling—a thicker-set Kylie Minogue.

"Well, well, well," I nodded meaninglessly. "Yes. That's her."

"Can't see any family resemblance," said Lavinia, grabbing the photo.

"Nah," agreed Rodney.

"I can," said Jude quietly. She took the shot back and handed it to me. "Keep it. I've got others. And now, Lavinia, I think we'll go, if it's all right with you. Please."

Lavinia was quite nonplussed. "If we must," she said. "But we're missing sweets."

She whirled around, kissing everyone good night and apologetically saying, "I'll kill her," while Jude waited patiently at the door. For all Lavinia's domineering style, it was plain who called the shots in this relationship.

As we sat eating our extra portions of Peach Melba, Roland mused. "You can never tell about dinner parties, can you? I thought the opera connection would make for bright conversation, and instead of that you drove her right out the door!"

"Me?" I said.

"Odd girl, though. I shouldn't think those two will last five minutes. Lavinia doesn't take kindly to being pushed around."

"Do you think Jude and Jennifer were having a fling?" I asked.

"It seems like it. What do you say, Ng?"

Ng looked inscrutable. "No, darling, she like men. More dessert?"

"Yes, thank you," I answered. "It's lovely."

"No worries. You come again." He winked. "Uncle Mike."

CHAPTER 8

*I*t was dark and hazy, and I could scarcely make out the shape or form of Rodney's room. I was sitting on a bed. Slowly, the door opened and there he stood, backlit by the soft light wafting through a tiny window. He wore a towel loosely draped around his taut waist. No, lower.

"Is this what you want?" he asked.

"Yes." My voice was hoarse and heavy. He casually rubbed his tanned, sculpted chest.

"Why are you here?"

"I'm a fraud," I said. "I'm nobody's uncle. I'm a detective."

"You don't look like a detective."

"No. It's because of the cortisone."

"Well, Mr. Detective, why don't you investigate this?"

He whipped the towel off and flung it in my direction. I made no attempt to catch it but sat mesmerized as he slowly walked toward me. He was inches away. I closed my eyes.

Abruptly I opened them again. I was sitting bolt upright in bed, my own bed. Rodney was nowhere to be seen. My eyes and ears strained in the dark, and I felt my erection melting away. Damn! It had been so real!

There was a soft click somewhere downstairs. I couldn't quite work out what it was. An intruder? I was suddenly petrified. I sat completely still for about half an hour, then garnered all my intestinal fortitude and looked sideways at the clock. It was 3:20 in the morning.

I waited till 4:20 but heard nothing further. So, with a great show of noise and light and a lot of self-encouragement, I got up. I clomped downstairs and one by one turned on every light in the house. The first thing I checked was the laundry window: It was shut fast.

I put on an opera CD, softly because of the neighbors. A wind was blowing outside. *That's all it was,* I thought, and made myself some chamomile tea.

As I walked past, I saw the red light flashing on my answer phone. I mustn't have checked it when I got in from dinner. I ran the tape back. The message was from Paul.

"Can you talk, caro, or have you got your mouth full at the moment? Ha ha. It's Paul. It's, uh...12:30 or so. I'm up the road and about to have fun. I hope! Look, I've got those piccies of you-know-who attending the you-know-what at you-know-where. God knows if they're any use, but they're well worth a look, I can tell you! Actually, there's one...well, I'll show you tomorrow. I'll call bright and early. Ciao!"

Twelve-thirty. Only Paul would casually call up at that hour. I must have just missed him. I leaned down to run the tape back but stopped myself. There was a second message. I waited as the machine played through fifteen seconds of silence and then, with that familiar click, shut off. I played it back, with the volume up on full. There was distant background noise, but I couldn't tell what it was. Even so, somebody had certainly rung.

Well, it happens, I said to myself as I put the lights out one by one. *Not at 3 o'clock in the morning,* I replied. *Kids,* I suggested. *It was the murderer you fool,* I snapped back. *We don't know that,* I argued. *You want to find out, I asked sarcastically?* Neither of me did.

I didn't sleep a wink from then on. Nor could I manage to conjure up the vision of Rodney in or out of his towel. I was finally nodding off in the pale light of dawn when the first jumbo jet of the day blasted its way overhead. Exhausted, I arose and made coffee. My hand shook with fatigue, splashing boiling water onto my leg.

I fell to thinking about Jennifer and going over the facts, as we detectives always do. Fact number one: Jennifer's room was now occupied by Rodney. I should have found some way to get in there to have a look around. She may have left something behind—one of those suicide notes, for example. I could go back on some pretext, but what? Maybe I should tell Rodney the truth—tell him straight out that I'm a detective. He'd be so impressed—excited, even...stimulated. I gulped down the coffee to wake myself up.

My list of suspects, previously consisting of one name, now included at least two more. Jude from finance was heading it, and amazingly, she had the same motives as Mr. Other Lloyd Webber: lovesickness and jealousy. I assumed she'd been present at Dame Norma's bash, though I hadn't confirmed it.

Then there was Dame Norma herself, about to be forcibly retired. What a blow to her reputation, her status, her income, if she were no longer Girl of the Golden West, but just another Golden Girl. Would she go so far as to kill? Why not? Operatic sopranos kill approximately three times a fortnight. And didn't somebody say Dame Norma had discovered the body? That in itself was fishy: How could the grand hostess of an exclusive party manage to escape on her own long enough to go poking around the cliffs?

This was presupposing Jennifer was the new discovery and love interest of the chairman of the board. From what I was beginning to discover about the dear departed, I had every reason to believe my 'niece' was a scheming little minx. (She didn't get it from my side of the family!)

Then there was the critic who visited her after hours, bald and middle-aged. Could it be the same one I had met in the café—Charles Mignon? Jennifer didn't strike me as his type, not at all, but you never know. Mind you, there are dozens of critics about, and nearly all of them are bald and middle-aged. Even the women.

I looked at the snapshot Jude had given me. "Take it," she had said. "I have others." Where and how did she get them? The obvious answer was from Jennifer herself.

Jennifer's pert face gazed up at me, smiling that radiant showbiz smile. She certainly had good teeth. I covered them up with my palm and looked at the eyes: The effect was startling. Her eyes bored into me, fixing me with a cold stare. I couldn't outstare her; admittedly, she was frozen in a snapshot so her eyes weren't likely to blink.

I took my hand away and held the photo up to the light. Now she looked weird. She seemed to have a jagged scar across her neck and right shoulder. I stared at it in horror, until I realized it was merely some writing on the back of the picture. *My God*, I thought, *I've really got the creeps this morning!* It was her name, and a date. This snap was taken only three days before she died.

I gazed at it for some time. The smile seemed to me more triumphant than radiant now. The girl in this photo was genuinely pleased with herself.

I took note of her clothing: She was wearing a cream top with an open waistcoat—Italian-looking I was pleased to note—and dark red slacks. She had a headband of some kind, small earrings, a bracelet, a love bite…a love bite? I looked closer at her neck. It was either that or an odd shadow.

I pinned the photo on my kitchen board, next to my VISA bill and out-of-date sale notices from the Italian Furniture Warehouse. Perhaps if I looked at her every day, she would start to tell me something. Meanwhile, my head was telling me to go back to bed. I did, and slept like a log until there was a loud knock at the door around 3 o'clock in the afternoon. It was Paul.

"You're not still in bed, are you?" he gasped.

"I slept badly last night," I grunted.

"Well, let's mobilize, whatever that means."

We sat at the table and sipped the dregs of some flat champagne.

"Paul, did Jennifer ever tell you any details about her love life?"

"Darling! Nonstop!"

"Was she seeing a woman? A woman from the Opera?"

"What, my girlfriend? Pussy-bumping?"

"For heaven's sake! Did she ever mention Jude?"

"Nope. Jude remains obscure."

"What about the chairman of the board? Fred something. Hang on." I looked up an old opera program. "Here he is. Sir Fred Mathieson. Was she stepping out with him in a more-than-friends, less-than-Siamese twins kind of way?"

"I wouldn't put it past her, but Jen was pretty tight-lipped about naming names. She talked about everything else, though. We used to laugh over the intimate details—feather dusters up the bum, how someone couldn't get it up, funny old things like that."

"You won't think it's funny when you get to my age."

"Oh, what's wrong, caro mio?" he pouted. "You're not getting enough sex and you're grumpy."

"How can I, when boys like you take twice as much as they need? How are all those affairs of yours going? Are you still a wanted man?"

"Depends what you mean. I'm still avoiding Stephen. Geoffrey and Rodney have split, so I guess Stephen will be in a bigger tizz than ever! I knew those two wouldn't last."

"Wasn't it only a week ago this relationship started?"

"Three days is a golden wedding anniversary for Rodney. He's a megaslut."

"I believe I had dinner with him last night." My head throbbed unexpectedly.

"Where?"

"I went to visit Roland Greaves's apartments. If it's the same Rodney, he's moved into Jennifer's vacant rooms."

Paul was fuming. "The lousy little opportunist! No respect for the dead or anyone else. Did he wear that cutoff *Cats* T-shirt?"

"Yes."

"That's him. Great big biceps and pecs, but his dick is infi-ni-fucking-tesimal!"

"Oh."

"I've gone right off him," he added, rather unnecessarily.

"I got the impression he was once on the game. You know Roland's building used to be a brothel?"

"Sure, El Torro. Well! Rodney's one of the El Torro Old Boys, is that sooooo?" Paul purred with impure delight. "He must be good for something, he sure as hell can't dance."

"Well, anyway. Show me these pictures of the party!"

Paul suddenly became strangely fidgety. He stood and paced, then abruptly sat down again.

"You should get out more, Marc—like me. Last night I went to a fabulous new sauna, 9-1-ZERO. Do you know it?"

"No."

"It's brilliant. It's got everything, including Americans. There's a real sexy black masseur who sometimes does freebies. Mm-mmm!" He literally licked his lips. "I think we should go this very night, you and me. Two for the price of one. Monday's 'Buddies Night.'"

"I don't think so, I'm tired."

"That's OK. You could watch the porn. And, um…you could help me look for the photos."

"You lost them in a sauna?"

"I know, I know. You think I'm an idiot."

"Never," I lied.

"I was positive they were in my locker."

"Did anyone else see them?"

"A few people. Oh, all right, I flashed them around. There was a beauty of me with Dame Norma. You know, brush-with-fame kind of thing. But I definitely locked them away. I think."

"You didn't have them on your person?"

"Where, darling? When did you last go to a sauna? They don't make you wear neck-to-knees anymore."

"How are we ever going to get to the bottom of this if you spend your time hanging around gay bathhouses?"

"That's the only way, caro. Anyway, don't turn on me!" he snapped. "What have you achieved? Supper with a bit of old trade! Well done!"

"I've learned a lot."

"Ha! Did you interview Dame Norma yet?"

"Oh! I completely forgot to call."

"Too busy basking in Rodney's afterglow. Well, there's no time like the present."

Harrumph. Dr. Watson never spoke to Sherlock Holmes in that petulant fashion. Slightly piqued, I picked up the phone and dialed the number for the City Opera.

I asked to speak directly to Dame Norma. I was put on hold and eventually found myself speaking to the director of subscriptions, the hat buyer for wardrobe, and the head mechanist respectively. I rang again and asked for publicity. This time they put me straight through, and I went into the *Opera del Mondo* rave, requesting an interview with the diva. I was put on hold, passed over to the canteen and back, and ended up speaking to a Ms. Cropper.

"Of course we're familiar with your magazine, Mr. Petrushka."

"Petrucci."

"If you'd like to leave your office number with us, we'll get in touch with Dame Norma's secretary for you."

"Perhaps I could ring Dame Norma's secretary myself. I've met the great lady many times. In fact, one of our staff covered her recent party."

"Err, it's not our policy—"

"I'm a personal friend of the chairman, although I hate to bring that up. But Fred did say if I had any problems…"

"Of course. I'll just put you on hold for a moment."

I waited.

"Sydney City Opera. Who were you wanting?"

"I was speaking to Ms. Cropper in publicity."

"I'm sorry, Ms. Cropper is in a meeting."

"I was just speaking to her, and I was cut off!"

"One moment please."

"Hello?"

"Who's this, then? The tea lady??"

"This is Adele Cropper speaking."

"Oh, I'm sorry, it's Mr. Petrushka here."

"I thought you'd hung up. I have the number you were wanting. Before you publish, we'd like to check the copy."

"Yes, of course."

She gave me the number. I grinned smugly at Paul as I dialed.

"Hello, Tim Boston speaking."

"Is that Dame Norma Clutterbuck's secretary?"

"I'm her personal secretary, yes. Can I help you?"

"My name is Marc Petrucci from the international opera magazine *Opera del Mondo,* based in Milan."

"Oh, yes?"

"We're doing a series of interviews under the generic title 'Splendid Sopranos of the Century.'"

"'Splendid Sopranos'? It sounds better in Italian, I presume."

"Si. Anyway, naturally we're interested in speaking to Dame Norma."

"Naturally."

"An overview-type piece—the past, the future, any funny little party incidents, that kind of thing."

"I see."

"I am the official Australasian correspondent for *Opera del Mondo.* I've written many articles…"

"I don't believe I've seen your byline."

"Sorry, my what?"

"Your name."

"I…uh, I use a variety of different names. Bylines."

"Who else have you interviewed for this series?"

"Renata Tebaldi…"

"Tebaldi? She doesn't grant interviews."

"She gave me one. The signora and I are great friends. I exposed the fake Tebaldi in London a few years ago. Do you remember the incident?"

"I think so."

"Oh, it's a wonderful story. This old duck was giving singing lessons and taking cortisone, but I saw right through her. So I rang up my friend Renata..."

"Yes, yes, I recall. Well, Signore, you appreciate that Dame Norma gets a lot of these requests. She has to pick and choose."

"Of course. Fred Mathieson was very anxious that she talk to us."

There was a pause.

"Was he? She'll be pleased to hear it."

"We are based in Milan, you know. Same as La Scala."

"Ah," he purred. "I understand what you're getting at. I'm sure there'll be no problem with the interview. The question is, when? At this stage"—I could hear pages ruffling faintly—"it will have to be next year. Dame Norma has some time available in early May—no, no, even better, April."

I came back to earth with a thud.

"I was thinking along the lines of later this week."

He laughed lightly.

"I'm sorry, that's impossible. Look, I'll make it as early as I can. Ten o'clock on the morning of April the 1st. The Opera Room at the Belvedere. How does that suit?"

"Fine. Thank you very much."

"A pleasure, Signore Petrucci. And, just off the record—"

"Yes?"

"Don't neglect your homework. Dame Norma doesn't suffer fools gladly. Ciao."

I was a mite depressed as I hung up and spied Paul's expectant face.

"You going to interview her?"

"Yes," I replied. "Next April Fools' Day."

I made coffee. As we drank it, I told Paul all about Jude, Ng, and partly about Rodney. I didn't mention the late-night phoner for fear of seeming paranoid.

"I wish I'd gotten into Jennifer's room," I mused. "A real detective would have."

Paul stood behind me and gave me a tender, reassuring hug. "We'd better not go into business as private eyes," he said. "I guess the police looked in her room anyway."

"Probably. But don't forget, they thought it was suicide."

"Yeah…" One of those expressions came over his face. The ones I have learned to dread.

"We can go there tonight!" he squealed.

"Oh, I don't think so—"

"But we can! There's a big party on after the show. It's the 20 millionth performance or something. Rodney's bound to be at the party. I'll remind him. Then while he's away from home we can sneak in and ransack the place!"

"We've got no right! What if he's got other plans?"

"If I know Rodney, they won't involve spending the night at home."

"Don't you want to go to this party yourself?"

"Of course, but I'd much rather go snooping! Whoo! I'm getting all moist just thinking about it."

"I don't know. Weren't we off to the sauna?"

"We'll go there later. It's not jumping till 2 or 3 A.M."

"Who cares if it's jumping? We're looking for the photos."

"You might be, sweetie."

"Paul, sit down!"

He grabbed me by the ears and shook my head rapidly from side to side, another habit I didn't associate with Dr. Watson.

"Caro," he said, "stop saying no and help me work out how to do a break-and-enter."

CHAPTER 9

The wind had come up again, and the overcast sky hinted at a shower. Over my oldest, warmest track-suit top I wore a gray raincoat, mainly for the camouflage of its dark color. Paul wore a flimsy T-shirt and jeans. (Naturally.) It was midnight. We were sitting on a seesaw.

The former house of ill repute, El Torro, was flanked on two sides by a children's park. This park was of the typical inner city variety. It contained a swing, a seesaw, a bin overflowing with garbage, rocks, weeds, syringes, and offcuts of building material. A car with one door and no tires was parked behind the swing, close to the high back wall of the apartment block. Paul's plan was to climb onto the car, hop over the fence, then scuttle around to the front gate and let me in.

Paul knew Jennifer's flat well, having once slept on her bathroom floor after a party. I had reluctantly agreed to let him do the snooping while I kept watch. I had no choice, since he was the only one of us capable of climbing in. One of the windows had a latch that wouldn't close; reputedly, several of Jennifer's nocturnal visitors had made use of it.

Of course, I was still extremely dubious about all this cloak-and-dagger stuff. Although we'd had a successful dry run at Paul's flat a few days before, it was a different matter hanging around someone else's apartment building at midnight in a raincoat. If I were cornered, I could hardly claim to be looking for a Mrs. Smith. The signal of whistling *La Traviata* had likewise been dropped. Instead, at the first sign of trouble, I was to make a noise like a cat.

"What if I'm the one in trouble?" I had asked.

Paul had thought for a moment, then said, "Still make the noise."

The reason I was prepared to go through with this risky and illegal act was simple: Jennifer kept a diary. Paul claimed to have seen it several times. What's more, he knew she kept it in an unusual place, though he couldn't remember exactly what this unusual place was.

"I'll know when I see it," he said.

Finding Jennifer's diary was our only hope—and not a very strong one, considering she no longer lived here (or anywhere). Rodney, however, had not struck me as especially decor-conscious. If he'd made any changes to the flat, I was sure they were minimal. A few pinups and the odd piece of home gym equipment would probably be the extent of it.

The diary, if it was there, would be our first piece of decent evidence. At least I hoped so. Considering I was no closer to any of the major players, and my showdown with Dame Norma was months away, I pinned all my hopes on that final entry: the one that read "Opera Party today. Am about to be murdered by So-And-So." I would be satisfied with nothing less.

We languidly seesawed and went over the details of the operation for the umpteenth time.

"Will you keep still?" I whispered irritably. "This seesaw squeaks."

"Sorry," said Paul. He leapt lightly to his feet. "Then let's do it!"

"Now?"

"No, in fifteen years."

"OK, OK. Anyway, I don't like sitting in a park at night like some old sleaze-bag."

"You are some old sleaze-bag."

"That's beside the point. Let's get moving before the police come along. They patrol places like this."

"I doubt it."

"Well, they should! Criminals might be hanging around."

Paul clambered up on top of the old bomb with remarkable agility. All those months as a cat had prepared him for this moment.

"I'll be over the top before you can say Errol Flynn," he called.

"Shut up," I suggested.

He jumped and grabbed at the top of the brick wall with his fingertips, but couldn't hold on. As he landed back on the roof of the car, his feet slipped from under him. He came down on his bottom with a thud.

"Whoops!" he squealed. "That was a bit girly!"

He tried once more, but this time didn't even manage to reach the top. The rusty old car creaked and rattled.

"Come up here, Marc, and give me a leg up."

With as much care as I could muster, I took his outstretched hand and scrambled up next to him. With a sudden bang the car roof buckled into a dent under my weight.

"Damn, it's even lower now. You must go on a diet, caro! All right, now, I'll climb on your back." As he did, I felt my knees buckling.

"Get off, get off!"

"What's the matter?"

"It's my knee."

"Oh, you're hopeless! What's wrong with it?"

"I've had a few knee injuries over the years."

"Too much kneeling as a young lad."

By now I'd lost interest. "Let's go home," I pleaded.

"Open your legs."

"Why?"

"We're in a park, it's night. We may as well have sex. Come on!"

All of a sudden Paul's head was between my legs, and I was being hoisted into the air on his shoulders. I tottered.

"Now get yourself to the wall!" he shouted. "Sit on it! Go, Humpty!"

Twisting painfully, I levered myself off Paul's back and onto the top of the wall. There was a dark garden with a path next to the building on the other side.

"It's a long way down," I whispered.

"Don't whine, I'll help you. Pull me up!" he called.

I reached out my right hand for him. To steady myself, I firmly planted my left hand on the wall. A jagged piece of broken glass was there.

"Ow!"

Paul jumped, but I was distracted by the sharp pain and missed him. He did manage to pull my shoe off, before he crashed back onto the car.

"Aaaaaargh!"

The air was filled with a sickening, terrifying scream. I was so shocked I rocked backward and started to fall. I reached out into the void. There seemed to be a tree next to me, and I desperately lunged at it with both hands. I grabbed a branch, which immediately cracked and broke off. The branch and I plunged to the garden below, smack into a clump of bamboo.

An outside light clicked on, blinding me with its rays as I lay in the garden. I kept completely still, which at that stage of the evening required no great effort. Soon the light, which was apparently automatic, snapped off again, leaving me in utter darkness. "Aunty Em?" I whimpered.

I took some little time to regain my equilibrium. The drop was not as far as it had seemed from above. Twenty feet, rather than sixty. I struggled to my feet. My raincoat was ripped. I felt the blood soaking through my sock where the bamboo had cut my foot.

I took a few tentative steps along the path. Before long my shin discovered a tap on the side of the building. I washed my hands and foot, and splashed water over my face.

"Pssst! Marc?" I heard Paul's stage whisper from the other side of the wall.

"Yes! Are you all right?"

"Yes! Are you?"

"Yes! What the hell happened?"

"There was an old drunk in the car! He's gone back to sleep now. Go to the front gate and let me in."

"Which way? Right or left?" I called, but he'd gone.

I edged my way gently around the building, fortunately leaving a trail of bloody footprints in case I should need to retrace my steps. I passed a couple of small high windows. Perhaps one of these was the one with the broken latch. I felt in my raincoat pocket for my pen-size torch. Miraculously, it had survived the fall. I shone it up at the windows. They both looked solid and freshly painted. *Just my luck*, I thought, *if security conscious Roland had had the damn thing fixed.*

I continued on my cautious way until I ran up against some large metal object. I flashed. It was either an incinerator or a very old-fashioned barbecue. Either way, it blocked the path entirely. That meant there was only one way out, possibly something worth knowing.

I returned, passing the windows, the tree, and finally rounding the corner to the front of the building. This area was well lit. I stepped behind a bush and wondered whether I would be seen if I opened the gate.

As it happened, there was no need to try. I heard a key turning, and the gate swung open to reveal Paul and Roland.

"Paul, isn't it?" Roland was saying.

"Yes. I've been buzzing Rodney's apartment but I guess he's not home yet."

"Well, don't stand out here, dear boy. You'll catch your death in that rather attractive ensemble. Come up and wait in my flat. I'm sure Rodney won't be long."

"Oh no, it's so late—"

"I insist. We'll have a nightcap. Warm you up."

"OK," said Paul, looking around frantically. "Just the one."

They disappeared into the building. I overheard Roland say, "Close the door behind you, my dear. We don't want undesirables getting in!"

The light was extinguished. I stood still for a while to get used to the darkness yet again. Now what? This looked like the end of our plans for the time being. The whole escapade had been conceived as a two-man operation. I would have to wait until Roland had finished with Paul and let him go before we could continue. I hoped they weren't about to indulge in prolonged foreplay.

Of course, if Rodney returned before Paul came down again, it would all be a waste of time. My instep would have been skewered to no purpose. Not only that, there was every chance Rodney would find himself face-to-face with the new unofficial doorman: me. I considered waiting for Paul outside on the street, but if I let myself out, the only way back in was over the wall again. It would be a crying shame to repeat that painful saga.

I thought I might as well take another look at Rodney's windows. I inched carefully around the building, picking up a discarded broom on the way. The windows were certainly high off the ground. I would never get up there with style and grace. Climbing is not my forte: I'm one of those hardy souls destined to linger back at base camp and get tea ready. No, Paul would have to do the heroic stuff.

The windows looked as solid as ever. As an experiment, I prodded one of them with the broom handle, but the window remained fast. I tried the other, also with no result. It occurred to me that I should try pushing the top of the frames, in case they opened out from the bottom. To do that, I needed to stand on something. I groped about and found a bucket, which I upended and gingerly stepped upon. From there I could just stretch the broom to the top of the frame. I braced myself and pushed with such effort that my foot went right through the rusty bucket and I careered over, back into the garden.

When I looked up again, I saw that the window had opened a fraction. *At last,* I thought, as I extricated my bruised leg from the bucket, *things are starting to go right!* I reached up with the

broom and tried to lever the window open further, but I could-
n't manage it. Still, it was open, should Paul and I ever be in a
position to pick up where we left off. I went back to the front
door to wait for him.

Much to my surprise, the door was ajar. There seemed to be
some object propping it open. I moved closer. The object was
my shoe. Paul must have put it there when Roland told him to
shut the door. The crafty little hussy had left the way open for
me!

I cautiously crept into the foyer and crouched out of sight.
The process of putting my shoe on was slow and painful, but
worthwhile—these brogues were Italian leather! I could hardly
afford to leave half of them behind.

I looked about. There was the familiar locked stairwell. A
peculiar arrangement, probably a legacy of the good old whore-
house days to stop customers getting in or out of their own free
will. Behind the stairs was the door to Rodney's flat, a tasteful
wrought-iron 1 adorning it. I tried the door, and it opened!
Rodney must have forgotten to lock it, or more likely he didn't
bother, with all the other security doors and gates all over the
place.

The flat was pitch-dark. I stepped in and silently closed the
door behind me. No one was there. I took several deep breaths.
My head was pounding. I hadn't been so on edge since my
school days, when Father Michael the math tutor outed himself to me in the sports storeroom. (That's another story.)

With a stumble and a thud, I found an armchair and fell into
its arms. Only then did I realize how uncomfortable I'd been for
the last hour or so. I got out my little flashlight and peered
around. The flat was spacious and disappointingly ordinary. A
stain on one wall indicated the presence of rising damp. Still, I
wasn't buying the joint, merely casing it.

There was a TV, couch, dresser, lamp—all the usual
things—and a pin-up from last year's Golden Boys of Rugby
calendar. A bottle of Wet Stuff Personal Lubricant stood

brazenly on top of the television. None of these personal effects appeared to be Jennifer's.

The window in the sitting room was shut, but through the nearby bathroom door I could see the second window, slightly open. Along the windowsill was an incredible collection of tubes and bottles. Intrigued, I got up to investigate. Every kind of skin conditioner, gel, makeup remover, cleanser, toner, and perfume were there, alongside remedies for cold sores, crabs, sunburn, and other indignities affecting the young man about town.

The shower curtain sported a cartoon depicting two grotesque creatures, whom I knew from one of Paul's T-shirts to be Ren and Stimpy. A towel on the rack showed a pink and white triangle pattern and the words STONEWALL '94.

I saw a pair of beady eyes on top of the shaving cupboard glaring at me. Panicking, I dropped my torch, and had to scrabble around the floor to find it. Shakily, I pointed it back up at the cupboard. The eyes were attached to a revolting toilet-roll cover in the form of a troll doll. *No wonder he put it up there,* I thought. *You could never use the toilet with that thing staring you in the face.*

In fact, the troll's grin was so mocking, so smart-arsely superior, I felt a spurt of anger. After all I'd been through, to be sneered at by a lavatory accessory! I reached up and grabbed it roughly, tossing up whether to throw it out the window or into the toilet bowl. As I shook it, Jennifer's diary fell out and landed at my feet.

At that moment, there was a quiet tap at the front door.

"Rodney?" somebody called softly.

I stuffed the diary and the torch into my pocket and hopped into the shower recess. I was still holding the troll.

"Rodney. You here?"

I heard the door open and then close again. I waited. No light was switched on. I couldn't hear anyone in the next room. Then again, I didn't hear anyone walk away from the door either.

Who could hear anything at all while their heart was performing the timpani part of *Also Sprach Zarathustra*? All I could do was nothing, which I did.

After a while I decided the coast was clear and it was time to go. Rodney would certainly be home before much longer. I sneaked out of the shower and poked my head around the bathroom doorway. In the gloom, the lounge room was as I had left it. I saw the dark bedroom opposite. Just as I was getting ready to beat it, something moved in the bedroom.

I jumped out of the doorway and squeezed myself up against the wall.

"Is somebody there?" called a distant voice.

I was adjacent to the window. Could I climb out? No, it was impossible without moving all the cosmetics. I pushed the window open a bit further, and two or three bottles fell out, crashing onto the path outside. "Meow," I added as an afterthought.

A light flashed on in the next room. I fumbled in my pocket for the diary and dropped it out the window.

A figure appeared at the door. It was Ng, looking as fierce as a Hong Kong film star and naked except for a pair of cotton briefs. He assumed a fighting stance.

"Hello there, Ng! What a surprise."

He stared for a moment, then exhaled slowly.

"It's me, Marc," I added casually.

"What you doing here? How do you get in?"

"Umm, I came through this window."

Ng stared past me at the window, which was open about six inches. He looked at me in disbelief.

"That's a crime," he said.

I didn't know whether he meant it was a climb, or he was pointing out the illegal nature of the act. I kept quiet.

"This is very awkward situation, Uncle Mike," he said, and shrugged his shoulders. "What you doing here? What am I doing here?" He giggled. "Same thing, I think."

"Why, what are you doing here?" I asked.

"Waiting for Rodney, like you. Yes? We are having an affair, Rodney and me. He leaves the door unlocked so I can come in."

"Oh, I'm sorry. I had no idea! I just...err..." Inspiration struck. "I just had to see him again. You're right. I was so taken with him at dinner last night, I didn't sleep a wink. I was dreaming about him." Strangely enough, that was true. "I think I'm in love and—well, you know what love is like. You become irrational. You climb through little tiny windows and so on. I couldn't help myself. You understand."

Ng looked horrified. "Don't be in love with Rodney! No good for you. Come, sit down." He actually ushered me inside.

"Yes, you're right, it's utterly stupid of me," I agreed too quickly. "It means heartache and pain and—I think I'm over it. I'd better go now."

"You bleeding."

"What?"

"Your leg. You injured?"

"It's OK. I've had worse."

"Let me see." I took my shoe off. "Ooh! Very bad!" He looked at me. "You crazy man! I fix it, no worries."

He fetched a bowl of warm water and disinfectant and carefully bathed my foot in it. Once or twice he looked up with an expression of deep sympathy and clicked his tongue.

"I think there something fishy with you," he said as he performed his ministrations.

"What do you mean?"

"You not Uncle Mike of Jennifer. I know."

"I'm not?"

He giggled. "Too butch, I think."

"Ah." I didn't quite see where this was going. "Too butch. That's very interesting. Um, in what way, exactly?"

"You kidding me? Ah, don't worry. I don't care."

"She had hundreds of uncles! I happen to be one of the butch ones. Ours is a big family."

"Oh, very big, yes. She from New Zealand, you from Italy.

But I mind my own business. No worries. I know why you come to dinner. I understand."

He winked.

"You do?"

"Same reason you here now? Yes?"

"Yes. What's that?"

"Love, sex, whatever! Rodney very attractive boy. Slut city, but very cute."

I breathed a slight sigh.

"Yes, he is. But I had no idea you and he were lovers."

"Now you know."

I glanced at my watch. Any minute Rodney might turn up, and God knows what would happen. A threesome, perhaps, the way things were going.

"Does Roland know what's going on between you two?" I asked.

"Maybe," said Ng, looking uneasy. "I don't talk about it."

"Better not," I counseled. "It merely complicates things. Let's make a deal. I won't tell anyone about seeing you here, and you tell no one you saw me. Then there's no trouble for anybody. All right?"

"Sure," he said. "I live here. You breaking and entering."

"Whoa, wait a minute. I told you why! It was my heart!"

Ng giggled. "I not press charges," he said. "There. Now your foot is clean."

"I'll be off, then," I said, sounding as if I'd popped in for a crumpet.

Ng gave me a kiss on the cheek. "You can stay if you like. No worries. Stay and watch." He winked.

I had to think about it.

"No, I forget!" he said. "You are in love. It would only hurt you more. I'm sorry, you must go. Better for you. Go to sauna maybe."

"Precisely what I had in mind."

"Sure! Enjoy yourself and forget Rodney."

"Yes, yes, I will. Good idea. Um, bye-bye then. It's been special."

"You go out same way you come in?" The color left my face. "Just kidding! Go this way. Front door is on the right. Good night. I'm hopping back to bed." He ran off, giggling.

I was finally out of there. As quickly and silently as I could, I left the building, ran down the path, and hurried out the gate into the street. I sat in the gutter and let out a deep breath. I never wanted to go through such an ordeal again. I headed off in the direction of my car, then I remembered: I'd left the diary behind! I stopped in my tracks, completely at a loss.

"Marc! Hey! Caro mio!"

It was Paul, running after me. I fell into his arms.

"I thought you'd gone! Marc, guess what?"

"Paul, I'm so glad to see you. What?"

"Guess."

"I don't know."

"I've got Jen's diary! It literally landed in my lap! It was incredible! I got away from dirty old Roland—heavens, I've changed my mind about him. What a slime-bag! Anyway, I couldn't find you anywhere so I went around to climb in Jen's window and somebody opened it and chucked aftershave all over me. Here, smell it—what do you think? I don't hate it, do you?"

"Huh?"

"Oh, never mind. And then what should come sailing out next but the fucking diary? I tell you, caro, if robbery is this easy, we should be going after the crown jewels or something!"

I felt a strong urge not to explain. "Fancy that," I remarked.

"Then I looked everywhere for you again, and here you were outside! What an excellent night's work. On to 9-1-ZERO!"

"Must we go to the sauna? I couldn't."

"Why not?"

"Well, I'm wearing a raincoat for one thing."

"Caro, don't be silly. We have to look for those piccies

tonight! Somebody might clean the place up and throw them away, if they haven't already."

"They probably have."

"No, think positive!" He waved the diary in my face. "This is such a good omen."

I tagged along defeatedly as Paul sang "I Feel Pretty" all the way to the car.

CHAPTER 10

A strong smell of chlorine was the first thing to greet us as we approached the sauna. I got a whiff of it a block away.

In suburban swimming pools the tang of chlorine is supposed to inspire confidence: The water must be clean, goes the reasoning: No germ could live in this! I beg to differ. Anyone who has ever sat in a tepid consommé of rubbers, pubes, sweat, moisturizer, and chlorine has renounced cleanliness (and probably godliness) forever.

I don't care for "the tubs" as we used to call them. I never had sex there, even in the years when sex was all the rage. I made a few attempts, but for some reason I was never able to let myself go. Too worried about tinea, I suspect. Those slippery, warm, wooden floorboards, rife with itchy little infections, bothered me constantly. I couldn't get my mind above the level of my feet. Well, not without a great deal of encouragement. And that's the other thing about saunas: They're so public! You might as well be in a glass case at a museum. Every flaw and imperfection, every asymmetrical, unacceptable aspect of your body is on show. You can't tie things around yourself, or trick yourself out in some fetching color to divert the eye. You can't fatten up interesting areas with football socks, and you can't atone for physical shortcomings with sparkling repartee because you're not allowed to speak. It's an unwritten, unspoken rule.

Because all the other saun-ees regard your body with such close scrutiny, you are forced to confront things you were blissfully taking for granted. Like the unmistakable signs of aging. Like the slow but unstoppable progress of your body hair's migratory patterns: over the shoulders, across the back, out through the nose and ears. Like sagging: If your stomach juts out and/or sags you can suck it in (though not for extended periods), but you can't suck in your bum. All you can do with that is hold it together, cupped in both hands, though you're liable to attract some very strange looks.

The other alternative is to find a warm, damp, wooden seat, and use your saggy bum to sit on it. In spite of the ever-present risk of tinea, this is my preferred option. On my infrequent visits to these steamy dens, I try to find somewhere comfortable out of harm's way. Paul, on the other hand, is all over the place hopping in and out of cubicles like a jackrabbit. His success rate is parahuman. He always seems to latch onto some body-builder from out of town or a television heartthrob experimenting between girlfriends. He radiates confidence, and it helps that he's young and his bum doesn't sag, though even Paul (like almost everybody) looks better dressed than he does nude.

I can't see why, but he thinks I have an attitude problem. "Try to pretend you're enjoying yourself, caro! " is his advice. "If you can't look drop-dead sexy, at least smile. It's a Turkish bath, not a Turkish prison!" I have been to a sauna with him exactly twice. I cramp his style, though it's typically sweet of him to drag me along. "Mr. Right might be waiting there for you, treading water in the spa," he says—and actually believes it. I don't know if I would recognize Mr. Right in a steam room; these joints are a touch murky. And let's be honest: Most Mr. Rights my age have retired gracefully and gone into native land-scaping. A bit late for a lifelong relationship when your life is more than halfway over.

I don't even know that I want such a thing. Paul automatically assumes that there's a someone for everyone, but his opinions were formed by women's magazines and the lyrics of old show tunes. I'm set in my ways. I enjoy the odd adventure—I was certainly getting a kick out of playing detective—but the grueling challenge of a relationship? Too much like climbing Everest: You practically kill yourself to get there and for what?

Five minutes of light-headedness, followed by a long, slow freeze.

Of course, I haven't been single all my life. I was in a relationship with my ex, Andrew, for six years, in and out of it for another two. Together we had some wonderful holidays, memorable dinner parties, loads of sex, the odd good cry. He certainly copped an earful of me whining about teaching, but he never complained about his own work. He's a sales rep for a drug company. We had samples from one end of the place to the other. Even now, eight years later (my God!) it irks me to pay good money for Berocca.

I thought he was a bit straitlaced. He thought I was sloppy. We broke up sensibly: He wouldn't have it any other way. Now he works in Brisbane. He lives with Neil, who is one of the dreariest men I have ever met. (I'm not the only one who says so either.)

So there you are. Mr. Right may have already come along and gone. Andrew had the best shoulders. Of course, there are plenty of good shoulders walking around, to cry on or lean your ankles against or whatever else you may like to do with them, but love's not so easy the second time. You're too wary. You can't lull yourself into some fantasy state and ignore those little irritating details. And breaking up: Is it worth it? It takes so long and on a purely practical level it's such a damn bore! I don't want to wade through that emotional sludge again. I'm not unhappy with my single lot.

I hadn't thought about Andrew for ages. I was drifting into a reverie, getting myself in absolutely the wrong mood for the sauna, so I was only half aware of Paul in the passenger seat reading out sections of Jennifer's diary.

"Only two days before! What do you think of that?"

"What?"

"Caro, aren't you listening?"

"I'm trying to get us there in two pieces. We'll have a good long look at that diary in the morning."

"I don't know if I'll let you."

"What do you mean?"

"There's stuff about me in here!"

"Oh yes? What kind of fascinating and revealing stuff is that?"

"Embarrassing stuff. 'April 12th. Supper w. Paul. He slept in due to hangover, missed *West Side Story* audition.' I wouldn't want that to get out!"

"Well, we're not going to publish it, for God's sake. And leave it in the car. We don't want it ending up at the bottom of a Jacuzzi."

"Good idea. I'll hide it on the floor under the Street Directory, OK?"

"If you must."

Needless to say, after the demoralizing escapades I'd been through at Roland's, I was hardly in the mood for any more. I hoped against hope that the man on the door at 9-1-ZERO would take one look at Paul, smack his forehead and say, "Hey, did you leave these photos behind?" before we had a chance to part with our $24. No such luck.

The doorman was a tough-looking but rather sexy youth with black hair close-shaved, tattoos, broken teeth, and a cut above his right eyebrow.

"Yikes, what happened?" asked Paul (a bit tactlessly, I thought) as the young man languidly took our money.

"Bashed," he replied.

"Oh, my God. Where?"

"Just outside here."

"Shit." Paul was all sympathy. I was horrified.

The doorman shrugged painfully. "Not the first time."

He handed us our locker keys. They were attached to a piece of elastic, to be worn at all times around the thigh or, if you were suitably muscular, the forearm.

"You're in Locker Room 5. Toilets are next door. Coffee shop and TV viewing area on the first floor—"

Paul cut him short. "Second floor, ladies underwear and accessories. Listen, I was here last night and I misplaced something. A packet of photos. I might have left them in a locker."

"I wasn't on last night. I'll have a look." He ducked behind the counter but came up shaking his head. "Cleaner didn't leave anything."

"Is he honest, your cleaner?" I asked.

"Dunno. He just come out."

"Come out? How sweet!" Paul fluttered, getting all sentimental.

"Come out of jail. He done three years for embezzlement."

We wandered to our locker room. It was lit in bright dazzling neon, not the ideal ambience in which to disrobe before strangers. Luckily, no one was around. The sound system was blaring house versions of '80s hits.

I folded my clothes neatly before placing them in the locker. Paul, more impatient, rolled his up and chucked them in. He wrapped a towel round himself and practiced several provocative poses.

"How could you lose those pictures?" I puzzled. "No one had the key to the locker but you."

"I sort of accidentally misplaced it."

"You didn't tell me that!"

"It came off. There was a fair bit of horsing around. You know, gents in the Jacuzzi, soap in the showers, gorillas in the mist. My key slipped off somewhere between arsehole and breakfast. It got handed in."

"Oh, Paul! For Christ's sake! Who handed it in?"

"I don't know."

"Did the doorman say where it was found?"

"Not exactly. But he wouldn't touch it without rubber gloves."

"Will you stop being stupid!" I was getting hot under the collar, or rather, the towel. "If somebody stole the photos, they'd hardly leave them lying around! You've brought me here under false pretenses."

Now Paul was getting cranky, too. "We don't know they were stolen, yet. Lighten up, caro! Let's enjoy ourselves."

"You know I don't like these places."

"Don't be so negative! That's all I'm getting from you: negative, negative, negative! By the way, the negatives were with the photos. They're gone as well."

I was fuming. "I'm leaving," I said.

Paul suddenly grabbed both our towels and flung them onto a chair. I felt naked.

"Come here, Marc!" he snapped. "Give me a hug."

I did.

"Closer! Mmmm. Feel good?"

"Yes!" I snapped.

"Good! Then let's go and get some more!" He grabbed my hand and the towels and dragged me upstairs.

The coffee shop and TV viewing area was vast, murky, and subdued. The room was decorated in the style of a 1920s movie palace: potted palms, chairs with velvet cushions, plaster statues of Greek gods in discreetly lit alcoves, a tiny fountain. Everything reeked of chlorine.

"I might have a coffee before I start," I said.

"All right, I'm going upstairs," said Paul. "I'll be in the maze or the steam room—and I expect to see you there soon!"

Off he bounded. I bought a coffee from another languid youth and took it to a raised area where there were several tables. Most of them were empty. At one, an elderly man sat intently poring over a crossword puzzle. On the other side, a youngish businessman sat, legs crossed, yapping on a mobile phone. Unwatched, a television was playing a Chinese kung fu movie.

On the pretext of making up my mind where to sit, I examined the tabletops and chairs for stray packets of photographs. I even gave the crossword man's table a cursory once over. He didn't look up.

There was no sign of the snaps, of course. I finally stretched out in a velvet love seat. My shins were quite bruised, I noticed. As I sipped my coffee, as slowly as humanly possible, I couldn't help but eavesdrop on the businessman's phone conversation.

"I'm still here at the office, can you believe it? It's that fucking Austcare thing. We'll never get it done by…Well, I'm sorry the baby woke you up, have a cup of tea…That? That's the cleaners, they've got their radio on…I might as well work through. I've got a meeting at 8:30 in the morning… Yeah, I know…"

He glared at me. I decided to pop upstairs.

They had gone to a fair amount of trouble decorating the walls and ceilings of this new venue, but I really wished they hadn't. It was fake stonework, made out of papier-mâché, the kind of thing you might see in a fun park sideshow: the Enchanted Castle or (more likely) the Chamber of Horrors.

On the first floor was a maze, painted black and consisting of tiny open cubicles connected by a twisting narrow corridor that led every so often to a dead end. As a sideshow attraction, this maze put me in mind of the Ghost Train: It was very dark, and every time you turned a corner, some old specter would spring out of nowhere and scare you half to death.

I had no idea how many gentlemen were in the maze. I could see them come and go in the distance, especially the pretty ones, but when I got to where I thought they were, they'd be gone. Paul didn't seem to be around. I found myself a quiet little cubicle at the end of a cul-de-sac and sat down on the hard bench. The hallway here was dimly lit by a small purple globe. There was a round hole in the wall to the cubicle next door, big enough to pass a watermelon through.

I took a quick look under my bench for the photos, knowing it was a waste of time. To my surprise, there seemed to be something there. I groped around and came up with a bunch of scrunched-up paper tissues. Disappointed, to put it mildly, I threw them through the hole in the wall. I closed my eyes and listened to a dance track that sounded like an industrial-strength cappuccino machine malfunctioning. A slave to the rhythm, I dozed off.

I was awakened by the feeling that all was not well. Something luminous was moving back and forth across my thigh: It was the face of a digital Rolex. Adjusting to the light, I saw that the Rolex was attached to an elderly wrist and presumably a hand, although that had disappeared under my towel. I slapped the wrist, more out of shock than anything else, and the arm whisked itself back through the wall. A face appeared in the opening.

"Pardon me!" It said.

I stared at the neat white mustache, the pale blue eyes in the tanned old face. "Anton?" I said.

"Why, Marc!" he said. "The stars are out tonight! Dear me. I've not seen you here before."

"I haven't been here before. Isn't the decor odd?"

"Neo-Butch."

"How are you?"

"Very well. Yourself? You're a gentleman of leisure now."

"More or less," I agreed.

"Well, well. Fuck me dead. Are you on your own this evening?"

"No, I'm with a friend."

"The love of your life? Or one of those studs that pass in the night?"

"Just a friend. What about you?"

"I'm with somebody, but she's off somewhere. Let's go and get a drink before my neck seizes up."

"I've just had a coffee."

"Have a whiskey and we can talk. You're supposed to keep quiet 'round here."

"Do you know the way out?"

"Like the back of my hand. Come along, Marc. How brilliant to see you like this."

He grabbed me by the arm and wrenched me out into the passageway. My towel unwound and slid to the floor.

"And like that!" he added.

We made our way to the bar. (There was one on every floor.)

Anton and I have known each other for over twenty years, ever since we worked together in Grace Brothers' department store. He was head of menswear; I was slumming it behind a counter during university break. They started me off in appliances, but after several bloody and off-putting demonstrations I was placed out of harm's way to keep an eye on enormous bolts of gray material. It was an easy job, since they never seemed to sell any. Anton made regular passes at me, as he did with all the young temps, in a discreet way of course. It was only later that I learned of his brilliance with a sewing machine and his huge reputation amongst Sydney's drag queens. Although he never got into a gown himself, Anton was known as "Queen of the Sequins."

"So what are you up to?" I asked as I sipped my whiskey and he lapped up a brandy Alexander. "Designed any shows lately?"

"Don't do those anymore. Heavens, that was sooo long ago! When's the last time I saw you?"

"I can't recall."

"You'd just split up with that salesgirl with the nice tits. What was her name?"

"Andrew. That's eight years ago."

"My god, no! The children must be in big school!"

"Four of them are. So you retired as Queen of the Sequins?"

"Very nearly. I was run off me feet there for a while. I wasn't sorry to see the joint burn down. Neither were the owners, for that matter! But Mardi Gras brought me screaming out of retirement. Now I'm working harder than ever."

"On the parade?"

"*Absolument*. It's a matter of principal. The parade's been getting a wee bit drab over the last few years, a bit PC, a tad plain. It's time sequins made a comeback! Fortunately, lesbians are learning to embrace glamour, but it's been an uphill battle."

"Will you be appearing on a float?"

"If I can find something to wear! I may be too busy anyway. Victoria's been at me. You remember her? She expects me to build her a cossie from scratch—from the ground up! It could take the rest of my life. But if ever I were tempted to make an appearance, it's this year. My friend Tammy—where is she? I thought she'd be here." He looked around the bar and sighed. "Timmy is his real name. He's an opera queen, and they're making a Diva float. It will be fabulous! Come to think of it, you're an opera queen yourself, aren't you?"

I demurred. "An opera fan—"

"Fuck it, you'd be wonderful, Marc! Tam needs an older woman to play Melba! You must do it!"

"I couldn't."

"Don't be such a wuss! It'll be the highlight. Tam's gonna be Callas. There's a Sutherland, a couple of Kiri Te Kanawas— they're all frocked up as Tosca, standing around the battlements, and there's one girl who keeps jumping off, only where she is it looks like a cliff face. Apparently some soprano just jumped off a cliff." He chuckled.

I was profoundly shocked. "That's tasteless."

"I suppose. Since when did taste matter at Mardi Gras? Nobody would know. It's an in-joke."

"I'm sorry, Anton. The idea doesn't appeal to me."

"Tammy!" he cried suddenly. "At long last! Maybe Tammy can talk you into it."

A chubby young man with a mousy face and wispy blond hair ambled over to us. Anton embraced him.

"Marc," said Anton, "this is Tammy."

I don't think in my whole life I had ever seen anybody who looked less like Maria Callas.

"Tim Boston," he said, and jabbed me in the stomach with

his hand. "Sorry, I can't see properly without my glasses. I meant to shake hands."

"Sorry," I echoed, and took his hand. "Have we met? The name sounds familiar."

"I can't say," he replied, squinting at me.

"Oh, you must have met each other!" said Anton. "Tammy is Norma Clutterbuck's personal secretary."

I froze and said nothing. Had he recognized my voice? He couldn't have. He was still squinting—or to be more accurate, wincing.

"Excuse me," he said, "you're crushing my fingers."

I realized I was still holding his hand. I dropped it abruptly.

"Anton's been telling me about the Mardi Gras float," I remarked in a voice strangely unlike my own.

"Ah."

"Yes, wouldn't Marc be stunning as Melba?" Anton gushed.

"Mmm," said Tim. "Do you look like her? We're only interested in look-alikes."

"I'm afraid I don't," I said. "I'm Italian."

"Don't be ridiculous, Tam!" interrupted Anton. "What about you? Who are you going as—Shelley Winters?"

"My Callas is world famous," sniffed Tim. "If you'll excuse me, I'll check out the maze."

"What's the point if you can't see anything?" said Anton, but Tim was striding away. "Oh, she's fucked," he added wistfully.

"Are you two in a relationship?" I asked.

"We try. She's away with Madam half the year. They're very close. That's why Tam refused to let a drag play Clutterbuck on the float." He sighed and finished his drink with a gulp. "If there is a relationship, it's incestuous. Tammy looks upon me as a surrogate grandfather."

"Oh, well." I leaned forward. "The interesting thing is, you see, I spoke to him only today on the phone!"

"To Tammy?"

"I need to see Dame Norma. I have very good reasons, but I

can't go into them here. I rang Tim—Tam—your friend for an appointment, but Dame Norma won't see me till April."

"What's in it for her?"

"For Dame Norma? Nothing."

He smiled wickedly. "That's why she wouldn't see you, dear."

"I have to speak to her!"

"Why?"

"I can't tell you."

"Marc! Tsk, tsk. You don't have to tell me. It's obvious."

"It is?"

"You obsessive opera queens—and don't deny it this time, you are a fucking Grade A Opera Queen in Spades!—you'll do anything to meet your idols. Believe me, Marc, it's more fun meeting an auditor from the tax department."

I decided to go along with him. "I'm desperate," I exclaimed. "She's my idol, as you say. Do you think you could swing it? I told Tim I wanted to interview her for an Italian opera magazine."

"And you don't, I presume. Whoo! She'd have seen through that in no time. She subscribes to everything and knows everybody."

I appealed to his nostalgic side. (Everyone connected with drag has a nostalgic side.) "Anton, for old time's sake. Remember the fun we had at Grace Brothers? What a tragedy that beautiful old store is closed. It breaks my heart. I wonder what they'll do with the building."

"Turn it into a gay retirement home in honor of all the girls who worked there over the years." We laughed.

"Anton?"

"All right, I'll get you in to salivate all over Dame Norma. But you must do something for me."

"Yes. What?"

"If Tam wants you on the float, I'd like you to say yes."

"Oh." It hit me like a bolt from the blue. "You're not going to suggest—you're not going to tell him I want to play Dame

Norma on a Mardi Gras float? He wouldn't let me, anyway."

"He's very loyal. But if he thought you were her greatest fan in the whole wide world—it may come to that, that's all I'm saying."

"Please think of some other way."

"I'll make you a gown! Do you want to see the old bitch or not?"

"I do, but—"

"Marc, your face! It's a fucking picture. Look, I'll try and think of something else, but if it goes that way, you're in. Deal?"

"Yes, all right. I want to be heavily made up."

"Naturally! You'll need to look decent! I knew old Dotty would come across."

I shuddered.

"What's up? Somebody walk over your grave?"

"Somebody drove a steamroller over it."

"Because I called you Dot? Ha! You remember that party then?"

"Vaguely. I need another drink. Same again?"

He glanced at his watch.

"I really ought to winch Tammy out and skiddoo. Some of us still work for a living, you know!" He gave me an affectionate hug. "I'll call you soon. We have a deal! I may need your measurements!" He winked. "Have a good night. Give 'em one for me. Now where is that girl? I wonder if she ever made it to the maze?"

I ordered a double. Perhaps the alcohol loosened me up, but I began to feel more relaxed. Mardi Gras was, after all, months away; the whole thing might be solved by then, especially if I could talk to Dame Norma ASAP. And then, what was wrong with camping it up on a float with a lot of opera queens? Nothing! My gut reaction was the result of shyness, a fear of making a fool of myself, a thing I often seem to do. But what was I worried about? This was Mardi Gras. I would be one of hundreds! Nobody was asking me to dress up as Tosca and run through the middle of a football match. *Au contraire,* I would be among friends, possibly very sexy ones.

By the time I'd finished my fourth or fifth drink, I was feeling supremely confident. Things were moving along. I had Jennifer's diary, and Dame Norma was more or less in the bag. It had been a hell of a night, though, and I was ready to drift off to dreamland, preferably in my own comfy bed. It was time to find Paul and drag him away from whatever activity was occupying his attention.

I was surprised not to have seen Paul already; he gets around. I tried the spa on the top floor, but there was no one there at all (unless they were fully immersed). Several men, mostly Asian, were in the showers. Paul wasn't among them. Surely he would not have left without telling me! I checked the coffee shop and TV area again to no avail. The only places left were the cubicles and the two saunas. These regular cubicles were, unlike those in the maze, lockable. About six were occupied. I didn't really feel like going on a door-knock appeal, so that left the saunas.

I entered the 'wet' sauna. It was almost entirely unlit and very steamy. I collapsed onto a wooden bench next to the wall and waited to get my bearings. There was nobody there. After all, it was very late. I didn't leave, however, overpowered as I was by tiredness and the heat.

As I stared into the darkness and became acclimatized to the low visibility, a figure began to take shape on the bench opposite mine. I was not alone. He was so still I hadn't noticed him. He wasn't asleep, though, and he was staring at me intently.

Gradually I could make out his features and, I have to say, they were well worth making out. He had what the ads refer to as a swimmer's build: strong, defined, but not pumped up to resemble the end result of an avalanche. His legs and arms were long, his chest hairless. He had short-cropped curly dark hair. The most interesting part, strangely enough, was his face: His eyes were large, penetrating, and set farther apart than average. He had a wide mouth and ears that were slightly on the pointy side, giving him a puckish look. He grinned, showing a set of beautiful even teeth, one of which was whiter than the rest. He was, well, intriguing.

"Hello," I said.

He didn't answer, but put his forefinger to his lips in a shushing pose. His towel was draped loosely across his lap. He stood and the towel fell to the floor. The phrase "hung like a horse" flitted across my mind. As he walked over to me, I had a feeling of déjà vu, along with other more pressing feelings. He sat on my lap, straddling my legs, and took my head in his hands. We kissed, deeply, for about 150 years. It was the simplest, most affectionate, horniest moment I could remember for a long time.

"I'm Marc," I said, coming up for air.

"Reg," he said. Even that failed to douse the flame.

"It's late, I have to go home." I said.

"I'm coming," he whispered. I looked down. "Coming with you—may I?"

"Please."

We kissed again. Et cetera. Twenty minutes or so later, we left.

CHAPTER 11

*N*eedless to say, the investigation took a back seat. Reg lurched into my life in a way that, moments before, I had thought impossible.

I had entertained visions of myself rocking on the verandah, cozy in my worn gray cardigan, staring blankly at the magnolias as they stirred lazily in the summer breeze, my mind occupied by ghosts: strapping men of decades long past, all fallen in some great war. Occasionally, perhaps, one of the young homosexuals playing French cricket on the lawn might run up to ask me the time or offer a cup of tea. "What, dear?" I would ask. "Oh, yes, that would be camp," I'd add and drift gently back into my ancient reverie.

In other words, I thought I was past it. Well, how wrong can you be! Here it was, after 4 in the morning of a jam-packed day, and I was brimming over with all the enthusiasm of a complete novice. (Neither of us was that, I might add.)

"Here we are!" I announced as we arrived home.

"Nice place you've got here," remarked Reg with a delightful lack of originality. Such an endearing addiction to cliché.

"Did an angel whisper?" I asked. During the trip home I had grown a mite poetic.

He smiled wanly. "Let's go to bed," he suggested.

"*Bellissima!*"

The answering machine was blinking fit to bust.

"Where's the loo?" asked Reg.

"Through there," I indicated. While he was completing his ablutions, I played back the message, suddenly anxious in case Breathers Anonymous had called again. I was quite relieved to hear Paul's voice.

"Caro mio! I'm sorry I didn't wait, but I had to go! Stephen and Geoffrey were both there—in the Jacuzzi! I can't believe they're back together, can you? No place for this little black duck to hang around. I tried to tell you—actually, I found you in the maze but I didn't like to wake you up so I tiptoed away. No pix, worse luck. God knows what happened to them. I'll try to write down every trivial little thing I remember about the party. Anyway, at least you've got the diary. Can't wait to read it! Don't start without me. Call me tomorrow morning— no, afternoon. Late. Sweet dreams. Did you score? I hope so. Ooh, there might be a gentleman there right now! I'll shut up then. Bye!"

"What are you doing?"

I felt Reg's arm around my neck as he smooched up behind me.

"Nothing. Just listening to the ravings of some demented queen. I'll never do it again. Let's go."

And we did. It may not have been a case of love at first sight, but it was definitely a case of making love at first light. We snuggled up as the sun rose. Somewhere out there in the world, people went about their business as though nothing had happened, unaware of the earth-shattering revelations taking place at chez Petrucci. As for me, my priorities were absolutely redefined. Jennifer who? Dame Norma which? They might have been figures in a comic opera, for all I cared.

The night was fantastic. It's a tonic when you find yourself involved in the sort of adventures that only happen to bulky bleached blonds in R-rated videos. All you can do is go for it in a big way, hold nothing back, and do your utmost to remember all the details so you can call everybody ASAP. With this in mind, I gave the usual conversational gambits the flick.

Reg, too, had little to say. He didn't need to: He was socially equipped in other ways. In tactile terms, he was as eloquent as Socrates. Also much younger.

In old films, back in the days when they couldn't show a

couple making love, the director would indicate what was going on by focusing on two drips of water dribbling down a window-pane. Halfway down, the two drips would join up, becoming one stream. All I can say is, if Reg and I had been in that movie, our window would have looked like a Jackson Pollock.

Eventually we lay in a state of blissful postcoital delirium. I stared lazily at the ceiling, trying to decide what time of the day it was. A birdie chirped. A 727 aircraft whooshed benignly overhead. It seemed like midmorning: time for Renata. I was about to suggest we gather round the old gramophone when Reg sat up.

"Let's do something," he murmured.

"So soon?" I was somewhat fatigued.

"I mean let's go somewhere. For lunch."

"Is it lunchtime?"

"Will be shortly. You want the first shower?"

"Oh, all right."

I staggered out of bed. It might have been fun for us to shower together, but I didn't protest: Old habits die hard. I'm used to having my own personal space. It's a feature I look for in a bathroom.

Reg blew me a kiss. "Don't be long."

But I took my time. My body ached from head to foot; all my underused muscles screamed in protest at the workout they had undergone. Plus, I wanted to make myself as pleasant to be with as possible. Several liters of moisturizer and aftershave later, I slipped into the hall, a new man. Halfway up the stairs I spotted Reg in my study, snooping. (Just what I would have done!) He looked very cute.

"Curiosity killed the cat!"

I think he jumped slightly. "Oh, hello. You finished?"

"Mm."

"You've got a lot of books. They're in Italian."

"You know Italian?"

"A little. From my singing."

"You're a singer?"

He blushed prettily.

"Not now. I...sang in a choir."

"Really. The Gay and Lesbian Choir?"

"No, no. A school choir. St. Thomas's."

"Ah, well, nearly right. Just wrong about the lesbian component." I laughed heartily. Reg didn't appear to get it.

"No, we were just kids. Our voices hadn't broken." He sighed and looked faraway and wistful.

"Don't get all maudlin," I said. "Hit the showers and we'll be off."

We decided to observe the wonders of nature in the Botanical Gardens. There was also an excellent restaurant there, a converted rotunda situated bang in the center. It wasn't particularly busy; the only other customers were two businessmen who never spoke to each other but talked on cell phones all through the meal. Reg and I were virtually the guests of honor. A blotchy-faced headwaiter beamed at us with matronly delight. I suspect he'd seen us holding hands under the table. Whatever the cause, he inundated us with roasted capsicum, Camembert, and Chianti. We talked very little, but it didn't feel awkward. Chat is just a form of camouflage anyway; it's terribly overrated. I drank wine instead.

It was with a slightly cloudy head that I fell back into bed late that afternoon. I snuggled up to Reg's warm contours and prepared for a doze. He'd have none of it. Now he felt like talking!

"Do you have a job or anything?" he asked.

"No, I'm retired."

"Retired! How old are you?"

"Oh, I retired early. I'm in my forties. Mid to late forties. I've got a small private income."

"Ah."

"And I do some tutoring in Italian. I get by."

I sounded incredibly dreary. I toyed with the idea of telling

him about my semiprofessional sleuthing activities. "I do a bit
of investigative work," I confessed. "Undercover."

"I noticed!"

He didn't seem remotely interested in the subject, so I
dropped it.

"What about you?" I asked. "You must have a job."

"Yes, I've been slack today. Hope I don't get sacked. I work
at Virgin."

"How incongruous."

"In the T-shirt department. It's only temporary. Maybe I
should ring them. It's late-night shopping, the busiest night.
They probably need me."

"Go ahead."

I lay there watching the dust particles swirling in a ray of
late afternoon sunshine. There was something timeless and
romantic about the sight. I reminded myself not to neglect the
vacuuming.

I turned over the situation in my mind. This was such an
unexpected turn of events. I hadn't felt so excited, so singularly
focused on another human being since I first met Andrew.
Indeed, this was even more compelling: With Andrew, we took
our time to ease into the relationship, whereas Reg exploded
onto the scene in more ways than one. How odd: I hadn't
given Andrew a thought for ages and here I was, com-
paring him with Reg. Did this mean I considered us a couple?
I hadn't planned such a thing; it wasn't part of some grand
scenario, it just seemed to be. Happened overnight, as it were.
As the idea took root, I cast my eye over the wardrobe, wondering where I could put half my clothes so Reg's would fit.
Pack them in an old suitcase, I supposed. Why not? I didn't
plan on going out for quite some time.

I wondered whether Reg knew any opera. He seemed a
sensitive boy; ripe, as it were, to experience the delights of the
soprano voice in full flight. I imagined the pleasant evenings
we would share, listening and exchanging expressions of rap-

turous amazement—our own suburban coven of Tebaldiani. But I would have to play it gently. I didn't want to frighten him away. The best approach might be to wait, see how things turned out. We could have sex first. We'd already had it, of course, but the best thing might be to have more and more. Hmm. The dust particles were swirling fit to bust. Where was he? He'd been on the phone forever.

I ambled out of bed and threw on my oxblood toweling bathrobe. "Darling?" I cooed as I stumbled down the stairs. "Reg?"

He wasn't on the phone. I checked the bathroom, but he wasn't cutely scrubbing away at his smooth firm limbs in the shower (as I had hoped). He wasn't under the couch. His clothing, which had hit the floor long before we'd reached the bedroom, was gone, and the front door was open. He had left.

Oh.

I guessed he had scampered off to work. But without telling me? Come to think of it, I'd paid for our lunch, too. I began to feel like a fool. It looked as if I had been taken in by a pretty face and a night full of sweet nothings. At least I wouldn't have to pack up my old clothes.

I made some tea, put on the "Death of Butterfly" and sat cross-legged in the middle of the floor. I felt an unfamiliar but not unpleasant prickling behind the eyes. Tears, however, weren't forthcoming. *Humph! It's this sort of experience that turns people hard,* I thought, as Renata performed hara-kiri in the background.

But there was no use moping around. I busied myself clearing up around the house: To be honest, it was a mess. The bed was unmade, the dishes unwashed. Even my study looked as though a cyclone had passed through, what with papers strewn over the floor, desk drawers open and so on. I couldn't believe how I'd neglected the place in the past week, going off on my wild-goose chases. I felt a domestic fit coming on, and very timely it was.

When I had finished, everything was spic, span, and well stacked. I'd even scrubbed away the prehistoric sauce stains burned into the top of the stove. Unfortunately, in my enthusiasm I'd gotten a drop of all-purpose cleaner in my eye, and it stung mightily. (Eyes were apparently not included in the "all-purpose" label.) I lay on the couch with a damp washcloth crushed into my face. Now the tears were copious.

The phone rang. My heart leapt. Of course, it was Reg ringing to explain—although I didn't recall giving him my phone number. I stumbled blindly toward the receiver and knocked it to the floor. I grabbed it.

"Hello? Hello?"

"Who is she?"

"Paul! Is that you?"

"Who else, caro? Look, it's after the half-hour, I can't talk for long. What I want to know is, who's the pert little brunette?"

"What do you mean?"

"Don't be coy! I thought you'd be falling over yourself to tell me! Did you pick him up at the sauna?"

"How did you know?"

"Darling, my spies are everywhere, especially in the Botanical Gardens. You were seen, caro."

"By who?"

"By whom."

"Don't you correct me! Who saw us?"

"A little fairy under a Christmas bush!"

"They always blab."

"Actually, an actor friend of mine sometimes drives the choo-choo train 'round the Gardens. Didn't you notice him? Tanned, long hair? Driving a train? He's very sweet. Jock. Shithouse actor. You met him at the party I threw last year."

"I didn't notice a choo-choo train."

"From what I hear, you wouldn't have noticed if it had run over you! So who is it?"

"The boy's name is Reg."

"Reg? Christ!"

"Possibly. I don't know his surname."

"Why waste time on formalities. Did you get on well?"

"Like rabbits."

"Fabuloso! You've broken the drought. Is he there now?"

"No, he's gone to work."

"Good, 'cuz I thought I'd come 'round after the show. We have to go through Jen's diary with a fine-tooth comb. You've got it in a safe place, I hope."

I hesitated. Where had I put it? Nowhere! It was still lying in the car.

"Of course it's safe!" I huffed. "Really, Paul, you're hardly one to talk."

"Don't nag me about the photos. I've got to go."

"Wait. Don't come 'round tonight. I need to sleep."

"Ah, I understand. At your age you can't go without your regular nye-nyes. Now hop into a scented bath, have a cup of beef tea, and curl up on a lovely warm Reg. I'll be over in the morning."

"That would be better."

"Oh, bugger, bugger, bugger!"

"What's wrong? Are you addressing me?"

"I just missed the opening number. Damn."

"I'm sure it didn't suffer too much."

"Probably not. Better go then. I'm on again in twenty-five minutes."

I almost flew to the car, which as usual I'd left in the nearest vacant parking space, about eighteen blocks from the house. All the car doors were unlocked. (The things you forget when you're in a horny hurry.) Fortunately nothing had been disturbed: Thieves prefer a challenge. The diary was still hiding safely under the seat.

Soon I was sitting up in bed, all ready to examine Exhibit A. The first thing I noticed was the title page with the simple word: "Agenda." Much to my amazement and delight,

Jennifer Burke's diary was Italian, printed in Florence! Like all Italian diaries, it named the saints for each day of the year. My heart warmed. Even though I'm a nonbeliever, I felt this to be a good omen.

The book was clearly a personal document. Most of the entries seemed pretty cryptic. Many were single words only; for example, the entry on the day of the party simply read "PARTY." Well, we already knew that! (Incidentally, she died on August 20th, Saint Bernard's Day. Even he couldn't save her! I had a momentary vision of a huge dog with a brandy barrel round its neck lunging through the bemused guests.)

In the middle of the previous week, on the Wednesday, there was an intriguing entry. "F.M. 11 A.M." was written at the top, but was crossed out brightly in red and the words "OH YEAH?" added. Jennifer was big on capitals. There was also another word, definitely not for publication.

Elsewhere were longer entries, sometimes quite rambling. I glanced at one that seemed to be about Randolph Lloyd Webber. It read, in part, "Randolph getting obsessive. Why, why, why, WHY must these people do this? Threatens suicide. Not worried. Anyone who talks about it is ALL TALK! Period today. Do TAX by 31st. Washing powder." Then, in a different ink, "Uncle taking care of R." I presumed R was Randolph; was the "Uncle" Uncle Mike?

I remembered Ng saying Jen had spent Christmas with this person, my doppelgänger. I scoured the earlier months for references to him and came up trumps three times, in January and March. The March entry (on Friday the 4th, the day of Saint Cunegonde) was the most explicit: "LUNCH, TREVISI'S, 1:15. UNCLE MIKE." Trevisi's is an exclusive sea-view restaurant. Paul would undoubtedly know all the waiters, I mused, either socially or biblically. Perhaps we could track this uncle down. Where was he now? How had he reacted to Jen's death?

The word "SEATON" occurred once or twice; wasn't that the name of a small town? It certainly sounded like it in a random entry, "SEATON INSUFFERABLE. CAN'T WAIT TO LEAVE." I made a mental note to look up Seaton in the directory.

My eyes were still sore, and I felt sleep creeping upon me, rather as Reg had done the night before. (Sigh.) I was about to close the diary when I noticed an elaborate diagrammatic entry toward the back. Under the heading "MEMORIZE THIS!" was a graphic representation of the various management levels and power blocs of the Sydney Opera. The board members were listed, with Sir Fred's name underlined several times, and many other names I didn't know. Each section was boxed and titled. Finance was there with Edward Quinn (administrator) at the head and three others including Judy Lecoq, whose name was ticked twice. The artistic director had a box to himself, as did the technical director; there were lists of more names under these two, presumably staff, some of whom were ticked and others crossed out. I noticed Adele Cropper of publicity in there.

Connecting various people from one category to another was a series of wavy lines and arrows. No two ways about it: This girl had been seriously, professionally ambitious. I stared closely at the diagram, feeling that I was missing something obvious, but I was too tired to think clearly. I gave up, and slid the book under my pillow for safekeeping.

Before long I was dreaming of wandering through the Botanical Gardens. I was alone, frantically searching for something amongst the Christmas bushes.

CHAPTER 12

*B*y 11 o'clock the next morning, there was still no hint of Paul's feet tap-tap-tapping at my front doorstep. The croissants and freshly brewed espresso I'd prepared for our intensive diary-fest were cooling rapidly and would soon be old news. It was annoying but not unusual. Paul rarely turned up on time, especially if it was important that he should—a habit that had failed to endear him to the representatives of Cameron Mackintosh, amongst others. Even so, I was surprised. I knew he was itching to get his paws on Jennifer's memoirs, if only to see what she'd written about him.

I sipped my moderately iced coffee and set the diary before me. I planned to take an analytical approach. Jennifer had carefully noted important meetings or tête-à-têtes at the bottom of every page: Sometimes there were names, but mostly just initials. My first task was to identify them.

R.L.W. was clearly Randolph Lloyd Webber. The meetings with him were concentrated in one period of a few weeks in June, around the time of the *Phar Lap* performances. The words "RUBBISH," "CRAP," and "SHIT" also turned up during this period, evidently a time of stress for all concerned. By July, R.L.W. had disappeared, although as I had already observed, his obsession with Jennifer dated back at least to February.

The history of her year with Sir Fred was easy to plot. He first appeared as Sir Fred Mathieson, then as Sir Fred, Fred, Freddy, and, finally, a few days before she died, as F.M. (with the additional "Oh yeah?" etc.) This seemed to bear out the theory that they'd had an affair—one that had soured in the two weeks prior to her tragic demise. Why had she undergone a change of heart? There were no clues that I could find.

The saddest page of this journal was a list, written a month before the murder, of operatic roles suitable for a lyric soprano: Mimi, Manon, Liu, even the ubiquitous Desdemona. In any one of these roles, Jennifer would have probably made her reputation. Coincidentally, all these characters come to an untimely end. *Was that significant?* I wondered. If I were a real sleuth, would I see some pattern emerging from the pages of this diary?

As it happened, the only pattern emerging from the pages of the diary was one made by coffee that I spilt all over it. (I often knock cups over when I work; it helps me think.) I left the book standing open on the table to dry and popped upstairs to change my pants.

Paul apparently was not going to appear before dusk, so I prepared to go out to do the banking and other mundane chores. Just as I'd locked the door behind me, the phone rang. I fumbled with my keys and got to the receiver just in time. The caller had not hung up, but no one was speaking.

"Hello?" I said.

The silence continued. Damn it, this had happened before! Somebody was either playing a joke or trying to scare me.

"Paul," I snapped, "if that's you, fuck off! You're too late, and I'm going out."

You idiot, I thought. *If it's a burglar, you just told them you were leaving the house.*

"That is, I'm not going out right now," I added in a hasty postscript, "but sometime this week—probably. And I'm not saying when! Um…woof! Woof! Down boy! Get down! I'll feed you tomorrow."

"Who's Paul?" said a voice.

"What? Who is this?"

"It's Reg."

"Reg!"

"Marc?"

"You left! Without a word."

"I know. I'm sorry. Is Paul your lover?"

"Paul Who? Oh no! Just a friend. Silly old bloke. Rice queen. I hardly know him. Are you coming back?"

"I'd like to see you again."

"Well, I'd like to see you, too!"

"I had to go in to work last night."

"I thought so. Well, look, are you working tonight?"

"Oh, yes. It's late-night shopping."

"That's what you said last night. It's only Wednesday."

"Did I? Ah."

"Reg, we had a wonderful time yesterday. But if you don't want to get together again, why did you call?"

"I do want to." He paused.

"Are you still there?"

"I thought I better tell you: I've got a boyfriend."

So that was it. "One of those modern open relationships?" I asked hopefully.

"No. He's real jealous. Protective. He's older than me."

"Who isn't?"

"He was away when I met you. He's back now. I don't really know when I can get out, you see."

"Mmm. I understand."

"But sometimes he works odd hours. Could I—do you think I could call you up, you know, like at a moment's notice?"

My heart hardened. "That's hardly a very satisfactory way to have a relationship."

"No," he sighed. "OK, forget it."

"Wait. Look, you never know. Why don't we try it? Call me anytime you like. How about that?"

"That'd be good. Darling."

Darling! I had to sit down.

"Reg, this wouldn't be one of those times, would it?"

"Um, no. Although I might be free in a bit. It depends."

"Right. Well, let's just chat away until you find out.

Um...so. What's the weather like over there?"

"Where?"

"Wherever you are! Where are you, by the way?"

Clunk!

"Reg? Did you hang up? Answer me! Hello?"

He'd gone. I was stunned. Was it something I said? In alphabetical order, I ran through every emotional reaction known to humans—anger, bathos, confusion, dribbling, etc. What was the matter with that peculiar, gorgeous boy? Had he changed his mind again? His social graces and phone technique hadn't improved one iota. But perhaps the jealous boyfriend had walked into the room: Was Reg being pistol-whipped (or worse) at this very moment? I seethed: If that fiend laid a hand on him...well, I wouldn't be at all surprised.

The phone rang. Ah! It was simply a mechanical malfunction. We'd been cut off in our prime.

"So!" I said. "Where were we, darling?"

"You're getting a bit camp in your old age," replied Paul.

"Paul! I was expecting you hours ago."

"I know, but something very exciting came up."

"Oh, really?"

"Now listen carefully, I've only got a second. Meet me up the road in ten minutes exactly. You got that?"

"What?"

"Write this down."

"Hang on."

"Never mind. Shit, he's coming. Look—I'll meet you outside Boyz Klub in ten minutes, OK? Act like it's a chance meeting. I'll be with someone. Don't mention Jen or any of that stuff, OK? I'll explain later."

"I can't go out, I'm expecting a call. Paul? Hello?"

I was a trifle bored with being summarily dismissed. Nevertheless, I would show Paul that one of us at least could be reliable. After adding a few more "pleases" to my phone machine message, I chucked the soggy diary into the backseat of the car and headed for the trendiest clothing shop in the Inner West.

By the time I found a parking spot I was running late. It was eleven minutes by the clock, easily. I was breathless when I got to Boyz Klub, but peering through the window I was relieved to see Paul inside, trying on an outfit. He seemed to be alone.

Boyz Klub was not a store into which I had ever set foot. Looking inside, I remembered why: Everything about the place was intimidating. Three of the walls consisted entirely of mirrors, so the store seemed enormous with enough stuff to clothe an army, whereas in reality they only stocked three or four items.

The outfits on show were made from denim, leather, and chamois, which had seemingly been blasted to smithereens in a large metal container. The remnants had been draped artistically over three models—who were live, paid to simply hang around and pout. Underneath their threadbare creations, these petulant boyz wore perfectly laundered, dazzlingly white singlets and loose underpants.

Along one wall were several larger-than-life-size photographs of naked young men, sitting in Old World leather armchairs while smoking cigars and sipping cognac. In one picture, a young man was being waited on by an elderly (nude) retainer who greatly resembled William S. Burroughs. It struck me as odd that a clothing store would feature pictures of nudes, but considering the clientele, I suppose it was the right move.

I waved to Paul. He ran to the door.

"Caro, you're late. I had to try on this hugely expensive camisole thing. What do you think? Not that it matters—even God couldn't afford it."

He spun around. He was wearing jeans and a white T-shirt in need of a dry clean.

"It looks like an ordinary T-shirt."

"Naturally! Don't you know anything about street fashion?"

"Paul, what are you doing here? What am I doing here?"

"We're...never mind, here he comes." He broke into a social beam. "Marc! Do you know Seaton?"

A tall and very fat young man had joined us. He offered me a chubby hand.

"Seaton Frith," Seaton announced. "Babe," he whined, turning to Paul, "it's just as I thought. The largest size they've got wouldn't go round my big toe!"

"Never mind, Seaton. Isn't this the coincidence of all time? I've just run into Marc Petrucci, one of my dearest friends."

Seaton sneered politely. "Paul and I were tossing around the concept of a coffee. I hope you're not too busy to join us?" he asked, without much enthusiasm.

"I'd love to," I replied.

He looked thoroughly put out. "Marvelous!" he lied. "Where shall we go? Do you know Café Poisson? It used to be a fish market?"

"I've never tried it," Paul replied. "I heard it stinks of fish. They can't get rid of the smell."

"Oh no, it's fine!" gushed Seaton. "They've hung garlic and onions all over the place. So now it smells like a rather good zuppa del mare!"

Paul removed the street fashion, boggled at the price tag, and told them he'd think about it—"But not for long, or I'll give myself a tumor!"—and we found ourselves being dragged along the street, literally, by this large florid man with the intriguing name.

Café Poisson was indeed fishy, and very large. It was also crammed to the gills with customers. We found a table in a back corner—the sort of space the proprietor muses over and thinks, *Oh, yes, I can squeeze one more table in here*. We were remarkably uncomfortable, thanks to Seaton's girth. Unable to move my head in either direction, I looked up. Above us hung a massive string of garlic, swinging in the breeze. We would be safe from vampires, but if it worked loose and fell on us we'd be dead.

"I gotta have a twinkle," Seaton announced. "If the waiter comes, I'll have the crabmeat burger with guacamole on the side and a mega iced coffee. Thanks, babe." He kissed Paul and wobbled off in the direction of the mens' room.

"Babe?" I queried with some amusement.

"Caro, what a handful! The lengths I'll go to."

"Yes, I know all about that. Seaton, well, well! The name turns up in Jennifer's diary you know. I thought it was a country town."

"He's as big as one!"

"Did she know him?"

He looked at me with astonishment. "Marc, are you serious? Seaton's the fiancé!"

I sat aghast.

"But wait a minute..." I was struggling with this information. "Him?"

"Seaton Frith, up-and-coming conductor and musical whiz kid."

"But he's a great big girl!"

"You're telling me, caro. I don't think that would have actually bothered our Jen."

"Obviously she was broad-minded, as opportunists go. So how did you find him? I thought you didn't know him."

Paul looked sheepish. "I didn't, till last night. I met him at a bar. He cruised me shamelessly! When I discovered who it was, I levered him into a taxi and went home with him."

"You what?"

"I did it for us! God, I'm exhausted. I feel like I've climbed the Matterhorn. Or Vesuvius might be closer."

I could see Seaton returning, with some difficulty, from the men's room. He was finding it hard to get past the tables, and needed to ask people to move. This led to long convivial conversations with most of the customers. (They seemed to think he was the owner.) I anticipated we'd have about thirty minutes before he got back to us.

"Did you learn anything useful?" I asked Paul.

"Yes, as a matter of fact. I think fatties are more tender round the nipples than your average queen."

I remained deadpan. "About the murder, I mean."

"*Niente*. Let's face it, the murder of your bride-to-be is not the best subject for pillow talk. But that's why I brought you into this. Should we do the opera magazine routine again? It worked with Randy, and it's lots of fun."

"I don't know. Dame Norma's secretary saw through it. I'm starting to worry that I'll get trapped by one of these lies. The "Uncle" story was a monumental mistake!"

"Well, we have to get him talking somehow. If I'm going to get a reputation as a chubby-chaser, I want it to be worthwhile."

"Hallooo! I'm back!" Indeed he was: I felt all the air squeezed out of my lungs as Seaton rejoined us. "What was that about a chubby-chaser? You little devil!" He pinched Paul painfully on the cheek.

"Hi, Seaton. We were just having a tiny argument."

"Oh, dear."

"Nothing important."

"Oh, I'm sure," said Seaton, "I meant, 'Oh, dear, the food's not here.' Did you order yet?"

"No."

"Waiter!" he screamed.

"Even the owner can't get served," remarked a woman at the next table.

A waiter came scurrying over. She was about twelve years old, her hair and makeup a total mess.

"Are you ready to order?" she whined. "Hold on, I gotta get my pad."

She started to wander off.

"You can remember it, girlie!" roared Seaton after her. "I'll have a crabmeat burger and an iced coffee. Extra cream!" He pointed at Paul and me. "They'll have two short blacks." He beamed at us. "Hope that's OK."

"You must be a mind-reader," Paul answered sarcastically.

"Isn't he cute?" cooed Seaton.

"Marc is a great fan of yours," Paul blurted.

Seaton nearly burst with pride. At any rate, he grew even bigger. "Of little old me? Brill! What in particular?"

"Err, let me think..."

"*Phar Lap*," Paul ventured.

"You saw that? You liked it? You mean to say you actually enjoyed it?"

"Yes," I mumbled unconvincingly, "though it didn't seem quite...ah...finished."

"It was a work in progress. Randolph will never finish it, in my opinion. He fiddles with an aria here, a few bars there, tinkers with it, but he ignores the main problem: the horse! It's staring him right in the face, and he doesn't even see it! Nobody is interested in an opera about a quadruped."

"I thought that was a difficulty with the piece," I improvised.

"You're so right, Marc! It's an unnecessary expense, for a start: It needs two people to play it. When Quinn found out, he said, 'We're not paying two singers to stand onstage all night unless we hear them!' With the ludicrous result that the bloody animal had a voice coming out of each end. The back end, a very promising baritone, couldn't see me at all, so the arsehole never came in with the rest of it! Hopeless."

"You mentioned that, I remember," Paul said to me.

"Animal operas are a waste of time," Seaton continued, "even when they're good. I mean, *The Cunning Little Vixen* pisses all over *Phar Lap*, and no one wants to see that either! Still, as you say, I did excellent work. I've got a Rossini next year, you must come to opening night. Should put me on the map!"

I didn't want to let him change the subject.

"The only good things in *Phar Lap* were you and that poor girl who died."

Amazingly, he never batted an eyelid.

"I know, she had a glorious voice. I was training it. She had picked up all sorts of bad habits from singing that commercial trash."

Paul began to go red in the face.

"I read somewhere," I interrupted, "that you and she—Jennifer, wasn't it?—were linked. Romantically, as it were."

He looked away into the distance. "Aren't they ever going to bring my meal? Who on earth recommended this place? I'll murder them!"

He turned back, all smiles. "That romantic stuff was all rather exaggerated. We went out together a few times—it didn't do either of our careers any harm, eh?" He patted Paul's hand patronizingly. "Now, babe, don't you be jealous."

Paul looked furious.

"Engaged to be married," I continued relentlessly.

"Oh, come on. Neither of us were ever serious about it! I called it off, if you must know. Simply not me, if you understand what I mean!" He winked lasciviously at Paul. "I'm sure you do!"

"You fat fucking pig!" shouted Paul.

The room fell silent. All eyes were on our table.

"Please continue eating, everybody. It's under control," smiled Seaton, addressing the crowd with aplomb. In spite of myself, I was impressed. No wonder this man had enough nerve to face a mob of orchestral musicians.

"He handled that gracefully," observed the woman on the next table. "He deserves to do well here."

Seaton turned back to Paul. Now there was an unmistakably murderous glint in his eye. "I didn't like that outburst very much, babe. You've changed. I'm beginning to think you're unbalanced. Are you on some kind of strong medication?"

I could see Paul was infuriated by Seaton's glib dismissal of Jennifer, and my gut feeling told me there was trouble ahead. The situation called for creative ad-libbing. Seaton was the last person we wanted to cotton on to our investigation.

"Seaton, could I speak with you privately?" I asked. "Paul, do you mind..."

"I'm going to the toilet," announced Paul. "There's a nicer class of person there." He stormed off.

I leaned across and spoke in an intimate whisper. "I think I know why Paul's acting so strangely."

"Why?"

"Well, I don't know if he mentioned it in passing, but Paul is gay, as indeed am I."

"So?"

"I'm glad it doesn't bother you. You see, we're lovers. He is, I'm proud to say, my lifelong partner."

He looked slightly confused.

"I had no idea—" he began.

"Don't apologize," I said. "I wouldn't expect a straight person like yourself to pick up on our subtle sexual undercurrents. The fact is, Paul stood me up last night. He never came home and he knows I'm not happy about it. Spent the night at a friend's place, he says." I laughed a bright yet threatening laugh, like Boris Karloff performing Noël Coward. "But you needn't concern yourself with that."

"Err, no."

"He's such a silly, impetuous boy. We are actually married, officially if not legally. We went through a beautiful civil ceremony."

"Really?" he squirmed.

"Yes, indeed," I smiled. "A week ago last Saturday."

"A week ago! Is that all?"

"It's not long, but it's just the beginning of years of happiness and loving commitment."

By now, Seaton was sweating with guilt.

"Both families were there, even some of my Calabrian relatives. Everybody was so supportive; it was very moving. Oh, and let me add my apology, Seaton, for bringing up the subject of your fiancée. It was insensitive of me, especially as she committed suicide after you broke off the engagement. You must have been through hell."

"I was very upset, naturally. It played havoc with my digestion."

"I don't doubt it, but it's none of my business and I apologize. Now, knowing Paul, I daresay he'll be crying his eyes out in the men's room."

"You think so?"

"I must go to him. After all, I've dedicated my life to making him happy. Bye-bye, I'm sure we'll meet again."

He took my hand limply.

"Isn't it a coincidence?" I mused. "Paul and I first met in a toilet! Have a nice day," I added to the woman at the next table who had just spluttered cappuccino foam all over her companion.

I felt very pleased with myself as I ambled into the mens'. It was empty apart from one occupied cubicle.

"It's OK," I said smugly, "you can come out."

The door opened, and a very embarrassed boy in school uniform scrambled past me and fled toward the exit.

I finally found Paul standing by the cashier's desk.

"The self-satisfied—" he began.

"Watch your language."

"I was only going to say cunt."

"Oh."

"Let's go."

"I've smoothed it over, so give him a wave as we go."

We raised our hands, but Seaton didn't notice. He had just been served his meal and was tucking in with such ferocity I was relieved not to be any closer. Several diners around him were leaving hurriedly.

As we ambled back to the car, I gave Paul a dressing-down.

"We'll never find out anything from him now, thanks to your outburst! How could you be so stupid?"

"I'm sorry."

"And after you went to all the trouble of sleeping with him to get him on side."

"I couldn't help it. Nobody orders black coffee for me without asking! And did you hear the way he talked about poor Jen? As though she didn't mean a thing to him!"

I had a theory about that. "I'm not sure it wasn't mere bravado. In the diary she says, 'Seaton insufferable, Can't wait to leave.' I think Jennifer's the one who broke it off."

"She didn't tell me."

"Perhaps she didn't want the world to know. And Seaton's name never crops up again after that entry. Did she love him?"

"She said so, but it's hard to believe! I should know, I've been there. He's not the most adroit partner in bed. A case of eats, roots, and eats more. It took him ages to get it up last night."

I glanced at Paul. "That could be your fault, of course."

He came to a sudden halt and glared at me. "Don't be idiotic, caro! That's not funny!"

"In any case," I continued, "she dumped him. I'm under no illusions about this girl. She had a better offer—an affair with Sir Fred—and she went for it. Fait accompli! Seaton must have known. He's my number one suspect."

"You say that about everyone!"

"I'm convinced I'm right. He was so smug about Jennifer just now."

Paul raised his eyebrows. "All right then, smarty-pants, what's your theory on how he did the murder? Considering he wasn't even there!"

I must admit I'd forgotten that minor circumstance.

"Yes, tricky one. We don't know for certain he wasn't there."

"I never saw him! You couldn't miss him too easily."

"He might have been hiding in the house. Maybe he sneaked in and murdered her while everyone thought he was in Brisbane."

"Caro, a man that size doesn't sneak anywhere! What did he do, disguise himself as a swimming-pool accessory?"

"I don't know the details as yet."

"If Seaton wanted to murder her, why dress up as a beach ball and do it at a crowded party?"

"Because he knew there'd be dozens of people there who would all love to kill her."

"I still think it's farfetched."

We reached the car. Paul thumbed casually through the diary as we crawled along. The traffic was at its usual worst.

"But don't you think," I asked, "that of all our suspects so far, Seaton is the most likely to be a murderer?"

"I guess so—apart from that terrifying drag queen who runs the florist's."

Paul's comment hit me like a sock full of sorbet.

"But of course! You said she was there!"

"Where?"

"At the party!"

"Yes, pissed and asleep most of the day."

"She's very big! The resemblance is striking!"

"Caro. You think she and Seaton are one and the same? That's impossible! Victoria is a well-known identity 'round town. She's twice his age."

"I don't mean they're the same person, but maybe on the day of the party...we must find out if she was there."

"If she says no, then it was Seaton behind those Long Island iced teas! But yikes! You mean we have to go back and see her? We're not her all-time favorite duo."

"No, she wouldn't give us the time of day."

"How about we break into her shop at night—climb through the skylight—and look up her appointment book?"

A shudder ran through me. "We're not doing anything like that again. I'll think of something else."

We arrived home. Paul came inside to make a nuisance of himself.

"Caro, this place is a mess! I can't stay here!"

"Who asked you to?"

I looked around. He was right: The house was unusually untidy. Hadn't I just cleaned up that morning? I ran to the study.

"Paul, somebody was here! Person or persons unknown have been going through my things." I checked the laundry window. It was open. There was no doubt. "I've been interfered with!" I screamed. I felt sick and cheapened.

"Is anything missing?"

I made a quick appraisal. Although things were skew-whiff, everything seemed to be in its place. "I don't think so."

"Is the sling OK?"

"Paul, don't be flippant. This is terrible. Wait! My Tebaldi collection!" I zoomed to the CD cupboard. "No, they're all here."

"Good. You'll live. Was there money lying around anywhere? A friend of mine leaves a hundred bucks in a saucer on the floor every time he goes out. His Burglar Money, he calls it."

"That's ridiculous."

"Don't be too sure! One night he was short of cash and had to borrow some out of the saucer. He came home, and there wasn't a stick of furniture left in the house! It served him right, he said, he'd made the burglars angry."

"I don't leave money around! I haven't got any!" I was seething with hostility. "Who did this? What on earth did they want?"

"I think they were after one of your rare first editions, caro." Paul held up Jennifer's diary. "This one."

CHAPTER 13

*I*t was a few days later that the totally unexpected summons came. Paul had persuaded me to lend him Jennifer's diary.

"Those desperados will be back, no question," he had said. "If I were you, I'd move out for a while. Rent a fabulous harbor-view penthouse for a couple of weeks and throw parties nightly. Can I bring a friend?"

"I don't think the burglars will come back: They looked everywhere for the diary and didn't find it."

"All the more reason to try again! Next time they'll slip down the chimney and tear up the floorboards."

"They can't. The chimney's fake."

"They'll come through the gas pipes, then. This diary's a very exciting read! It must be—the pages are sticking together."

"I spilt coffee on it."

"Mucho clumsy. How is your hand, by the way?"

"Fine. Don't change the subject, Paul."

He threw himself at my feet.

"Oh, please, let me borrow it! *Prego! Pregissimo!* I won't lose it. I won't go near a sauna for a week."

"Liar. All right, study it and see if anything rings a bell, but remember: It's our only evidence."

"So far! Who knows what may turn up next?"

There was something suspicious about this. "What do you mean?"

"What do you mean, what do I mean?"

"I mean…what do you mean!"

"Oh, nothing. I thought I might visit a local flower seller, and I don't mean Eliza Doolittle. Bye!"

With that, he bounded off. Instantly, I felt anxious. He had already mentioned the idea of a clandestine break-in to Victoria's shop, which could be disastrous. Even if he planned to confront the gal herself in broad daylight, you can bet he'd make a hash of it. Still, he was welcome to try: I certainly had no wish to find myself squirming under her baleful eye.

The loss of the diary left me with very little sleuthing to do, so I rescheduled my Italian 'students'—whom I'd lately been neglecting—and placed an ad in the local rag for more.

I considered calling the police over the burglary but decided against it. I didn't want to drag them into my murder investigation, then have them take all the credit. (That's what they do in books.) Besides, nothing had been stolen.

I was lounging around on my balcony one calm sunny morning, reading my well-thumbed Elsa Morante, listening to the mellow chirping of birds and the mind-boggling blare of jumbo jets. In the back of my mind, I thought it would be a good time for Reg to discover he had five or ten minutes free.

My Tebaldi CD had finished. I popped inside to replay it, but then I thought about Dame Norma. Surely I had a scratchy old record somewhere of hers: In the interest of research I dragged it out. It was Strauss's *Four Last Songs* (a luscious work, which, to the best of my knowledge, Tebaldi never recorded). I had just whisked it onto the rarely used turntable when the phone rang.

"Mr. Marc, err, Petroosy?"

"Petrucci. Yes?"

"I beg your pardon, my Italian! Never was any good. Well, we meet at last! Speak, I should say."

"Who's this?"

"I thought you might recognize the voice! Rrrrrrrrrrrrrrr!" she trilled. "It's Norma Clutterbuck here."

"Dame Norma!"

"Call me plain old Norma."

"I couldn't!"

"Are you surprised to hear from me?"

"My word!"

She chuckled operatically. "Good. I love surprises. Do you?"

"Err, yes and no. How did you get my number?"

"I sort of looked it up. Aren't I clever? I heard about you from Timmy. He's my little private secretary."

"I know."

"Ooh, you know all sorts of things! Well, Marc—may I call you Marc?"

"Please do. This is a great honor—"

"Yes, yes. Listen, love, we need to talk. Nobody knows I'm calling you. Timmy didn't want me to, he's so protective—he's a dream. But I'm disobeying orders for once. I think we should meet, considering everything, don't you?"

"'Considering everything?'" I asked tentatively. What was "everything" supposed to mean?

"I don't want to speak about it over the phone, I'm sure you understand. We have so much to talk about! I should tell you, I know what you've been up to!"

"You do?"

"Goodness, is that me in the background?"

"Oh, yes. *The Four Last Songs.*"

"Ugh! German! Cow of a language. No wonder I didn't keep them up. Now then, do you know my place at Palm Beach?"

"Vaguely."

"Come tomorrow at 10. We'll be all alone, I promise."

"OK. Where is it, exactly?"

"You know, northish. Just tell your driver to keep heading north on the cliff road. It's got a foreign name: Castel Clutterbuck. That means Clutterbuck Castle in Spanish or something, but of course it's not a castle, it's a weekender. I'll see you tomorrow! Ooh, I feel like such a naughty girl! Ten on the dot. Toodle-oo!"

I replaced the receiver. It's no exaggeration to say I was utterly mystified. I had hoped Anton would put in a good word for me with the diva's private secretary, but this effusive conversation was straight out of left field. What's more, the rendezvous appeared to be her own idea; she gave the distinct impression Tim was against it. The poor woman must have been in desperate need of meeting a fan, even though she had millions all over the world. Why did she want to see me alone? I might have been one of those lunatic fans who tie their idols up and knit very big jumpers for them! And what did she mean when she said, "I know what you're up to?" Surely that subtle crack could only refer to my poking around in the affair of Jennifer's death.

Nevertheless I couldn't resist the opportunity to talk with "plain old Norma" and see for myself, finally, the scene of the crime.

It was overcast and humid the next morning when I instructed my driver—namely, me—to head north up the peninsula. I had rung Paul before I left, letting him know where I was going. His machine answered; either he was still in bed (singly or in groups) or hadn't yet moved back to his flat, so I had to wait through thirty interminable seconds of Liza Minnelli before leaving the message. I told him to call as soon as he was disengaged.

As I neared Palm Beach, I stopped at a local fish-tackle store to ask directions. There was no one in attendance. Behind the rows of fishing rods and shelves full of sophisticated, highly priced gizmos designed to annihilate harmless sea creatures, there hung a signed photograph of the Dame herself: The scrawl read, "To darling Guido, Dame Norma Clutterbuck." I'd obviously come to the right place.

"Hello?" I called.

"Comin'!" yelled a voice, and into the shop ambled a bronzed god with thick black hair and mesmerizing dark eyes. His grubby singlet set off the powerful chest and bulging, tattooed arms. This was presumably Guido, man-god of the lagoon.

"Hi," he said. "I was getting the boat ready. D'ya wanna be taken out?"

A mental picture flashed before me: a candlelit supper, champagne, petit fours...beer and prawns for Guido...

"Oh, err, maybe later, thanks."

"I'm goin' now."

"I just wanted some directions. I'm looking for Castel Clutterbuck."

He smiled a broad smile. "Got her pitcher on the wall," he said.

"I noticed. Does she do a lot of fishing?"

"Nup. She only been in once, to give us the pitcher. All the shops from here to Barrenjoey got 'em."

"Why?"

"Dunno. We didn't want it, but it's OK. The guy who works for her...Tim? He gets all his stuff here."

Surprise me, I thought. "So Tim's the fisherman."

"Guess so."

"Anyway, Castel Clutterbuck?"

"You want the cliff road. Take the next right up the hill, then right again—it's hidden so watch for it—that'll bring you up to the gate. Wanna beer?"

"What?"

"Wanna beer with me?"

"Now? It's 9 o'clock in the morning!"

"Just bein' friendly, mate. Bit quiet today. I usually have one or two before I take the boat out. Sure you don't wanna come out? Bit of fishin', bit of a talk, coupla beers?"

Damn and blast, he was practically throwing himself at me, and I had an unbreakable appointment with a coy superstar who was possibly also a deranged murderess!

"Sorry," I said, and I deeply was.

"Too bad." He looked disappointed. "Just tryin' to drum up some business."

"Thanks anyway."

"Ay," he called after me as I left. "If you see Tim up there, tell him I got a fly he might wanna look at."

I made a mental note to pop back in on my way home.

As you approach Palm Beach, the peninsula narrows and grows steeper. Left of the main road, the terrain slopes down to the calm waters of the inlet; to the right is the high ridge where sheer cliffs drop away to the Pacific Ocean. It was through this dense, steep bushland that my good-natured jalopy struggled until we reached the ornate stone gates of Castel Clutterbuck. All I could see behind the gates were tall thick trees, partly obscuring a very large metallic-gray water tank. I buzzed the intercom.

"Yes?"

"It's Marc Petrucci."

"You came, how thrilling! I'll be right there."

And she was! Almost immediately, Dame Norma stepped out from behind the gates and dragged them open. I'd apparently interrupted her in gardening mode; she wore shorts, a filthy old lumberjack shirt, and a large pink straw sun hat, and she carried a lethal pair of garden shears. I felt overdressed in my shot silk slacks and flowing full-sleeved shirt. She directed me to a parking area and dragged the gates shut as I surreptitiously rolled up my sleeves for a more casual look. (First impressions are so important.)

I hadn't made up my mind how to play this particular scene, but I presumed I had been represented as Dame Norma's greatest fan. I didn't know if the Mardi Gras float idea had been floated, so I decided not to bring it up. My plan was to wax enthusiastic and be generally awestruck. This wasn't difficult when the first thing she did was to kiss me full on the lips.

"So you're Marc Petrucci! Weren't they horrible to keep you from me all this time!"

"They who?"

"Well, Timmy for one. Fancy him knowing all about you."

"I'm you're greatest fan."

"No question of that, love!" She laughed as loudly as an ambulance siren in my ear and took my arm. "Let me show you 'round the old place."

We walked up a flight of stairs, rounded a bend in the path, and there it was—but what was it? Paul was right about the garden: It was dazzling, chockablock with tulips and other non-native bulbs, all presented symmetrically to set off the thing I had thought was a water tank but now appeared to be a vast silo.

"What do you think?"

"The garden's beautiful."

"Thank you, you're sweet. And what do you think of the house?"

"Ah...is that it?"

"It's won awards, you know. It was designed in the '50s by Harvey Krautenheim."

"Really?"

"Yes, the great formalist. You know him?"

"I've heard of him."

"He designed the famous cement *Mastersingers* for Bay-reuth, and he built my little weekender! I've quite grown to like it over the years."

As we got closer, a tennis court came into view further down the other side of the award-winning house.

"We'll go in the back way. You can have a drink by the pool while I change into something dignified. I was gardening when you arrived."

The northeastern side of the house was totally, delightfully different. It opened out to a large tiled area where there was a swimming pool and, resort style, hundreds of banana lounges and umbrellas. A person could have a hell of a party around that pool. The house itself boasted wide picture windows on the second story, where Paul must have watched the poolside poseurs. Unlike the austere gray of before, here everything was canary yellow and turquoise.

"Well, this is so...vivid!" I enthused.

"Yes, isn't it? It used to look like the front, but I had to do something before the National Trust put some sort of embargo on the place. Don't tell Krautenheim! He'd sue if he ever found out!"

"And the cliff—" I said, pointing toward the rugged bush-land, "is over there somewhere?"

"Yes, there's a little lookout farther up."

"The view must be spectacular!"

"Oh, it is! Come, we'll have a tiny peep before I change."

With that, the diva dragged me into the thick bush. We twisted and staggered up the track for a couple hundred yards. Almost without warning, I found myself perched on a weathered wooden platform, built out over the edge of a pre-cipitous cliff. A strong ocean wind hit me full in the face and I grabbed the wooden railing tightly. Dame Norma, squeezing my arm tighter than ever, suddenly let rip with a full-throated high C. I nearly changed the color scheme of my shot-silk slacks.

"Exhilarating, isn't it!"

"It certainly is," I gasped.

"This lookout was here even before the house was built," she shouted over the sound of wind whistling around us and waves crashing below.

I gazed left and right, following the line of the peninsula up to the lighthouse at the end and all the way back to the main-land. I stared over the ocean to the horizon. In fact, I looked everywhere but down.

"This must be where that poor girl committed suicide," I said.

Dame Norma grabbed my arm even more tightly and dragged me back down the track.

"I can't talk about it," she wailed, but she did. "It was such a shock. I was the first to see her body, you know. I was awfully distressed, and as for the party, it was just ruined! Luckily it was late in the day. Poor child, she had so much potential." She turned and gave me her most sincere look. "The great stars, and I suppose I am one—"

"You are!"

"I know. Well, when we get to a certain age we feel a desire to pass on the mantle of greatness to the next generation..." Her eyes hardened. "When we're ready."

"Was that girl going to be your successor?"

She smiled brightly. "We'll never know, will we? Now come inside and make yourself comfortable. I'll only be a minute."

She swanned up the staircase as I relaxed onto the tiger-skin divan. Looking around, I noticed one or two objets d'art and plenty of objets de trash. If Liberace had been a soprano, his poolside room might have looked roughly like this one.

There was, for instance, an ornate and elaborate chandelier hanging from the ceiling; also a white baby grand piano with a vine of gold leaf festooning its way around the perimeter. Next to it, however, was a pure-kitsch 1950s cocktail cabinet, all green glass and chrome. The effect was disconcerting, likewise the neon Coca-Cola clock on the far wall juxtaposed with the Rubens. Opera memorabilia was rampant: The walls displayed several posters of Dame Norma's appearances, each displayed in a large gilt frame, and a few genuine collector's items. One of these was a signed letter from Puccini to his publishers, demanding a larger advance. I examined it with interest.

There was no sign of the Grande Dame, and much as one hates to snoop, that's exactly what I decided to do. I particularly wanted to take a look through those picture windows on the second floor. I crept upstairs, to be confronted by a kitsch-filled hallway: I didn't have time to notice much except a glass case containing a revoltingly posed stuffed corgi. She sported a big pink bow around her neck and had that expression dogs get when they've been unfairly chastised.

There were doors off to the right and left of the hall. The first door was slightly ajar. I hoped it wasn't Norma's boudoir. I peeped in: It was definitely a bedroom—a neatly made, queen-sized bed stood within, flanked by the wide windows beyond. The absence of memorabilia suggested this was a guest bedroom, and I was about to step inside when Dame

Norma's unmistakable form ambled across in front of me. She was half dressed and humming a little ditty that I think was a Bellini aria, though it sounded for all the world like "We're in the Money."

I sprang back. She couldn't have seen me. I speedily crept to the next door, which had a sign marked PRIVATE. I tried the handle; it wasn't locked, so as quietly as I could, I opened it and stepped inside.

This room was a neat little office, so tidy that it looked as though no one had used it for years. There was a desk, the old-fashioned rolltop style (currently making a comeback amongst people who have no practical use for a desk), two gray filing cabinets, a fax, and a small photocopier. I tried the desk. Naturally, it was locked.

A signed photograph of Dame Norma graced the wall (the same picture, but more garishly colored, that I'd seen in the fishing store); this one was autographed "To my darling Timmy, who takes such good care of me!" Next to it was a framed diploma: a bachelor of accounting from Bond University. Evidently, this was Tim's office when in residence. I glanced around, looking for diaries or interesting little notes—anything—but he was far too anal to leave such stuff lying about.

At the end of this room was another large picture window, identical to the ones in Dame Norma's room. A wooden slat blind kept out the light. I sneaked over and peeked through. The pool below was too far to the left to be visible. What could be seen from here, however, and probably not from Dame Norma's room, was the track up to the cliff. Indeed, from my vantage point, I could clearly see the lookout itself. If the murder had happened while anyone was peering through this blind, that hypothetical person would have seen everything.

I heard the next door shut and Dame Norma trundling downstairs. "Wooo!" she warbled. "Where are you?"

I waited for a second, then hurried after her. She was looking out at the pool. She turned to see me; an alarmed expression flitted across her face.

"Where have you been, you naughty boy!" she said.

"I was...err...looking for a toilet."

She relaxed. "It's the last door on the right."

"Yes, thanks, I found it."

"You were very quiet!" she remarked. "Hope you didn't forget to flush! Well now, come and sit down. How do you like my outfit? Much better, eh?"

She had thoroughly transformed herself from a large plain woman in gardening clothes to a large plain woman in a tent. Her black hair was combed into a bun, and she had stuck two chopsticks through it, à la *Butterfly*. Any further resemblance to a butterfly was nonexistent.

She threw herself onto the couch next to me. She took my hand in hers, and it was clear that we were getting to the crux of whatever this summons was all about.

"It's not an easy life on the opera stage, you know," she confessed humbly.

"I'm sure."

"I mean, God! You work like a navvy, you do your best, and your old triumphs are thrown back in your face as soon as you put a bloody foot wrong! Critics, ugh!" She shuddered massively.

"I never liked them."

"Look at today's paper. The first of the summer season, *Marriage of Figaro,* and it's been absolutely trashed by that dreadful Charles Mignon! I can't bear him."

"I gather he was at your party," I murmured.

"Oh, yes, naturally. I'd have been mad not to invite him. That's what I mean—these people have got a stranglehold. We're only the poor old talent, and we're at the mercy, the whims of these...these..." She took a deep breath as she tried to think of the most vile term she could politely use. "These critics!" she snarled.

"What do they know?" I added.

"Well, they know when you're having an off night, but do

they have to tell the whole world? It's so petty! All right, I don't have the same voice I had at thir—twenty. But so what? My artistry is at its peak! That's the important thing, surely—especially in this day and age when they video every bloody thing you do! Of course, I don't let it get to me. God, no! I'm above all that. I don't care one bit!" She shook her head briskly, causing one of the chopsticks in her hair to poke me in the eye.

"Ooh!"

She turned back, all solicitous. "Why, there's a wee teardrop in your eye! You really do care for me, you sweet little man."

Before she started suggesting the two of us shack up for a lifetime of bliss, I felt it wise to bite the bullet.

"Norma, I'm a great fan of yours, but you have so many fans. Why did you ask me here?"

She assumed a serious expression.

"You and I have to talk about Fred."

"Fred Mathieson?"

"Marc, I'll put my cards on the table. You know what Fred's like—he's a law unto himself." She lowered her voice. "I'm sure you know we were lovers, 'were' being the operative word. It was a perfectly good arrangement all 'round, until he fell in with that Burke girl. She threw herself at him. I saw it happening right under my nose, but what could I do? I couldn't go public, his wife would have objected. A scandal is the last thing anyone wants. Then he tried to put that mere child into *Girl of the Golden West*! My opera! My production! She had a pretty voice, but a role like Minnie needs maturity. I could hardly believe him capable of such a thing, but that's what men are like: They think with their dicks. Oh, I'm sorry."

"No, no. I'm sure you're right."

"I'm dead right, but it wasn't a genteel thing to say, was it?" She grinned mischievously. "But we know what happened. It was taken out of Fred's hands—the opera, I mean, of course. He couldn't do a thing without that donation." She chuckled gleefully and pinched my cheek.

"Ouch."

"Then that girl jumped off my cliff. She must have been unbalanced."

"Literally."

"Very unfortunate but fortuitous, if you catch my drift." She winked.

"Yes. So you wanted to talk about Fred?"

"Oh, well, Fred's been impossible ever since. He won't take my calls or anything. He acts as if I picked up that bloody girl and chucked her over the edge myself!"

Something along that line had also occurred to me. "Did you?"

"You're a little devil!" She giggled. "Anyway, bugger him. I've found you, and I wanted to let you know I'm available." She snuggled closer, stroking my hand maniacally. "Ready, willing, and pretty damn able!"

I gulped.

"Well?" she asked.

My mind boggled.

"Well, what do you want me to do?"

"You could talk to Fred, I suppose. Or you could go straight to Ed Quinn. That might be best."

"I don't know him."

"No problem there. I'll put you in touch. Unless you'd rather see Fred—protocol and so on."

What was she on about?

"I'm afraid I've never met Sir Fred."

She dropped my hand and stared enquiringly at me. "Then how," she asked, "did you give him the money?"

The usual expression is, I believe, "the penny dropped." This time, however, it wasn't a penny, it was several million dollars. Dame Norma had invited me over because she thought, or had been led to believe, that one Marc Petrucci was the anonymous billionaire who had been funding special opera productions for her! She thought I was her benefactor, and she'd been buttering me up under false pretenses. This was a serious error. I tried to get my mind around the situation.

"You're very quiet, dear," she said.

"Dame Norma," I replied. "What have you been told about me?"

"Nobody knows anything about you. You're awfully mysterious. I heard you were Italian, an opera-loving playboy who'd inherited the family fortune. Are you titled, by any chance?"

"No. Look, um, shall we have a drink?"

"Oh, yes, you must think me a terrible hostess. Something Italiano! Sambuca! That'd be gorgeous."

"I'll get it."

"It's on the cocktail bar over there."

I took my time pouring two tumblers of the sticky liquor, as I wondered what to do next. I would have to tell her the truth.

"There are coffee beans there. Matches, too," she called.

"We're going the whole hog are we?"

"Why not?" she trilled.

I plopped a coffee bean into each glass and, on about the fourteenth attempt, managed to set the drinks alight.

"What a man of the world," she cooed. "Bring them over here, love."

It was now or never.

"Dame Norma," I said, "it's not me."

"What's not you, dear? Sambuca? You could have something else."

"No, not that. I—oops!"

I hadn't seen the step down from the bar area. Desperately juggling the two flaming drinks, I stumbled. The hot sticky liquid swished out of the glasses, splashing onto my hands.

"Whoa!"

I dropped both the glasses. Sambuca poured all over me. At least the flame had gone out.

"Sorry, sorry!"

I lifted my hands up to see, with horror, that they were

outlined in a purplish blue flame. My hands were on fire! I screamed, though not as beautifully as Dame Norma, and beat my fists against my shot silk slacks. This merely served to transfer the flame to my trousers, which were soaked with the lethal liquor. The fire shot up and down my right leg.

"Aaagh!"

Any second I would be a sizzling statistic.

"The pool!" cried Dame Norma.

I raced past her and hit the water in a fiery swan dive. I stayed under for as long as I could (mainly through embarrassment). Back on the surface I looked like a pile of garbage somebody had chucked out of a coal barge. My hands were numb and my leg was black. The pungent smell of roasting hair was in the air, but I was no longer burning. I climbed awkwardly to my feet at the pool's edge and what little was left of my shot silk slacks fell off.

"I think I'd better go," I suggested.

Dame Norma was very good, I must say. She dried me off gently and, after giving me a swig of unlit Sambuca straight from the bottle, she popped my blisters and bandaged my hands up.

"I was training to be a nurse, you know," she chatted amiably as I cringed in agony. "That's before I discovered my great talent."

"Dame Norma, I'm not your anonymous benefactor. It's someone else."

She sighed wearily.

"Timmy said you'd deny it, but I thought in private, just between us..."

"I'm afraid it's true."

"Very well. Have it your way. But when you see Mr. Benefactor, you tell him from me that he's a sweet, lovely man, and there's no need to withhold the money any longer, because Jennifer Burke's unavailable and the finest Minnie since Tebaldi is back! All right, dear?"

"You like Tebaldi, too?"

"I idolized her. There, that should heal in a few days."

As it happened, I didn't call in to see Guido on the way home. It would have been fun, but my hands were killing me. Also, I was wearing one of Dame Norma's rather large dresses.

CHAPTER 14

"Cocktail injuries are on the increase again. I read it somewhere. Now eat this, caro. It's best for baby and best for you."

Paul brought me a bowl of sludge.

"I don't need all this attention. Is this what I think it is?"

"It's nutritious pork-flavored two-minute noodles. Why, what did you think it was?"

"Unacceptable."

"Come on, eat. I'll admit I forgot about it and cooked it for twenty minutes, but all the goodness is still there."

"Is that the goodness floating on top, or sticking to the bottom?"

"Look, if I can stand it—" He grabbed my spoon and shoveled a portion of slop into his mouth, grimacing in disgust. "See? Enjoy!" he choked.

"No."

"Caro, you're the pits. You ought to be grateful to have a sexy houseboy around in an emergency."

"I can look after myself."

"Darling, your hands are so heavily bandaged you couldn't hold a conversation! Now relax and I'll tell you what I found out."

I dropped my head back onto the pillow. It was true: I was genuinely inconvenienced. It was a few days after my visit to Dame Norma's home. The burns had started to heal swiftly as she'd predicted, until they took a turn for the worse overnight and became infected. As a result I was laden to the brim with antibiotics and swathed in kilometers of adhesive bandage.

Paul told his tale with relish. "I didn't want to go back to the florist's in case Victoria remembered me, so I went to her other shop."

"The sex shop?"

"No, there's another one. She's part owner of Crystal-Packin' Momma. New Age accessories. And just to be sure she made no connection, I went in drag!"

"You did?"

"Yes, it was a hoot! I borrowed a few things from the girls in the chorus and ad-libbed the rest. I aimed for that sort of '60s Goldie Hawn look. I must do it again."

"Why, apart from your own perverse pleasure, would you do a thing like that?"

"I thought Victoria would be more simpatico with a tranny. I mean, she's one herself, after all. And I was right! We nattered away like great old mates."

"I can't imagine it. Not that gorgon?"

"She was a different woman. All I did was lend a fascinated ear to her New Age psychobabble and nod my head once in a while. You must have rubbed her up the wrong way, caro."

"She probably *was* a different woman! Did she go to the party or not?"

"She thinks so."

"What?"

"She doesn't know. She has blackouts."

"Alcohol or drug related?"

"Both, I expect, though she blames them on the transit of the moon or something. I forget how it works; it sounded quite plausible at the time. Anyhow, I told her I'd seen her at Dame Norma's shindig, and she said she hoped she hadn't made a fool of herself. She remembered nothing about it."

"That's convenient."

"But she certainly knew the place. I asked her all kinds of trick questions like where did she park and isn't the house beautiful. By the way, isn't the house hideous!"

"She could have gone out there anytime. Nothing very positive there."

Paul pouted. "Well, excuse me! I should have thrown Sambuca over myself and tried to burn the shop down!"

He stomped grumpily out of my bedroom. I felt chastened.

"Paul?" I called out. "I'm sorry."

He returned, sipping a glass of champagne.

"None for you: You're recuperating. So, did Dame Norma do it? Did she go all operatic and slaughter her ambitious young rival?"

"Well, she could have. She benefits from Jennifer's removal. Or she would if I was who she thinks I am."

"Who is this generous patron, I wonder?"

"That's the $800,000 question. But I've been thinking while I've been lying around here. In my opinion we can wipe Dame Norma off our list of suspects."

"Give reasons."

"OK. Firstly, she said she idolized Tebaldi, so she's automatically vindicated of any wrongdoing."

"First reason sucks. Next?"

"Next, she said to me, quote, there was no need to withhold the money any longer, Jennifer was unavailable and she, that is, Norma, was back!"

"Sounds like an admission of guilt."

"No, because at the time of the murder the money had already been withdrawn. The production was off. Dame Norma only has a motive if the opera was going ahead without her."

"Sorry, I'm confused."

"Let's recap. Sir Fred hopped into the cot with Jennifer and in the course of their congress promised her the lead in *The Girl of the Golden West*, the next show to be bankrolled by the anonymous donor. But the donor, who is Norma's all-time greatest fan, got wind of this last-minute cast change and pulled out. Sir Fred told Jennifer the bad news, and she was livid: He'd promised her this big star part, and now he was forced to renege. If anything, Jennifer had a reason to shove Dame Norma into the briny, not the other way 'round!"

Paul looked thoughtful.

"Yes, all right," he said. "But when did Dame Norma find out the money was withdrawn? She might not have known until after she'd murdered Jen."

"Only three people could have told Norma the money was being withheld—the donor, whom she doesn't know; Sir Fred, who she was no longer speaking to; and Jennifer herself."

"I bet Sir Fred is the donor!"

"I don't think so. Dame Norma doesn't either, and she must have examined that avenue pretty thoroughly. If it was Sir Fred's money, he could have gone ahead with the new production starring Jennifer. But he didn't: He told Jennifer it was off. Why?"

"Because he was blackmailed into it!" Paul grinned triumphantly.

"By whom?"

"By Dame Norma, threatening to go public with their affair. The current affairs shows would love it! 'Sleazy Aussie Businessman Sex Slave to Cultural Icon.' I'd watch it religiously."

"Aha!," I countered, Holmes-like. "But if she blackmailed him successfully, she had no need to kill Jennifer."

"Except as insurance. So Sir Fred couldn't change his randy old mind again."

"Hell of a risk to take when you've already achieved your goal."

"All right then, who did it?"

I sighed. "I haven't got a clue," I admitted.

"And who's playing Daddy Warbucks?"

"I don't know, but whoever it is, he must have a contact in the opera, and it isn't Norma."

"All very vague, caro."

"Well, forget that for a second. This is the other thing I've been thinking about: Someone's trying to get their hands on Jennifer's diary, right?"

"Don't know why. It's not the saucy bedtime read I thought it would be."

I was exasperated. "Yes, but they don't want it because of what is in it. They want it because of what they think is in it. There may be clues to the identity of the killer," I mused. "What else could she have known that she might have confided to her diary?"

"Um, her PIN number? A secret family recipe?"

"She could have known the identity of the donor! There's lots of people after that particular info—Dame Norma; Sir Fred, too, if as I suspect, he doesn't know; and undoubtedly the rest of the opera company management. Everyone would like a rich patron, Randolph especially. It's the only way he'll ever get his stuff performed."

"Would he murder for it?"

"He might, if he were also insanely jealous, which he is! And there's something else bothering me."

"Wow, your little pink cells have been working overtime, caro!" Paul smiled as he poured himself the last of the champagne.

"I thought it was time I came to a few conclusions. Who told Dame Norma about me, and who gave her the impression I was her long-lost benefactor?"

"Wasn't it your friend's idea? What's his name?"

"Anton."

"Yes. He told his friend Timmy, alias Tammy, the private secretary."

"Right, and Tim told Dame Norma, but he also told her that if she confronted me I'd deny it. Why would he say I'd deny it, unless," I leaned forward for emphasis, "he knows it definitely isn't me? And if he knows it's not me, he must know who it really is!"

"Brilliant! I bet it's Anton. Isn't he a rich old queen?"

"He can find any fabric at less than cost, but I don't think he's necessarily well off."

"Then if Tim's not covering for his boyfriend, why is he lying to Dame Norma?"

"I don't know. Of course, all this may have nothing to do with Jen's murder at all."

"It's a mystery, caro."

I didn't think that was very helpful.

"We have to narrow it down. For Christ's sake, Paul, you were at the damned party. Don't you remember anything? Or were you on steroids or whatever all afternoon?"

"I remember Dame Norma screaming like a—I don't know, a superstar doing a mad scene when she found the body."

"So it was a bit overdone?"

"Huge."

"She might have beefed it up because she was secretly pleased. Anything else?"

"I remember that slimy Charles Mignon trying to get into my pants—and everyone else's! Blech!"

"He seems so nice."

"What else? Nothing, I don't think. I was having too much fun!"

"Who was it Jennifer wanted to speak to before she left?"

"She didn't say." His eyes lit up. "Wait! I wanted to go, but she said she had to speak to someone, and I said, 'Who?' and she said, 'Mind your own business,' and I said, 'Well, hurry up,' and she said, 'I have to get him alone. I can't just barge up to him—he wouldn't like it,' and I said, 'I know the feeling. Is he gay?' and she laughed and said, 'He's on your team but he's not your type.' Then I went off somewhere and that's the last I saw of her."

"Well! She doesn't sound very suicidal."

"Not a bit."

"'On your team but not your type'—Charles Mignon, do you think?"

"Why would she want to get him alone? Besides, I'd seen her chatting to him earlier. Networking."

"Then who?"

"Seaton's not my type. Maybe he was there, like you said,

hiding somewhere, and she saw him. That would fit!"

"You know, Paul, there must have been something or somebody in one of those photos you took. Why else would they get stolen?"

"No one was in them except a bunch of pretty waiters and all the people we've been talking about!"

"Nothing struck you as odd when you looked at them?"

"My hair was a tad messy."

"Tell me about the waiters."

"Spunks of all sizes. Smorgasbord! Blond, dark, shaved— all cute. Types you see up and down Oxford Street any time of day or night." He glanced at his watch. "Darling, I have to go. I've got a show at 5. Will you be all right here with no hands? I'll drop by after midnight."

"No, don't do that. I want to sleep."

"All right. Well, if you need me, I've moved back to my flat."

"What about Stephen the Avenger?"

"Oh, it's a long story, but we effected a rapprochement, as they say. It happened the other night in the women's toilet at the Phoenix Bar. That is, I think it was Stephen. It's very dark in there! Bye!"

I heard him slam the door, and before long I was dozing peacefully. My awakening would be abrupt.

CHAPTER 15

*T*he telephone exploded next to my ear, shattering several million synapses and causing temporary deafness. This often happens when you're dozing, partially asleep, your mind wandering through dreamscapes vaguely sexual and usually unsatisfactory. In this instance I dreamed I was being date-raped by a gorilla that bore a certain family resemblance to Seaton Frith.

Sitting upright in a mild panic, I grabbed for the bedside phone but missed and slammed my bandaged hand into a chest of drawers. I gently lay back, throbbing quietly, and let the machine downstairs record the message. I drifted back to sleep.

When I woke again, it was 7:20 in the evening. I staggered to the bathroom, pausing in the kitchen just long enough to take in at a glance the incredible mess Paul had left behind, and proceeded with the aid of cold water and moisturizer to turn myself back into a civilized human being. I was washing down a handful of Panadol with strong black coffee when I remembered the phone call. I replayed the message: It was young Reg.

"Marc? I was hoping to catch you. It's 5:30 now. I'm finishing work in half an hour, and I've got a little free time. I thought—if you liked—well, anyway, you're not there. Um, well, I might go to the sauna, you know? 9-1-ZERO, where we met. If you get this message in time, come and join me. Sorry I haven't seen more of you. I wanted to, but things made it hard. I do think of you. You're so—"

The message cut out. So what? So what? Damn it! So gorgeous? So thrifty? I checked my watch: 7:30. Would he still be at the sauna? Possibly. I looked at my hands. The idea with bandages was, of course, not to get them wet, but did that include steam? I considered the question for half a second and decided steam didn't count: After all, normal air is probably full of it. Mainly, the thought of Reg getting off with some sexy older man other than me was all I needed to spur me into action. I ensured my hands were bound as tightly as possible, gobbled an extra couple of painkillers and called a cab.

Within fifteen minutes I found myself slinking through the door of 9-1-ZERO. The same doorman I'd seen last time was on. His hair had grown slightly and was now inexpertly blond-tipped. The scars from his bashing seemed to be no better, though he might have been one of those people who get bashed habitually.

"You're in Locker Room 3. Toilets are down the hall. Coffee shop and TV viewing area upstairs—"

"Excuse me," I interrupted, "but I'm looking for someone special."

He scowled. "That's what it's for, mate."

"Have you seen a young man come in tonight? Moderately tall, brown hair?"

"Seen plenty of 'em."

"No, this one's…well, beautiful."

"I wouldn't know. You goin' in?"

He buzzed the door open and the fetid atmosphere hit me. I spluttered. It was as if somebody had lobbed a few punnets of overripe raspberries into a blender with a liter of liquid chlorine.

"What's that smell?" I asked.

"New scent." He shrugged. "We had complaints from the ice-cream joint next door. Now we smell like them."

As the door closed behind me, the doorman leaned over his counter and grabbed me roughly by the arm. He looked utterly menacing.

"I hope you find the bloke you're lookin' for," he snarled, "but remember somethin': You only need one man in your life."

"Oh. Really?"

"Our Lord Jesus Christ." He flashed the broken teeth. "He's the one, mate."

He let me go, and I scurried off to the comparative safety of the tubs. I was into my towel in a flash and raced to the top floor. Gingerly, I approached the wet sauna where Reg and I had originally met. I tenderly pulled open the door. As before, it was dark and steamy; I stood there expectantly, waiting for the apparition to appear as he had done the last time. I replayed the scene over in my mind.

Five minutes passed before I accepted that this time I was definitely alone. I tried waiting there for a while—the sauna was certainly the spot Reg would make for if he arrived—but it was getting awfully humid and sweat was running down my arms into the bandages. Disappointed, I trudged back down to Caesar's Palace on the first floor. Nobody was there except a tall young thing behind the coffee bar. I ordered a cappuccino.

"Where is everybody?" I asked.

"Yessir, it's very quiet," he beamed, an escapee from McDonald's. "Lotsa talent here before. I guess we'll fill up again 'round midnight. Sugar, sir?"

"No, thanks."

"Big dance party on tonight, maybe that's it. Guess our boys are getting' ready for that, ay."

"You have an accent," I commented. "American?"

"Ontario, Canada, sir. Name's Rusty. I'm working my way 'round the world." He shook my hand briskly, which under the circumstances was quite painful.

"Sorry, I thought you were American," I winced.

He sniffed. "No offense taken." He stared at me closely. "I know you, don't I?"

"Don't think so."

He smiled. "Yessir. I served you at the Mapplethorpe opening. Don't you run a casting agency? Movies, commercials?"

"Not me. Sorry."

His smile dropped perhaps a thousandth of a millimeter. "My mistake, sir. Enjoy."

I sat at a table sipping my coffee (which was scaldingly hot and piss weak). The television was on and I found myself drawn by a strange program. I don't watch TV regularly; I haven't really enjoyed anything since 1986 when SBS showed Renata Tebaldi in a special about famous Toscas, so I was taken aback to see what must have been a prime time show playing amateur videos of shocking car accidents.

I was mesmerized as a huge removalist truck collided with a combi van on a deserted intersection out west of Nowhere. The van was virtually rent in two. A studio audience laughed itself sick as the smarmy voice-over chortled, "Oops! Looks like that holiday was cut a bit short!" The crowd screamed at this; then the announcer adopted a somber tone to add: "Fortunately, no human beings were seriously injured in this accident." The audience applauded and we went to a commercial. I heard a faint sniggering next to me, as Rusty collected my empty cup.

"Gross, ay!" he said.

"The world is sick," I said, "and I can't work out whether programs like that are a cause or a symptom."

"Yuh," he said, blankly. "Another coffee?"

"No," I replied. "I might go upstairs. You coming along?"

"Hey!" he beamed. "You do run a casting agency!" We laughed. "Apologies," he added, "I'm on duty. Have a nice night, sir."

I was having no such thing, however. Clearly, I was wasting my time and it looked increasingly as though Reg and I would never meet again in our lifetimes. I decided to take one quick promenade around the premises, then head for home.

I checked the showers and the maze, none of which were overpopulated, then, in spite of the overwhelming aroma of raspberry frappe, I braved the Jacuzzi room. An elderly white-haired man sat against the wall. He was holding a thick walking stick, ornately and tastefully carved to resemble a penis. He looked up and, on seeing me, put down his stick and opened his arms wide.

"At last!" he croaked.

"Oh...I'm...I'm looking for someone," I stammered.

"Beg your pardon, my boy, I thought you were staff. Help me into the pool there, will you? Good lad."

Ever the Good Sauna Samaritan, I sprang to his assistance. He seemed stronger than I was (ex-Army, I guessed), but I supported him while he steadily descended the steps into the hot spa.

"Thanks, sonny," he wheezed. "Leave my stick nearby, would you? And come back in ten minutes!"

Dismissed, I left him soaking and closed the door. The two saunas were nearby. I took a quick look in the dry sauna, but it was vacant. I'd checked the wet sauna already, of course, but out of sentiment I couldn't resist a return visit. It was still, seemingly, empty. I sat near the doors for a moment, once again reliving the original meeting with Reg, and once again feeling let down.

This is ridiculous, I told myself. We Italians are famously emotional, although I sometimes feel I'm the exception to this rule, but that's no reason to stalk around the place obsessively like Anna Magnani. *I must look a sight,* I thought, haunting this virtually deserted sauna with my long face and bandaged hands. *Anyone who saw me would run a mile.* I was depressed, uncomfortable, and hot.

I closed my eyes. The steam was fatiguing; I shouldn't have even been there in my condition, all the antibiotics were getting sweated out. It was time to go. With a considerable effort I hauled myself to my feet, but swayed and reached out to steady myself against the wall. It really was incredibly, dangerously hot! I staggered to the door. It would not budge.

I pushed it harder, leaning against it with all my weight, but it didn't open. I kicked it: It rattled but remained firm.

It was a push/pull double door, with the handles on the outside, solid wood incorporating two small glass panels. I wiped away the condensation with my towel and peered through the glass, trying to catch somebody's eye. No one was visible. I happened to glance down and, to my horror, saw that a wooden object had been shoved through the door handles. It was the old man's walking stick. I broke out in an extra layer of sweat as it dawned on me: I had been trapped in here deliberately.

I charged against the doors again, but the stick was too thick to break; besides, I was running out of steam even if the plumbing wasn't. The sauna was hotter than ever. I groped around in the dark looking for a thermostat but could not find one. It was obviously located somewhere else for safety. Great, I thought. I whipped off my towel and threw it over the steaming vent, but there was no change in the atmosphere. I collapsed onto a bench and started to cry for help; just at that moment the muzak sprang to life with a loud rendition of "I Will Survive."

Feeling woozy, I stretched out on the clammy bench. My bandages were unraveling and my hands ached. "I will survive," I muttered under my breath along with the beat. My eyelids grew heavy, and I tried desperately to stop them from closing. Before long, however, I must have passed out.

I don't know how long I was unconscious, but as I came to I felt something cool on my lips: chilled chlorinated water. I gulped it down and opened my eyes. There was no more steam, but I still lay on the bench, my towel draped modestly over me and my head on something soft. The smiling, attentive face of Rusty from Ontario hovered above me.

"More water, sir?"

I struggled to speak. "Trapped…old man…tried to kill me… I will survive…"

"Relax now, sir. Here, drink some more. You're dehydrated."

"Where? The penis stick. Want the penis stick…!"

"Sure, OK, just drink."

I gave up the struggle and sipped the welcome beverage.

Rusty chatted on. "You gotta be more careful, my friend. You don't wanna go off to dreamland in these kinda places— it can be bad for you, ay? I guess we woulda checked on you earlier but we had a little emergency. An old gentleman in the Jacuzzi suffered a heart attack. One of the regulars, too. He was a politician, so I guess they'll say he died at home."

I gasped. "Is he dead?"

"I believe so, sir."

I sat up. The doors to the sauna were wide open.

"Was his stick with him?"

"Stick, sir?"

I tried to stand. "He's got a stick like...like a dick!" I sat down abruptly with a thump. "I'm dizzy," I said.

"I don't think you're ready to go yet, sir. Now you lie down again. Here, put your head on my lap. OK?"

I noticed Rusty had changed into the regulation uniform: a towel. I did as I was told. He gently stroked my hair.

"What did you do to your hands?"

"Burnt them."

"Oh. Not your day, is it, huh. When you feel better, we'll go downstairs and have a good strong coffee on the house."

"Oh, no, I must go. I only came here to look for somebody."

"Oh?" he mused. "Say, is your name Marc?"

"Yes, it is."

"We had a message earlier for you. From...uh..."

"Reg?"

"Reg, yuh. Phoned to say he couldn't make it. He's gonna call you."

"When was this?"

"An hour ago, maybe. Normally we don't pass on messages."

I didn't know what to make of all this.

"Rusty, did you find me in here?"

"Yuh. I thought, like, oh, no!—two heart attacks in one evening! Yikes!"

"How did you get in?"

"The doors. How else?"

"They weren't locked?"

"They don't have a lock, sir."

I carefully sat up. "The heat in these saunas: Where is it controlled?"

"The thermostat's in the control room on the ground floor, just by the office. It's carefully monitored. Are you feeling OK now?"

"Yes, thank you very much for looking after me."

"Pleasure." He smiled. "I finished my shift at 10:30. We can have sex now, sir, if you want."

"No, thanks. You're very kind, but I've got to get out of here."

He helped me downstairs and into my clothes. I had the shakes. As I exited I noticed a different doorman was now on duty.

I'd hoped I would calm down when I hit the street, but in fact I felt more vulnerable than ever. I couldn't go home until I'd thought out the full implications of what was happening. I needed to talk rationally to someone about it—you have to be convincingly rational when suggesting you're the victim of attempted murder—but I no longer knew whom to trust...except Paul, of course. I sighed; he was the least rational person on earth. Still, his show would be finishing any minute and the theatre was only five or six blocks away.

As I strode through the city streets, I tried to reconstruct what had happened. The least likely scenario was this: The old man had followed me, shut me in, wandered back to the Jacuzzi, and promptly expired. I rejected that idea straight away: far too decisive for a politician. No, someone must have been watching me as I visited the Jacuzzi and then the sauna. Probably he was hiding in one of the toilet cubicles close by. It would have been an easy matter to take the old man's stick away and slide it through the door handles. After that, Mr. X must have dashed downstairs to turn the heat up, which meant he knew where to find the thermostat and how to go about it. Perhaps he had an accomplice? The boy who talked about having Christ in your life? I never trust those born-again people: Most of them believe implicitly in homicide.

But why didn't my would-be murderer leave the premises? The dreadful truth hit me: He must have killed the old man to create a diversion so he could sneak back into the sauna and finish me off once I'd passed out! Smother me, for example, making it seem like an accident!

Something had gone wrong with that plan, I surmised. Maybe there was too much fuss nearby and he'd been forced to remove the stick and make himself scarce. But where to? Of course, back to the toilet cubicles! He had probably witnessed my rescue by Rusty and everything. *He might still be there,* I thought, *or he might be following me at this very moment.* I glanced cautiously around, feeling extremely paranoid, and quickened my step.

Before long I recognized the dazzling lights of the Criterion theatre. One of the two oldest theatres in Sydney, it had recently been snatched from the jaws of a bulldozer and lavishly refurbished. The upgrading had been funded through a government initiative of staggering vapidity: They had leased a ten-mile column of air space above the block to an enterprising firm of commercial skywriters.

Poor but happy patrons were streaming out from the theatre's main entrance, humming the scenery of the mega-production they had scrimped and saved all their working lives to see. Musicals are not my personal cup of syrup, though I keep my opinion to myself when Paul waxes lyrical on the subject. Frankly, though, anyone who is fond of opera can hardly understand what all the fuss is about! Paul got me a good seat for a preview of the last show he was in: It was sweet of him, and I only went without food for a few weeks as a result, but within ten minutes of the start I had nodded off. Me, a man who has been held spellbound on the edge of his seat through hours of Verdi and even Wagner!

I wandered around the flashily painted cultural edifice looking for the stage door. It was in a back alley, next to the garbage bins of twenty or so restaurants. Young actors and dancers were leaving in droves. I entered and found an old stage doorman behind a partition. He was wearing a gray boiler suit and had thick greasy gray hair and a gray mustache. He was browsing through the paper.

"Is Paul Silverton still here?" I asked.

He didn't look up. "Who?" he said.

"Paul Silverton. He's in the show."

"Christ, how would I know?" he muttered in a rough Abruzzi dialect. "These faggots…"

"*Signóre,*" I answered, also in Italian, "I'm a friend of Cameron Mackintosh, and if you wish to keep this worthless job beyond tonight, you will locate Paul Silverton for me. Pronto."

He sniffed, raised his eyes to heaven, closed the paper, and consulted a computer printout.

"What name?"

"Silverton. Paolo."

"Seelvertown… " He moved his finger slowly down the list, yawning.

A lithe young man with receding hair tapped me on the shoulder. "You won't find him here, love. You've got the wrong concert."

"What?"

"Paul's at The Royalty."

I frowned. The Royalty was right up the other end of town. I looked at my watch. "How inconsistent. His last show was on here!"

"He'll have gone by now," the boy said. "They come down before us."

I cursed in Italian. The stage doorman grinned to himself.

"You could try Fireworks," the boy suggested.

The Fireworks Bar, alias the Joe Cahill Hotel, was so named because right through the '70s and '80s it had been repeatedly gutted by fire. This, in some obscure way, enabled the owners to keep the place running at a profit. For as long as I'd been aware, the Fireworks had been a popular, cruisy rendezvous spot in the Sydney scene. My ex, Andrew, had practically lived there before I met him. I also knew it to be a post-show haunt of Paul's, one among thousands.

I cabbed it up there and, I must admit, when we turned into Oxford Street I felt more relaxed than I had been all evening. Safer, too: At least around here one merely had to worry about random bashings and police sniffer dogs. I entered the hotel, which looked resplendent in its new coat of fire-truck red. They'd even hung a fire-bell over the front door; it was festooned with limp bunting left over from Mardi Gras nine months earlier.

The bar was absolutely packed, filled to capacity with smoke, noise, beer, leather, and singlets. Even if Paul was here, there was every chance I wouldn't find him. I elbowed my way through the throng, crossing from one side of the bar to the other, an activity that took me over half an hour. By then, I'd worked up a thirst. I bought a light beer and retreated to a vacant stool near the window. I gazed unseeing into the crowd and concentrated on a single thought: *My life was in danger.*

"Marc! Hoy there!"

I looked up as a familiar face came into view. It was Anton. He raised his glass in greeting.

"Out again!" he shouted in my ear. "I don't see you for decades and now twice in a row. Goodness groceries! Do you come here a lot? I've just learned to face it again. I gave it a big miss for years after they stopped doing drag shows."

"I haven't been here for a long time either."

"Still very cruisy! Mother of us all, look at that!"

"What?"

"Him! Look at that butt. Ooh, I'll wrap it up in cellophane for tomorrow's lunch."

"Tim's not here with you, I gather."

"Not tonight, Dorothy. Which reminds me, I'm so glad I caught you! There's a diva meeting Saturday next week about the outfits. We must get moving! It's almost Christmas, half the other floats are finished, and we've done fuck all! I'll be taking measurements, dear, so if you're thinking in terms of losing weight, do it this week or not at all."

"Anton," I shouted, "I saw Dame Norma."

"Good! Happy to oblige. Did the earth move?"

"Tim didn't mention it?"

"She never said a word, but she's a bit secretive when it comes to the Great Dame."

I leaned closer. "Exactly what did you tell Tim about me?"

"What else? I told him you were a huge fan." He looked a little uncomfortable.

"Dame Norma thought I was the person who's been bankrolling her productions. The anonymous donation man!"

Anton turned to me and smiled. "Guilty!" he chirped.

"How could you!" I snapped.

"Don't get into a frenzy, Dot," he cooed. "Getting you in there wasn't the easiest request in the world, and anyway it was a fucking fabulous idea! I laughed myself stupid when I thought of it! She's been looking for Mr. Moneybags forever: She's investigated every cunt with six figures after his name in the BRW top 500! I suppose you told her it wasn't true. "

"She didn't believe me."

He roared with laughter. "Oh, don't worry, she's heard it before. She'll latch onto somebody else. Good on Tammy for following through. You owe me one now, Marc. You've got to go on the float."

"Does Tim know who this person really is?"

"No, I think not. He'd have told Dame Norma long ago if he knew. He actually likes the old cow! Personally, I couldn't care less. Whoever it is, they're an idiot. A fool and his money, my dear!"

"One thing I don't understand," I said. "If Tim is so protective of Dame Norma, why does he want me to play her in the parade?"

"He doesn't want her to feel left out. They have such a sense of billing, these divas. He loathed the idea at first, but now he thinks it's pure heaven. Of course, I've told him how brilliant you are at that sort of thing."

"Thanks a lot!"

He laughed again and patted me on the back. "Well, I'm going to mingle till I die. Don't forget the meeting. I'll ring and remind you. Are you in the book?"

"Yes."

"How old hat! Ciao, my darling." He kissed me and disappeared into the crowd.

Suddenly I felt ill. Tonight had been a trifle heavy. I saw no sign of Paul anywhere. Leaving my unfinished beer, I pushed, shoved, and apologized my way out of the bar. A row of vacant cabs revved eagerly outside. I hopped into the first taxi, directed the driver to take me away from all this, and promptly fell asleep.

CHAPTER 16

*T*he next morning I was up early, after sleeping fit-
fully. I tried to lose myself in *Otello*, but I could-
n't concentrate. In fact, the opera got on my
nerves. Fancy Otello falling for Iago's story about the hanky.
How could anyone be so stupid as to believe that? Especially
coming from Aldo Protti, the most wooden Iago ever to stand
still on stage. He couldn't tell you the time convincingly. And
then to strangle Desdemona because of it! Shows you how
low tenors will stoop.

I switched off the music and spontaneously flicked on the
television. A cartoon was showing. At least it sounded like a
cartoon: The characters hardly ever moved. The hero was a
muscular environmentalist named Captain Clean. He was
fighting an evil scientist, a woman who wanted to blow up a
virgin rain forest. Captain Clean dealt with her by the envi-
ronmentally unsound method of blasting her to bits. His
sidekick, a streetwise parrot, found this act of annihilation
hugely amusing.

When the cartoon finished, a strange half-dressed teenage
girl appeared and spent five minutes laughing and failing to
string a sentence together. I pointed my remote at the TV girl
and, cartoon fashion, blew her away. Five minutes viewing
and already I'd picked up violent habits!

I didn't seem my usual self today.

I decided I'd have to see Paul. It was not yet 10 o'clock, far
too early to ring, so I locked up the house and drove over to
his flat.

He lived in a tiny dark flat in a nondescript red-brick
building, one of several blocks built in the 1930s. At that
time they were probably regarded as cheap-looking and ugly,

but in later years they had been overtaken by even cheaper and uglier home units, so now they looked Old World and quaint.

The frosted-glass front doors were unlocked, and I was able to walk straight up to Paul's door. I heard no sound of activity. I knocked softly, but nothing stirred. I knocked a little louder. I was about ready to buy myself breakfast up the road when the door opened. There stood Paul, wearing only a pair of Calvin Kleins and a sleep mask pushed up onto his forehead.

"Caro mio! What are you doing here?"

"Can I come in?"

"Natch!"

He closed the door silently behind me. The room looked like Apocalypse Recent. Chairs were tipped over, every surface littered with magazines, ashtrays, and empty glasses. The lumpy couch onto which Paul hurled himself was awash with pillows and blankets.

"I'm less than fabulous right now," he muttered. "Please don't take advantage of me."

I cleared a pile of old newspapers off a chair and dragged it over next to him. "No push-ups this morning?"

"My back's buggered."

"Are you sleeping on the couch?"

"Just for a few days. I've got guests."

"Here? There's not enough room to flutter an eyelash."

"You're telling me. It's Rodney and some friend of his."

"Rodney? You're always saying how much you dislike him!"

"Shh, keep your voice down! Of course I can't stand him, but we're friends. That's showbiz."

"I'll never understand you theatrical types."

"The three of us did some drugs last night," he explained sheepishly. "It got a bit wild. We're dancers, don't forget!"

I looked askance. Several generations of the Bolshoi couldn't have created turmoil like this.

"What have you been up to, caro?"

"Let me make us a coffee and I'll tell you."

"With those filthy old bandages? I'd better do it. How are your fingers, anyway? Been resting them, I trust." He winked salaciously.

"Not exactly, but they're feeling better this morning. The dead skin is cracking, I think it should peel away in a few days."

"More than I needed to know, thanks."

Paul stumbled across to an overflowing laundry basket and yanked out a Chinese dressing gown from the bottom of it. As he pottered around the kitchenette, searching for jars of instant coffee and sugar, I told him of my adventure in the sauna, making it as dramatic as I possibly could. To give him his due, he seemed genuinely concerned.

"Caro! An attempt on your life! Brilliant! I knew we were right."

"About what?"

"About Jen being murdered, of course! But you must be *très* careful from now on."

"Thanks for the advice," I remarked. "That's precisely what I intend to do. In fact, I'm thinking of calling it a day and hanging up my deerstalker."

Paul's mouth fell open. "You're wimping out?"

"I'm not good in the role of dead person."

He dropped everything and rushed to my side.

"Don't let it affect you like that. You're being silly. We'll simply watch our step! No more of this solo detective work. We'll do it together from now on, OK? Besides, I'm jealous! Sounds like I'm missing out on all the daredevil stuff."

"You can have it."

"Bad Marc! Stop that talk! Here, drink your coffee."

He looked so crestfallen, I had to laugh.

"Where do we go from here, then?" I pondered. "There's so much to unravel, I don't know what to do next. Except avoid steam rooms."

In response, Paul put his hand down the back of the couch

and pulled out our only plum, to wit, Jennifer's diary.

"I've been rereading the good book," he said, "and I've learned all sorts of interesting things!"

"Such as?"

"Well, for instance, did you know there's a Saint Andrea Dung-lac? That means a lake full of dung, doesn't it? Spooky thing to name a saint after. It was her day yesterday."

"Is that all? Andrea's a man's name, by the way."

"No, that's not all. Look."

He held the diary up by the top of its spine and dropped it to the floor.

"I see," I said. "It doesn't bounce."

"Now watch closely," he whispered, and repeated the trick.

"You'll wreck the bloody thing!"

"It always falls open at the same page! Very significant, caro. This page must be extremely important."

I was impressed. "What's written on it?"

He shrugged. "Nothing."

"Nothing at all?"

"Nope. Nothing on either page."

He handed it over. I examined it carefully.

"Well, that hardly tells us anything, does it?" I said, exasperated.

"Something might have happened on those days," Paul suggested, "that was so important she couldn't even write it down. Or was afraid to!"

"Rubbish!" I said. "It only tells us that Jennifer had a couple of dull days on…" I consulted the diary. "On June the 8th and 13th! Paul! That's why it fell open here: A double page has been torn out!"

He bounded over, positively glowing.

"Wowee!" he squealed. "Where?"

"Here, the 9th to the 12th. This is just before *Phar Lap* and all the references to R.L.W. Dear me, another mystery. Why would she rip pages out of her diary?"

"Girlish high spirits?"

"Maybe."

At that moment, the bedroom door opened. In a flash I snapped the diary shut and shoved it back under the cushions. I turned to see Rodney step hesitatingly into the room. He was tousled, sleepy, and bountifully naked.

"What's the fuckin' time?" he asked.

"You haven't missed the matinee," Paul answered. "I'll make more coffee. You know Marc, I think?"

Rodney stared at me for a moment. "Oh, yeah, hi. You're the photographer guy, right? How're they selling?"

"Oh, not bad," I answered.

"How's what selling?" asked Paul.

"The, err, photos," I said.

"Did they turn up?" he exclaimed. "I thought we lost them. Whom are you selling them to?"

"Not those photos, other ones!"

"Which ones?"

"The ones I take for a living!" I said with unusual emphasis.

"This is the guy Paul I was telling you about," said Rodney. "I guess you found him."

"Yes, I did. Thanks."

"This bloke's Jen's uncle," Rodney said to Paul.

"I know," said Paul. "Why don't you take a shower, Rodney? The coffee's not ready."

"Yeah, OK" he answered and, turning back to me, said laughingly, "Paul's got this theory Jen was murdered."

I was stunned, unable to speak.

"Not really," Paul said lightly.

"Yes you do!" Rodney replied. "He told us about it last night. He's investigating the murder, like Agatha...um, Lansbury."

"Is he?" I said, glaring at Paul. "Is he really?"

"Yeah," said Rodney. "Better watch you don't get bumped off, Paul!"

"I'd say that's looking more and more likely," I muttered.

"Take a fucking shower," Paul snapped.

"All right, all right," said Rodney. "Come on, babe," he called into the bedroom, "Come and do things under the shower with me!"

"No worries," said a voice, and there behind Rodney in a pair of skimpy black shorts stood Ng.

"Oh!" he cried as our eyes met. "Uncle Mike? You here? You follow us here?"

"Follow you? No, no! Of course not."

"You follow Rodney everywhere. You tell me this! You very sick man."

Rodney looked puzzled. "Is he following me?"

"Cover up," Ng shrieked, and held a newspaper up in front of him. "Cover up, this man sick. All too much for him!"

"Don't be stupid," Rodney said, grabbing the paper from Ng and flinging it into a corner. "Mike's a photographer! He's seen guys with their gear off before." He hit a stirring muscleman pose.

"Marc," I corrected.

"Go to shower," screamed Ng, pushing Rodney away.

"Why does everybody want me to take a shower?" Rodney complained. "Do I stink or something?"

"Yes," Paul answered.

"Oh. OK." He ambled off to the bathroom.

"I join you in a minute," said Ng, stepping over to me. He frowned. "I am not being nice to you no more now. You sure you don't follow us?"

"No, honestly! I came to visit Paul. He's a friend of mine."

He shook his head. "Don't understand. You always turning up!"

This was becoming irritating.

"Well, what are you doing here, more to the point?" I said. "Did Roland find out about your little fling with Adonis?"

"Adonis?"

"With Rodney!"

"Yes," he sighed. "Roland throw us out. Only for a week, I think. After that I go back. This happen before. Always a week, tops."

"He just needs time to cool down," said Paul.

"Pah! Roland is old man, not thinking like young man!" mused Ng. "No big deal, sleeping around. Rodney sleep around all the time! Every day, I think, bring man home. I don't care, but he is using a condom, so no worries!"

Suddenly, Ng's expression darkened. He lunged at me, his hands tightly clasping me around the neck.

"You Roland spy!" he cried. "You tell Roland about us!"

"No," I choked. I tried to pull his hands away, but the bandages made it awkward. He was throttling me!

Paul bounded across the room and leapt onto Ng. "Stop it," he screamed. The three of us tumbled onto the floor, knocking over a dead pot plant and a pile of CDs.

"You tell Roland," Ng shouted, "so you get Rodney for self! Sick spy man!"

"No!"

"Get off!" shouted Paul and finally dragged Ng away in some kind of wrestling hold and forced him into a chair.

I fought for breath. "I'm not Roland's spy," I panted. "I don't even know the man. I haven't seen him since that dinner party. Believe me!"

Ng relaxed, all his manic energy suddenly evaporating. "Sorry," he said.

Cautiously, Paul let go of him and hopped back to the kitchen. "Let's all have a drink," Paul suggested. "A brandy, caro?"

"*Grazie,*" I breathed.

"Very sorry," repeated Ng, looking ashamed. "Ng losing control, like stupid Australian."

"It's all right."

"How your leg?" he inquired brightly.

"Better thanks."

"But your hands injured now!"

"I burnt them."

"Tch-tch-tch. I fix with herbs."

Rodney stuck his wet head out the bathroom door. "Hey, come on!" he called. "I'm getting all wrinkly."

"Couldn't have that, could we!" shouted Paul.

"Sorry," Ng said once more as he squeezed past me and disappeared into the steam.

Paul brought two glasses of brandy over and handed the one with the least in it to me. I scowled at him.

"I can't believe it," I said.

"Me neither," he said. "She's a loony!"

"What I can't believe," I corrected him, "is how stupid you are!"

He assumed a hurt demeanor. "Caro! I just saved your life!"

"Temporarily! Why on earth did you tell them Jen was murdered? And that we were investigating it?"

"I didn't. That is, I didn't mention you. I may have mentioned I was looking into it myself. In an offhand sort of way."

"Thanks a million! My life is in danger," I ranted, "and you make it worse!"

"What's the harm? It's only Rodney and that maniac. They've got nothing to do with Jen."

"How do you know? It was Rodney's room I was in when I found the diary! They've both got everything to do with it!"

"You found it? I'm the one who found it!"

"I threw it out the window!" I fumed. "You just picked it up."

"Did you? But why didn't you hang onto it?"

"Because someone was coming, and I didn't want to be caught with it in my hand!"

"Oh. Did Rodney spring you?"

"No, Ng! That's why I knew about the two of them!"

"I see." He started laughing. "No wonder he thought you were Roland's spy. How delicious!"

"It wasn't delicious at the time," I said grumpily. "It was a close shave, and I was petrified."

"Never mind," he said, patting my bandage in a conciliatory fashion. "It was worth it. Help me put away these CDs you knocked over."

"You knocked them over, too!"

"While saving your life."

We got down on our knees and scrabbled around in the mess.

"They're out of order now!" Paul whined. "They should go alphabetically."

I looked around. "How? They're all Streisand!"

"Yes. *The Broadway Album* is B, *Color Me Barbra* is C, et cetera. On second thought, just whisk 'em under the couch and we'll get some breakfast."

"What about Rodney and Ng?"

"They'll find a way to occupy themselves. 'Scuse me while I throw on something casual yet exquisite. Bring the diary."

I was happier than usual to get away from Paul's flat and so, I suspect, was Paul: I'd never known him to dress so quickly. Ng and Rodney did not reappear, even though the shower had stopped running some time ago.

"I think I'd like to eat something today," I said to Paul. "Let's not go to the place where they don't serve you."

"Café Butt? That closed. It went out of business."

"I'm not surprised."

"Oh, it was very popular, but they had a ton of robberies. No glass in the windows."

"I recall."

"We'll go to the Austral. It's ultra-trendy this week."

We made our way down to the older part of Oxford Street. Here were three or four stores left over from times gone by: Jewish tailors, purveyors of hideous Indian artifacts, and a shop that sold huge knives and chef hats. The stores huddled together (as well they might) for mutual support against the advancing onslaught of boutiques, nightclubs, and Internet cafés.

On the corner, hidden between a pawnbroker's and a porn-broker's, was the Austral, a cavernous old milk bar. It had been sitting there deserted since Armistice Day but recently had been reinhabited. I couldn't remember ever having been inside. Still it looked incredibly familiar: It was exactly like every milk bar I'd ever passed on school holiday trips to "the country." There were booths for the patrons, separated by walls of polished ply, each booth with its own coin operated jukebox. The floor was a grubby, curly linoleum, possibly yellow originally. Tabletops were green Laminex. Each table boasted an individual bottle of tomato sauce and a tumbler of toothpicks.

On the walls were beloved Australian commercial icons: the Arnott's Biscuits cockatoo, the Vegemite logo, posters advertising beer and Chad Morgan. A hand-colored shot of Princess Elizabeth II had pride of place. A big old fan was the centerpiece of the ceiling, majestically still and sporting cobwebs that must have been over a hundred years old.

The place was crowded, but Paul and I found a table at the back, near a glass cabinet displaying today's cakes and a few dead blowflies.

"The flies are plastic," Paul enthused. "Camp, isn't it! I just love it—It's so Period!"

"What's available on the jukebox?" I asked.

"They don't work," he explained. "They're only for effect."

"Pity," I replied, as a speaker somewhere nearby pumped out the latest dance music. In this one respect, authenticity had been abandoned.

The milk bars on which the Austral was modeled were invariably run by European families, often Italian. (Southern Italian: My parents looked down on them.) The Austral was run by a council-funded collective—middle-aged hippies and unemployable youth.

Our waitress boogied over and efficiently cleared the table, balancing three plates, cups, and saucers along her freckled arm. She wore loose Indian slacks with a thin satin top, and had short gray hair and round tortoiseshell glasses.

"Good monning," she said. "Two bretheths?"

"Sorry?" I said.

"Yes, two breakfasts," answered Paul brightly.

"Cothee or hubble tea?"

"Coffee, thanks."

With her free hand she swiftly wiped down the tabletop and disappeared.

"What an unfortunate speech impediment," I whispered sympathetically.

"I think it's due to the piercing," said Paul. "Didn't you notice? She has a ring through her tongue and bottom lip."

While waiting for our order, we reexamined the diary at the torn out section, especially the entries before and after, but nothing significant leapt to the eye. References to the weather, shopping, and Paul all seemed utterly trivial.

"Even so," I said, "It's our only piece of evidence, except the photo Jude gave me."

"Speaking of photos, what was Rodney talking about?"

"Roland kept introducing me as a photographer. I don't know how it started," I said. "I wish your party snaps had turned up."

"We're not in a strong position with clues, are we? Shame we didn't see the suicide note."

"I've wondered about that. Do you know what was in it?"

"Other than heartfelt regrets, no."

"Where was it found? Who found it?"

"Dame Norma. She picked it up at the cliff edge, she said."

I scoffed. "That's impossible! I've been there, it's windy as hell. Any scrap of paper would have blown away."

"Maybe she put a rock on it, or stuck it on a tree."

"Who, Jennifer?"

"No. The murderer, I suppose."

The same thought occurred to us at precisely the same instant.

"Caro!"

"Yes! The torn out page!"

"Jen wrote practice suicide notes, she told me! It was her quirky feminine way of letting off steam! Her therapy!"

We reexamined June 13th (coincidentally, the day of Saint Antony of Padua, patron saint of sea creatures).

"It looks like something was written on the missing page," I said. "Have you got a pencil?"

"No," Paul replied. "But wait a minute!" He reached up to the top of the booth partition and ran his fingers along it. He examined them closely: They were black.

"Just as I thought," he said. "It's filthy up there. Remind me to complain to the council!"

He smeared the grime gently over the page and, miraculously, a faint ghost of the original message began to appear. It was not completely decipherable, but it was clearly what we were looking for. "Dear Seaton," it began, "By the time you read this I will be dead. Life sucks." There were several lines we couldn't make out, then, "Before you are satisfied. You fat fucking pig."

"Jeez," said Paul. "That's what I called him, too!"

"Great minds think alike," I said.

The message finished, "Goodbye forever, Jennifer." We reread it.

"What do you think, caro?"

"I think she'd had some kind of falling out with Seaton."

"Discovered he was a big help to his mother."

"Then someone got hold of this note, written two months earlier, and used it to make her death look like suicide. In fact, if you were to tear off the top of the page, you'd lose the date and 'Dear Seaton' and be left with a useful all-purpose farewell!"

"Except for the fat pig bit."

"Mmm."

"But how did this person get it? We're the ones who found

the diary, and I know we didn't do it!"

I was stumped. Paul grabbed my hand. "Of course!" he crowed.

"Of course what?"

"Rodney's the murderer! The diary was in his room. Oh my God, he's loose in my flat at this very moment! We'll all be killed!"

"Calm down, for God's sake. There must be another explanation. Did Jennifer carry the diary around?"

"Sometimes, I guess."

"She wrote her appointments in it. She may have taken it along with her."

"Makes sense."

"Any of the people she met could have had an opportunity to rip out the message. It would only take a second."

"You'd have to be quick."

"That's true. You would have to know what you were looking for. Who else knew she wrote practice suicide messages?"

"I don't know. Her agent? People she worked with..."

"Rodney?"

"I don't think they ever did a show together. She would have complained about him."

"Why?"

"'Cause he's slack and untalented."

"Or it could be someone she saw frequently, somebody who had plenty of chance to browse through the book in her flat."

"Seaton!"

"Yes, or Jude or Randolph or Sir Fred or...somebody else."

"Well, caro, we know it wasn't Jude!"

"How do we know that?"

"She might be a dyke, but I bet she's not butch enough to get into a men's sauna to try and kill you."

"That's if it was the same person who murdered Jennifer."

"It goes without saying! Unless you've got squillions of enemies out there waiting to pounce."

"I just mean we don't know."

"It lets out Dame Norma as well."

I felt uneasy. "I don't think Dame Norma's the murderer," I said, "but I'm sure she has more to do with this whole business than we know."

"You're right, caro. That mysterious benefactor of hers! Who is it?"

"If we knew that, we'd be ahead."

Paul's eyes lit up. "There's one way to find out."

"How?"

"Flush him out! Dame Norma thinks it's you, so tell her it is! Tell anybody who gives a shit! The real guy's nose will be so out of joint he's bound to come out of the closet!"

"And kill me," I suggested.

"Don't worry, I won't let him."

It actually didn't seem like a bad idea. If they all thought I was the opera-loving billionaire, I'd be able to meet everyone: Sir Fred, Edward Quinn, the lot. I wondered if it was against the law to claim to be a billionaire if you weren't. I could probably fool people as long as I didn't write a lot of checks. If pressed for money, I could claim I'd lost interest in opera and was going in for cutting-edge street theatre instead.

"Two bretheths."

Our lacerated waitress was back. Onto the table in front of us she slammed down two enormous plates piled high with food: hard fried eggs, burnt bacon, spicy sausages, mushy tomatoes, scorched hash browns, and chilled maple syrup.

"This is huge!," I said.

"Good, I'm starving," Paul remarked and dove in.

"I've been thinking," I said between mouthfuls of runny, gooey tucker. "I might move out of my place for a while. After last night's business."

"Good idea. I'm afraid we're full up *chez moi*."

"There's a couple of friends I can try," I said. "I'll let you know where I go."

"Do stay in touch!"

"And don't forget, we're expected at Roy and Shaunna's place next weekend. Though, on second thought, I might cancel. I've got other plans: living, breathing, things like that."

"No! I want to go!" Paul squealed. "I'm so excited about it!"

"Can you get time off from the show?"

"Don't worry. Rodney can cover on Saturday. He owes it to me, for putting up with him and his crazy boyfriend."

"You know," I mused, "your friend Jennifer was pretty weird herself! Writing practice suicide notes is a strange hobby."

"Nonsense, caro, it's *très* sensible. One day you might genuinely want to end it all, but you'd be far too depressed to fiddle around with a note, getting the grammar and spelling all perfect! This way, you've got the hack work taken care of, and you can concentrate on the important things. Like your hair."

I sighed. "And what would you write in your farewell message?"

"I don't know," he answered. "Something deep. 'Bury me by the river'—something with a country feel."

"Any special river?"

"Phoenix."

With that, we stopped chatting and got down to serious breakfasting. I didn't pause for breath until my plate looked like it had been zapped by Captain Clean himself.

CHAPTER 17

I don't see much of my cousin Gianna, though when I do, we always have a few laughs. She's in her mid thirties and owns a high-rise apartment on the north side of the harbor. From her balcony you can see a section of the city skyline and a lot of other high-rise apartments.

Gianna's the only one left in the family who still talks to me, probably because she was too far removed to have any claim on my inheritance. She's single but used to be married to an opinionated bastard who writes a weekly newspaper column called "Opinion." They were divorced years ago, but she still reads the column avidly and starts every conversation with, "Did you see what that arsehole said about..." Once off the subject of her ex-husband, she's fairly pleasant.

The simple reason we don't get together is because she never goes out. Gianna's an obsessive fan of daytime television; she leaves the video on "record" while she's at work, then watches the day's programs at night. Her friend Annie, who lives eight floors below, comes up to watch with her. Gianna claims this lack of socializing saves her money and she is indeed a saver: Twice a year she and Annie take a trip to some exotic location. (Last year they went to Tahiti and Aspen, Colorado.) Judging from the holiday snaps, they have a ball and spend most of their time roaring drunk. She claims they meet hundreds of men abroad, but there's never the remotest sign of one in her apartment. Still, I don't like to pry.

Gianna was delighted when I rang to ask if I could stay at her place for a while. "Sure, Marc," she said, "on one condition. You've gotta tape my favorite shows while I'm away."

"You won't be there?"

"Don't sound so happy about it!"

"Oh, I'm not!"

"Annie and me are off to Mexico for a fortnight. Tequila, here we come! Whoo!"

"Enjoy yourselves."

"I'll leave a list with the times and channels, but check the guide in case they change. And the keys I'll leave with Mrs. Takahashi in 328. She's boss of the Body Corporate."

"Thanks for this, Gianna."

"When will your floor be finished?" (I had told her I was renovating.)

"About a week."

I moved in straight away, bringing a minimum of goods and one or two chattels.

On my first morning, I settled down with the Sunday papers. As if to deliberately remind me of my precarious position, they were full of articles concerning Maurice Littlechild, the politician who had expired in the sauna. He had been so eminent, respected, and well liked that everyone had had to save up the dirt until he was dead. Now it came forth in a torrent: questionable financial deals, conflicts of interest, even an old incident with a neighbor involving a nine-iron and a restraining order. The cause of death was ambiguously described as heart failure. No mention was made of the deceased's whereabouts at the time of departure.

I had decided to lay low, even if it meant my students gave up on me for good. I didn't want to let Rodney and Ng get hold of my new number, so I rang Paul's theatre (the right one, this time) and left the number for him there. Then I settled down with *The Young and the Restless*.

Speaking of which, I naturally thought about Reg. I missed him severely, but had no way of contacting him. I wasn't even sure it would be a good idea anyway. I had asked myself many times why he had failed to come to the sauna, and I'd more or less settled for the "boyfriend" answer, but I was beginning to recognize the truth: We'd fallen into that no-man's-land where relationships go to die. It had been fun while it lasted, but, as young men are wont to do, he wearied of it. When he said on the phone he'd been thinking about me, he meant he'd been thinking about how to call it off. Anyone with a bit of experience under their belt can read the signs. These liaisons don't end the way they do in grand opera, with suicide pacts and top notes; they just sort of wilt. It was over; the fact that I had not heard from him since Sauna Night confirmed it. Five entire days! *Finito*.

I fidgeted around Gianna's flat. I was edgy. It may have been due to the sound of the planes: I missed them dreadfully. Every morning at 6 A.M., I'd open my eyes to bewildering silence. The roar of heavy traffic, a distant dull hum at this height, was quite inadequate as noise, so I couldn't get back to sleep. It put me out of kilter for the whole day. Then, at 11:30 in the evening, just when I settled down for a good Renata fix, I would get a call from Mrs. Takahashi ordering me to turn off the opera. Totally bamboozled, I would slink off to bed only to lie awake for hours, serenaded by an eerie cacophony of car alarms.

It was during one of these wakeful periods that I worked out a way to follow up Paul's suggestion. It was his idea for me to pose as the generous soul who had bankrolled Dame Norma's triumphs, but how? Norma herself already believed it, but was not about to tell the operatic world in case they beat a path to my bank account. Neither was there any point in talking to Tim, whom I suspected of knowing the benefactor's true identity. Who did this leave among my opera company connections? Jude from finance.

She was well up there on the list of murder suspects, but, as Paul had pointed out, she can't have been the one who gave me the dim sum treatment. That had to be a man, and Jude didn't seem the type to act in collusion with anybody belonging even remotely to the opposite sex. What's more, she thought I was her beloved Jennifer's uncle, and had given me Jen's photo to boot. She'd taken a fancy to me.

I called her at the Sydney Opera and, unlike last time, was put straight through.

"Hello?"

"It's Marc Petrucci here."

"Yes?"

"You remember, we met at Roland's? I'm Jennifer Burke's uncle."

"I know who you are. I'm very busy."

"Oh, sorry. Look, I wonder if we could meet: Do you eat regularly somewhere?"

"Well, in the park mostly. When I get a spare moment."

"I wanted to thank you for the picture you gave me."

"No need, really."

"And I wanted to tell you something which may intrigue you. In private."

There was a pause.

"This isn't harassment, is it?" she asked suspiciously.

"What?"

"Are you coming on to me?"

"Certainly not! I'm—well, I'm not interested. I mean, I thought you had a lover."

"I do. Lavinia. That wouldn't stop most men."

"Oh? Well, it would stop me! I've met her."

"What's that supposed to mean?"

"I mean—what I mean is, I just want to talk to you," I said exasperatedly.

"About Jennifer?"

"Yes!"

She sighed. "I'd rather not, but if you insist. You know the Opera offices?"

"Yes."

"There's a park a block away, corner of Edgeware Parade. I'll meet you there tomorrow at one."

"Right. Thanks."

"I don't have a lot of time for lunch."

I got myself to the spot promptly at 12:50. It was a small park, pleasantly laid out with swings and a slippery dip, the big old solid variety. The slide was warped from weathering, very tall and shiny, guaranteeing a life-threatening ride for any kid foolhardy enough to risk it. To block out the traffic, thick shrubs had been planted and wooden seats, painted a dull crimson, had been placed adjacent to them. Checking that the paint was dry (I've been misled before), I sat myself down to wait.

By 1:30 there was still no sign of Jude. I was disconcerted; I'd expected her to be punctual. I had no newspaper to read, and nothing to do.

By and by, I noticed a strange man. He was of indeterminate age, wearing dark clothes and an overcoat in spite of the warm weather. He had a neatly trimmed mustache and beard. He wandered past the park, eyeing me closely, and disappeared around the corner. Minutes later, he wandered back and crossed into the park, loitering amongst the shrubs. I caught his eye; he winked and nodded slightly. No mistake: I was being cruised!

He was attractive in a Middle European way, but this was the last thing I wanted to deal with right now. I sat still and stared at my feet. When I looked up again, he was still lurking in the bushes, rubbing his crotch with one hand and frantically beckoning with the other. I shook my head vigorously. He smiled and began to amble over.

I wanted to leave, but I risked missing my appointment with Jude. I would have to try and ignore him.

The strange man arrived at the bench and sat next to me, immediately placing his hand on my thigh.

"Look, I'm sorry, but I'm waiting for someone," I said.

He merely continued to smile and rub my leg.

"No!" I snapped, and stood up. I walked briskly to the next

seat. He followed. I got up and moved again, but he followed again. Eventually we were back where we started; this was getting ridiculous.

"What do you want?" I said (as if I didn't know).

From inside his overcoat he produced a polystyrene tray of frozen pork chops, the kind you buy in a supermarket. It was plastic wrapped and still had the price on it. The man smiled broadly and nodded, pointed to the meat, then replaced it in his coat. Having done that, he returned his hand to my leg. He laughed—a rich, deep chuckle.

At that moment, Jude appeared. She marched across the park with a fixed smile. "Marc?" she called. "I'm sorry I'm late."

"It's all right," I replied, rising to greet her.

The strange man rose as well, smiling and nodding.

"Been making friends?" she asked.

"No," I said. "I've no idea who he is! He just wandered up."

"It's Sergei Petrovich," she said. The man laughed again and attempted to embrace her but she neatly sidestepped him. Undaunted, he embraced me instead. He smelt of pork, not surprisingly. "He's with the opera," she explained. "A visiting bass-baritone from the Ukraine. He has a big reputation over there."

"He's going to get one over here, too," I said.

"He's supposed to have a minder." She sighed. "I'll have to take him back. What do you want to see me about?"

"Well," I said, "I'll only be a minute."

The three of us sat on the bench.

"As I said, I wanted to thank you for the photo. I think you're one of the few people I've met who really cared for my niece." I smiled warmly.

"Thank you. I cared for her deeply."

Sergei chuckled. "Da," he said.

"I'm sorry?" I turned to him.

"Don't bother," said Jude. "He doesn't speak English. He's a pain in the arse."

"Mm. Well, the thing is, I've always been an opera fanatic, as I told you. I'm quite wealthy, my family owns a lot of valuable real estate, investments—"

"*Da*," agreed Sergei.

"And I've been making contributions to the opera for some time. Anonymously."

Jude eyed me slyly. A knowing smile flitted across her lips.

"So it's you?" she asked. "I wish I'd known a year ago."

"Why?"

"No reason, really. Curiosity. We've all been wondering about Dame Norma's secret admirer. You must have been livid when I slagged off at her."

"I thought you were a bit harsh, but I knew what you meant. She was stunning in her prime. Those years are over, I'm afraid."

"You said it."

"I saw her back in the '60s. I'll never forget the effect she had on me. Even so, I had decided to cancel my opera donations: Then, by chance, I discovered my niece's involvement. I had no idea of Jennifer's aspirations."

"Jen never told me she came from a wealthy family," said Jude. "Quite the opposite, I thought."

"Um...well, yes and no. That is—I'm sorry, but Sergei has his hand in my lap."

"Sergei Petrovich!" she barked. "*Nyet!*"

He frowned and withdrew his hand.

"Anyway," I continued quickly, "I've decided to set up a fund for young singers. The Jennifer Burke Scholarship. What do you think?"

"I think you owe it to her."

"Um, right."

Jude smiled. "And I think it's a lovely idea."

"Good!" I exclaimed. "I want the Sydney City Opera to be involved in the selection of candidates and to guarantee the winner a professional debut. The fund would cover expenses and send the scholars to study, perhaps at Juilliard, or even better, La Scala! I have connections there." I leaned toward her, as did Sergei, and emphasized, "Of course, I will be doing this anonymously, but I thought you at least should know where it's coming from."

"Thank you."

"I'm sure I can trust you with our little secret."

Knowing her penchant for gossip, I was convinced this would get my name zooming from one end of the opera company to the other by late afternoon.

"Have you told anyone else?" she inquired.

"I've spoken to my solicitor about it. He'll be getting in touch with Quinn. I don't wish to go through Sir Fred with this one."

"He'll be ropable when he finds out!" She and Sergei laughed heartily. "I hope I'm not around. The chairman has a foul temper! Now I'd better take this idiot back." They laughed again.

We stood, and I shook her hand.

"It's the least I can do for Jennifer. It could never make up for what happened."

"No."

"It's what she would have wanted."

"Excuse me," Jude said sharply, "but it's not! Jen didn't give a stuff about other singers, or anyone else for that matter. To be a star: That's what she would have wanted! That's all she wanted."

"Well," I stammered. "This is the next best thing."

"*Da*," whispered Sergei and, taking my hand, pressed the tray of pork chops into it. He smiled and winked, shaking his head when I tried to give it back.

"He likes you," Jude remarked sarcastically. "I can't begin to tell you how much we paid to bring him over."

I could hardly wait to tell Paul of my cleverly executed plan. I still hadn't heard from him, so I made a clandestine detour home to see if he'd rung me there. I took all due precautions, parking in the next block and scanning the street for potential murderers before I quickly and quietly let myself in. I was relieved to see nothing had been disturbed.

The phone machine was blinking away, as usual. What did people do in the days before these things took over our lives? Spoke to each other, I suppose.

There were four messages. The first was from Paul.

"Caro! Where are you! You never call, you never write! Like the gorilla in the old joke. Sorry, I can't remember it. If you're not dead, I guess the weekend is still happening, n'est-pas? Don't get all girly on me and refuse to go! I've arranged with Rodney to take over my leading role and be mediocre. Ciao."

I realized he had received neither my message nor my new number.

The second message was from Roy.

"It's Roy, you old sodomite! Oh, Jeez, I better watch myself. Now listen, I'm gonna get Shaunna to give you directions. I won't do it myself cause I'm on the mobile and it'll cost me. Plus, I can't be bothered. HAR! But I'm looking forward to you coming. Wait till you see the place: We've got a new vat, fully computerized, varies the temperature automatically. It's a bloody marvel! Bring your little mate along and don't worry, it's a broad-minded bunch. See you Saturday."

The third message was from Shaunna.

"Hello, Marc, Shaunna Coxedge. It's been too long! I'm so looking forward to this weekend. I'll personally make sure you both have a fabulous time! Roy's called already, he says. Now, this is how you get here. Got a pen?"

Her directions were crisp, clear, and efficient, as I knew they would be. Then, at the end of the message, she added a postscript: "One other thing, Marc. I wonder if you would be a sweetheart and give someone a lift? His name's Seaton. He says he's met you, so I gave him your number. He's a musical genius, but I'm sure he won't bore you. If he does, I apologize in advance! See you soon, my love!"

The last message was from hell.

"Marc? Seaton Frith here. No hard feelings, eh? Looks like we're about to get all cozy in the country. Sounds like fun! Tell your friend to take it easy. I'm sure Paul has cooled down by now—he's a sweet boy, really. Well, you know that, don't you! Pick me up outside the Opera offices at 10:15. Cheers!"

As I shoved a few pork chops onto the griller, I considered the turn of events. *So this is how I avoid danger,* I told myself, *by spending two days in the close company of our number one suspect!* Close company was right: I remembered Seaton's bulk. It wasn't going to be a very comfortable journey.

$\mathcal{P}$aul was ecstatic (in the nontoxic sense) when I told him I'd spoken to Jude about the Jennifer Burke Scholarship.

"This is a huge step forward for mankind in our investigation," he crowed. "We're getting close!"

"You don't know the half of it," I said and then told him about our traveling companion. I heard startled gasping down the phone.

"I've been a devoted fan of Shaunna Campbell's all my life," Paul moaned. "How could she do this to me?"

"I don't think she knows Seaton too well."

"Obviously not. Well, forget it. Have fun with fat boy. Make my excuses."

"Who's wimping out now? I'm the one whose life is in danger. If I can cope with him, you can!"

"I guess that's true, caro. He could be our murderer, and we've got the whole trip to grill him. By the time we get to Malanga we'll have a signed confession!"

"Hmm."

"But I'm not sitting next to him. You can put him in front!"

"He won't fit."

"We'll see. I'll bring a crowbar along!"

"You don't own anything as macho as that!"

"No, but I know a bit of rough trade who does."

When I picked Paul up on Saturday morning, he brought with him a portable cassette player, a dinner suit in a plastic bag, and six or seven Louis Vuitton cases. I helped him stuff them in the back of the car.

"Aren't they divine? I got them in Bangkok on the Southeast Asia tour of *Flower Drum Song*. They're fake, natch.

Only classy French call-boys can afford the real thing."

"They take up so much room!"

"Too bad, we'll have to dump big fat Seaton overboard."

"What's in these bags? We're not moving up there permanently, you know!"

"A change of clothes, personal toiletries, and few dozen porn videos to amuse us if it rains. It's less than it looks."

He climbed in the back next to them and we chugged off toward the offices of the Sydney City Opera. Outside stood Seaton, as promised, resplendent in large tan slacks, a straw fedora, a flowing cream silk shirt, and something I'd thought I would never see again: a paisley cravat.

Paul hooted. "She's a Merchant Ivory nightmare!"

"Shh!" I cautioned. "Just because he's dressed funny doesn't mean we can trust him."

Seaton had more bags than Paul. By the time they'd all been crammed into the car, Paul had virtually disappeared. I did the loading while Seaton stood by, radiating an easy camaraderie that I didn't entirely trust.

"Hallo, Marc. Paul, are you in there? What a lot of baggage. Make sure mine's on top, I don't want it crushed! Ooh! Tight squeeze! Still, beggars can't be choosers. Do you know the way, Marc? Don't go the highway, it's dreary. I'll show you a back road. You turn off before Gosford."

I started the engine and reached over for the gear, but instead got a handful of Seaton's massive thigh.

He slapped my wrist. "Naughty!"

"I was trying to find the gear stick."

"Were you, indeed!"

I realized I would probably have to choose one gear and stay in it for the whole trip.

We drove for an hour, and the city gradually gave way to rolling grassy fields stretching as far as the eye could see. A lot of these fields had once been farmed but were now earmarked for retirement village development. What will happen, I wondered, to these cute little roadside stalls selling honey, oranges, and potatoes? They'll fade into the mists of history, alongside milk bars and one-pump service stations, to be replaced by retirement village stalls flogging knitted tea cozies and biscuits you couldn't crack with a jackhammer.

How exhilarating it was to see the greenery; to feel the warm wind blowing through my hair. Even with the window shut I felt a breeze. It came from Seaton. He never stopped prattling from the minute we set off, keeping up a constant stream of chat. He talked about every subject under the sun, and on every one of them he regarded himself as an authority. We'd been through opera, film, food, clothes, wine, religions of the world, international diplomacy: everything, in fact, except the demise of Jennifer Burke.

We were thundering down a man made canyon, past one of those areas of freeway where the workmen had made a mistake and built an exit leading to a wall of sheer rock. Abruptly, Seaton grabbed my arm, almost sending us headlong into the aforementioned wall.

"Next left, next left!" he cried.

"What? Where?"

"It's coming up, you have to watch for it. The sign says Upper Fairlight Ridge. It's the back way. Authentic country road, much more attractive than this expressway! There! Now!"

"Mary, Jesus, and Jason!" shouted Paul as I skidded across four lanes of speeding maniacs and lurched onto the exit road. I slowed as soon as possible, though my heart was still dangerously over the speed limit.

"Where to now, Seaton, seeing we're still alive?"

"Just keep to this lovely old dirt road, there's a turn to the right at about fifty kilometers, just after a picturesque little potters' gallery. We might stop there. It's absolutely marvelous, pots of every shape and size."

"Good," said Paul, "I'm busting for a piss."

"We're going west now, aren't we?" I said. "I thought Malanga was north."

"It's northwest," Seaton announced confidently. "And this country is so beautiful. We may add a couple of hours on the journey, but it will be worth it. Just drive on, I'll tell you where to go."

"God," remarked Paul, "You are such a bossy, opinionated person! Except in bed."

Seaton flushed scarlet. "Now, don't be silly," he spluttered.

"I'm not being silly," Paul continued. "I should know!"

Seaton turned to me with an inane smile. He was sweating visibly. "Paul will have his little joke!" He laughed halfheartedly.

"A joke?" Paul exploded. "Sex with me wasn't that bad, was it? It's not my fault if you didn't rise to the occasion!"

Seaton laughed harder and more mirthlessly. "Stop it, Paul," he said, "or Marc will start believing you. Think of your vows!"

"What vows?" said Paul. "I'm not one of the Sisters of Perpetual Indulgence. Just because I slept with you doesn't make it a vocation!"

"Stop it!" said Seaton through gritted teeth.

"Give it a rest, Paul," I said, enjoying every second. "He's straight, and you're deliberately embarrassing him."

"Straight? Straight like Joan Crawford's coathanger!"

"Could we drop the subject?" Seaton snapped.

Luckily, Seaton was so put out by this exchange that he not only dropped that subject but all others as well. We had twenty minutes of blissful silence to enjoy the scenery without his commentary.

We passed by the hamlet of Upper Fairlight Ridge, which consisted entirely of a dog and two contradictory speed-limit signs. Eventually, the road wound down the mountainside and, to our left, a vast pale-green valley opened out. I saw, with dismay, our road meandering haphazardly through the valley toward more hills in the distance. There was no indication of a turn-off.

"Ahh," breathed Seaton. "Look at that vista! I could write a symphony about it, but Beethoven already has."

"Too bad," said Paul.

"Mind you, I don't know that he quite captured it."

As we got nearer, I could make out a small cottage by the roadside, with two cars parked outside, a land rover and an open BMW sports.

"Is that the potters' gallery?" I asked.

"Yes," said Seaton, "it must be. It's ages since I passed through here."

"Or anyone else did," added Paul, who gets more and more uncomfortable the farther he travels from Oxford Street.

"Pit stop coming up," I announced as I swung into the parking area. The cottage was, indeed, as Seaton had described it, picturesque. Deliberately so. It was painted pale pink, had a blue door, and chintzy white curtains that would have done Enid Blyton proud. A vine, copiously sprouting flat variegated leaves, climbed tenaciously up one wall and halfway across the roof. A gleaming white picket fence completed the picture. The whole effect was studied and unreal; I almost expected June Allyson to come prancing down the path.

"It's changed somehow," muttered Seaton.

We walked up the path and I spied a small wooden sign that clarified all. In Gothic lettering it read: *THE QUEEN'S TEA ROOMS*. The apostrophe in *Queen's* was a pink triangle.

"We're here, we're there, we're everywhere!" sang Paul delightedly.

Inside were a dozen or so tables with starched muslin cloths and a small vase of wildflowers on each one. Flock wallpaper of a tasteful canary-yellow brightened up the room, which was just as well because at one end, perched on the mantle above an antique fire grate, stood a horrifying portrait of Queen Victoria. The royal personage was clutching her scepter and staring viciously at the diners, daring them to misbehave in her presence. She looked, as ever, like a malevolent feral pig.

Two chunky girls in denim sat at a far table, smoking, laughing, and drinking enormous pink milk shakes. They evidently belonged to the land rover. We seated ourselves, our backs to good Queen Vic, and perused the menu. Loganberries featured prominently. There was a loganberry salad, loganberry health shake, loganberry tea, loganberry pie, and homemade loganberry ice cream served on a loganberry coulis. As an alternative, summer berry pudding was also available.

"What's with the loganberries?" asked Paul.

"We grow 'em, pet."

The waiter/owner had materialized out of nowhere. He was the thinnest man I'd ever seen, with a hawk nose, an old-fashioned pencil mustache, and long, thinning black hair. He wore jeans and a pink T-shirt, covered by a long apron. The apron was stained here and there with splashes of dark red; loganberry, I presumed, unless our waiter was also the village axe murderer.

"They're in season," he continued. "Come March, everything'll be raspberry. Are you eating?"

"Ooh, yes!" said Seaton, rubbing his hands together. "A good healthy meal is just what the doctor ordered! I've been driving for days!"

"Just a coffee, thanks," I answered.

"I'll have the jumbo iced chocolate," said Paul.

"Well! Where to start? I'll have the pie and the ice cream thing, a jumbo loganberry frappe, and a Vienna coffee," smiled Seaton. "And I need to use the bathroom."

"And so you shall!" Paul quipped.

"Through the kitchen and out the back," said the waiter, indicating with a bony finger. Seaton hauled himself up and followed the waiter into the kitchen.

"Don't be long," Paul called after him. He turned to me.

"Caro, this is hideous. He's a superhuman bore, and we've found out fuck all!"

"I'm afraid so," I admitted. "I'm beginning to think Seaton has nothing to do with it. How could anyone talk so much and not give something away?"

"Blah blah blah! No wonder Jen threatened to top herself. He would have driven her to drink."

"Or into the drink. Perhaps it was suicide after all."

"Oh, you don't think that, do you? Not after what's been happening over that diary!"

"No, no. My brain's numb, that's all. Let's get things clear. What would we like to know about Seaton?"

"Whether he was skulking around like a hippo in the grass at Dame Norma's."

"Right. So we need to ask him what he was doing in Brisbane that weekend. He'll have some convincing story prepared."

"Yeah, and it'll probably include the whole history of the place."

"We could ask about his and Jennifer's engagement. Who proposed to whom?"

"Jen did the propositioning, I'll bet."

"Why?"

Paul smirked. "Well, in my limited experience, Seaton's not too hot at making the first move. And what's this coy act about sex, all of a sudden! He's so embarrassed. He must think I told you all the gory details."

"Didn't you?"

"Not all. Some things are professional secrets."

"I wouldn't like it if some young stud went around telling the world I couldn't get it up."

"Did I say that? I just said it took ages! He'd eaten too much. He got there in the end."

"How romantic. But he's really embarrassed because he thinks we're a heavy couple."

"You and me?"

"Yes, and that I'm the jealous type. He's frightened I'll discover the truth!"

"Oh, come on! That's ridiculous!"

Paul can be so insensitive. I was insulted.

"What's ridiculous?" I retorted. "That we could be a couple? Get stuffed! I'll have you know I've got a boyfriend younger than you! Or did have, for a couple of days."

Paul looked chastened. "I didn't mean it to sound like that, caro. You know you're an attractive man. I often get horny just thinking about you."

"You do not."

"I do. On a bus, usually. Come on now, kiss and make up."

He took my head in his hands and planted a big wet one on the lips. It went on and on!

"Paul," I gasped, "put that tongue away!"

"Why?" he answered, dragging me back. "I feel like it. What are friends for?" (Sometimes he can be very sweet.)

Queen Victoria practically burst out of her frame with rage. "Slut!" she announced. I looked up hastily. It wasn't Her Majesty who had spoken but our waiter. He'd materialized again, this time with a tray of steaming coffees and loganberry nibblies. Unlike the queen in the picture, he was smiling. "Your pie will be ready in a minute," he added, and glanced across at the kitchen door. There stood two figures who had been watching us. One, of course, was Seaton. He had the most extraordinary look on his face: a mixture of fear, disappointment, and lust. The other was the trim, well-groomed figure of Charles Mignon.

Paul's expression was a textbook study of a queen confronted by the two people he liked least in the universe.

Charles took the initiative, beaming and holding out his hand as he approached us. I shook it; it was limp.

"Well! *Quel* surprise! Marc and Paul. I knew you'd be joining us this weekend, but I didn't expect to meet you so far off the beaten track. Developed a loganberry fetish, have we?"

"Actually, I'm allergic to them," Paul said dryly.

"You don't know what you're missing."

Charles seated himself between us, patting Paul paternally on the thigh. Seaton looked put out, but brightened up completely when his pie was served. He tucked into it in full Billy Bunter fashion. Charles, meanwhile, chatted away cheerily.

"Don't forget our devious little plan. Consider yourselves recruited."

"What plan was that?" I asked.

"To work on Roy, remember? I want him to take the plunge and produce Gluck's *Orfeo* at next year's festival. There's a disused barn on the property that I've had a look at, and I think it will make a perfect 18th-century style theatre. The proportions are excellent. The acoustics, too."

"Why should he spend all that money?" asked Paul, who was feeling contrary. "His festival's a success already."

Charles sighed. "Yes, yes it is—at a provincial level. My plan would put it in the forefront of the international festival circuit."

"Sounds reasonable," I commented. (Charles always sounded reasonable.)

"At the moment the festival's only as good as the individual performers, and their standards can vary, as I know too well! But with my theatre, Malanga would become an institution, attracting the top talent from all over the globe. Once it's up and running, we could stage a new opera every year. There are hundreds of beautiful works waiting to be revived—by the right people, of course. Naturally, I would be involved in a consultative capacity, and, " he winked smarmily at Seaton, "I trust our most promising young conductor will be the musical director."

"A privilege," mumbled Seaton, spitting tiny flecks of pastry everywhere.

"Is your protégé here?" I asked Charles.

"Young Raoul has a singing lesson this afternoon. He'll be coming up later. He's very dedicated to his craft." As he said this, Charles stared pointedly at Paul.

"So am I!" Paul protested. "I happen to have a sore throat and I won't give my public less than one hundred percent."

Charles sniffed.

"Would you produce the operas?" I asked in an attempt to avoid unpleasantness.

Charles smiled. "I believe I could. I know more about them than anyone else. So you've begun to admire the old masters, have you? A man of taste!"

"I haven't entirely given up my loyalty to Renata!"

"To whom?"

"Tebaldi."

His smile faded. "I'd best be getting underway. It's quite a drive back to the expressway."

"Oh, don't go that way," said Seaton, spraying us with his last mouthful. "There's a better route not far from here."

"Always looking for a better route," said Paul.

"Are you certain?" said Charles doubtfully. "I don't know it."

Seaton bubbled with enthusiasm. "Just follow us!"

"Well," Charles suggested to him, "why don't you come in my car and direct me? It must be a squeeze with three of you."

Seaton looked confused. "Oh...err..."

"Yes!" Paul exclaimed. "We don't mind."

"OK, I will. It'll be fun! I won't bother changing my bags over. You'll take them for me won't you?" he simpered to me.

"Of course," I said.

"Anything," said Paul.

"Come along then," said Charles, getting up. "See you there!" He waved airily and they left. As I heard Charles's BMW starting up, I realized we'd been lumbered with the bill for Seaton's loganberry indulgences.

"They're going," I said. "We'd better hurry if we want to follow them."

"Fuck that," Paul replied. "Let's head back to the freeway."

"I'd love to."

"You know, caro, I'm starting to think Charles is our man."

"Oh yes? What's your reasoning?"

"I've only got one reason, but it's a beauty. He's an arsehole."

Once back on the road, we made up for lost time. The gorgeous weather and the unexpected loss of Seaton put us both in a lighthearted mood. We gossiped at length about people who weren't connected to our investigations: Paul told me how he'd sorted out the famously volatile Stephen and Geoffrey situation. Basically, Paul had called a summit meeting and the three of them, reunited in their raw contempt for Rodney, had bitched enthusiastically for a whole day. As for Rodney and Ng, they had moved out of Paul's flat leaving at least some of the furniture in one piece, so he was happy.

Before we knew it, we arrived at Malanga and the Cox Wines Estate.

The place was divine. Vineyards stretched in every direction from the central homestead, built on a slight incline and protected from wind by a row of majestic cypresses. The house itself was a two-story colonial mansion, lovingly restored, settled behind a vast semicircular driveway. Nearby were old stables converted into garages, and a short way off I could see several sheds of varying sizes, some enormous, and a large tank traced with a scaffolding of narrow metal ladders and walkways. The sight of this monolith was softened by the nearby presence of a beautiful white gum. Surrounding the entrance to the homestead were immaculate lawns and tamed wild gardens, through which an ancient bumpy path wended its way.

As we got closer, the house became even more charming and welcoming. The windows in the second story were of the old colonial style, and appeared to have a slight yellow tint about them. They stretched right across; there were evidently many rooms.

"Paul, my God. It's heaven!"

"You're not wrong, caro. I'm speechless."

"Have you ever seen a house like it!"

He glanced at me. "The house? Oh, yeah, to die for. However, I was referring to that!"

He pointed. Over on the far side of the grounds was a young man pushing a manual lawn mower. He was tall and very tanned, with dark curly hair. He wore a reversed baseball cap, jeans, and a sweaty khaki shirt with the sleeves ripped off (as if by wild animals). His arms and legs were like tree trunks. As I pulled up near the homestead, he dropped the mower, waved, and leisurely strolled over.

"Hello," he said, a boyish smile revealing a sexy gap between his two front teeth.

"Honey, I'm home!" Paul crooned.

"Uh, sorry?"

"Take no notice of him," I said.

"You guys have come the wrong way for the cellars," he said. "It's the other entrance, but the sign come down." He had the sexiest Irish accent.

"We're guests," I replied. "I'm Marc Petrucci, this is Paul Silverton."

"Hi," said Paul.

"Shaunna and Roy are expecting us."

"Oh, right," he smiled. "Sorry 'bout that. You can park in the second garage over there, and I'll help you with your bags. I'm Brendan."

"Hi," said Paul again. "Marc can take the bags and you can carry me. I'm paraplegic."

Brendan looked confused.

We parked. "Paraplegic!" I snorted. "You're insane! I'm amazed you didn't just wrestle him to the ground and get right into it!"

"Darn. Why didn't I think of that?"

Brendan insisted on looking after our baggage, and directed

us down the bumpy path to find Shaunna. She was bustling about in a large well-stocked kitchen. When she saw us, she wiped her hands on a towel and ran over, giving me a tight squeeze.

"Darling, hullo!" she said. "You've made good time. No one else has arrived yet. I'm doing a little prep for tonight, but I'll bung on the kettle right this minute! How good to see you here at last!"

"It's great to see you, too," I said. "This is my friend Paul."

"You're my greatest fan!" he gushed as she hugged him.

"Isn't that nice! Am I really? Now sit down at the table, which I should tell you is a priceless piece of ancient history, and tell me all. What have you been up to?"

"I'm doing some private coaching. Nothing very exciting, I'm afraid." (*Why do I always sound so boring?*)

"What a life!" she laughed. "And what do you do, Paul?"

"I'm in show business," he said. "Mega-musical spectaculars."

"Terrific! Leading roles, I trust."

"Any day now."

"Hang in there, darling. I know it will happen for you."

Paul took her hand. "I hope you'll be coming back into showbiz soon."

"Thank you, but I don't miss it. I've got my Logie Award, and I think I'd rather be a real person!"

"Can I see your Logie?" he asked in a hushed tone.

"Darling, you can sleep with it if you like." She stopped in her tracks. "Oh, did you get my message? You were supposed to bring Seaton!"

"Don't worry," I answered. "He went with Charles Mignon. They're going the back way."

"I see," she said. "What back way?"

"Hey!" Roy barged into the room, slamming the door behind him. "Brendan told me you were here! Welcome!"

"Hello, Roy. You remember Paul?"

"'Course I do! HAR HAR HAR!" He slapped Paul on the back so hard I thought the musical comedy star might throw up.

"I'm just making tea," Shaunna said.

"Tea! This isn't the bloody vicarage! A glass of red, that's what we're after. I thought we'd start 'em off with the merlot. It's just peaking!" He grabbed a bottle and filled four glasses. "Here we go! Cheers." Roy drained his glass in seconds flat; Shaunna, I noticed, was not far behind.

"Mmm. Bloody good! Ay?"

I took a sip. "Excellent!"

"You can say no," Shaunna laughed. "He'll have you comatose by 5 o'clock if you don't!"

"What's wrong with that? That's what they're here for! We don't care, as long as you don't piss on the carpet. Come on, I'll give you a tour of the cellars."

"They haven't even seen their room, yet!" Shaunna protested.

"Ar, they can play hide the sausage later! Ay?"

"Roy!"

"HAR HAR!"

For the next hour we were literally dragged from one end of the property to the other. Roy showed us the different vines, with a well-researched lecture included on each variety of grape, its history and characteristics. Naturally, we sampled them all.

We toured the cellars, which were much bigger than they seemed from the outside, although we weren't allowed amongst the vintages. They were locked in their own select alcove.

"It's for me as much as security," barked Roy. "If it was open, I'd' have finished the bloody lot by now!"

We also glanced into the old barn Charles had mentioned. I could immediately see his point: It was perfectly proportioned for theatrical purposes.

"I dunno what to do with this barn," Roy said. "We have concerts here during the festival, the indoors stuff anyhow. I'd as soon hold 'em outside. Charlie wants me to build a theatre."

"It's the right shape," Paul pointed out.

"The acoustics are good, too," I added. "Listen how our voices carry."

"Yair. It's a thought. There's a few other ideas floating around. To tell you the truth, I like it the way it is now—useless! HAR! A good place to sneak away to when everything gets a bit much. All these nooks and crannies—a bloke can disappear for a while. I've got a nice pinot noir stashed 'round here somewhere. Let's find it."

At the back, next to a makeshift stage platform, the barn was divided into a series of small rooms.

"These were stables," Roy explained. "The whole joint was an inn, you know, back in the 1870s. It was on the main road and they got all the passing trade goin' through to Queensland. The house was a pub. Still is, I reckon. HAR HAR!"

We sniffed around three of these rooms; in the third we found a cupboard stocked with wines and glasses.

"Ah! Here we are!"

For Roy, every new bottle opening was a celebration. He had a corkscrew around his neck on a string, the way normal people carry their specs. The pinot noir, not usually a great favorite of mine, was delectable. Before long, the three of us had drained two whole bottles of it.

"Come on!" Roy thundered. We staggered to our feet, and he led us to the base of the big metal vat. I gazed up at the crisscrossing ladders and felt less than excited.

"This is for the mass-produced stuff. The thing's computerized. It monitors the temperature, controls sediment levels, picks up bloody Sky Channel! We gotta climb up to the top—the view's one in a million. You first, Marc!"

"I'm not good with heights," I protested lamely.

"Me either," mumbled Paul who was atypically quiet and looked pale.

"Jesus, what a couple of girls!" Roy boomed. "It's nothing! Just don't look up, down, or to either side! Brendan and me are running up this thing like rabbits every five minutes. He's there now."

I looked up again, and saw Brendan smiling and waving to us from a great height. The color miraculously returned to Paul's cheeks.

"Oh, let's give it a try," he chirped.

"Not me," I said. "I'll wait here."

I sat on the lower rungs while Roy, followed cautiously by Paul, began their ascent. I was sure the view was magnificent; I was equally certain what view Paul was interested in.

I stared out across the vineyards and let my mind wander. A feeling of contentment rolled over me. The place was so calm and peaceful and slightly out of focus! I breathed more easily than I had for a week. This would be an opportunity to put the question of murder to one side, a welcome respite from recent life-threatening escapades.

There was no one here to worry about. I had virtually changed my mind about Seaton: He was too self-centered to notice another person, let alone murder them. He might kill for a second helping of dessert, but nothing less. As for Charles, Paul's dislike was not enough to condemn him in my book. He had no discernable motive and was far too reasonable to be a murderer. Anyway, I reflected, why go to the trouble of killing someone 'live' when you can draw and quarter them in print?

No, it was people closer to Jennifer I should be considering—Jude, for example. If there was a way to discount the sauna incident, then Jude was my prime suspect. She was insanely jealous, that was quite clear—jealous of Seaton, of Randolph, even Sir Fred. But how could she sneak into 9-1-ZERO? Would she pass for a man wearing only a towel? Plenty of the men in there wouldn't!

Then there was Sir Fred himself: the central character in this whole business, whom I'd never met. Did he have a motive? His affair with Jen turned nasty, judging from the last diary entry, but exactly how nasty? Was blackmail involved? He had told her the deal was off, but in the photo of her, taken not long after, she seemed very pleased with herself. Was it Sir Fred whom she wanted to see alone at the party, perhaps to threaten him in some way? Of course, Sir Fred wasn't 'on our team' (to the best of my knowledge—one never knows), but maybe Jen had made that remark to put Paul off the track. I wouldn't blame her; Paul never keeps his trap shut.

"Hoy! Look out!"

The panic in Roy's voice scattered my thoughts. I jumped to my feet and glanced up to see Paul, halfway to the top on a tiny platform, leaning over and clutching the railing. "Marc!" he called and, without further ado, threw up an excellent merlot, a very good pinot noir, a dozen other vintages, a jumbo iced chocolate, and his breakfast. I leapt to one side: Unfortunately, it was the wrong side.

There was horrified silence for a moment, then Roy burst out laughing. "Bull's-eye!" he cried.

I had no alternative but to remove my pants and shirt. Brendan was down in a flash and quickly procured a plastic bag for me to seal them in, prior to burning. He then helped Roy fetch Paul, as I stuck my head under a tap. We headed back to the house: me in a vile mood and not much else, Roy roaring with laughter, and Paul, pale and sylph-like, cradled in the rock-solid arms of Brendan. Due to public demand, I walked apart from the others.

I was relieved to find that the other guests still hadn't arrived. Shaunna showed us up to our room, and Brendan proceeded to tuck Paul into bed: a queen-size bed. Paul gazed up at him with moist doe-like eyes and whispered a thank you that would have done Marilyn Monroe proud. I took a long, hot shower in the tasteful en suite.

"I'm terribly sorry," Paul whispered as I crept out to unpack some clean clothes. "I tried to warn you."

"What a cheap way to get into Brendan's clutches!" I observed. "You had better sleep it off."

"I will. Is anyone else here yet?"

"No. Seaton and Charles must have gotten lost."

"I wonder if Seaton's baggage is next door."

"Why?"

"You could go through it. You might find something."

"No!"

"Just a thought." He yawned. "Ooh, my head."

"Try not to be sick in the bed. I have to sleep in it later, you know."

"Shaunna must think we're lovers. Everyone does!"

"I'll see if I can change the sleeping arrangements."

"If we get a choice, put me in with Brendan."

"You're sounding much better."

I closed the door quietly and stepped into the hallway. It, like the rooms, was authentically restored in the period style with wallpaper, light fittings, and a tiny bureau all complementing each other perfectly. In fact, it was as tasteful as Dame Norma's decor was garish.

The silence was palpable. I loitered for a millisecond of indecision, then carefully tried the next door. It opened into a similar bedroom and there, stacked against the wall, were Seaton's bags. I closed the door and sat on the bed, staring at his flowery luggage. *I do have some snooping rights*, I thought. *My car carried it all this way.*

I tried the smallest bag first, but it was locked. A second one was jam-packed full of music, vocal scores of operas. I quickly browsed through: They were all scholarly new editions of works by Monteverdi, Handel, Purcell, and Gluck. No sign of the Rossini, which Seaton had told us was his upcoming project for the Opera.

I decided to go for broke. The largest bag had catches and a zipper. After putting up a brief struggle it sprang open easily and sprayed shirts, socks and big underpants all over the place. There seemed to be nothing else of interest, and I was hastily cramming them back in when I found something wrapped in a particularly repulsive pair of mauve slacks. It was a plastic bag containing a video—hard-core porn in a mountain setting, entitled *Hot, Hung, and Himalayan*—and two leather-bound, cylindrical containers. In the smaller of these was an ivory conductor's baton. In the other nestled an enormous black dildo.

I was examining the latter massive piece of equipment when the door opened and in strode Jude's friend, Lavinia.

"Ew!" she said. "Yuck!"

"Lavinia! Hello again."

"Hello! Well! I guess I've stopped something very titillating from happening just in time."

"No, no, this isn't mine."

"I can see that,' she answered dryly. "It's black and unattached."

"What a coincidence. I didn't know you'd be here this weekend. Um, were you invited?"

"No, I broke in. Of course I was invited! And I did know you'd be here, though I sure didn't expect to meet you in my room with a salami up your arse!"

"Oh. Is this your room?"

"I always stay here. I like to face west, I don't want the sun waking me up at some ungodly hour. It does that in the country, you know. Christ Almighty, will you put that dick away?"

"Sorry."

I hastily repacked the bag as I tried to make casual conversation.

"Is Jude here with you?"

"No, she had to work, she says. I don't think she cares too much for Roy."

"I suppose he might be pretty overbearing to someone like Jude."

"What's 'someone like Jude'?"

"You know…ah, a lesbian."

"Is that what she is?" she bellowed. "Well, lucky I'm fucking her!" She screamed with laughter.

"That came out wrong," I mumbled apologetically.

"I don't find Roy overbearing," she said. "But then, he is my brother."

I might have known! They were like brother and sister.

"I thought your name was Cooper," I said.

"I changed it, of course. Coxedge! I refuse to wear a moniker with the word 'cock' in it. It's just not where I'm coming from."

"Roy never mentioned you at university."

"Is that where you two met up? In those days we weren't on speaking terms. I was an early feminist, he was a shit. We're mates now, though."

"Good."

"I'm the one who's mellowed," she barked. "Not him! Roy thinks my work is utter crap. I don't suppose that surprises you."

"No."

"Why? Do you think it's crap, too?"

"No!"

"Buy something and prove it. Now tell me: Is this your room or not? I was told you were next door!"

"I am. My friend Paul's asleep in there."

"So you thought you'd pop in here and get down and dirty. Fair enough. Are these your bags?"

"Not really."

"They're not? What are you doing poking around in someone else's luggage?"

"I…err…they belong to Seaton Frith, a friend of mine. I lent him something. He's not here yet and I needed this… thing urgently."

"Not that ugly black thing?"

"No, another thing."

She snatched the videocassette off the bed.

"Is this it? *Hot, Hung, and Himalayan*?"

"Err, yes."

"You're a filthy pervert, not that I care." She sniffed the air. "What's that?"

"What?"

"It's you! You must have stepped in some shit or something. Check your shoes."

"Oh. It's not my shoes I'm afraid, it's me."

A look of utter disgust came over her face.

"Maybe I'll get another room," she said. "You keep on doing what you're doing."

"No, I've finished. I mean, I'm not doing anything. I was just going downstairs for a drink. My friend's been sick."

"I'm not surprised."

I'd had enough of this. "Listen, Lavinia, you're misunderstanding the situation. These aren't my things—"

"Sit down," she said.

I did.

"Now, Doll, you listen to me. I don't give a rat's if you want to root around in somebody else's boxer shorts for your own weird sexual kicks. I expect the guy wouldn't be thrilled to find out, but I can keep a secret. OK? And you can do me a little favor in return. I've got plans for an old barn Roy isn't using."

"I've seen it."

"Yeah? Well! Don't you reckon it would make a first-class gallery? It's big, it's light and spacious. It'll be perfect for my pieces, and with the Malanga festival I'll have a captive clientele. All I want you to do is back me up; just sit there agreeing and repeating the words 'fabulous idea' over and over. Not too hard. Deal?"

"Charles Mignon wants to turn it into a theatre."

She bared her teeth. "I know all about that. But we're not going to let him."

I felt an urge to display a little of the fabled Petrucci independence.

"I think," I said nonchalantly, "it would make a delightful little theatre."

Lavinia's eyes narrowed, the light glinting menacingly off her nose-ring. "You think that, do you?"

"I do. Yup."

"And are you planning to underwrite it?"

"Err, no."

"Well, you better change your plans. Because when I tell Charles Mignon who you are, you'll never get him off your back."

"Who I am? You mean Jen's uncle?"

"Jen's rich uncle who throws three quarters of a million bucks a year at the opera. That particular uncle! And it won't only be greedy, smarmy old Charles: They'll all be after you, as you well know."

"Jude told you."

"Did you think she wouldn't?" She reached into her bag and brought out a neatly rolled joint.

"Cigar?" she asked, lighting up.

"No, thank you."

"Well, I'm going to change, Uncle Scrooge. So piss off and take those bags with you."

CHAPTER 19

*S*haken and stirred by my confrontation with Lavinia, I was only too happy to accept a glass of chilled Chablis from Roy. The moment I set foot in the stately sitting room, he materialized.

"A lovely little drop, just the shot to loosen us up before dinner."

He handed me a glass that held roughly a gallon and plonked the dripping bottle down on top of the grand piano.

"How's your lily-livered mate?"

"Sleeping like a baby with a hangover."

Shaunna soon joined us. Bottles were emptied, one after another, as we spent a very pleasant hour reminiscing. She recalled the days when she and Roy were first married and living in an inner-city terrace. I'd forgotten, but they used to throw extravagant parties that were the talk of the social pages. A party at Coxedges' was the favorite haunt for rich entrepreneurs and long-legged soapie stars who wished to exchange favors. I didn't belong in either of those groups, but I went as an onlooker and always had a hysterical time. My ex found the crowd intimidating, so we stopped going.

Eventually, 5 o'clock loomed and our fond memories began to wear a bit thin, as memories do. There was still no sign of the other guests.

"Where's Lavinia?" asked Shaunna. "I thought she was joining us."

"Thank heaven for small mercies!" roared Roy.

Brendan appeared, carrying a reasonably sized suitcase.

"Charles is here," he whispered to Roy, as the aforementioned disgruntled critic swept in.

"Greetings at long last!" said Charles, seething beneath his calm exterior. Seaton followed. He looked unusually contrite.

"What kept you?" I inquired brightly. "Been on a jaunt through the countryside?"

Charles eyed me with undisguised hostility. "You were wise not to follow us," he sneered. "It so happens there is not, never was, and from all appearances never will be, a back way!"

"I thought it sounded odd," said Shaunna.

"We traveled hundreds of miles, right to the edge of nowhere and back. Not only that, he insisted we stop at the Queen's Tea Rooms again!"

"Their loganberry layer cake is very more-ish," Seaton muttered uncomfortably.

Shaunna presented her best ex-television, current-top-hostess smile. "Why don't you two unpack, have a rest and a drink, and we'll get dinner underway as soon as you're ready."

"Yeah, let's eat at twilight," said Roy romantically, "before we're all shit-faced."

I didn't want to wake Paul by sneaking into my room, but if I stayed drinking with Roy downstairs, I wouldn't survive beyond the hors d'oeuvres. I was standing in the hallway, being indecisive, when Seaton came bustling along.

"Ah! Marc! Would you help me drag my bags inside? Thanks so much!"

I wasn't greatly desirous to do this, since I'd only recently dragged his baggage into the hall, but I could hardly tell him that, so I obliged. His new room was at the other end of the house. By the time we got there I was exhausted.

"Just over against the wall, Marc. You're a gentleman!"

"Mind if I sit down for a moment?"

"Not at all. Actually, I thought we might have a little chat."

He closed the door and flung himself down on the bed (and, I feared, almost through the floor.)

"It's about Jennifer Burke, my ex-fiancée."

My ears pricked up. Was this the long-awaited confession?

"What about her?"

"Charles tells me she was a close friend of…of your wife's."

"Paul took her to the party at Dame Norma's."

"So Charles said. Well, I hope I didn't give you both the wrong impression, that day we first met. I may have been a bit offhand about poor Jennifer. The fact is, I liked Jen very much indeed. I thought we'd make a sensational team, artistically speaking. I was awfully upset when she dropped off the twig. The cliff, I should say. I can't help thinking if I'd been there, I may have been able to prevent it."

"Why didn't you escort her to the party yourself?"

"We had called off our engagement by then, although we hadn't gone public. The strange thing is, I was expecting to see her in Brisbane that weekend! I was going to play for her; she'd even bought me a plane ticket! Her favorite uncle had died and she wanted to sing at his funeral. I was supposed to meet her at the service. We'd rehearsed the "Pie Jesu" from Faure's *Requiem*."

"And she never showed up."

"Very strange. I thought I'd gotten the time wrong. You know, it's never the time it ought to be in Queensland! I spent a day sitting through one funeral service after another. I was positively grief-stricken by the end! When it dawned on me I'd been tricked, I was absolutely livid! I couldn't eat!"

"My God."

"But later, of course, I realized she was simply getting me out of the way so she could end it all."

"Very sensitive of her."

"I thought so, too. That's the kind of caring relationship we had. I have a lot to thank her for. She introduced me to Charles."

"Jennifer knew Charles?"

"Oh, yes, my word. She was very interested in his scheme, and he was keen to use her. Plan B, she called it! She was terribly organized."

"Plan B?"

"The idea was she'd gain a reputation in 'authentic' repertoire. There are some fantastic roles for a soprano in some of those old operas, just as dramatic as Verdi in their way. Charles convinced her she'd make a huge splash. He has a long-term vision, you know. He says so himself. He talked about critical acclaim, massive publicity and enormous public interest, private funding, all that. He's very convincing."

"Did Jennifer have a Plan A?"

"Do you know, it never occurred to me to ask!" He jumped up and hoisted the large suitcase onto his bed. "Of course, I had no inkling of the desperate act she was contemplating. I would have stopped her! I'd appreciate it if you would tell that to Paul. He seems to have turned against me."

"Has he? All right. What will I say?"

"I don't know, say…Oh! Shit!"

"What is it?"

"Someone's been through my things! Look! All my best clothes are crushed!"

They're your best? I thought.

"Brendan left your bags in the hall, exactly where we found them."

"Who could have done this?" Seaton muttered as he slid the dildo swiftly under his pillow. "Who else is staying here?"

"There's Paul, Charles, me, Lavinia—"

"Who's Lavinia?" he asked, as he quickly kicked *Hot, Hung, and Himalayan* under the bed.

"What are you doing?"

"Kicking off my shoe. Who's Lavinia?"

"I met her at a dinner party. Do you know a girl named Jude who works for the opera? She's in finance."

"I certainly do. She was a friend of Jen's. Dreadful person." He pulled a face. "A lesbian, you know."

"Well, Lavinia is Jude's girlfriend."

"The 'friend' friend?"

"Yes. In a big way."

"But she's a raving maniac! Jen told me about her."

"What did she say?"

"Just that this pushy dyke was hanging around like a vulture. She threatened poor Jen a couple of times. What's she doing here? Why would she go through my things?"

"Was Jennifer having a sexual relationship with Jude?"

Seaton slammed the suitcase shut. "I don't know. That was entirely their business, I would say."

"Yes, of course."

He strode to the door.

"Please excuse me. I'm going to have it out."

"What?"

"This bag business. Where is this Lavinia person?"

"Ah...I wouldn't mention it if I were you. Is anything missing?"

"I don't think so, but—"

"Then you mustn't say a word."

"Mustn't I? Why not?"

That was a good question.

"It's...not done."

"It's not done for lunatic lesbians to rifle through a man's personal effects!"

"What I mean is, it's dangerous to aggravate people in her condition."

"She has a condition?"

"Yes, she's psychopathically unstable. It runs in the family. Shaunna told me that they asked her up this weekend to help her recuperate. It's very peaceful here: the scenery, the quiet, the alcohol...a calming influence. It may do the trick."

"Recuperate? I'll help her recuperate!"

"Shaunna is concerned Lavinia doesn't turn violent."

Seaton bit his lip.

"Violent?"

"It's touch-and-go, apparently. Any confrontation could tip her over the edge. She could lose it completely. She lives under the flight path; a lot of those people suffer from this condition."

"What's the condition called?"

"It's called"—I wracked my brain—"jumbo jitter syndrome."

"Never heard of it. Sounds ghastly!"

"Unspeakable. I'm glad I could warn you in time. Now I must go and wake Paul with a gentle kiss. See you at dinner."

I tiptoed back to my room. Paul was already up, though not quite up and about. He sat on the bed, humming to himself and gently rocking back and forth.

"How's your head?" I asked.

"Not brilliant, but I'll be OK. I've taken pills for it. By the time dinner is served, I should be at my sparkling best."

"Well, I've had a couple of interesting conversations. You remember Lavinia, Jude's girlfriend? The artist I met at Roland's?"

"You mentioned her. I've never met her."

"You will tonight, and I want you to try and remember if she was at Dame Norma's party."

"Ooh! Is she a suspect?"

"She is now! Seaton told me she was hanging around Jude and Jennifer like a vulture. As soon as Jen was out of the way, she swooped!"

"Aren't lesbians sluts!"

"Look who's talking."

"Is she the type who'd push a girl off a cliff out of jealousy?"

"I'd say she's the type who'd push a girl off a cliff to get a better look at the view."

"Tough, eh?"

"Formidable. She's Roy's sister."

"I get the picture. Why were you talking to Fat Features?"

"A mix-up over bags. By the way, he can't understand why you've gone off him."

"It's entirely personal. Let's change the subject, I don't want to throw up again!"

"Please don't. And go easy on the wine tonight."

"But of course. I never mix."

He stood up, swayed, and abruptly sat down again.

"Are you sure you're OK?" I asked.

"No, but these pills are guaranteed to do their stuff. My head is clearing with every throb."

I glared at him dubiously. "Move over," I said. "You're not the only one who's been hitting the piss." I lay beside him.

"Caro," he murmured.

"Don't go back to sleep," I cautioned him, closing my eyes for a five-minute nap.

Of course, we both drifted off into a wine-sodden dreamland. A loud knocking at the door abruptly woke me.

"Dinner's on, lads!" called Brendan.

"Be right there!" I croaked. I sprang up and quickly changed into something casual and Italian. Paul was already awake, but hadn't dressed. He was sitting on the floor next to his bag, holding a black T-shirt and staring meaningfully at it.

"Hurry up," I said.

"This is beautiful. This is so-o-o-o beautiful!" he murmured.

"Put it on, then."

"Have you ever really looked at this T-shirt, caro? I mean, looked closely? The way it all fits together: It's just incredible." He turned to me beseechingly. His eyes were strangely dark, the pupils wide, deep, and black. "Come and see. The light, the shade...it's all so...mmm."

I knelt next to him. "Paul, if you're still under the weather—" I began.

"Even the sleeve," he said. "See? Isn't that the most fantastic sleeve?" He carefully pulled the T-shirt over his head and stood. "I feel excellent!" He smiled. "Caro. Caro mio. Caro mio! That means "my friend," doesn't it?"

"Sort of. My dear one."

He put his arms around me.

"You're such a dear friend to me, Marc. You're the best

friend a girl ever had. So incredibly friendly. You!"

He licked me gently on the nose.

"Take my arm," I suggested. "Let's go."

"What a sensible idea. You're so sensible, caro. Remember when I was robbed by some piece of street trash and I had a huge party happening that night and I was a mess and everything was fucked and I came crying to you and you organized my whole life? You lent me your blender. Only a true friend lends his blender."

"You broke it. Let's go to dinner."

"Hmm? OK. I'm not hungry, really."

The dining room was yet another tribute to Shaunna's good taste. It was exquisite: the table a vast slab of mahogany, formally set with a bone-china dinner service and the Coxedge family silver. A silver candelabra graced the antique sideboard. The cloth and serviettes were in matching hues: creek-bed beige flecked with ochre. In fact, the room sported more heritage colors than you could poke a burnt stick at, yet the effect was not at all forbidding or artificial. It was individual and, above all, comfy.

The table was set for eight. I noticed each place setting had five wine glasses of various shapes and sizes. The other guests were already present and well underway with their guzzling. Roy sat at the head, Shaunna at the other end. Lavinia had taken the seat nearest to Roy, and Seaton had placed himself as far away from her as possible. Charles sat opposite him.

"Well! Here they are at last!" bellowed Roy. "Don't let a lousy little dinner interrupt anything interesting! HAR HAR HAR!"

"Sorry, we dozed off," I apologized.

Paul sat two down from Seaton, opposite Lavinia. I pulled out the chair next to his.

"Oh, no you don't!" said Roy. "No couples together! You sit over there, Marc. Red or white?"

"White, thanks. Just a half."

"A crisp little Riesling, you'll like it."

So I found myself uncomfortably sandwiched between Charles and Lavinia, staring at an empty chair.

"Raoul not here yet?" I asked Charles.

"I can't think what's keeping him." Charles seemed very put out, still suffering from his long trip, no doubt.

"Red or white, Paul?" Roy asked.

"White, yes. White. White is right."

"Are you sure?" asked Shaunna. "How are you feeling?"

"I feel pretty," Paul sang.

"We haven't met," boomed Lavinia.

"Lavinia Cooper, Paul Silverton," I said.

Paul smiled lovingly at her. "You are an absolutely extraordinary person!" he announced.

"Yeah? You're pretty damn unusual yourself."

"I'll serve the soup," said Shaunna, standing. "Charles was just telling us about the castrati."

"The first and greatest stars of musical theatre," he said.

"Not a very pleasant subject to discuss over dinner," joked Seaton.

"Hope we're not having meatballs!" added Roy jovially.

"As a reconstructed neo-feminist, I can't approve of male castration," said Lavinia. "But speaking as a woman, it rather appeals to me."

"It would," said Roy.

"Even in the age of the great stars, castration was never a legal practice, though the church gave it their unofficial sanction," Charles explained. "The last of the castrati, Alessandro Moreschi, sang in the Sistine Chapel choir."

"He made a recording, I think," said Seaton.

"Oh, yes, but it's a travesty."

"Literally!" Lavinia chortled.

"He was very old," Charles continued, "and his technique was shot to pieces. He sounds like Shirley Temple on a bad day. Moreschi's record is no criterion to judge the famous castrati of the past. They had range, power, technique to burn."

"Look!" said Paul. "The wallpaper's unbelievable!"

Charles froze, mid-lecture.

"In that film—what was it?" I asked.

"*Farinelli*?" suggested Seaton.

"Yes. Didn't they merge two voices by computer, a man's and a woman's, to get the castrato effect?"

Charles sneered. "And that's precisely what it sounded like. A soprano's top—"

"And a man's bottom!" chuckled Seaton.

"A ludicrous film; it quite misrepresented the life and the art of Farinelli. Not a shred of nobility in the staged performances."

"Wow!" exclaimed Paul, who was now looking at the ceiling. All heads turned to him.

"What?" said Lavinia.

"That spider, see, up in the corner? That tiny, tiny spider? Just look at it!"

"What about it?" asked Seaton, turning slightly pale. "Is it deadly?"

"It's amazing," Paul cooed. "Just fucking amazing."

We all stared at the amazing spider, then at Paul. No one spoke.

"I'm starving," Seaton mumbled. At that moment Shaunna returned with a steaming tureen, and Roy filled our clean glasses with the soup wine.

"Minestrone," beamed Shaunna, "*Eccola!*"

"*Brava!*" I echoed.

"Not for me, thanks," said Paul.

"I'll have yours," said Seaton.

"So," I said to Charles as we all tucked in, "you didn't like the Farinelli film?"

He smiled in an oddly grateful way. "I'm not that interested in Farinelli," he said. "He was regarded as a freak, they got that right at least. No, the supreme castrato in my book was Gaetano Guadagni. He and the composer Gluck were at the forefront of the reaction against Farinelli's mechanical, florid style. Guadagni created the role of Orfeo in Gluck's opera in Vienna. By all accounts, he was very good-looking and a strong dramatic presence. You might say he was the Maria Callas of his day: In Guadagni it all came together—drama, music, and the whole superstar syndrome."

"A man with no nuts, a matinee idol?" scoffed Lavinia.

"That's the interesting part," continued Charles patiently.

"Not to me."

"Castrati were literally a race apart. They were gods. Of course they were matinee idols! They had been chosen, singled out from other mere mortals. They sacrificed themselves for Art."

"Bollocks," said Lavinia.

Charles ignored her. "And they were extraordinary singers. We have no way of recreating the impact they made on their contemporaries. Computers, heavens! That's exactly the wrong way to do it! We have to forget our 20th-century gizmos and think ourselves back into the 18th century before we can begin to appreciate such great art."

"One thing you can say in favor of wine," Roy remarked. "We get the same pleasure from it—and the same bloody hangovers they got hundreds of years ago. It hasn't changed. Comes from the very same vines, quite often!"

"In music we're not so lucky," Charles opined. "For our so-called renaissance of Early Music, we've had to recreate old instruments—there aren't enough of the genuine article left and most of those have worn out or deteriorated. Have you heard Beethoven's piano?"

"Neither has he," quipped Seaton.

Charles glared at him. "But the human voice, that's a constant," Charles continued. "Every generation is born with the same vocal chords. The only difference is in what we do with them."

Lavinia laid down her soup spoon and sniffed.

"Well, you've just shot down your own argument," she

crowed. "You're right, we can't go back 200 years, and why the bloody hell should we? Art's function is to reflect and shape contemporary society. Who cares what a bunch of eunuchs were up to at the Court of King Kong the Fifth? It's got fuck all to do with my life! It gives me the shits when I see public money being poured into these museum pieces. We should be nurturing our own young talents, and, I might just add, specifically women, since we've had such a rough deal for the last 5,000 years."

Seaton watched her closely, his eyes wide with apprehension.

Charles smiled benignly. "That might be a valid argument," he admitted, "if modern art wasn't bogged down by fashion, trendiness. and pretentiousness—not to mention the corporate mentality. But it is, with one inescapable result: It's crap."

"Are you saying my work is crap?" she snarled.

"Nobody's work is crap," said Paul. "Everyone's work is wonderful."

"Shut up," snapped Lavinia.

"I think your work's rubbish," laughed Roy.

"Let's have the next course," stammered Seaton nervously. "Lavinia, I, um, I think Charles is actually talking about contemporary music which is, um, a different thing altogether."

Shaunna collected the bowls. "Promise me you won't come to blows till I get back!" she trilled.

"OK," said Lavinia, relaxing. "Anyway, I'll admit I don't care about music. I've got a tin ear. Totally tone deaf!"

"It never ceases to amaze me," crooned Charles, "how people will tell you they're tone-deaf as though it were something to be proud of! It's extraordinary. No one would ever boast: 'I'm incapable of dressing myself,' or 'I don't know left from right,' yet where's the difference? The truth is, tone-deaf people are several rungs lower on the evolutionary ladder. In more enlightened times we'd have had them put down."

"You pompous shithead," snapped Lavinia. "I might as well tell you, I don't have much time for critics."

"I'm a reviewer," Charles drawled.

"You're all so full of yourselves, yet you're entirely irrelevant! Where do you fit into the creative process? You're just an unwelcome spectator, a professional voyeur! It must rot your insides. No wonder you've got bad breath."

Charles blinked. "There's no need to get personal," he said, unconsciously licking his teeth.

"I'm going to help Shaunna in the kitchen," Lavinia replied. She punched Roy on the shoulder as she passed. "I'll talk to you later!"

Roy laughed heartily.

Seaton leaned nervously toward Charles.

"Charles," he whispered, "Please don't criticize her. She might turn ugly."

"Too late!" said Roy, who was enjoying himself immensely.

"My dear Seaton, what are you talking about?" inquired Charles.

"She's pathologically violent."

"Violent? Nonsense. Lavinia's just pathologically opinionated."

"No, she's nuts! She's got this condition. It runs in the family. They're all lunatics, apparently."

"What?" said Roy.

"Yes! Surely you knew? Mumbo jumbo I believe it's called. And she has no respect for other people's property."

"You're talking about my sister, mate."

Seaton opened his mouth and closed it again. He gulped.

"Where on earth did you get this idea?" asked Charles patronizingly.

"Aaaah!" Paul cried, his voice harsh and fearful. He'd broken out in a sweat and was literally shaking. "He's right! She's violent. She scares me! Caro, I'm frightened. Don't let her hurt me." He lunged over the table and grabbed my wrist.

"What's gotten into you?" I said.

"She killed once and she'll kill again!"

He started whimpering. I got up and stood behind his chair, gently massaging his temples.

"Calm down, Paul."

"Ah! Ah! Can't stay here. Frightened. Caro..."

He sprang to his feet and threw his arms around me tight.

"Gawd," remarked Roy.

"It's all right," said Seaton. "They're married."

"Come on, I'll take you upstairs." I smiled awkwardly. "Back in a minute," I said breezily.

I dragged Paul into the hallway, and shook him. "What is wrong with you?" I snapped.

"Nothing," he said ingenuously. "Hey, how about this room! It's brilliant!"

"Come up to bed."

"I don't want to. I want to explore."

I started to drag Paul upstairs.

"No! I'm sick of going to bed. Boring!"

"Anything the matter?" said a voice. It was Brendan.

"Brendan!" exclaimed Paul, like a child seeing Santa Claus emerge from the chimney. "Brendan-Brendan-Brendan-Brendan."

"I'm taking him up to bed," I explained. "He's not himself."

"I'm fine," said Paul. "I've just had a couple of E's, that's all."

"Ecstasy?" I asked.

"So I wouldn't be dreary. I wasn't dreary, was I?"

I sighed.

"I'll take care of him," said Brendan. "You go back in to dinner."

"Yes!" squealed Paul. He put his hand on Brendan's shoulder and pulled us both in close to him.

"You three," he said, "are my best friends. Marc is my best oldest friend"—(kiss)—"Brendan is my best newest friend"—(kiss)—and...." He looked confused. "And Brendan's here, too!"—(kiss)—"I'm incredibly happy to have such wonderful, beautiful friends. I really mean this—it's not the drugs talking.

Let's always, always stay together just like we are now."

"Come on, Paul," said Brendan. "I'll take you."

"Faaaab! Bye-bye, caro! Love you!"

The dining room was silent when I returned. Charles was in a foul mood, Roy was quietly sozzled, and Seaton looked like he'd prefer to be conducting a walking tour of Sarajevo.

"He'll be all right," I said. "It's some kind of reaction to a drug."

"Thought so," said Charles.

"A prescription drug," I hastened to add. "Paul gets shocking hay fever in the country."

"Never mind," Charles scoffed. "Ecstasy does wonders for hay fever."

I sat in the chair Paul had vacated.

"Mmm," I said. "How's about a drop of red?"

"Help yourself," said Roy disinterestedly.

I did, somewhat surprised by his lack of enthusiasm.

"Roy," I asked. "Have I done something wrong?"

"I thought we were old mates!" he whined. "Oh, I know we don't see each other that much, but I have to say I'm a bit pissed off!"

"Why?"

"You didn't invite us to your wedding!"

"What? I didn't have a wedding."

"Yes, you did," Seaton piped up. "You told me there was a big civil ceremony and everybody was there. Both families. Even the Mafia."

"No, no!" I backtracked. "It was nothing. Really. We're not even a couple. We don't sleep together. He has his own place. In fact, I'm seeing someone else!"

Charles raised his eyebrows.

"I'm sorry if it's gone bad," said Roy. "I'm still pissed off."

"There was no wedding ceremony!" I shouted. "I lied!"

"Why would you lie about a thing like that?" asked Seaton.

"Wishful thinking, that's all. Honestly, Roy: If and when I have a formal ceremony of any kind, you and Shaunna will head the list of invitees."

Roy beamed, and refilled my glass. "Apologies, Marc!" he grunted. "I don't understand you shirt-lifters sometimes. Ay!"

Seaton looked more flustered than ever.

"While we're all in such a good mood," said Charles to Roy, "I'd like to speak to you about my plans."

"Yes, well," said Roy.

"I've finally got a foot in the door at the Sydney City Opera, and I think somebody important may be coming around to my way of thinking. It was only a matter of time. Naturally, the board members are entrenched and conservative, but they'd be interested in coproductions. It could be beneficial all round. The productions would originate here in your theatre, Australia's Glyndebourne so to speak, which would be marvelous for prestige, and we'd have some of the company's resources to play with. Then the most successful productions would transfer to a bigger theatre, which means you'd be getting your money back. With interest, probably. Plus an ever-increasing audience for the festival."

Roy drained his glass and refilled it. "What if the show flops here and they don't want to take it?" he sensibly inquired.

Charles smiled confidently. "I don't think that will happen, not with talents like Seaton and Raoul involved." Seaton glowed at this. "And you wouldn't be taking the whole risk yourself. Besides, your festival's already a success. An audience is assured."

"It's still a hefty outlay. What do you reckon, Marc?"

Charles turned to me encouragingly. I glanced up to see Lavinia, standing in the doorway holding two plates of food. She had a suspicious look on her face. I don't know how long she'd been there.

"Here we are," announced Shaunna, shunting Lavinia into the room. "Good old-fashioned roast pork. Where's Paul?"

"He's not himself."

"No, he seemed a bit out of it." She winked at me. "I'll put his food in the fridge in case he gets a dose of the midnight munchies."

The pork was melt-in-the-mouth wonderful. Paul couldn't have praised it too highly, even with the help of ecstasy. The wine complemented the meal perfectly.

"You calmed down now, Lavinia?" Roy asked. "Seaton tried to tell us you were sick in the head!"

"Me? Sick?" she drawled. "I'm not the one who watches videos of shagging Sherpas."

Seaton turned purple with embarrassment.

I affected an air of nonchalance. "The meal is superb!" I said.

"I was just talking to Roy about our plans for the new opera theatre," Charles confided to Shaunna.

"You mean the barn?" she asked.

"You mean the gallery?" barked Lavinia.

Charles pursed his lips and stretched them almost to breaking point. "Gallery?" he drawled.

"It's perfect for me," Lavinia grinned. "I'll have a rich clientele on tap. I charge for my work—you can be sure of that—and I get what I ask. I'm very hot at the moment. Naturally, there'll be a commission going to the festival: That should help cover the expense of putting those bludgers up and feeding them. Whaddaya say, Roy? Keep it in the family, right? I'm so confident about this, I'll pay for the renovations myself. You'll have no outlay whatsoever. If the punters don't go for it, you'll lose nothing."

"Well, yeah," said Roy.

Charles interrupted. "Roy, I have a long-term vision for this place. Paintings can be hung anywhere—in the halls, in the frigging toilet! What you're running is a music festival!"

"Yeah, well, I've got something to say about that, too," Lavinia butted in. "Where's our indigenous music? Opera, string quartets, and what-have-you—that's not our heritage! That stuff was brought here by this country's oppressors, along with the rabbit and the Indian mynah bird! It's the language of tyranny! We have a great and ancient culture under our very noses, the culture of the true Australians. I should know, aboriginal art is a radical influence on my work. Why don't we subsidize our own ancient music? Tap into the song lines."

Charles remained calm, like the eye of a cyclone. "I might have known we'd hear that kind of patronizing twaddle from you," he snarled. "You're a complete fraud! 'Tap into the song lines!' Tap into this week's trendy arts-babble, you mean. While you're trying to invent the alphabet, I'll be reading Shakespeare, thank you very much!"

"My views may be trendy, but that doesn't make them wrong! Is Shakespeare Australian? Are Freud and Walt Disney Australian? No, but we let these patriarchal icons rule our bloody lives! Well, I say bugger 'em!"

"Yes, let's be narrow-minded and primitive. Let's learn nothing from the world! You want to drag us back from civilization to the level of cave dwellers. How good would your pork taste if it were raw and covered with red dirt?"

"You're a snob. You're living in a fucking ivory tower that somebody else built!"

"Maybe," Shaunna interrupted, "we should think in terms of what's best for the festival. After all, Charles's plans are innovative and Lavinia's work is important. There's a case for both sides." She smiled sweetly.

"No question what's best for Roy," Lavinia said. "Charles, you might think you're sitting on a gold mine, but you'll get a rude awakening."

"I don't have much of a cash flow," Roy said. "It's all tied up in the running of the place. Vineyards don't grow on trees."

"That's why I'm working on the City Opera, convincing them to come in on it," said Charles.

"Oh yeah?" snarled Lavinia. "Who's arse are you crawling up there? Won't do you any good. They've never made a profit in twenty-five years. There's no way they can—opera's a cash-eating dinosaur."

"What would you know about it?" Charles sneered.

"My lover works there. In finance."

Charles sniffed. "I'm not dealing with some clerk. I've been talking to the chairman of the board of directors."

Lavinia roared. "Fred Mathieson? He's a paper tiger."

"He raises money."

Lavinia stared straight at me as she spoke. "The only bread he ever got came from an anonymous donor and Mathieson doesn't have the foggiest idea who it is, silly old bastard. You're wasting your time."

Charles fumed. Ugly veins pulsated rhythmically in his neck.

"We'll see about that," he whispered vehemently. "I know about those donations, and I confidently expect to discover the source. Don't you worry!"

"That would make a difference," said Roy.

"Meanwhile, we're going with the gallery idea," said Lavinia. "What do you think, Marc," she asked sarcastically, "as a disinterested observer?"

"Yes, Marc," Charles smiled. "We were about to hear your opinion. You know all about the opera." He eyed me stonily.

"I…is there any more wine?" I turned to Roy and held out my shaking glass.

"Here you go," he said. "Now what do you reckon? Who's side are you on?"

I turned back to face two bloodthirsty predators. I checked the room: All potential exits were cut off.

"I'm not really a disinterested observer," I said. "Opera is my great love."

Charles grinned.

"That old castrated stuff?" asked Lavinia.

"No," I admitted.

"Ha!" she crowed, triumphantly.

"But," I continued, "opera is not only music. It's a—you know, a visual medium, too. It needs sets and costumes, and having seen some of your historical women, Lavinia, I think you'd be an excellent designer."

"Fantastic idea!" exclaimed Roy. "Best of both worlds! Marc, you should be in politics."

Lavinia and Charles were utterly dumbstruck. Lavinia was the first to regain her composure.

"It might suit you," she said to Roy, "but I have my integrity as an artist to think about. I won't be selling out!"

"Thank Christ for that," said Charles. "I was envisaging Orpheus climbing up the side of an enormous tit and Euridice dressed up as a wombat!"

"I thought it was an interesting suggestion," murmured Shaunna. The two protagonists looked horrified. "Roy and I can discuss it later. Now, who'd like some steamy fig pudding?"

"I—"

"Yes, I know you would, Seaton."

Lavinia leered at me, then turned to Charles.

"Charles, there's something I ought to tell you about that anonymous opera queen you're so hot to track down."

"Yes," I interrupted. "I'm sure I know what Lavinia's going to say. She was about to suggest that if you find the donor—"

"*When* I do."

"When you do, you'll be in a much stronger position. You're so very persuasive, I'm willing to bet the shady old philanthropist will be one hundred percent behind you and will instantly finance your entire plan—as soon as you discover who it is."

"I certainly expect so," he replied.

"That's what you were about to say, wasn't it?" I asked Lavinia.

She was utterly checkmated. "Ah, go and stick a big black dildo up your bum," she quipped.

Seaton, who was at that exact moment sipping his dessert wine, fell forward onto the table, spluttering and choking. I clapped him on the back. Lavinia broke into paroxysms of mirth.

"Are you OK?" I asked.

"Uh-uh," he panted. "Sorry. It went down the wrong way."

"I'll bet!" Lavinia screamed.

Meanwhile, Charles was looking over my shoulder, grinning from ear to ear. "Raoul!" he said. "At last!"

"G'day, Raoul!" cried Roy. "You're in time for pudding."

I turned around, curious to finally see what all Charles's hype was about, and there in the doorway behind me, looking gorgeous, vulnerable, and a bit tired, stood my recently beloved boyfriend Reg. He stared at me guiltily. I stared back in amazement. Our eyes asked a million unanswered questions, all starting with "what the fuck?"

"R—" I said. He quickly shook his head. "Ra-oul?"

Charles introduced him around, and I suddenly found him sitting next to me. He offered his hand.

"Pleased to meet you," he muttered.

"Likewise," I responded incoherently. "So you're the singer I've heard so much about."

"Mmm."

"Charles's protégé. You!"

"Yes, indeed," Charles gushed. "And a perfect Orfeo. Raoul, my boy, we've just been kicking around ideas for the production. How about a quick aria, hmm? To give the whole thing a human face?"

"He just got here!" Roy protested.

"I'm sure he won't mind. Singing is his life. Would you play, Seaton?"

"With pleasure."

"I'm pretty tired," Raoul protested.

"Just do it!" growled Charles under his breath.

So the pudding was postponed, and we all adjourned to the lounge, sitting around the grand piano in large comfortable chairs. I felt alienated and confused.

Raoul handed Seaton a copy of the aria "Che farò senza

Euridice" from *Orfeo*. Lavinia snorted contemptuously and fiddled with her nose-ring. Seaton struck up the simple yet affecting accompaniment, and Raoul/Reg began to sing.

"Che farò senza Euridice? Dové andrò senza il mio ben..."

Roy, Shaunna, and Charles were utterly rapt. Lavinia simply looked depressed. As for me, tears gathered in my eyes. It wasn't Tebaldi, but it was the most beautiful thing I had ever heard in my whole life. The sound was otherworldly, intoxicating, beyond reality. I was deeply moved. I wished I really was the opera donor so I could give everything to this boy. But that's not so surprising: After all, I was head over heels in love.

CHAPTER 20

*T*here was a stunned, respectful silence when Raoul finished, of which Charles took instant advantage.

"You see?" he enthused. "This music speaks to us here and now in its purity. It's an antidote to the overhyped, cheap culture we're force-fed every moment of our lives. Admittedly, opera's a European tradition, but in Europe they've inherited a lot of old baggage with it; they stagger under the weight of their history, whereas in Australia we're in a position to take what we choose from that tradition and bring to it a unique freshness and objectivity. And with talent like this," he patted Raoul fondly on the buttocks, "I'll make the world spring up and take notice!"

"How are you planning to let the world know," asked Shaunna, "if you don't believe in media promotion?"

Lavinia smiled wanly.

Charles raised his eyebrows. "Who said I don't believe in it? I do, very much so. I have many exciting promotional ideas. No, my complaint is with the product we are sold. It's faulty. If you need an example, look at the current crop of populist musicals: these elaborate, elephantine packages that contain nothing but a bloated, half-remembered Anglican hymn where the inspiration should be. 'Media mountains made from oft-mined molehills,' to quote one of my more famous reviews."

"People seem to enjoy those shows in spite of your reviews," remarked Lavinia.

"Exactly my point. If the publicists can sell such garbage, they can sell anything. My product has the bonus of artistic purity, of unassailable integrity. Yes, Raoul?"

"Oh. I was wondering...where's my room?"

"I'm so sorry, darling!" said Shaunna, jumping to her feet. "Brendan should have shown you. I'll take you up now."

I took the initiative. "No, I'll go," I said, standing. "I have to get a handkerchief anyway."

"Thank you, Marc," said Shaunna. "Raoul's next door to you, on the right."

We walked upstairs together in silence. On the top step he gave me a hug.

"Hello," he whispered. I froze.

"What's the matter?"

"You never told me you were Charles's boyfriend!"

"You didn't ask."

"You lied to me! You said your name was Reg!"

"It is. Raoul's a name Charles thought of. I didn't lie." He looked over his shoulder, then turned back and kissed me. "I didn't lie about anything."

"That's your room over there," I said coldly, as I turned to go.

"Wait," he said. "Please, Marc. You don't understand about me and Charles—our relationship. It's...funny."

"Hysterical."

"It's just that I'm part of his plans and everything. Oh, we can't talk here!"

"I'll see you downstairs."

I trudged down. I was bewitched, bothered, and betrayed. It was shattering to discover that Reg, my Reg, was sharing his delicious favors with Charles Mignon in some kind of 'funny' relationship. Funny in what way? Were they into S/M, W/S, F/F, and all those other sleazy parts of the alphabet? Were they close blood relations? My mind boggled. On top of that, the boy had the voice of an angel. There was something bizarre about the whole arrangement. I felt it in my vital organs, one in particular. Or was this feeling simply plain old-fashioned adolescent-strength jealousy? Not impossible.

Charles Mignon! The loathsome, bald, self-important, pompous old perv. I was seriously coming round to Paul's way of thinking on that subject! I made up my mind by the time I reached the bottom step to throw all my weight behind Lavinia (so to speak). However, the question of her gallery never came up again; when I got back, she was not there, but had taken herself off for a walk in the moonlight.

Charles was in full flight once again, relating the plots of several ancient operas to a less-than-enthralled gathering (except for Shaunna, who was delighted to find parallels in the story lines of her past soap operas). Roy and Seaton, both well and truly drunk, were on the verge of tearing off after Lavinia, to make sure she hadn't ruptured herself falling over a grapevine in the dark, but Charles never gave them the chance. He seemed not to draw a breath, even when Reg joined us to sit quietly at his side. It was well after midnight, and umpteen glasses of port, when the company staggered off to their respective bedrooms.

I thoughtfully snuck in without turning on the light, so as not to disturb Paul's psychedelic dreams, but I was no sooner inside than I tumbled arse over tit. Paul's suitcases were lying all over the floor, some wide open. Struggling to get up again, I deftly overturned a small table with a vase on it, spilling water into a bag of Paul's Calvin's.

"Sorry if I woke you up but it's your own fault," I whispered, "leaving all your bags open like a slob."

When I eventually switched on the reading lamp, I discovered the bed cold and empty. Paul had evidently not come back here at all. I was hardly surprised and, in fact, was secretly relieved to have the bed to myself. I wriggled in, ready to do some serious thinking about Reg, and promptly slipped into a deep sleep.

"Shhh."

A strange shushing noise sounded next to my ear as I rolled groggily over.

"Where've you been?" I yawned.

"It's me, Reg. I can't stay long."

He cuddled up close and put his arm over me. His feet were freezing.

"Reg? Oh. Ohoohoohoo! Your feet."

"Sorry."

"Reg, I'm asleep. I don't want to talk just now."

"Neither do I," he said, crawling way down under the bed-clothes. It was a while since I'd thought about our first bliss-ful night together, but in the ensuing moments it all came flooding back. "Oh," I panted. "And you...can sing...too!"

When we finally lay face-to-face, I said, "You have a beau-tiful voice."

"Thanks."

"You might have mentioned it!"

"Yeah, I should have told you about my singing. I know you like opera. But I felt like being ordinary again. I get sick of 'Raoul' sometimes, and I need to escape. Charles never stops going on about it. 'Course, I'm grateful for what he's doing for me. It's gonna be amazing."

"But," I choked, "do you love him?"

He smiled and kissed me. "Not like I love you."

My heart swelled and exploded, sending torrents of hot blood to my brain where they settled into a bolero rhythm.

"It's a funny relationship," he went on, "like I said. I thought I loved him at first, but it's not that. He's just—I don't know, he's the boss. I have to do what he says. Everything."

"No, you don't. You're a grown man. Let me add, 'And How!'" I gently tickled his tummy.

"No, really. Legally, I have to obey him: It's in the contract."

"The contract?"

"Yeah. I signed this contract for ten years, renegotiable after five. It says I have to obey him—everything he tells me—without argument, and he'll make me a star. If I break the contract—I don't know, something terrible happens. I go to jail, I guess."

"And you do not collect your $200?"

"Huh? I get lots more than that."

"Do you want to be a star?"

He took his time answering. "Charles says I have a gift."

"But Reg...this is ludicrous! It's farcical! It's tantamount to slavery! What does he make you do? Do you have to lick Dairy Whip off his old army boots and things like that?"

"Oh, no. I don't think he's got any."

I laid it on the line. "Do you have to have sex with him?"

"He never asks me, but I do anyway."

"What on earth for?"

He looked surprised. "For fun!"

"Well, what does he ask you to do?"

"Oh, stuff. I can't tell you."

"Of course you can. I'm fifty, I've heard everything."

"You said you were late forties."

"Fifty *is* late forties. Tell me what he makes you do!"

"I can't. I can't tell anyone. He told me not to."

"You're disobeying him now, aren't you?"

"No. How do you mean?"

"By coming here. By making love! Did Charles tell you to do that?"

"He didn't tell me not to."

"But he'd be furious if he knew, wouldn't he? Hell, I would! Surely that's the point?"

"Do you want me to go?" he asked dejectedly.

"No! No, no."

"Look, I just have to do what he says. That's what the contract is. I don't have to worry about what he likes or doesn't like, you know? If he doesn't say anything, I'm OK."

"Will you tell him about popping into my lovin' arms at 4 A.M.?"

"Well, if he asks me, I have to. I want to get back before he wakes up."

"This deal is extremely unorthodox. It's almost a case for the United Nations. After all, you're a citizen. You have human rights."

"Charles says I signed them away. But I'm getting plenty in return. He works very hard on the opera thing."

"That's all very well." I was exasperated. I tried another tack. "I don't see much future for us, Reg, if you're in the business of being a professional kiss-and-tell."

"I know. That's why it's been difficult, but I love you. You know?"

I melted. "And I love you. I honestly do. I never expected anyone like you to wander into my life. I've had relationships before, but this is so different. I can't put it into words— I sound like a soppy old pop song."

"It's OK," he purred.

"Aha. What's happening down here?"

"I should go."

"Mmm. Not yet."

We were just getting reorganized when the door opened. Reg scurried under the covers. A figure, which I recognized in the dim light as Paul, hopped across the room, removing his T-shirt and jeans en route.

"You awake, caro? Let me in!"

He scrambled into bed, on the opposite side to Reg.

"Have I been having fun! Come on, move over a bit!"

"Paul...I...oh! Your feet."

"Give us a cuddle, caro. Warm me up. Fuck, what's that? Caro, I'm sorry. It's a lovely thought, but forget it—I'm not in the mood anymore."

"It's not me," I said.

"Who's he?" said Reg, coming up for air.

"Aaaaah!" screamed Paul. "It's a man. A strange man in our nuptial bed! Eeek! Hello."

"Oh, that's great. Fine." Reg was angry. "You call me a liar!" He slipped out of bed and pulled on a pair of shorts. "Good night!"

"Wait," I said, "It's nothing. This is only Paul! We've never slept together before."

"Yeah? That's even worse! Jeez! Give me a contract anytime. You know where you stand with a contract!" He slammed the door quietly—don't ask me how, but that was the effect—and was gone. I switched the light on.

"Only Paul?" Paul pouted. "*Charmant.*"

"Oh, shut up."

"Was I interrupting something precious and special?"

"What do you think?"

"Sorry, caro. Who is he, by the way?"

"Reg."

"Reg, the boy you picked up in a gay male sauna full of homos? What's he doing here?"

"He's here because he's Charles Mignon's boyfriend."

"No! Whacko!"

"'Reg' and 'Raoul' are one and the same."

"Tarnation! Land sakes alive!"

"I notice the drugs haven't worn off yet."

"I'm much better, though. That big brute Brendan has healing hands."

"And you've been on the end of them, I take it."

He whooped with laughter. "While you've been gorging yourself on filet Mignon! It couldn't happen to a nicer critic. When the cat's away, the mice will lie on their backs with their tails in the air!"

I grabbed him by the face. "Are you quite finished? I don't know why you're so gleeful about it."

"'Cause I hate Charles, that's all. I'm proud of you. Well done, well done indeed. 'Do it again,' to borrow a phrase from Ira Gershwin. Does hubby know about it?"

"Of course not."

"Honey, he soon will. I saw him prowling around not ten minutes ago."

"What? Where?"

"Outside. We passed in the night like ships."

"What were you doing outside?"

"Returning from my assignation, what else? Brendan and I did it in the barn like a coupla stud stallions! Then he went home to his primitive mud-brick dwelling and I came back to Tara."

I hopped out of bed and threw on a silk dressing gown. "I've got to find Reg before he tells Charles everything!"

"Suit yourself." He stared at the floor. "What were you looking for in my bags?"

"Nothing."

"Then why are they open?"

"I thought you left them like that."

He was up in a flash, kneeling over his cases and fossicking through them frantically.

"Oh no!" he cried. "I've been robbed."

"They were open when I came in from supper. Anyway, it's tit for tat. You didn't mind the idea of going through Seaton's bags."

"Caro, stop talking about tits and help me look."

"What for?"

"I had drugs in here. Very expensive drugs!"

"You used those already."

"Did I? I'm a bit hazy on that. Still, if you say so—wait, caro! Fuck a duck, the diary's gone! Jen's diary is gone!"

"Are you sure?"

"It was here, and now it's not."

I sighed. "Well, that's the accepted definition of *gone*."

Paul drew himself up and looked grim. "That boy took it."

"Reg?"

"Yes. Reg, alias Raoul, alias my number one suspect."

"Don't be stupid."

"He was in here, wasn't he?"

"Paul, I can vouch for him. He had his hands full."

"Hmm." He frowned. "So who took it? Who absented themselves during dinner?"

"Everybody! We drank so much, we were all racing to the toilet every five minutes."

"Whoever it was needed time. I've got a lot of luggage."

"Well, let's see. Shaunna was in the kitchen most of the time. But it can't have been her! You and Brendan were away the longest!"

"What about Seaton?"

"He went to the toilet pretty often."

"Good. I'm glad he's not eliminated. In the morning we'll check their rooms. Caro"—he grabbed my arm dramatically—"does this mean one of these characters is the murderer? And he or she has been snooping around in this very spot?"

"Don't jump to conclusions. But, err, come with me now, will you?"

"What for?"

"In case there's any trouble."

I couldn't imagine what kind of trouble we'd get into, but, frankly, Paul had unnerved me with his cheap melodramatics. I didn't wish to creep around an old house in broad darkness, and he obviously felt even less enthusiasm for remaining behind. So we held hands and hit the hall.

The room Charles and Reg shared was next to ours. The door was ajar; there was no light within. I tapped Paul on the shoulder and indicated in dumb show for him to be quiet while I crept in and looked around.

"What?" he said.

"Shh!"

I didn't expect to find anybody there. I was certain that if Reg had returned and found Charles absent, he would have been too agitated to sleep. Also, people rarely sleep in a strange house with the door open. Nevertheless, I was ready with a story: If I were caught, I would pretend to have mistaken their room for mine in the dark.

I poked my head inside. It was utter blackness, nothing was visible. I listened hard for the sound of breathing. All I could hear was a distant arrhythmic thump: the sound of my heart desperately pumping adrenaline into any anatomical extreme where it might prove useful. After holding my breath for longer than was recommended by health authorities, I tried a whisper.

"Reg?"

There was no answer. I took one tentative step inside. Images were becoming clearer. There seemed to be a lump of tangled sheets on the bed, but I was fairly sure it wasn't a human form.

Then, quite unexpectedly, I felt a hand in the small of my back. It gave me an almighty shove into the room. The door shut swiftly behind me. In total darkness once more, I stumbled onto the bed, which luckily was unoccupied as I'd hoped.

"Oh! I thought I'd seen a ghost! What are you doing?"

It was Seaton's voice outside the door.

"Nothing, Seaton!" answered the voice of Paul. "Taking the night air."

"Why are you shouting? You'll wake everyone, though most of them seem to be up and about anyway."

"It's Marc, you see. He snores. A lot of men do at his age." I gritted my teeth. "When it gets too bad, I get up and...stand outside. Like this."

"But this isn't your room, is it?"

"And what are you doing wandering around, may I ask?" Paul continued, loudly.

"Oh, I've been visiting the kitchen. Did you get any of Shaunna's fig pudding? It's even nicer cold."

"No, I missed out."

"Of course, you were stoned or something. You seem much better now."

"I am, thank you."

"To tell you the truth, I'm on the lookout for that gorgeous hunk Brendan. I wonder if he lives in the house?"

"I've got no idea. Why?"

"Nothing. Oh, well, I can tell you I suppose." He giggled. "Last time I was here we had it off!"

"What?"

"Isn't it divine? He's so sexy. So are you, of course. He wasn't as good as you."

"Now, Seaton, calm down."

"You know, Pauly, I can't think why we never got together again. It was fun, wasn't it? I could help your career, such as it is. I'm extremely well connected in musical circles."

"Seaton, no. My...my lover is asleep next door. I couldn't betray him. I never should have slept with you in the first place. Marc's no chicken. Any sudden shock could mean the beginning of the end."

I made a mental note to wring Paul's neck.

"Well, Marc's not exactly loyal to the core, let me tell you!" Seaton replied. "He was very cavalier about your so-called marriage this evening."

"That's just his funny old ways. Who else is up? Reg?"

"Who's Reg?"

"I mean that boy who sings. What's his name?"

"Oh, Raoul! Yes, I saw him downstairs. And Lavinia is in the sitting room, the frumpy old bitch. You want to avoid her, Pauly, she's a mental case. Do you know she went through my bags the minute she arrived this afternoon?"

"No!"

"Really! She didn't take anything but they were a total mess. I was most curt with her! Anyway, I'm going to bed. You should, too. In fact, why don't you come with me? I don't snore, as far as I'm aware."

"You do, Seaton."

"Oh, come on, give us a kiss."

"No. I think I hear someone coming. It's Marc, I think."

"I can't hear anyone. Kissy!"

"Stop it! Marc is definitely coming!"

"He will if you shriek like that. Never mind then. Nighty-night!"

There was a brief pause. The door slowly opened and Paul peeped in gingerly.

"Don't worry," I said, "I'm alone. Why in heaven's name did you shove me in here like that?"

"I panicked! Someone was coming. I thought it was Charles but it was only Seaton."

"So I heard."

"I was practically raped. Thanks for all your help and support."

"We old fellers don't like to interfere with you youngsters."

"Oh, that! Can't you tell when I'm kidding? I thought you'd be amused."

"I just about burst my colostomy bag laughing."

"Let's go back to bed."

"Let's find Reg."

Paul shrugged and we slunk downstairs. Whether it was fear or overexertion I don't know, but I was sweating profusely.

"Warm night," I whispered.

"Hot as hell," he replied.

The dining room was uninhabited. We had no need to switch on a light; the whole room was flooded with moonlight, streaming through a lavish picture window, which had been curtained off during dinner. The atmosphere was eerily unreal, like an Act III opera set. I couldn't help but stare at the sharply lit buildings outside, all strange shapes and sizes, casting long unnatural shadows.

"Blu-u-ue moon," crooned Paul softly.

"Who's that?" snapped an apprehensive voice. I stepped into the hall and saw Lavinia standing at the door to the sitting room.

"Only me," I said. "When there's a full moon, I can't sleep."

"Pipe down then." She stomped off. Through the doorway behind her I saw a pale, flickering light.

I returned to Paul, who was still staring out the window.

"I think Lavinia's made a fire!"

"Caro, look! Down there, behind the cellar."

"Where?"

"There! Second one."

I continued to peer into the gray shadows and was suddenly aware of a figure leaning against the wall. Whoever it was stood quite still. I almost began to believe it must be some object, turned vaguely human by a trick of the eye, until the figure stretched. Now I could see it was a man. He stepped into a shaft of moonlight, which gave his face an androgynous mask-like aspect.

"That's Reg!" I exclaimed.

"Why's he lurking down there?"

"How would I know? Come on."

"Must we? I don't think he's looking for company."

"I have to explain things to him."

Paul kept staring. "I've seen that face somewhere, I know it."

I yanked Paul away from the window and we crept along the hallway. As we passed the half-open door to the sitting room, Lavinia called out.

"Marc, are you still there?"

"Y-yes."

"Come in here for a second, could you?"

"Shit!" I muttered under my breath, then said to Paul, "Go back to that window and keep an eye on Reg."

The sitting room was exactly as I'd left it: the chairs in a semicircle, the grand piano open and the aria from *Orfeo* lying open on top of it. Lavinia was sitting on three-quarters of a love seat next to the grate in one corner of the room. A brilliant fire was crackling away.

"It's summer! Why have you built a fire?" I asked, as she glared into the flames.

"I have a low metabolism."

"What do you want?"

I looked down and saw, to my astonishment, that her hands were clutching Jennifer's diary. I drew up a chair.

She looked me straight in the eye. "You're not going to bankroll Charles's idiotic schemes are you?" she asked.

"I don't know," I said. "I suppose not."

"I know you boys stick together. God, the arts industry is a gay Mafia! But Charles's grandiose ideas are a very unsound investment. Quite honestly, he has no idea of the contempt he's held in by the arts community. Believe me, I'm doing you a favor telling you this."

"He always seems so pleasant and reasonable."

She shook her head. "He's neither. How naïve are you?" She snorted and continued. "That boy's a good singer, I suppose; good enough not to need Charles behind him. Take Raoul out of the equation and what's left? Nothing but a lot of hot air."

Taking Reg out of the equation was an idea that appealed to me hugely.

"Let me tell you something about the world," she continued. "There's only two types of artists who can get projects off the ground. The first are young, unknown geniuses: They succeed because all the tired old hacks fall over each other to discover them first. They have a dream run for two or three years before the same hacks turn 'round and put the boot in. Then there's the second type, geniuses whose time has arrived: drooling, senile farts who haven't produced a thing for decades and everyone thought they suicided in the '60s. Those old buggers have got it made! For the rest of us it's one long arse-lick, day in, day out." She smiled wistfully. "Don't mind me, I'm in a bad mood."

"I'll have to go in a minute," I hinted. "You're updating your diary, I see."

"Yeah. This! No wonder I'm cranky. I s'pose I ought to show it to you, since you were her uncle."

"It's Jennifer's? Where did you get it?"

"I was given it. Look here, you get a mention. Though why she calls you Uncle *Mike* I can't fathom."

"It's a family nickname."

"*Mike* is a nickname for *Marc*? Bloody unimaginative family!"

She handed me the diary. I pretended to read the Uncle Mike entry with great interest. Something (my sleuthing instinct?) told me the solution to this whole investigation was close by.

"Ah, that's right, we had lunch at Trevisi's. It rained, if memory serves."

"You said you'd never met her."

"I...err, hadn't gotten to know her. You know," I ventured, "this diary might contain some clue as to why she did away with herself."

Lavinia snatched it back. "It does," she said. "The fool of a kid blames me!" She flipped through till she found the final entry. "Here it is, August 19th. 'Finally broke up with J.' That's Jude. 'She's in love with Lavinia Cooper, a PUSHY, MEDIOCRE artist. Lavinia's welcome to her. Very depressed. Feel life's not worth living.'"

Lavinia's voice was more shaky than the handwriting. She found it difficult to read and contain her temper simultaneously. "'Pushy and mediocre,' am I? Nasty little twat! And this isn't the only time she shit-cans me."

I didn't know what to say. I would have sworn on a stack of Tebaldi records that August 19th had previously been blank.

"This is crap," Lavinia railed. "I want you to know that! Sure, Jude was mooning over her like an imbecile, but Jennifer gave her the cold shoulder from the beginning. She only kept in with Jude to help her precious, pathetic career! Poor Jude would've had a breakdown if I hadn't come along."

"Yes, well. A person's own private diary is...um, private. You know."

"And now every fucker is going to think I drove the kid over the edge!" She jumped up and began pacing around in a terrific rage, kicking obstructive furniture out of her way. "Stupid cow!"

Paul opened the door. "Everything OK?" he asked tentatively. At that moment Lavinia found herself standing next to the fire. She unceremoniously dropped the diary into it. Sparks flew.

"Good riddance," she said.

"Wait!" I cried. "It's not your property."

"Touch it, pal, and I'll thump the shit out of you."

"Oh! The diary!" screamed Paul, and he bounded over toward the grate. Lavinia, however, headed him off and knocked him gasping into an armchair with a deft karate chop to the windpipe.

"Listening at the door, were we?" she snarled. I slowly sat down again. "I didn't do the Lesbian Co-op Self-Defense Course for nothing," she added.

For five or so minutes we sat there, speechless, while she stood guard over the smoldering evidence. Soon there was precious little remaining of Jennifer's thoughts for the day, ghostwritten or not.

"*Finito*," said Lavinia. "It was the best thing to do, for all concerned. It's why I made a fire in the first place." She grinned at me as she poked the embers around. "I'd advise you to forget all about it. You might as well. You know, you've gotten a hell of a lot of free advice from me tonight!" With that, she marched out of the room.

Paul sat grimacing and rubbing his throat. "I'll never sing again," he croaked. "Is she the murderer?"

"I don't know, Paul. I don't know what to think. If she is, she just destroyed the only evidence of it. I'm so confused! There was an entry in the diary blaming Lavinia for Jen's suicide, but I'd swear it was new."

"Caro, can we leave first thing in the morning? I'm getting cold feet. I don't want the rest of me to follow!"

"We need to have a long think. What's Reg up to? Howling at the moon?"

"That's what I came to tell you. He was waiting for Charles. They went off somewhere toward the cellars."

"Odd."

"Maybe they were sneaking away for a quiet poke."

"Don't be stupid, they share a bedroom! Show me where they went."

"You don't want to follow them?"

"Coward! Are you coming with me?"

He leapt to his feet. "Of course. I adore a good eavesdrop."

We struck out into the night. The moon had changed from big, yellow, cheesy mode into a searing white pin-spot. I felt as though we were wandering through a silent German expressionist film.

"*Nosferatu*," I said.

"Bless you."

"I wasn't sneezing, I...never mind."

All the buildings, including the barn, were dark and forbidding. I had expected Charles to head for his beloved soon-to-be theatre, and was disconcerted to find it apparently empty. We scrounged about the outskirts, far too petrified to consider gaining entry.

"This is a waste of time," I muttered.

"Wait, caro, there's light somewhere over there."

Paul was right. A dull glow was visible, coming from a window in one of the wine cellars. We snuck across to it. The main door was open, the light deep inside. We entered.

"They're in the vintage room! The one Roy keeps locked!" whispered Paul.

He was right. The metal door was ajar, propped open by a crate. Ghostlike, we wafted through. Inside were several long rows of shelves filled with hundreds of wine bottles. Roy must have started this collection long before he ever bought the vineyard. Peering down the center aisle, I spied Charles and Reg sitting at a small wooden table. They were drinking. I pulled Paul back and we tiptoed up the furthest aisle until we were close enough to hear their conversation without being seen. Charles seemed to know all about Reg's nocturnal visit.

"Are you positive?" Charles was asking.

"Yes! I've seen his home, he's not rich."

They were discussing me! And my house!

"Then why the hell? Oh, this is so irritating. That dreary dyke was dropping hints like there was no tomorrow. I was so sure we'd finally found him. She did it deliberately. I'll bet she knows who it is and she's trying to throw me off the scent. But I've got her right where it hurts, don't you think?"

"I don't know."

"Sorry, I forgot: You don't know anything! You're just a set of vocal chords with a dick attached."

"Charles—"

"Shut up. Pour me some more. This stuff is delightful. I thought there was none left in the entire country!"

"If Roy finds out—"

"Well, he won't. He never comes in here. Anyway, it's the least he can do for me, the vulgar Philistine."

"That boy Paul is sleeping with Marc. I didn't know they were lovers."

"Not only lovers, they're officially married, so Seaton tells me. There was a civil service. God knows why anyone would bother."

"I...I don't believe it."

Damn, I thought. Reg sounded upset. Charles obviously hadn't noticed; he merely kept on yapping about his operas. *How tiresome he must be to live with,* I mused. *You'd have to be legally bound in writing just to put up with it!*

"Come on, cheer up, dear boy. I know you're impatient. I'm getting that money one way or another. As soon as our first production's off the ground, the hardest part will be accomplished. And when that's ready to go—"

"Yes, I know."

"Remember your contractual obligations."

"Yes!"

"All right, relax, don't start worrying about it now. But it is important. My entire plan is useless without it."

"Yes, Charles."

"That's better. Smile, come on, God damn it, I told you to smile! Good. Now let's go to bed. And I might take another bottle of the Grange with me. Do you have the key?"

"Here."

There was a shuffling and grating of chair legs as they got up. Paul and I flattened ourselves against the wall. After a moment the footsteps receded and we were plunged into darkness. I heard the metal door shut with a clink.

"Charles is obsessed!" said Paul. "And he thinks you're the donor."

"Not now, he doesn't. I've lost my fortune and my boyfriend in one night. I wish I'd never said I'd married you."

"You don't love me anymore!" he whined. "I'm going home to mother."

He flounced off into the blackness. I followed cautiously.

"Caro? Mother will have to wait up! The door's locked."

"Is there another way out?" I asked hopefully.

"Didn't see one. All the windows are barred." He rattled the door, but it was shut tight.

"This calls for brute strength, caro. Break it down at once."

"Do it yourself."

"Where is Brendan when you need him? All right, we'll try it together. How far back can we get?" He began pacing it out.

"Paul, I don't know. We might damage something. Ourselves, for instance."

"Stuff it, I don't want to spend the rest of my life among cheeky little reds. Look, soon as we're free we'll sprint off to beddy-byes. Nobody will ever know who was in here. If the subject comes up, Charles and What's-his-name will look guilty as hell."

"Well..."

He rubbed his hands together—a useless move if ever there was one.

"Now," he said, "I've seen this done many times, always

with phenomenal success. We run at the door, then at the last second, jump, turn, and hit it with our shoulders. A snack! I did a similar routine in *Kiss Me Kate*. Ready? I'll count to three. One! Two!"

"Err..."

"Two and a half! Three!"

It was pitch dark. Paul executed his *Kiss Me Kate* step with panache, if not much heft. I, on the other hand, flung myself face first into the wall.

"Nearly right, caro. Now try it on the door. Facing away from the mirror!"

"What mirror?"

"It's a showbiz expression, darling. Ready? One...Two... Three!"

This time we connected with a jolt. I thought I felt the door give slightly, although it may have been my spinal column.

Instantly, the room was flooded with harsh neon light. A sound of loud, wailing sirens pierced the night air. I grabbed Paul in shock, trying to regain some sort of equilibrium.

"What was that?" he squealed.

"The sound of shit hitting the fan, I'm afraid."

A look of dismay dribbled across his face. I slid down the wall onto my haunches. There was nothing to do but wait for Roy to arrive, trusty shotgun in hand, to discover Paul, myself, two used glasses, and two bottles of priceless Grange Hermitage: one empty, the other missing.

CHAPTER 21

*D*awn was breaking as we staggered back to the house, but I had no inclination to admire its pink and orange hue. Paul and I were in utter disgrace. The loss of his prized vintages stunned Roy into a state of apoplectic catatonia; even Shaunna wore a pained expression as she bade us goodbye. Needless to say, we packed hastily and left. I promised to pay for the Grange Hermitage, not one drop of which I'd consumed, and decided to buy a lottery ticket: If I won first prize, it would almost cover the expense.

Our return trip was uneventful. Paul slept (and snored) the entire time. I didn't object. It gave me time to think, and as home grew closer I began to adopt a fresh perspective on the Jennifer Burke affair. Namely, I was over it.

The girl had certainly been helped to her eternal destiny, but the more I thought about that, the more it seemed like a good thing. Lots of people were infinitely better off without her messing up their lives, and I included myself in that group. I would let the investigation drop. Anyhow, with the diary destroyed, I could prove nothing.

I dropped Paul at home without mentioning my new resolution. I was too fatigued to get into an argument. No, I would simply retire and get on with my drab everyday life. Eventually I would pay off my debt to Roy and the events of the past month would be a bittersweet memory.

Buoyed up by this vision of normality, I checked out of Gianna's apartment. She'd be back within the week in any case. I left a note, explaining how my life was a shambles and apologizing for any episodes of *Days of Our Lives* I may have missed.

Home was warm and welcoming. I felt I had overreacted

by moving away. There would be no danger to me now that I'd bowed out of the murder business. As I unpacked, my ears twitched delightedly: Was it? Yes! That old Qantas quiver was in the air. A moment later I was shaking from head to bowel, and everything was engulfed in a sonic roar. A Venetian watercolor fell off the wall, and the glass shattered. I smiled as I swept it up.

I wandered up the road and found a pleasant café for a lazy, indulgent brunch. I browsed through the gay papers. It felt wonderful to be rid of that self-absorbed opera crowd. Even Reg. I temporarily consigned him to the too-hard basket. My heart backflipped when I thought about him, but my heart would get over it. It had before.

As I scanned the Classifieds, I knew I wasn't alone. Every boy and his dog were whining in print, desperate to find that perfect partner. Of course, people's ideas of perfection differ. I noticed the gentleman who offers to take out his teeth and give all comers an erotic gum-over was still advertising. Very sensible, I thought: Massage keeps the gums healthy.

I did some much needed shopping, specifically the ingredients for pavlova. It was high time I whipped up a frothy little number, and the much-maligned pavlova is one of my specialties. I love it because it can be gossamer-fluffy fabulous or granite-solid dismal, as the mood takes it, and you never know till you open the oven door which version you're going to get. All you know for sure is you'll have to live with it.

When I returned to Casa Petrucci, much to my joy, there were no messages. I pulled up my sleeves and started flinging foodstuffs around the old kitchenette.

Of course, when I say you can't affect how a pav will turn out, I'm not being one hundred percent accurate. You can guarantee a dud if you leave the preparation at any stage to do something else. I was separating eggs when the phone rang. And rang. That's why I had no messages: I'd left the machine off! The phone kept ringing.

It's not easy to put eggs down when you're separating them, unless you chuck the lot in the garbage. I had no choice.

"Yes?" (Crash.) "Sorry, the receiver slipped. Are you there?"

"Mr. Marc Petrucci?"

"Speaking."

"Mr. Petrucci, I'm Sir Fred Mathieson's assistant. I've been trying to get you all weekend."

"I've been away."

"Sir Fred would like to set up a meeting with you. As soon as possible."

This came as a surprise, to say the least. "What about?" I asked.

"I can't tell you. He said you would know."

"Ah. All right."

"Sir Fred is very busy, of course, but he asked me to suggest a possible time."

"Yes?"

"The SODS dinner is being held this Tuesday night in the Opera Room at the Koala Belvedere International Hotel."

"Hmm? What sods?"

"The Sydney Opera Devotees' Society dinner. It's an annual function."

"Oh, I see. Am I invited?"

"No, no. Sir Fred suggests you meet him after the meal for a drink. Say, 10:30?"

I was about to refuse—I was no longer interested in Sir Fred and company—but I sensed something in the air. Literally. It was the unmistakable odor of burning sugar.

"10:30, Mr. Petrucci?"

"What? Oh yes, fine," I babbled distractedly.

"You know the Barbirolli Bar?"

"I'll find it, thank you—goodbye!"

I slammed down the receiver and raced to the kitchen, but it was, of course, too late. Charcoal had set in. My light-hearted mood was shattered. New resolutions and pavlova:

both had sunk without a trace. Rather than scour the cajun style–blackened cookware, I chose the soft option: a late-afternoon stroll.

It was sunny and invigorating outside, a lovely day for window-shopping. The stores were mostly shut, with the exception of the newsagent/kebab stand and the local kitsch emporium, with its banner proclaiming CLOSING DOWN SALE. That must have been the registered name of the shop, because after eight years of service, the place still showed no sign of closing down.

I wandered in, intrigued by the mammoth floor-to-ceiling display of copulating lesbian Barbie dolls. I'm no great aficionado, but I swear I'd never before seen a Barbie with a shaved head. I was considering putting one on layaway for Paul when I heard a familiar panic-stricken voice demanding to purchase the store's full stock of glitter.

"Anton!"

"Hello, my darling." We air-kissed. "What are you up to, hanging around these purveyors of tack?"

"Passing the time."

"Cruising, ay? Well, you're just the woman I want to see. Come and help me carry this bulk glitz round the corner. You can have a look at our float! We're putting it together right now."

"Whereabouts?"

"Darling, the Mardi Gras workshop is a street away. Didn't you know? You should get out more."

He bustled me out of the store and down an ancient back alley strewn with litter. On the way, we discussed my Dame Norma outfit. I may have withdrawn from detective work, but the Parade was one activity I wouldn't get out of so easily.

"You don't have your own drag, I presume?"

"No, Anton."

"Extraordinary. You're the only one who doesn't. Well, not to worry. I'll have a word with Victoria. She's got a ton of old tat in her wardrobe. God knows, she puts on a hundred kilos a month! We'll find something that's absolutely you. And I might see if Tammy can swipe an item or two from Norma herself—that enormous hat she wore on the cover of her recital disc, you know, with the ostrich feathers?"

"An enormous hat sounds good. With an enormous veil."

"I wonder if he'd do it? Probably not. Ah, here we are!"

We veered out of the prosaic street and into a vast fairyland. The workshop was as big as an aircraft hangar. Every inch of space, high and low, was packed with all sorts of colorful artifacts: papier-mâché heads of politicians and celebrities, signs, streamers, giant shiny costumes, and assorted oddities left over from previous parades. A buzz of activity sounded as the multitude of volunteers sawed, hammered, glued, and gummed props together.

Anton hauled me over to a group gathered around a large platform. "This is our corner," he said.

Half a dozen strapping young boys and girls were mixing paint or daubing spots of color on large spreadsheets. On the platform itself was a naked wooden scaffold resembling the structure of the Big Dipper. The activities were being supervised by a thin, alert man in a wheelchair. His white hair was close cropped and, as he wheeled around, I was struck by the twinkle in his deep-set eyes. He grinned as Anton approached.

"It's going to be a dream," he said. "Did you get glitter?"

"I did, darling, and I also got Marc. Marc, meet Ozzie. He has the best eye in the business."

"Hi, girlfriend" said Ozzie, pursing his lips.

"Marc is our Dame Norma!" Anton announced.

"Sensational! You're the living image!"

A muscular red-haired youth in a denim shirt came over to us. He was carrying a pot of paint. Ozzie peered into it.

"Whaddaya reckon, Oz?"

"Not mysterious enough! Wants a dash more ultramarine. But don't drown it."

"Where are you thinking glitter?" asked Anton.

"Umm, what's finished? Take me 'round the back there."

As we wheeled Ozzie over, Anton described the layout of the float.

"We have three divas on each side, each with their own little bit of scenery from their own opera. For instance, Marilyn Horne will be there on the left as Carmen! And see that structure sticking out? That'll be a bull charging up behind her. Callas will be Tosca, of course, so she's up the top. That big lump's the Castel Sant'Angelo. We're hanging a curtain right down the center of the display, gilt-edged of course—goes without saying. But I think it should be transparent, so the crowd can see the whole float and not just one side of it."

"No, NO! It'll look like they're in the shower!" snapped Ozzie. "Especially if it rains again! We represent opera, not 9-1-ZERO. The curtain has to be velvet." He rolled out the words. "Crimson crushed velvet!"

"He's right," I said.

Anton sighed. "OK, then, if you both think so."

Ozzie winked at me. "You can stay."

"You're 'round there on the other side, Marc. *La Traviata*, we decided on for Dame Norma. Violetta is a famous part of hers, though she comes across about as consumptive as a Laughing Buddha!"

"And what about Jennifer Burke?" I asked.

"Oh, she hit the deck. Victoria put her foot down. She was at the party where it happened, apparently, and the idea upset her. Also, I can see her point. Who was the girl? Nobody will know—they'll just think we hate women."

"Never!" Ozzie was shocked.

"Oh, you and I know that, but a few Mardi Gras board members...anyway, who cares? We're going ahead. We even got private funding."

"Really?" I asked. "Anonymously?"

"Not at all. We got a big contribution from SODS, the

Sydney Opera Deviants Society. They love the float. They're all elderly bachelors and they're fucking loaded."

My interest in Tuesday's dinner greatly increased. The anonymous donor must belong to this organization! It looked like the murder investigation was on again.

Meanwhile, work continued on the float so I rolled up my sleeves and pitched in, working in tandem as much as possible with the delectable redhead, whose name was Matthew. We finished painting and carefully sprinkled glitter in areas specified by Ozzie. After that, we nailed two of the cloths up to a section of scaffolding, elaborately crisscrossing and bunching them together, and with very few adjustments (and no major accidents on my part) we miraculously transformed the pile of sparkly material into an exotic Arabian Nights scene, the backdrop for *Salomé*.

When it was finished, everyone stood back to admire and applaud the result. It had been such a satisfying afternoon's work. I was amazed to see, glancing through a window, that the sky outside was almost dark.

"More than nice and no less than fabulous!" enthused Anton. "It looks exactly like my boudoir at home!"

"It does, too," smiled Ozzie. He had been brimful of vitality directing the proceedings, but the minute the job was done every drop of his energy had dissipated.

"Come on, my loves," called Anton. "I'll treat you to cheap and cheerful Chinese."

"Not me, girlfriend," said Ozzie.

"Oh, yes! You must," Anton protested. "It'll do you good."

"Matthew will take me home. Ta-ta, kids! See you Wednesday." He took my hand. "Lovely to meet you, Marc. I look forward to seeing you in your outfit. May I suggest a deep sea-green?"

As we wandered back up the road, I took Anton aside.

"Your friend Ozzie's remarkable."

"True. Mind you, today was a good day. She can be plenty

of trouble when she feels like it. Listen, what are you doing later tonight?"

"Nothing really."

"Want to be my date, then? I'm going to a drag show, a fund-raiser. Victoria will be doing a number. We could see her afterward about your gear! She hardly ever performs anymore. Want to come?"

"Why not? I'd love to. But I need to go home and change."

"Goody! Dress smart-cas. In other words, polish your nipple studs. Meet you outside The Fireworks at 9:30."

I was in the mood for some more camaraderie, and by the time I strode through my front doorway I felt very chirpy indeed. I hadn't been to a drag show in years. Even the prospect of meeting up with Victoria again failed to dampen my spirits.

I breezily tidied up the kitchen, then picked out a suitable lightweight jacket for the excursion. In case of emergency, I slipped some earplugs into the pocket. I was in such a hurry, I nearly forgot to check the machine. At the last moment I remembered. The one message was from Paul.

"Caro! Where the hell are you? I've been giving this matter a lot of thought. In fact I thought about it the whole way back from Amityville. We must stop dithering around and accuse somebody! Who do you think is our man? I'm convinced it's Victoria. You know, the big drag queen? How could she not know whether she was at a party or somewhere else? It's beyond belief! Everybody remembers going to parties, even if they don't remember leaving. No, she is definitely hiding something. Guilty, guilty, guilty! Don't you agree? Now it's 2 o'clock-ish. I'm going 'round to her shop this afternoon in my 'disguise,' and I won't rest till I get to the bottom of it—the case, that is. Wish me luck, caro! I'm firing on all four pistols, or whatever you call it. Talk to you later. Ciao!"

CHAPTER 22

"*Y*ou're late, girl!" Anton grumbled. He was waiting on the busy corner, leaning up against a newsstand display of *Mandate* and *Inches* magazines. He wore a full-sleeved maroon shirt, trim black jeans, and a nifty little leather jerkin. His white hair was immaculate. I hoped I would be as stylish in fifteen years. (Not very likely; I'd never come near it yet!) As I bustled up the street, he glanced crossly at his gleaming Rolex. "The show starts at 10 o'clock, and it'll be packed. We won't see a thing below the neckline!"

"Sorry."

I had been sitting by the phone until the last possible minute, waiting for Paul to ring back, but he never did. I'd been aghast when I heard what he intended to do—and without even consulting me! Rushing off to accuse Victoria of the murder, all because he was getting impatient! And on what evidence? Simply because she didn't want to tell him details of her social life. Perfectly reasonable! I know we'd put Victoria on our list of suspects, but as far as I could see she had nothing whatsoever to do with Jennifer Burke. I crossed my fingers that Paul hadn't managed to catch up with her.

To my mind, Lavinia was a much more likely candidate for soprano-shoving status. She'd destroyed the diary in front of Paul and me deliberately. Why not simply suppress it? Why perform this ritual public cremation? There was only one answer: She knew I understood the diary's significance. It was her subtle way of telling me to back off, to drop my line of inquiry, and it almost worked. She'd written that new diary entry herself, to give her a handy motive to get angry and burn the book, but I saw through her little burst of neo-Nazism. The real reason for her actions was increasingly clear: She 'dunnit.'

My thoughts were interrupted by Anton, who grabbed my hand and frog-marched me across two intersections to the pub where the night's show was scheduled to occur. There were so many writhing, seething bodies on the pavement you could scarcely see the building. It had never been a particular haunt of mine. I only knew the place vaguely by reputation, as a bar that specialized in Chinese take-away.

"Come on," Anton said exasperatedly. "The show's in the front bar, but we'll never get in that way. We'll go through the piano bar and 'round the back. Elbows up!"

We started to squeeze our way through the crowd. Once inside, the music was thunderous. I was buffeted every which way, and just as we started making progress, I stumbled over some woman's foot. She sneered and shoved me roughly into the midst of the crowd, where I bumped the elbow of another girl, splashing her drink. A good-looking young man next to her turned to me.

"Watch it! Faggot!"

This remark rather took me by surprise. As I looked about more closely, Anton caught up to me in the crush.

"Anton, we've come to the wrong place!"

He started to say something, but was squeezed out of the way by a migrating flock of young women, all in hysterics and screaming out their drunken fragmentary conversation over our heads. They were girls who worked together in a travel agency, enjoying a hens' night out (as I discovered with absolutely no effort). As they passed, they shoved me aside and I fell almost into the lap of a sweaty boy and girl at the bar whose faces were virtually locked together. They seemed to be exploring the lining of each other's lungs, using their tongues.

"Anton!" I cried weakly. "Help!"

I reached out blindly into the hormonally overendowed rabble and felt Anton's tight grip on my fingers. He yanked me across to the wall.

"We'll rest here for a sec," he panted. "Girlie shows do bring in the riffraff these days."

"Times have changed."

"Not that much. In my day the straights behaved themselves and the queens were rude. Now it's the exact opposite!"

We set off again on our slow journey to the front bar. The closer we got, the more crowded and stifling it became.

"I feel like we're on our way to the gas chamber!" I shouted.

"Pardon?"

"I feel like...ah." I gave up and simply followed.

We edged our way into a large room mostly taken up by a circular bar in the center. Several contenders for the title of Mr. Universe, clad bewitchingly in brief Lycra shorts and assorted body jewelry, served drinks to the manic mass. So pumped up was one barman, I'd swear that two out of every three glasses he handled got deftly crushed into smithereens. The area around the bar was jam-packed; every travel agency in Sydney must have been represented! I had to concentrate to breathe.

In the middle of the room a hand waved frantically to us. It was Matthew, my redheaded workmate from the afternoon. He was standing on a raised area against the wall, and indicated that he'd make room for us. Anton and I barged our bruised way over.

"Hi," said Matthew.

"Darling, what a godsend you are. It's so straight tonight! If we stayed down there any longer, we'd get pregnant. Hello, Fenella. This is Marc."

"Mmmm."

Matthew's companion shook my hand vacantly. He was a tiny, slim slip of a boy. His face consisted of a dreamy smile and wide blue eyes with no ability to focus. I'd have estimated his age at around fourteen.

"Is he on something?" I shouted in Anton's ear.

"Probably, but she's always like this."

Matthew generously offered to fight his way to the bar and get us drinks—doubles, so we wouldn't need to go back too soon—and, chat being impractical, I settled down and waited to be entertained. A platform stood in the central area of the bar to accommodate the acts, leaving plenty of space for the barmen to continue selling liquor. Just as Matthew returned, the bar filled up with smoke, the lights dimmed, and a spot shone onto the stage. The smoke gradually cleared, revealing the full and forbidding figure of Victoria, holding a microphone.

"Good evening. God, look at this yuppie turnout. What a trendy, discriminating crowd. Are you discriminating? I can't hear you! Are you a discriminating crowd?"

"Yeah," they cried halfheartedly.

"Then stop discriminating, it's against the law."

There was a baffled titter.

"Never mind. Designer drugs *killed* audience participation! OK, where are the girls from Von Trapp Discount Travel?"

The group who'd passed me earlier screamed, as if in mortal agony.

"You giving discounts tonight, ya bunch of slags?"

The crowd snickered. Victoria was displaying a common touch she'd kept well and truly under wraps at the florist's.

"I know you're all pissed already, but every drink you buy during the show, the money goes to AIDS research. So enjoy yourselves, write yourselves off, and if you feel like shit tomorrow come 'round and see me at Crystal Packin' Momma's for a facial." She strode over to the hens' party. "Except for you, love, you're gonna need a full mudpack. And would you do me a big favor? *Never* take it off! All right now, we've got hundreds of acts for you, and it's such a big night some of them are even sober. Here's the first lot. Please welcome with open legs the lovely and talented Miss Helen Back!"

So began a series of turns. I'm no critic—I'm sure Charles would have had plenty to say—but I rather enjoyed the show. There was precious little room for choreography, so most of the artists spun around on the spot with varying degrees of poise. The music tracks they used were all new and hardly known to me. Matthew, a font of information, identified them as Madonna, Kylie, and others which, fortuitously, I've since forgotten. I agreed with Anton: We sorely missed the drama of, say, Shirley Bassey (a favorite of our generation).

Two particular acts stood out. One was a trio of rather tall girls known as Sophisticated Ladies. They performed an old song by the Pointer Sisters, "Automatic," an appropriate choice since one of them, the tallest, was unmistakably on automatic pilot. Whenever they had a move together, she would be late or end up the wrong way around and giggle in confusion. A few times she fell off her high heels and once she bumped into the bar, almost bringing a shelf full of spirits down onto her head.

The shortest of the trio looked daggers at her constantly, and halfway through the song, when yet another piece of choreographic business had been ruined, dropped out of Pointer Sisters lyric mode long enough to scream, "Drug fucked slag!" in her ear. The tall girl retaliated by shoving her Sister into a cash register; the cash drawer flew open, slamming her in the midriff. After that it was on: Punches and wigs went flying, the two girls locked in serious sibling combat.

The third Sister, obviously a true pro, worked around them, continuing as though everything was under control. Her smile and performance expanded impressively, and she had that "my big chance!" look in her eyes, familiar from musical films of the '40s. She shined!

When the others realized what was happening, they temporarily buried the hatchet and, against all odds, Sophisticated Ladies finished the number together. The cheering was unconstrained.

"They've got that routine down pat!" called Anton, above the applause.

The other act that made a big impact was an Asian girl, Miss Sigh Gone. Exquisitely made up in traditional style and dress, you'd have sworn she was female, except for a very slight squareness of the arms and shoulders. She performed in a bluish half-light a ballad called "Save the Best to Last," and brought to it the sculpted, spare movements of oriental dance. She mesmerized us, and the rowdy drunken mob grew quiet and still during her performance.

Victoria was the final act, and she was undeniably a presence. Making no concession to contemporary musical taste, she performed the theme song from a James Bond movie, *License to Kill* sung by Gladys Knight. Here was all the drama I'd missed in the other acts; shivers ran up my spine, particularly as Victoria stared straight at me each time she sang: "Got a license to kill, And you know I'm going straight for your heart." My intestines whipped themselves into slipknots. Perhaps Paul was right about her after all!

She was a huge hit. It was a big sound, a big woman, and a big performance. The crowd erupted.

"Buy more drinks, now—it's for a cause!" she announced. "We'll be back with new acts, new songs, and the same old tits in half an hour! That means an hour."

The music faded up and the mob started seething again.

"Wasn't she just fambulance?" Anton enthused. "She put the others to shame. Let's go and see her now! Come on. Matthew, push your way through."

We elbowed our way to a grunge-green door behind the stage entrance. It led to a stairwell heading down, although the bar was already at street level. The stairs took us to what I presumed was the pub's storage cellar. The smell of draught beer was overwhelming. In one corner, an area had been cordoned off by a stained, tatty hotel sheet hung from a line. Behind this sheet was the official dressing area for the artistes.

"Helloo? Fans!"

Anton brushed the sheet to one side, and we found ourselves in a tiny alcove crammed with mirrored dressing tables and costumes hanging in every available cranny. Some of the performers sat preening in front of the mirrors, including Miss Sigh Gone, whose face was coated with cold cream. Victoria was nowhere to be seen.

"Anton! Hello, pet," said one of the Sophisticated Ladies.

"You were great, Brett."

"Ta. Been doing it long enough, God knows."

"Where's Victoria?"

"Upstairs somewhere. Trying to flog her boring stupid old book."

Anton and Brett kept chatting, while Matthew and his strange boyfriend wafted over to see another girl they knew. Left on my own, I decided to pay Miss Sigh Gone a compliment. I tapped her on the shoulder.

"Excuse me," I said, "I enjoyed your act very much."

"Thank you, Uncle Mike," she replied. "No worries."

She finished wiping off her make-up and grinned at me.

"Ng! It was you!"

"You not recognize me? Good! I get into character for my act. Roland shows me what to do. Good acting, huh?"

"Certainly was. You were excellent."

"Ah, you nice man now. I'm glad you come here. Yes, this will be most interesting night, I think."

"Is Rodney here with you?"

His eyes blazed. "You must forget him! This is good advice."

"I have!" I said hastily. "He's all yours."

Ng sniffed. "We are not together now. Rodney is stupid boy, big dumb muscle Mary. No good for me. I go back to Roland like before. We throw Rodney out of his apartment. Everything very good now. So." He looked up and started giggling heartily. "Hi Victoria!"

I felt a heavy hand on my shoulder, forcing me down into a chair. I stretched around to be confronted by the formidable bulk of the evening's emcee.

"I want to talk to you," she growled.

At that moment, Anton came cavorting over.

"Darling, you were a marvel, you must do it more often!" he beamed. "Your public needs you."

"I'm a businesswoman now, Anton." she replied dryly. "I'm flat out."

"*Quel dommage!* By the way, this is Marc Petrucci, who'll be on the float with you. I was wondering if you had some old rag that might fit him. But don't worry if you don't."

"We've met," she said sweetly. Ng started giggling again, but Victoria silenced him with a look. "The two of us were just chatting about the float."

"Marvelous!"

She hauled me to my feet. "Come over here and we'll check out some cossies."

"Err, if it's inconvenient for you…" I mumbled.

"Not a bit! Anton, we'll be with you in a moment."

He looked puzzled. "I'll come, too, darling. It's my department!"

She held up her hand. "No. Girl talk first!"

With that she dragged me off to a farther dank corner of the storeroom. The walls were slimy with moisture. She slammed me with a jolt up against a beer barrel.

"We can talk here," she said, "but not for long. I'm on again soon."

"You were very good," I gasped.

"Never mind that." She leered into my face. "So, you nosy little prick, you think I murdered my own niece, do you?"

"Your niece? Jennifer was your—you're Uncle Mike?"

"That's right. I used to identify as male, believe it or not."

My throat contracted.

"Uh…oh! Well! I—no, I don't think you killed her… actually."

"Bully for you! Let me tell you something, Jack. My aura's a mess: It looks like somebody threw up a kilo of smarties. I should have been there for her; I'll never forgive myself. But that's none of your business, and I don't take kindly to your naff little friend accusing me of homicidal acts, or you buzzing around town telling people you're me. Now why don't you inform me exactly what the bloody hell's going on."

"I will if you let go of me."

She threw me into a moldy old armchair and loomed over me with her arms folded. "In your own time," she purred.

So, starting from the beginning, and leaving out irrelevant details like the Sambuca, I told her how Paul and I had set out to discover whether his friend Jennifer had been pushed and, if so, who pushed her. I outlined our main suspects and their possible motives, and I mentioned the suicide note torn out of Jennifer's diary.

"Have you got the diary with you?" she asked.

"No. Lavinia burned it."

"How did she get it?"

"I don't really know."

"Why didn't you take the evidence to the police?"

"I don't know. It wasn't very good evidence."

"It's no damn good at all now."

She sank down onto the arm of my chair, produced a tissue from her voluminous cleavage, and loudly blew her nose.

"Poor Jen," she said. "She was spiritually troubled."

I doubted that myself but kept mum.

"I tried to look after her. I took on that wimp Randolph at the shop to keep him out of her hair. She had a great future as a diva. She'd have been my successor—in her own sphere, of course. When she moved on, I tried to see it in cosmic terms. I knew she'd been summoned to the next life, that it must be her time. Now you tell me it was murder! If I find the son of a bitch who pushed her, I'll skin him alive with my bare teeth."

"Look," I said, "Paul and I are amateurs in the strictest sense—"

"I reckon!"

"But I'm sure we're on the verge of discovering the truth.

I can't help feeling it's staring me in the face."

She glared at me.

"But," I continued nervously, "what if we do find out? There's no evidence, there seem to have been no witnesses, the police are satisfied. There's nothing anyone can do."

Her eyes glinted with malicious intent. "Don't worry about that. Just find out who did it!—if you can."

She stood and straightened her clothes.

"I'll wear the same frock in the next set. I'm too emotionally challenged to change."

She started to stride away, then called back over her shoulder, "I'll be in touch. And tell your silly friend—"

"Paul."

"Tell him that's the worst drag I've seen in thirty-five years."

CHAPTER 23

*P*aul laid low over the next few days, and after making such a fool of himself, I wasn't at all surprised. I could imagine how graciously Victoria must have taken to his accusation of murder, especially if he'd presented the idea to her with his usual subtlety.

At first, I was ready to blast him for acting so recklessly, and to make it quite clear that in future when his friends got knocked off he needn't come bounding to me for help! But as time passed and my calls were not returned, I mellowed and felt sorry for him. Victoria must have given him one hell of a hard time! By the time Tuesday rolled around, I was quite happy to accept a simple apology, kiss and make up. "Paul will be Paul" became my motto.

When he turned up abruptly that afternoon, however, he was far from apologetic.

"At last we're getting somewhere, caro!"

"Come in. I've rung a million times. I think I should tell you, I saw Victoria on Sunday night."

"Did you? Bravo. A two-pronged attack, good thinking. My, look at the time. Cocktail hour. I think champagne's called for."

"What? Oh, yes, all right."

I poured us a glass each of flat bubbly. We did the housewifely thing and sat at the kitchen bench.

"I gather your interview didn't go too well," I said gently.

"I put the big sheila on the spot all right, if that's what you mean! It was fabulous."

"But didn't she hit the roof?"

"She sure did! She denied everything. Picked me up and threw me out the door on my butt, like in the movies. You should see the bruise. Look!" He jumped up and whipped down his Aussie Boys training shorts. There was a very nasty discoloration over most of his right buttock.

"Ooooh," I whistled.

"It's too sore to wear Calvin's. Specially just here…ow! Kiss it better!"

I did so. He grinned cheerfully as he eased himself back onto the chair.

"But Paul! You made a huge idiot of yourself. You were wrong!"

"About what, caro?"

"Victoria's not the murderer."

"Yes, she is! I'm more sure of it than my own hair color! The harder she denied it, the more she gave herself away. I mean, she was so angry! If she'd been innocent, would she carry on like that? No, she'd laugh it off. 'Get outta here!' she'd say. A playful pinch on the cheek—that kind of cutesy reaction. Not launch into the stampeding elephant number!"

I gave it a moment's thought. If Victoria was guilty, was she the type to break down and confess at the first sign of trouble? I couldn't see it happening this side of the Stonewall centenary.

"But why did she do it? She's the uncle, you know."

"Victoria is?"

"Yes! She's the Uncle Mike we've read about so often."

Paul considered this new information as he held out his glass for a refill. "Well, that confirms it!" he declared. "Family reasons! Most murders happen within the family. We were barking up the wrong lesbian."

"What family reasons?"

"How would I know? Let's think of some. Victoria would have to be the scourge of the Burke clan. No family would tolerate a monster like that in their midst, not even in New Zealand. Whereas, let's suppose Jennifer was the family pet, the little darling who could do no wrong, beloved by all and sundry. There you are! Pure jealousy!"

"Don't be ridiculous, there's thirty years between them. And uncles aren't jealous of their nieces."

"Not even uncles who wear frocks? What do you think, then?"

"I think she's innocent, and you fucked up."

"No, caro, can't agree. Cast your mind back to your little spasm in the steam room. Who, out of all our suspects, is most likely to have connections in that part of the world? Old finger-in-every-sleazy-pie Victoria, that's who. If she wanted to follow you in there, she could because she's a man, after all, and who would know her? Not you or anyone else! Have you ever seen a drag queen out of her drag? They're unrecognizable!"

"It never occurred to me."

"Me neither, till just now."

My glass trembled. I gulped down the dregs uneasily.

"I'm afraid I told her everything."

"Everything? Like what?"

"About our investigation. The diary. Whom we suspect. The truth, in other words."

"You blabbed? You told the truth?" I'd never seen Paul so testy. "How unprofessional! How—how unqueeny!"

"Yes, well. She was very intimidating."

"So what did she say when you told her all that?"

"She suggested I stay in touch."

"I'll bet."

"And let her know when I flush out the murderer."

Paul clapped his hands together in delight. "That's what we do, then! Tell her we've found him! Hand somebody over to her and tactfully withdraw! She'll relax, leave us alone, and we can trap her. Oh, I love it!"

"We can't do that to some poor innocent person! She might push them off a cliff!"

"How 'bout Rodney?"

"Not even Rodney."

Paul paced the kitchen, rubbing his arse absentmindedly. "Well, could we just say we'd narrowed it down to one suspect but we weren't one hundred percent sold on it? What about that? Somebody she couldn't easily get to."

"Like the Prime Minister?"

"Too far-fetched."

"I was being sarcastic! I still don't think she did it."

"Even so! We don't want her on our backs while we snoop around, do we?"

"No. Let me think. Oh, I'm meeting with Sir Fred tonight."

"Really?"

"His secretary rang and arranged it, out of the blue. I s'pose Dame Norma's been whispering. I'm going to the Belvedere; there's an opera function on."

"Pooh. Why didn't you invite me?"

"You're working. And I'm not invited either. I'm to meet him afterward."

"Well, he's perfect! He's almost the Prime Minister anyhow. Tell Victoria our main suspect is Sir Fred, and you're following it up tonight! See if she sounds relieved. She might let something slip. She might say, 'Whew! I'm off the hook,' or words to that effect."

"Sure."

"What do you think Sir Fred wants?"

"To find out if I'm the donor, I presume."

"What will you say?"

"That I prefer not to comment at this time. That's how businessmen operate."

"Excellent! Ring me first thing tomorrow and give me the goss!"

I sounded very gung ho, no doubt, but I felt much less sure of myself as I approached the evening rendezvous.

As hotels go, the Koala Belvedere International was nine parts Belvedere to one part Koala. It was plush plus. Situated adjacent to the C.B.D., it catered exclusively to the passing trade in multinational financiers whizzing through town to buy a few Aussie dollars whenever the pound looked shaky or the greenback took a nosedive.

The building itself was National Trust–approved. Recently, it had been the home of the State Government Treasury Department and, before that, a Methodist hostel for wayward women. Now, as an outrageously expensive hotel, it combined both its previous functions.

For the building's latest incarnation, designers of the pseudo-antique school had been at it with a vengeance. Nothing had been left untouched. Every surface from floor to ceiling was busy with archaic motifery; each article, down to the toilet paper holder, would have been cozily familiar to our forefathers. Every curlicue known to humanity was there, writ large. Such brazen ostentation might have made King Vittorio Emmanuel II blanch, and if that didn't, the bill certainly would. I can't say I felt right at home as I approached the gleaming red-carpeted entrance.

Two uniformed doormen—both, I noted, sporting zits—went to a good deal of trouble with their facial expressions to let me know I was regarded as a lesser being, and when they ascertained I was not staying in the hotel, they promptly closed all channels of communication and waited for me to return to the bottom of the food chain.

Of course, I'd dressed up in a rather swish blue suit, which hadn't had an outing in years, but perhaps the suave impression was spoiled by a nasty cut I inflicted while shaving. I'd cut myself on the earlobe (yes, it happens), a portion of the anatomy that serves no useful purpose and bleeds like Niagara Falls. Try as I might, I couldn't avoid the accompanying red polka-dot collar. Not a good 'look.'

Eventually, having dropped Sir Fred's name several times in a variety of contexts, I was allowed entry. The snobbier and more complexionally challenged of the doormen directed me up a vast staircase to the Barbirolli bar. It was empty, apart from a liveried barman who made no attempt to put me at my ease.

I ordered a glass of water. It came with a brown slice of pineapple and a green maraschino cherry, and cost $11.50.

A meeting was taking place behind ornate closed doors in an adjacent salon. This must have been the Opera Room, jam-packed with devotees. I strained to catch some snatch of conversation, but the low level of their high-pitched chatter was incomprehensible. I moved closer, but when the barman glared at me I casually retraced my steps. Every time he turned away, I went back to the doors, and quite a cat-and-mouse game developed between us. Finally, he tired of it, but by then it was too late: The doors opened wide. The meeting of the SODS had been adjourned.

An homogenous pack of opera lovers emerged. They were mostly male drones of fashionably late middle age. All had gray hair—widow's peaks were popular—and tanned leathery skin. They wore beige polo-neck jumpers or shapeless tweedy jackets with fussy little bow ties. Gold-rimmed glasses were also at a premium. The one or two ladies present were decidedly dumpy, and everything about them (including the odor of mothballs) bespoke a pre-War aspect.

They drawled or yapped away to each other happily as they made their way past me.

"She has such a tiny voice! You can't tell from recordings."

"No, she just had an off night. Wait till you hear her *Cosi!*"

"I bought the new *Trovatore* today. Stunning's not the word."

"Love to hear it. Who's the baritone?"

"The baritone! Who cares?"

I noticed in the room behind them the remains of a sumptuous dinner.

"Mr. Petrucci?"

A tall, large man had split from the group and strode over to me. He was well groomed and pale, almost cadaverous. He wore gold reading glasses on a chain around his neck Rupert Murdoch–style.

"How do you do?" he said. "Fred Mathieson."

"Hello."

He shook my hand warmly and indicated a table in the corner.

"It will be quieter over here."

We took a seat and ordered a couple of brandies.

"Mind if I smoke?" he asked convivially and, without waiting for an answer, lit up a cigarette. "Aah, much better!" he breathed. "I'm relieved that's over. They're a devoted lot—well, they're official devotees, aren't they!—but still, these functions can be trying."

"I'm sure."

"Now, Mr. Petrucci, I'll be brief. I've been hearing your name around the corridors of power in the Sydney Opera. You're something of a mystery man."

"Am I?"

He laughed lightly. "Indeed, yes. Tell me: What line of work are you in?"

This interrogation had gotten off on the wrong foot. He was asking the questions!

"I'm retired."

"Retired. That is, you inherited a small amount of money from the sale of some property, and I believe you live in a pleasant but modest terrace in the Inner West. I've been poking my nose around, too, you see."

"Well, really, I don't understand…"

He leaned forward. "Mr. Petrucci, how do we communicate? What is the setup that enables you to finance certain operatic extravaganzas?"

"The setup?"

"Yes. Does your money go through a solicitor? Do you use a courier? Is it a bank transfer? How does it work?"

"Err, I use a courier."

"Ah. Which company?"

"I don't wish to comment at this time."

He snorted, flicking ash onto the polished table. "Off the record."

"Oh. Off the record. Well—"

"You don't know. And why should you? You are *not* the source of those donations."

"Well...no. Not really. Who is?"

He relaxed. "I'm afraid I can honestly tell you I've no idea. May I ask you another question?"

"I'd rather you didn't."

"Do you wear women's clothing regularly?"

"Of course not!" He couldn't have heard about the Friends of Dorothy party, surely! It was aeons ago.

"Oh, you don't? My mistake. Then you cannot be Jennifer Burke's uncle. Her uncle, I happen to know, wears women's clothes and goes under the pseudonym of Victoria. So!" His voice took on a steely edge. "You are not the donor, and you are not the poor girl's uncle, even though you have personally led several people to believe both of those fabrications. Mr. Petrucci, you may well be in breach of the law."

"Oh. Shit."

"Quite. I don't care about that, however. What I want to know is: Who are you? Why are you concerning yourself in the fate of Miss Burke?"

"I'm a...an inquisitive well-wisher."

"Crap!" He slapped the table. The brandies shook. "I've talked to a few people about you. I'm perfectly well aware who you are."

"You are?"

"And I think it's utterly despicable, the depths to which you scribblers will sink. I can't say I've ever heard of *Opera del Mondo* magazine, but it does have a trashy ring to it, and if your journalistic methods are anything to go by, it must be a rag of the worst order! I know your game—I've dealt with your type before. God knows, it required all my skill and connections to hush up Jennifer's regrettable suicide, to keep the story off Sunday breakfast tables across Australia, and I don't intend to see it popping up now in the lurid European press or anywhere else.—if for no other reason then simply because Miss Burke and I were very close. I was like a father to her."

I began to see the light. He must have spoken to Randolph!

I quickly adopted the demeanor of a world-weary opera correspondent. I half-closed one eye, gazed enigmatically into the
distance, and swirled my brandy around in the glass with care-
less nonchalance.

"Will you watch what you're doing?" he snapped. "You're
spilling brandy everywhere."

I opened my eye. "So I am. Whoops." I coughed. "Well,
you're spot on, Sir Fred, alias Frederic. I am writing the story
up, and a hot little piece it's going to be. Would you care to give
us your own version of events?"

"No, I would not. I would like a guarantee from you that
you will suppress the article and start minding your own damn
business."

"I'm sorry, this is my business." I shrugged. "The story is
intriguing. A brilliant young singer is offered a starry debut if
she will sleep with a certain influential person: She does it,
only to find he reneges on the offer. In despair, she kills herself.
Makes interesting reading."

"That's not how it happened!" he protested but stopped
himself. He smiled broadly. "I'm no fool," he said. "I know it's
useless to threaten your sort. You are lowlife. Words like
decency mean nothing to you. I'll have to silence you the only
way I know how."

He reached into his coat pocket. I paled and shoved my
chair out from the table, ready to duck for cover.

"Where are you going?"

He had produced a printed document.

"I'm given to understand, Mr. Petrucci, that you genuinely
enjoy opera."

"Oh, yes. I'm a Tebaldi addict."

"Indeed. I've also noted that you are not a current subscriber
to our season. Well, I am about to buy your silence. If you kill
your story, I'll give you a lifetime subscription to the opera.
Two seats at any performance, every performance if you like,
for the rest of your life. We can't guarantee Tebaldi, but we have

some notable singers even so. My offer is set out in this legally binding contract. Would you care to peruse it?"

I was flabbergasted. I suspected some trick, but no: To the best of my knowledge, the deal spelled out in the document was exactly as he had said. He held out a gold-plated fountain pen. I signed on the dotted line as he ordered two more brandies.

"Good." He smiled as I handed back the contract. "May I have my pen, please?"

"Oh, sorry."

He rolled his eyes, took his pen, and deftly flicked his glasses on to examine the signature. Satisfied, he leaned back. "You keep one copy for yourself. Your subscription will arrive by courier tomorrow, Friday at the latest. The company is TNT, incidentally. Fill out the form; address it to me personally, care of the Opera."

He lowered his voice to a faint snarl. "Make no mistake, Mr. Petrucci, I intend to hold you to this. If anything further appears in print or any other medium about that business, and you have anything remotely to do with it, I'll hit you with the full force of the law: breach of contract, for a start, plus anything else I can think of. And there's plenty."

I put away my copy. "I promise you, Sir Fred, the story's dead."

"Dead. My word, it is. Now drink your brandy and piss off."

He stood and, without another word, walked out.

I was left stunned by this turn of events and sat awhile with my drink, in spite of the barman's three attempts to remove the glass before I'd finished.

I looked again at the contract, searching for hidden clauses with a catch. Any moment I expected to find that I'd agreed to offer myself in a virgin sacrifice, or willed my estate to the Cat Protection Society of Tasmania. But no, nothing was amiss.

The nagging question remained: Was Sir Fred the murderer? Was this agreement his attempt to compromise me? If I was legally involved in Sir Fred's affairs, and he was charged with murder, would that make me an accomplice? I didn't know, but there must have been some reason for this generous gesture. If he could find out my personal details, he could just as easily have discovered that *Opera del Mondo* didn't exist. Surely he would not have taken Randolph's story at face value without checking up: Randolph was famously unstable.

Sir Fred also didn't seem like the type to give away life subscriptions to the opera on a mere whim. Perhaps he fancied me. No, that couldn't have been it. Did he imagine I knew something he didn't want me to know? And if so, what? Did I know it? Did I know I knew it? Was I losing my mind?

These thoughts occupied me as I wandered back to my car. I'd parked in an alley in the business district nearby. It had been the only space I could find at the time, although by now the streets were pretty much deserted. So were the nearby buildings, two blocks of terraces recently occupied by the Department of Youth and Community Services before they moved to new premises on the 107th floor of the Sydney Tower. The terraces were boarded up and scheduled to be demolished. I crept up a passageway between the two blocks. Glancing at my watch, I saw it was midnight.

Dark back streets can look disconcertingly similar, and I've often misplaced my car in them. Luckily, not this time: There it was, snuggling under a dim street lamp up the other end. I whistled softly to soothe myself, a jaunty number from the third act of *Rigoletto*.

Out of nowhere a car drove into the street behind me. I heard the low hum of its engine, and turned. I couldn't see the driver or even what type of car it was, just the headlights. In an instant they flashed onto high beam, and the car jerkily accelerated. It was heading directly for me, bumping the gutter as it drove up onto the pavement. Blindly I looked around—nothing but brick walls. I ran like buggery.

Farther ahead, a metal garbage tin sat on the footpath. I

lunged blindly, trying to clear it, but my foot caught the lid and I fell. With the bin on top of me, I rolled down a set of steps and smashed against a small basement door. Under the impact the door burst open and I fell through to safety. A split second later, the rolling lid hit the front of the car close behind. With a bang, it sent the lid spinning after me. I sat up. I only had enough time to shut my eyes before the lid whacked me full in the face. Lying back in a daze, warm blood seeping into my eye, I heard the car screeching away in the distance.

I felt faint, and lay there for a minute, heaving and covered with garbage. I felt one or two cockroaches scurry over my arms and neck. With a shiver I climbed to my feet and cautiously hobbled out into the street. It was empty. I staggered up to my car, fell into the driver's seat, and locked myself in.

I cleaned my face up as best I could—the cut on my forehead was a lot smaller than it felt—and, taking a deep breath, I slowly drove to the nearest public hospital, some twenty kilometers away.

Fortunately, they weren't too busy. There were only three people ahead of me: a little boy with a fever, an old asthmatic woman, and a derelict with a split lip. The asthmatic woman glared at the derelict, then at me. "Drunks!" she wheezed.

The doctor was a young Chinese girl who looked very tired but nonetheless smiled at me reassuringly. "Shouldn't be more than an hour," she said. "Make yourself a cup of tea if you like."

While I was waiting, I phoned Paul. He immediately promised to jump in a cab. Within fifteen minutes he'd arrived, carrying a small overnight bag. When he saw me, he imitated *The Scream* by Munch.

"Ach! Caro! You look like shit. Lucky I brought slap." He patted my hand. "What happened? Who fucked who? Tell me everything."

I opened my mouth to speak, but no words came. Instead, to my surprise, I began sobbing.

"Oh, don't cry, honey," he said, putting his arms round me and rocking me back and forth. "Shh. Paul's here. Poor darling."

The asthmatic woman wheezed in disgust. "There's no call for that," she sniffed. In reply, Paul reached into his shirt pocket and pulled out a packet of cigarettes. He held them out to her.

"Fag?" he said loudly.

She grunted and turned away, then thought the better of it and took one. With a flourish he lit it for her, and she sucked on it greedily, gasping between drags.

Paul waited until she was clearly enjoying herself, then stood up. "Excuse me," he said, pointing to a clearly marked NO SMOKING sign. He leaned over, daintily pulled the cigarette from her lips, threw it to the floor, and stepped on it. Sore and sorry as I was, I couldn't help laughing at the look on her face.

"I've decided to move in and be your nurse and bodyguard," he said to me, sitting on my lap. "Until this murder stuff is out of the way. I'll be no trouble 'cause I don't eat a thing, and I won't try to manage things because I can't think."

"OK," I whispered. "Thanks." I looked down. "You didn't bring much."

"That's only for the next couple of hours. I'll get the rest of my essentials in the morning."

I looked at him slyly. "There wouldn't be anything in your bag remotely like a chocolate?"

"'Course there would."

"I love you, Paul."

"I love you, too, and I want to have your babies. What's your name again?"

The asthmatic woman spluttered.

CHAPTER 24

 hings were getting serious. Paul even let his customary devil-may-care attitude waver when I
described in bloodcurdling detail my escapade in
the dark alley. We decided not to tell a soul. We could no longer
trust anyone, not even our own mothers. (If my mother were
still alive, she'd wonder what the fuss was about: She often
used to drive along the sidewalk.)

Paul moved in, as threatened, and during the next few days
we agonized over the big questions; namely, who was behind
all this and what would we do if and when we found out who
it was. Painstakingly, we went through every possible suspect,
motive, and theory—and always returned to the same inescapable conclusion: Everybody involved was guilty as hell! I kicked
my wimpy old self for not intervening during Lavinia's bonfire.
If we had the diary at our disposal, I was sure a vital clue
would spring out rubbish bin lid–like and hit us in the face.

We had plenty of time to chat, as Paul had practically put
me under house arrest. He wouldn't let me go anywhere without him—and then only if he regarded it as a top priority, such
as a trip to the bottle shop. He made me cancel the lessons
I'd arranged, and he also took my measurements so I would-
n't have to go to the Mardi Gras costume meeting.

"Maybe it's just as well, love," said Anton over the phone,
when I told him I had a previous engagement.

"What do you mean?"

"Oh, well, Tammy will be there, and he's a little piqued
at you."

"At me?"

"Yes. Dame Norma sacked him—and after all these years,
too! Can't say I'm sorry."

282

"Why did she do it?"

"She was unhappy about her Mardi Gras appearance. She blames Tam. Tam blames you."

"But I never wanted to do it! You told me Norma loved the idea!"

"I thought she would. How wrong can you be? Listen, it's a long story, I'll tell you someday. It's all for the best, and there's a happy ending: When Tam got his notice, he was so shattered he went through her wardrobe and pinched her *Girl of the Golden West* outfit! You know, the black cowgirl suit with the gold beading? It's one of the few cossies she keeps at home; she actually makes the company rent it from her, the old bitch! Tam nicked it on a sentimental whim and I grabbed it! Wait till you see it! It suits your coloring, and I barely need to take it in!"

"Um, I don't know about this parade now, I can't make public appearances in stolen cowgirl suits. What if—"

"Don't worry, Dotty. It'll all have blown over by then. Got to run, darling. Be in touch."

It seemed as though my troubles were far from over, but I decided not to worry about Mardi Gras just yet. Somehow I doubted I would live that long.

Not that anything further happened. There were no more attempts on my life, no anonymous phone calls or anything faintly spine-tingling. Paul took the credit: His terrifying presence kept the forces of evil at bay. That was his theory at any rate.

Of course, he was not by my side twenty-four hours a day. He still had the odd performance to do. Not only that, but with Christmas fast approaching, the number of parties he was invited to (always a glut) increased markedly. He missed most of them, especially at first, assuming a martyred expression for hours afterward. Eventually, after having milked this virtuous pose from every possible angle, he tired of it and simply became grumpy.

On Sunday the week before Christmas, Paul was more than usually disgruntled. We were sitting in the kitchen, making steady progress through a pile of banana pancakes with Camp Maple Syrup.

"Pancakes are hateful," he grizzled with his mouth full. "They make me fat."

"Leave them then."

"Caro, listen to us! We sound like an old married couple."

"More like the two prisoners in *Kiss of the Spider Woman*."

"I'm the butch one."

"What a revolutionary idea. Sugar?"

He gave me his best pathetic look. "Nothing personal, caro, but it's getting me down. You're OK. You're happy to sit around with your divas."

"Wait a sec! I'm not keeping you here. You've been wonderful but let's not strain our happy, superficial relationship."

"Caro mio! Never! It's just that today's my last day off before Christmas, and there's four fabulous parties on and liters of new talent around. Why don't you come along? There's safety in numbers! It's true—it says so in *The Boyfriend*."

"No, but you go. I'll lock myself in and I won't answer the phone. I'll be fine."

No extra persuasion was necessary. Paul launched into the pancakes with renewed vigor.

"I'll call you now and then to check up. I'll leave uproarious drunken messages."

The mention of Paul's phone messages reminded me of something I had been meaning to bring up.

"Remember when you rang that first time you had the photos?"

"From the sauna? What about it?"

"Well, a couple of things have occurred to me. Did I tell you there was another call later?"

"No. Who was it?"

"Nobody spoke, but I heard background noise. I wonder if that call was from the sauna, too."

"Don't know. I used the blue phone downstairs. There were a couple of people waiting, I think. They could have seen me dial your number. Shit, don't tell me the murderer was standing right next to me! How creepy!" He ostentatiously crossed himself.

"Well, someone stole those photos, and it was no accident. You don't go near other people's snaps without a reason."

"Unless you've lost your mind."

I mused. "When you talked about the party shots you said something like 'Wait till you see them, there's one in particular.'"

"Did I?"

"Can't you remember? What was there you wanted to show me in particular?"

He rubbed his neck thoughtfully. "Some spunk, I s'pose. The waiters were heaven on a tray."

"Where were the pictures taken? From the pool? From the balcony?"

"Everywhere. Wait a minute, there was a really good shot of the house…was that it? I remember now; an excellent photo. I thought I really must do a course in photography, you know? The boy has talent. It was the back of the house from a distance, side view, so there were lots of people milling around. Victoria was in it, sitting by the pool in a hideous caftan. She was reading somebody's palm and whoever it was looked incredibly pissed off!"

"So it was a photo of Victoria? Why was that significant?"

"Think! Think!" He slapped his forehead.

"Whose palm was she reading?"

"I think it was Dame Norma's—wackadoo, I've got it! There was something else. Above all the activity, Victoria and Dame Norma and everyone, there was a guy at one of the windows on the second floor. A side window, and he'd half opened the blind and was just staring—standing completely still and staring out the window, not at the party but gazing off into the distance. Intense, you know? Like he was waiting for something. And it was all golden—must have been late afternoon. And, yes, that's it, it was one of the waiters. He shouldn't have even been up there."

"What was he staring at?"

"Well, he was looking in the direction of the cliff."

I remembered Tim's office, and thinking how someone could have witnessed the murder from there. Apparently somebody did, and Paul took a picture of him.

"Was he shocked? Stunned?"

"No, I don't think so. He was…just watching."

My pulse raced. "Paul, this is what we've been waiting for! If someone saw the murder, we can find him. What did he look like?"

"I don't remember."

"Try!"

He closed his eyes. "Sorry, I can't. Blond, maybe? It was a great photo."

This was the most promising lead we had ever had. Paul agreed to give it more thought at the four parties and scampered away that afternoon with a light heart. I settled down with *La Wally*, an opera that Tebaldi rescued from obscurity as a vehicle for herself. Strangely enough, the torturous plot is sorted out by the soprano helpfully flinging herself over a cliff. The resonance, as they say, was not lost on me.

I felt like an early night and prepared to turn in around 10. Paul hadn't called, which was no surprise. I had just put on the kettle for chamomile tea when there was a knock at the front door. I froze in my tracks. Should I answer? The knock came again. Renata was working the top of her range; they'd know somebody was home.

"Marc? Are you there? It's Reg!"

I opened the door. There he stood looking tousled, slightly sweaty and edible.

"Hello, Reg. I didn't expect to see you here!"

"Can I come in?"

"Err, yes, of course."

He stepped inside. I locked the door, and he almost knocked me to the floor in his puppy-dog enthusiasm.

"Oh, Marc, I miss you. Darling! Please, can we go to bed now?"

"What?"

"Please."

"Certainly. I was just about to."

"Come on!"

I hardly had time to think before we were up and into it—torrents of sexual energy explosively unleashed, the kind of lovemaking that forms the basis of major friendships and minor operas. I hadn't realized how much I'd missed him.

Hours passed before our passion ebbed to a manageable level. Even then, just the feel of his body against mine kept up a supply of warm tingles. He lay facing me in my arms, his head on my chest.

"Reg?" I whispered.

"Mmm?"

"My hand's gone to sleep."

"Oh." He shifted and turned over.

"Reg?"

"Mmm?"

"I'm in love with you."

"But you've got that boyfriend. Paul."

My impulse was to quash this distracting rumor once and for all, but on reflection I thought I could use it to my advantage.

"Yes, it's awkward," I ventured. "But things might change. Radically. If I had some sort of commitment from you. We must be completely open and honest with each other."

"I love you."

"I know." I kissed him lightly. "That's not quite what I mean. Does Charles know you're here?"

He turned over again, alert now. His eyes met mine.

"Don't talk about Charles."

"I just want to know if he knows."

"No. No, he doesn't." He pulled the pillow up behind him and sat up straight. "I've been thinking about that contract and stuff. It makes me nervous."

"Nervous? What are you nervous about? Your debut?"

"No. Well, sort of."

"There's no need. Your voice is wonderful."

"Oh, yeah, I guess."

"Why are you nervous? Is it something in the contract?"

"I'm not allowed to talk about it."

I sighed. "Here we go again!"

"I know, I'm sorry. I'll tell you tomorrow, I promise. Let's go to sleep."

"I won't sleep now," I grumbled. "I'll make some chamomile tea. Do you want one?"

"OK."

I crept down to the kitchen, boiled some water, and plopped in the tea bags. On my way back to the bedroom I noticed the light flashing on the answer phone. It took me by surprise: I dimly recalled hearing bells ring, but had assumed it was Love.

"Caro, it's me! I'm having the time of my life—I am a dancing queen! Listen, are you OK? Good. I've actually remembered something important. You didn't think I would, did you? Shut up, will you! Sorry, that's just Rodney. I—What? Yeah, he says hi. Yeah, thanks, the same again. Good, he's gone. Look, I remembered about the photo! The boy at the window was your friend. Reg! Ralph, Rhonda, whatever he calls himself now. He was a waiter at Dame Norma's party! I'm positive. I knew I'd seen him before, that night he was out near the barn, remember? That's exactly what he looked like in the photo. How 'bout that? We better talk to him. Oh, um, I may not be home tonight, there's a pretty good chance I'll get lucky. OK? You stay inside, lie low, and chew your food thoroughly. See you soon."

I sat at the table watching our drinks cool. My mind was a

blank. Was the key to this whole thing lying in a postcoital stupor upstairs in my bed? Had he seen something and, if so, did he realize what he'd seen? Was he in danger? I dreaded to think of the other alternative: that Reg might in some way be a party to the murder. I would need to approach this carefully. I went upstairs.

He was almost asleep again.

"Here's our tea," I said brightly.

"Oh. Ta." He sat up and I snuggled in next to him. "This is cold."

"Um, easier to digest that way."

"Oh."

"So," I said, "in our new spirit of openness, why don't you tell me everything about yourself and Charles." I cleared my throat. "I'm ordering you!" I added.

He responded at once. "OK! See, I've been thinking about what you said about the contract. It's true, he makes me do things. Bad things, you know. Sneaky things. That's not fair, is it?"

"He has no right to make you do anything."

"Yeah." He sounded dubious.

"What did you want to tell me? The thing you're nervous about?"

I waited.

"Well—it's part of his plan, see. He wants me to have the op."

I was all prepared to hear about murder. I didn't quite follow him.

"The what?"

"The op. The operation."

"What operation?"

"You know. The one they all had. The castrati."

There was dead silence.

"*What?*"

"He says it won't hurt."

"Charles wants to castrate you?"

"There hasn't been a real castrato since Moreschi, and he died a long time ago. It's for publicity, see. Charles says it'll be a talking point all over the world! It gives his plan—what is it? Legitimacy?"

"I don't believe it!"

"I'm not super-keen, but I can see his point. He says it will increase my vocal range."

"'Charles says!' 'Charles says!'" I cupped my hand protectively around the innocent furry little creatures. Reg smiled.

"That feels nice."

"Nobody can force you to give these up for art! It's inconceivable! Literally!"

"Well, the contract—"

"Bugger the contract. You'd be putting your life in danger. This is utterly sick! How does Charles propose to do it? Hire a barbarian?"

"He's got a doctor friend whose hobby is sex-performance art. Mutilation, all that stuff. He's interested in doing the op. He wanted to do it at a dance party, but Charles said no, it has to be done privately."

"Oh! How thoughtful! What a great humanitarian! Give Charles the Nobel Prize!"

"You don't think I should let them go ahead."

I held him as tightly as I could. "It's out of the question! Reg, this is your body. It belongs to you, not anyone else. That's the law! This scheme of Charles is worse than rape! It won't change your voice, and it will hurt, heaven help us! It's an idea that would only occur to an obsessive madman! No, no, *no!*"

He nuzzled me fondly.

"You really do care about me."

"I'm not letting you go back. In fact, you're never leaving this bed."

He turned over.

"OK."

I kept my hand there, carefully shielding the endangered

species, as Reg's breathing became regular and he drifted off to sleep, cuddling up to me instinctively. I lay still. My heart beat furiously; my limbs were taut with anxiety, my eyes wide open. I was resolved: Moreschi was the last of the red-hot eunuchs, and he was going to stay that way.

It must have been 4 in the morning when I heard Paul let himself in. Evidently he didn't get lucky at the four parties. Too bad, I thought, his ego could stand a few of life's regulation knocks for once.

Typically, Paul made quite a racket in the kitchen, but Reg didn't stir. I had half a mind to creep down and relate the grisly scenario I'd just heard, but decided it would keep till morning. I closed my eyes. A champagne cork popped. Really, this wanton extravagance had to stop! I wondered whether he'd brought some party piece back with him: I strained but heard nothing until Paul's voice rang out loud and clear. He was playing his message back! The vanity of show people!

At last I heard him head for his bedroom, or so I thought. Instead, the footsteps grew closer. The door of my bedroom drifted open.

"Ah, yes. I thought I might find him here. May I come in?"

There, backlit by the night-lamp in the hall, was the unmistakable form of Charles Mignon. He held a glass of my champagne. Without giving me a chance to answer, he wandered into the room and sat facing the bed in my rocking chair.

"Forgive the intrusion," he simpered.

"How—how did you get in?"

"Oh, we had a key cut long ago. Raoul!"

Reg jumped, startled into wakefulness.

"Charles! Oh! I—"

"Don't say a word," Charles commanded. "Go downstairs and make yourself a saucer of coffee or something. I have matters to discuss with Marc."

"Charles—"

"Do what I tell you!"

Without another word, Reg slid nervously out of bed, gathered his clothes up off the floor, and left the room.

"What—how dare you?" I blustered. "Get out or I'll call the police."

"The pen is mightier than the sword, my dear fellow," he replied smoothly. "But the gun is streets ahead of both. I have one and I'm pointing it at you."

I wiggled down under the blankets.

"Reg turned up out of the blue," I explained.

"You mean Raoul?"

"Raoul, then. He's over eighteen, for Christ's sake. There's no need for these amateur dramatics."

Charles paused. "You're very fond of him."

"Yes. And he's fond of me."

"I'm well aware of that. Yesss…all right. I'll be magnanimous. You can have him. Take him—in whichever way suits your fancy. The prize is yours; you're welcome to it."

"What do you mean?"

"I'm not interested in his body, not anymore. Frankly, I get bored after a couple of sessions. I prefer to move on. What I am interested in, very much so, is his career. Over that major part of his life I shall retain complete control."

I sat up and folded my arms. He sounded, as usual, fair and reasonable. But I knew better.

"I've heard all about your one-sided contract."

"It's nothing of the kind. Raoul will be a superstar. Even more than that, a legend. I've set my mind to it, and nothing is going to stand in my way."

What had he said that first time we'd met in Café Butt? It suddenly came back to me: *I'm too dangerous to ignore.* I was petrified, but I took a punt—a shot in the dark, to coin a phrase. I let him have it.

"Charles," I said. "You killed Jennifer Burke."

He rolled his head back and chuckled. "Nonsense! She suicided."

"You pushed her over the edge. Raoul was watching from a window on the second floor. He saw everything. I—I confirmed it with him."

"Oh, did you?"

"Yes, I did. Just now. Tonight."

"Before, during, or after your exertions?"

"Err, well, after."

"I know you're bluffing. Raoul hasn't the slightest idea what went on. He's an artist; he doesn't need to be involved in the sordid workings of day-to-day management. He only knew I was in an important private meeting with Jennifer and didn't wish to be interrupted. I sent him upstairs to keep a lookout. I could see him, too, don't forget. If anybody wandered up the track, he would wave to let me know. Then, after I'd given her a gentle shove, I returned and told him she'd jumped. I explained that I'd failed to prevent this dreadful accident, and it might be better for everyone's collective future if we forgot I'd ever been up there. I then sent Norma to the cliff top on some pretext. She discovered the note and thence the body. I suggested to Raoul that he call the police. So you see, you do *not* have a witness!"

"It was you! You're a murderer!"

I threw the bedclothes aside.

"Marc," he barked in a harsh tone. "It would be in your interests to stay put! Get back to bed."

I did.

"You've been such a thorn in my side! I have many more important things to do than worry about that girl. I was so annoyed when your idiotic friend Paul told me to my face that he didn't believe the suicide story! I'd seen him at the party taking pictures. Heaven knows what he might have captured on film. Needless to say, the photographs and the negatives have been destroyed. I got Raoul to follow him, to a sauna of all places, where it was simple enough to remove them from his locker. Then I set Raoul up with you."

"You set us up? It was deliberate?"

"I wanted to find out what you knew, what possible interest you could have in that girl's affairs. I still don't know, to be honest."

I was stunned. "You set us up? Me and Reg? I thought it was fate!"

"I was fate's agent. I've done you a lot of favors, you know."

I broke into a sweat. "You tried to kill me! What sort of favor is that?"

"I couldn't decide what to do with you. I realized if you went to the police, they might reopen their investigation, which would mean a lot of unwelcome time-wasting. Fortunately, you never seemed to contemplate such a sensible course of action. Anyway, please accept my apology. I got Raoul to lure you back to that sauna. I'll admit, I tried to engineer a little accident."

"And you killed an old politician in the Jacuzzi!"

"What on earth are you talking about?"

"The man whose stick you stuck through the door handles. He had a heart attack, or so they said."

"How unfortunate. They're far too hot, these saunas. If I were a politician, I wouldn't be caught dead there."

I scoffed. "Well, neither was I!"

"Which was a relief, because later I heard a rumor you were the elusive opera donor. You were worth much more to me alive. Of course, now I'm told you are no such thing."

He waved the gun around playfully. I thought it was about time I saved my life. "I might be the donor. How can you be sure?"

He mused. "I'm inclined to believe Fred Mathieson on this one. He certainly gave you your comeuppance! By the way, I am genuinely sorry about that business with the car. It was foolhardy of me, but you must understand, I'm getting very tired of you. You wouldn't even support my plan for a theatre in Roy's festival!"

"I do support it!"

Charles snorted contemptuously. "Too late now! He's gone cold on the idea. His self-promoting untalented sister talked him out of it. But I had my sweet revenge there! When I finally got hold of that bloody diary, I wrote all sorts of vile things in it about her! My dear, the phraseology was inspired. Some of my best work lost forever, albeit in a good cause. I must recycle it in my next review.

"I then had Raoul put the book in her room. I thought she'd throw it in the garbage. I never dreamed she'd be so thorough as to burn it! Brilliant! Ashes to ashes. I presume you discovered the diary's significance?"

"You tore Jennifer's suicide note out of it."

"Yes. A little ditty she penned in mild distress when she broke up with Seaton. It came in quite handy."

"But why?" I asked. "Why did you kill that poor girl?"

He stretched and took a deep breath. "Well. You never heard her sing, did you?"

"No."

"There were three young major talents in this country: Raoul, of course; Seaton—it stretches credibility, but he'll go far since he's very very good—and Jennifer Burke. She was easily the most extraordinary talent I've ever heard. She had looks, musicality, stagecraft, and a voice that'd make Norma Clutterbuck grab the nearest bedpan and head back to the hospice. Of course, those were early days for her vocally: She hadn't lost that purity of tone, which is essential for the old masters. Her next career decision would have been crucial.

"I was very keen to involve her in my plans. With those three, I could set the music world on fire! She was very ambitious, as you know, and with good reason. She fell in with my plans at first, but Fred Mathieson filled her head with grandiose ideas: She would become the next Callas, the next Tebaldi, and outshine them all. Trouble is, she could have! With me she was an asset, but against me she was a formidable threat. There's only so much limelight available in this business. It's as simple as that. I had to remove the threat. What a team she and Raoul would have made—in Handel, in Purcell. It'll be trickier with Raoul on his own, but naturally I have a game plan. Quite a fascinating one!"

"Oh? Tell me."

He laughed wickedly. "I'd rather not reveal it till everything's cut-and-dried."

My throat tightened. "Well, when did you decide to bump Jennifer off?"

"That's a pulp-fiction way of putting it! I visited her after one of the *Phar Lap* workshops. It was about the time she was losing interest in my scheme; she'd just finished with Seaton as well, so I couldn't use him to influence her. A bloody nuisance, all that. She told me to take the old masters and stuff them, basically. She was out of the room, and the diary was lying there open at the pages you mentioned. I kept them for later use."

"Why did you kill her at a huge party with so many people around? Wasn't that a big risk to take?"

He rocked the chair briskly, in a huff. "I don't do these things on a whim! It took me a while to settle on Dame Norma's as the best spot. I knew the layout there, of course, and I knew Ms. Burke's love life was an utter mess: Even a cursory glimpse in the diary showed that! So, if the suicide note was not accepted at face value, if the police suspected murder, at least there were several people in the vicinity who might reasonably have had a motive. It was insurance."

"And you arranged to meet her at the party?"

"Yes. I said I'd discovered who the donor was, that I'd talked him around and he'd agreed to sponsor her career. We walked up to the cliff; we couldn't risk someone overhearing this hot information! And then," he chuckled softly, "her career took an unexpected nosedive."

"Now I've heard everything."

He frowned. "Yes, you have."

I felt a nasty anticipatory feeling in the pit of my stomach, as though I'd eaten a bad oyster and was waiting for it to act up.

"So," I gulped, "I suppose you're going to kill me."

"I could, certainly." He toyed with the gun. "I like plans. The beauty of this plan was twofold: Nobody imagined it was murder, and there is no evidence. Even Raoul was unaware of it. But if I shoot you here and now, there will a body, an investigation, a witness—all those petty accoutrements. A huge bother. When I came here tonight, I still didn't know what to do with you. Now I don't think I need to do anything at all."

I breathed out (something I'd forgotten to do for some time). "Thank God. Why not?"

"As I said, there's no evidence. You could kick up a fuss, I daresay, but who's going to believe you? Certainly not Sir Fred. He thinks you're a muckraking journalist trying to beat up a story."

"How do you know that?"

"I told him what Randolph had told me. *Opera del Mondo*—for heaven's sake! I even suggested to Mathieson he buy you off with a subscription. Did he?"

"Yes!"

"Marvelous. You accepted it?"

"Well, yes. Why not?"

"How corrupt life is. I'm thrilled to hear that you yourself are well and truly compromised. Secondly, there is the matter of Raoul. At the moment, he has the prospect of a wonderful career, and you have the prospect of a wonderful time! But if you were to drag all this up and somehow make it stick, what would happen? My plans for him would be abandoned, and he would be arrested as an accessory to the murder. Jail would be a terrible trial for a sensitive boy like Raoul, fond as he is of anal sex."

"He didn't know what you were up to."

"I'm afraid I would be forced to admit that he knew everything. I'm very persuasive."

He stood and tucked the gun in his coat pocket. With a quick swig he emptied the champagne glass.

"Yes, I don't think I need to worry about you any longer, Mr. Petrucci. Our shared time this evening has been fruitful. You have no reason to make trouble and plenty of reason not to. And if you do, I can still find some way to get rid of you quickly and quietly."

He walked to the door. "Please don't get up, Raoul and I will see ourselves out. I'm taking him with me for debriefing. I suggest you use the time alone to mull over our discussion."

He tiptoed out and thoughtfully extinguished the hall light.

I lay there in a quandary for the few remaining hours of darkness. Charles was so right. I couldn't let Reg go to prison. Could I even let him discover what had been afoot under his very nose, so to speak? On the other hand, neither could I allow Charles to go whipping off my lover's testicles whenever the mood took him. It was a classic conflict of interests.

My other problem was Paul. Would I tell him what I'd learned? And what would he do if I did? He didn't give a damn about Reg. Yet he deserved to be told, and I could hardly keep such a major piece of dirt to myself.

Morning came and Paul, lucky as ever, hadn't returned. I felt enormously hungry, and toasted an entire loaf of yeast-free Italian bread.

It was a glorious day. I popped outside to pick some jasmine from the vine newly flourishing on my back fence. As I arranged the flowers in a yellow ceramic vase, an impromptu attempt to brighten up the kitchen, a solution of sorts occurred to me. I would explain everything to Paul, but not straightaway. There was someone else to speak to first. I opened the phone book and found the number for the Upstairs Nursery, Bondi.

CHAPTER 25

*M*y meeting with Victoria was not terribly satisfying. I don't know what I expected. I suppose I was hoping she'd take over and solve all my problems. We met that morning at the beachfront, a couple of blocks from her florist–sex shop emporium. I gazed at the flat ocean as I waited for her. It was a few days before Christmas, so most of the world was out shopping. The sunbathing fraternity had been reduced to schoolboys, Maori musclemen, and layabouts asleep in their ancient vests and overcoats.

I was roused from my lethargy by the approach of what looked like a walking rock melon. It was Victoria, and for one ghastly moment I thought she was naked. Fortunately, it was just a first impression: She wore an orange-pink sari.

"Apricot is my new color," she said. "It focuses the female spirit. Sorry I'm late, but we're very busy before Christmas, and a lot of new stock has just arrived."

She sat and turned to me expectantly. As accurately as I could, I told her what I'd discovered: the who, the how, and the why. She took it very calmly, much to my surprise.

"What are you going to do now?" she asked.

I said I had no idea, and I emphasized the uselessness of going to the police with an uncorroborated story. She agreed.

"I've never had much joy from the police. Still, thanks for what you've done for my niece. I believe I've misjudged you. Pop into the florist's on Christmas Eve: I'll give you a little something for your tree." She patted my hand heavily and was gone.

Paul showed up that afternoon, distinctly the worse for wear.

"I love Christmas, caro! There's so much goodwill toward men. After the party, everybody went to the Phoenix, then the

Taxi Club, then an all-day recovery party with a cyberfunk theme. I didn't sleep for twenty-four hours! Eventually, the drugs ran out and I taxied home. I was so tired, I forgot I was living with you, caro! Rodney came along for the ride and, well, to make a long story short, we're having an affair!"

I nearly dropped my coffee.

"You loathe Rodney!"

Paul looked sheepish. "I'm too quick to judge people. I used to think Rodney was this up-himself idiot, but he's just misunderstood! Mind you, it's easy to be misunderstood when you're that stupid." He winked. "He's back at the flat now. I came to get my toothbrush et cetera. Anything happen while I was out?"

I shook my head. "All very quiet."

"There you are, then. I'd say we're over the danger period."

"Absolutely. You go back to Rodney. He's very cute. Have one for me."

"I did. By the way, if you see him, don't mention that he used to be a prostitute—I'm saving that up for our first big fight!"

He sighed and put on a soppy face. "You know, caro, this may not be the big romance of my young life, but let's see what happens! I'm always prepared to commit myself emotionally, as many people will testify. We're giving it till Christmas."

"See you back here on Boxing Day."

"I love how you're such a cynical old bag."

I was in a festive mood that evening. Tebaldi never recorded a yuletide album—more's the pity—but Leontyne Price had a stab at one. I was jollying and ho-hoing away with it when Anton rang.

"Lovey, I hope you're not busy Christmas Eve!"

"No."

"Fab! I'm having a little do, a diva get-together. We can try on cossies and get pissed and giggle and be silly. Tammy will be here, of course, and so will Matthew and his friend. Ozzie's going to come, and there'll be a few drag queens and old window dressers like myself. Should be fun."

"Can I bring a friend?"

"Of course! Ooh, who is she, this mysterious femme fatale?"

"He may not be able to make it." I was thinking of Reg, although my only way of getting in touch was to leave a message at Virgin. I'd looked up Mignon in the phone book; the name was unlisted (a wise move for a critic).

"Oh, another thing, darling. Can you give Victoria a lift? She said you were dropping by her shop in any case."

"Sure."

"If you could pick her up there at 7, that would be gut-wrenchingly marvelous. Then come right over and don't bring a thing but your gorgeous selves. We're in Potts Point."

He gave me his address, a terrace overlooking the city: Anton had moved there long before it became up-market and sought after. In spite of escalating council rates, he was determined to stay.

I rang the T-shirt department at the Virgin store. A queen with a deep sonorous voice told me Reg had quit the week before.

"During the Christmas rush, too! We were so plain!"

I pleaded, and he unwillingly gave me a contact number they had for Reg. When I tried the number, it turned out to belong to an Upper North Shore Convent. The nun who answered was quite sweet but not much help. There had been a gardener named Reg working there in the late '70s, she said, but he'd retired. He'd be in his eighties now. I thanked her and hung up. Somewhere along the way, the phone number must have gotten scrambled. There was nothing more I could do.

Come Christmas Eve, I had time on my hands. I have so little family, Christmas is always a time of inactivity for me. I rang Gianna around 5:30, and we chatted vacuously about her holiday. She had contracted food poisoning; otherwise, she'd been having a great time.

I asked whether she had ever contemplated subletting her

spare room. It was for a friend, I explained, who might be needing to go underground for a few weeks. She said she'd consider it. I thought Reg could use a home away from home when Charles finally started sharpening the steak knives.

At 7 o'clock precisely I reached the Upstairs Nursery. Both it and the sex shop were shut. The lights were off. I climbed the stairs and rapped loudly at the nursery door. Massive uneven footsteps approached; the door edged open, and Victoria, dressed, high-heeled, and made up to the nines, peeped out.

"Right on time. Good. Come in, I need you to help me with something."

She locked the door behind me. The vegetation, lit by the dying rays of a summer sunset, took on a creepy life of its own. Leafy tentacles seemed to weave before my very eyes. Victoria grabbed me by the hand and dragged me in amongst the wet subtropicals.

"Over here," she said, a grim smile on her face. "I'm afraid there's been a minor tragedy."

We continued until we reached the cool room, where I had interviewed Randolph. The metal door was closed. Victoria produced a set of keys, unlocked the door, and threw it open. A neon light automatically flickered on to reveal Charles. He sat, very pale and still, on a metal stool in the corner. His arms were folded, and his legs were tightly clamped together, like an attentive churchgoer with a full bladder. He stared straight ahead. His face showed an expression of mild discomfort, as if he'd just detected a bum note in a Handel overture. He had nothing on but a big pair of stripy undershorts. The most notable thing about him, however, was a lush flowery vine winding around his legs, torso and neck. It had a thick, prickly stem and its flowers were a full, opulent, hermitage-red. The reddest, most lavish flower sat unashamedly on his bald head. The plant originated in a plastic bucket at Charles's feet.

"Charles?" I murmured. He neither saw nor heard me.

"Must be his heart," said Victoria, marching into the room. "He came in to get an orchid for Christmas and had a heart attack. I believe heart victims ought to be kept cool."

"I've never heard that," I gasped. "Is he dead?"

"In about fifteen minutes, I predict." She picked up a monstrous pair of rubber gloves and a yellow raincoat and began putting them on. "He can't stay here, anyway. He might stink the place out. Would you help me move him?"

"Have you called an ambulance?"

"Damn. I forgot. I'll do it directly. Now give us a hand."

I crept forward and reached out toward Charles's pallid, sweaty arm.

"Don't touch the vine!" Victoria snapped, as she started to gather it up with her thick rubber gloves. "It's from Central Africa—very rare, very expensive, and very toxic." She stared grimly at me. "It may cause an unpleasant itch."

I shuddered. "Is it poisonous?"

"Who knows?" she answered. "I've not had it in before. I know the Pygmies speak highly of it. They use it to subdue elephants."

She dumped the vine and bucket into a wooden crate and nailed it shut. Then she marched back over to Charles. He seemed to be trying very hard to breathe. She slapped him across the face with all her might. Four times. A pinpoint of color came to his cheeks.

"I think he's coming 'round," she said. "I'll try some smelling salts."

She reached down the front of her cleavage and pulled out a small brown bottle. She unscrewed the lid.

"This is the strongest one I stock. I got it from downstairs. Nitrate based. Cosmic stuff, I use it myself."

She shook the open bottle under Charles's nose, splashing much of the liquid up into his nostrils. His body gave a small jolt; his eyes rolled back in his head, and a dribble of white foam oozed from one side of his mouth. He appeared to have an erection. I could no longer hear him breathing.

"That's done the trick," she smiled. "Well, we needn't reproach ourselves. We did all we could. It was preordained: His time was up. Ha! Help me carry him downstairs."

We carefully picked up Charles's body. Victoria held the shoulders and I took the feet. He slumped somewhat in the middle. We lay him out on the floor while she relocked the cool room. laid

"I'm closing the nursery for renovations after Christmas," she announced. "You won't know it next time you come in."

She opened a trap door, which I'd overlooked. Inside was a narrow steel ladder. I climbed down first, balancing Charles's feet on my shoulders. I was about halfway down when Victoria called out, "Can you take him now?" and simply let go of her end. The dead weight of his body landed on me, loosening my grip, and the two of us crashed to the floor. The trapdoor above banged shut.

It was pitch dark. Charles's heavy, sour-smelling body lay on top of me. Something was sticking into my ribs, which I realized with horror was his penis. I scrambled to my feet. I could barely make out where I was, but it was evidently the back room of a sex shop: The whole place reeked of Victoria's smelling salts. We were adjacent to some thinly constructed cubicles. I dragged Charles by his feet inside the nearest one, and took a deep breath.

A single globe light snapped on and Victoria came waddling in.

"Sorry about that," she laughed. "I can't get down that way. I don't fit. Ah, you've put him in there. Good thinking. Before I call somebody, what about one of these?"

With a sweep of her arm she indicated a nearby display: a glass wall-unit filled to the brim with life-size Jeff Stryker rubber dildos. There were about two dozen of these monsters, in various repulsive colors.

"No thanks," I said. "I don't use them."

"Not you, *him!*" she snapped.

"Oh...no!"

"It's an excellent idea. It'll look like he's had a stroke in a fit of sexual frenzy. Come on, get those pants off him."

I froze to the spot. "I couldn't."

"Bugger you, I'll do it myself. Now what color? Black? Brown? No, I know—apricot!"

She opened the cupboard and lovingly removed the tremendous object.

"Stryker's not selling so well these days. It's his '80s karma. I s'pose I can afford to lose one."

I averted my eyes as Victoria went to work in the cubicle. I heard her struggling manfully and at one point she said brightly, "It's harder when they're dead, isn't it!" Finally, she emerged triumphant. "There we are. Push my niece off a cliff, will you? Happy Christmas!" She slammed the cubicle door shut. The whole partition rocked.

Victoria composed herself and glided over to a phone nearby.

"Hello?" she said. "Emergency? No, I'll wait." She examined her fingernails and hummed a catchy tune. I recognized it: the theme from *License to Kill.*

"Yes, hello? It's Victoria here from Wet Dream in Bondi. I was just closing up. I think one of our customers may have had a turn in the back room. He's in a cubicle. Yes, he collapsed. Oh! I don't know. Should I take his pulse or something? OK. You'd better send paramedics right away. I hope it's nothing serious. No, I'm afraid I don't know what he was up to. We don't like to pry, you understand. It's policy. All right. No, don't worry, I'll stay here. No, thank you."

She hung up and turned to me. "They'll be awhile—a lot of people tend to go *troppo* at this time of the year. You nick off to Anton's party. I've locked upstairs. I'll get a cab later."

"That sounds like a good idea."

She reached over and gave me a huge scented embrace. "Thank you," she said. "What a coincidence, eh? The workings of the universe are transcendentally inexplicable. Or is it inexplicably transcendental? I must look it up. Who'd have thought Charles would come back here to die? It's divine justice. Save me a handful of Anton's chipolatas."

I staggered into the fresh air and wandered down toward the ocean. It was one of those warm nights with people everywhere, all in a party mood. A group of young surfie boys with their girlfriends surged past me, laughing and swigging from beer cans. At the back of the group were two boys on either side of a girl, their arms all around each other, each with long salty-blond hair. The nearest boy, slightly intoxicated, veered into me. He looked up, caught my eye, smiled, then reached out and placed his hand on my cheek. "Merry Christmas, mate," he said. He patted my cheek and was off.

"Merry Christmas," I replied in a choked whisper.

I was in a state of shock. Knowing Jennifer Burke's murderer was one thing—but now I was a murderer myself. The man had passed away right in front of me, and I'd helped! This detective game hadn't worked out at all the way it was supposed to.

I had no idea what I would say to Paul, when he got over his latest boy-meets-boy interlude and started nagging me to relaunch our investigation. As for Reg, how could I ever face him, knowing what I knew, what I'd done? It was for him I'd called Victoria, well aware that she would deal with Charles in her own inimitable way and show no mercy. (She wasn't the forgiving type.) Tonight's fracas would save Reg a hell of a lot of bother and leg-crossing in the near future, but the way it turned out made my stomach churn. I couldn't think of Reg without seeing Charles's face as well, absolutely white, staring, accusing, lying there at the bottom of a filthy cubicle with that slightly exasperated expression.

Of course, everybody was better off now with Charles gone (except Charles). I needed to keep that fact constantly in mind. One thing was certain: I would never again, as long as

I lived, set foot in a florist's. Those places are death traps!

I considered returning home, alone and guilt-stricken, but couldn't face the prospect. The only thing to do was go to the party and drink a lot of alcohol with my old friend Anton and my new Mardi Gras friends. The thought warmed me.

It was exactly the kind of party I like: not sedate, just on the quiet side of hysterical. I renewed acquaintance with my float-painting workmates and spent the odd moment underneath the mistletoe with Matthew. (I wasn't the only one.) Gradually, I relaxed. When Victoria arrived, she looked immaculate and treated me as though we'd never met. Her haughtiness put me at ease even more.

A few times, when I stumbled into the kitchen for refills, I interrupted passionate moments between Anton and Tim, the diva's now ex-personal secretary. They didn't seem to mind. Tim had already taken me aside to show me my cowgirl outfit— (fabulous)—and apologized for any trouble he may have caused me with Dame Norma. With my usual good grace, I shrugged it off.

Very late in the night, when the party was in full swing, I found myself lounging on the terrace with Anton. I was wearing the cowgirl hat and boots, to break them in, and had my feet crossed up on the railing. Anton was stretched out on a cane lounge beside me, his white hair sparkling with strategically placed diamantés. We sipped whatever it was that was left, and watched the lights of the city and the harbor spread before us. The lights were fairly blurry.

"I'm so glad we've gotten chummy again," he enthused.

"Yes, me too. People drift apart. We shouldn't let this happen."

"No. Mardi Gras brings people together, you'll find."

"I can't wait. You and Tammy have patched up your differences, I'm pleased to see. Good news."

Anton took my hand.

"I must apologize, Marc."

"No need. Tim already has."

"No, no. For myself. I used you as a pawn in a little game I was playing. *Mille scusi!* I knew Norma would hit the roof about this parade appearance. Fact is, I hoped she would. I needed to get Tammy away from her before it was too late. And hallelujah, it worked."

"Why? Because he was getting obsessed with Dame Norma and ignoring Dame Anton?"

"Oh, yes, partly. I'll tell you because you were so mixed up in it. I was concerned for him. I didn't want the dizzy little broad getting into trouble. The thing is, he was fiddling the books."

"Norma's books?"

"Yeah. The old Dame made a lot of recordings in her prime. The annual royalties are enormous, or they were. She's lost track of them: The money's all over the place, mostly in Swiss banks. Well, Tam sorted out all these hundreds of accounts and started making withdrawals, shifting funds around. She's a clever girl at that sort of thing, and she was a bona fide signatory, after all. Norma's career was lagging a bit, and Tammy, feeling sorry for her, pulled together half a million bucks and sent it off to Fred Mathieson to keep madam on the payroll. Didn't say where it came from. And he kept on doing it!"

"So that's it! Dame Norma's her own benefactor."

"When you think about it, who else gives a flying Dutchman? And she never even knew she was her own greatest fan! 'Course, she may find out, and I don't know if she'd be too happy. Tam decided to stop when he found it getting harder to cover his tracks, especially after Sir Fred suddenly made up his mind to back a different filly.

"I finally had to take a stand: so butch! I encouraged Tam to break right out of the whole mess, jumble up all the accounts again and *scarpa*. With your help, that's what we've done, and we're both much happier within ourselves. So thank you, thank you, thank you."

My legs fell from their balcony position with a crunch.

"Oops."

"You're pissed, dear."

"And I suppose you're not?"

"Wrong again!"

"God, those bloody donations!" I said. "So many people would like to know what you've just told me in strictest confidence."

"Wouldn't do them any good: They can't get their hands on it!"

"That's right. They can't, can they! They're dead. Too bad for them. Let's have a party."

Anton looked around languidly.

"I'm bored with the party crowd. Same old faces. Same old butts."

"I like 'em."

"Let's go to the sauna!"

"What, now? It's—" I tried to consult my watch, but it refused to cooperate. I held my wrist out. "It's that time!"

"Darling, they'll be open, they're always open. Come on, 'tis Christmas Day. Someone's bound to be feeling charitable."

He hauled me to my feet.

"I can't drive," I slurred, "I'm true drunk. Too."

"We'll walk."

We started to leave. My head was spinning, as the city lights swirled around with jumbled images of cowgirls and Jeff Stryker and drag queens with a license to kill. Somewhere in there, too, was a beautiful boy with the voice of an angel, whom I secretly understood I wouldn't be seeing again. I sat down momentarily on the front steps of Anton's terrace house. I felt tired and emotional.

"Marc, darling, it's kicking in. Best to keep walking."

"Oh. Yeah." I stood shakily. "Where are we going again?"

"The sauna."

"Oh yes, yes, yes. The sauna. What for?"

"To get laid, dear."

And we did.